Embarrassment flooded her face. She wriggled beneath his hold and barely moved an inch. "Let me go."

The dragon propped himself up on an elbow. His electric blue eyes slid from hers, to the flesh her leather bodice failed to conceal.

"No."

Her jaw slackened. "Release me or – "

"Or what? Don't tell me you're frightened of me now?" His thumb began to draw lazy circles over the pounding pulse in her wrist.

"I'm not frightened of you," she said, the words coming out in a breathy sigh.

His wing coiled tighter, crushing her breasts against the warm barrel of steel he called a chest.

"Then why are you trembling?" He dipped his head below hers. "I can hear your heart hammering. Right here." A hot, open mouth covered the pulse beating beneath the skin.

"You're – " she stammered.

"Hungry. And you look tasty."

His dark head swooped

9030

MEAGAN HATFIELD

Shadow of the Vampire

Harlequin Mills & Boon policy is to use papers that are
natural, renewable and recyclable products and made from
wood grown in sustainable forests. The logging and
manufacturing processes conform to the legal environmental
regulations of the country of origin.

Printed in Great Britain
by Clays Ltd, St Ives plc

MILLS & BOON

DID YOU PURCHASE THIS BOOK WITHOUT A COVER?

If you did, you should be aware it is **stolen property** as it was
reported *unsold and destroyed* by a retailer. Neither the author nor
the publisher has received any payment for this book.

All the characters in this book have no existence outside the imagination
of the author, and have no relation whatsoever to anyone bearing the same
name or names. They are not even distantly inspired by any individual
known or unknown to the author, and all the incidents are pure invention.

All Rights Reserved including the right of reproduction in whole or
in part in any form. This edition is published by arrangement with
Harlequin Enterprises II B.V./S.à.r.l. The text of this publication or any
part thereof may not be reproduced or transmitted in any form or by
any means, electronic or mechanical, including photocopying, recording,
storage in an information retrieval system, or otherwise, without the
written permission of the publisher.

This book is sold subject to the condition that it shall not, by way of
trade or otherwise, be lent, resold, hired out or otherwise circulated
without the prior consent of the publisher in any form of binding or cover
other than that in which it is published and without a similar condition
including this condition being imposed on the subsequent purchaser.

® and ™ are trademarks owned and used by the trademark owner and/
or its licensee. Trademarks marked with ® are registered with the United
Kingdom Patent Office and/or the Office for Harmonisation in the
Internal Market and in other countries.

First published in Great Britain in 2010
Harlequin Mills & Boon Limited, Eton House,
18-24 Paradise Road,
Richmond, Surrey TW9 1SR

© Meagan Hatfield 2010

ISBN: 978 0 263 87821 9

89-0810

LONDON BOROUGH OF WANDSWORTH

9030 00001 1108 7	
Askews	29-Jul-2010
AF HATF	£6.99

To: Nan and Bump, for giving me not only a love of the written word, but raising me to believe I could do and be anything I set my heart to.

Lori Devoti, for not outbidding me and for being a mythbuster. Kristi, because a book not dedicated to you is just dirty and wrong. AVP, Kathy, Chris, Diane, Kathryn, Bev, Shari, Bobbi, Rachel, Heather, Andrea, Angie, Deb, Donna, Stacey, Mary Jo and the rest of the WI writing gang for all the help, support, inspiration and friendship.

Shawn, Jayne, Courtney, Kathy, Jenelle, Shelley, Virgil, Christine and the other gym rats.

Rosalind (and Raven), for being my first official dragon lovers.

The two best kids on the planet, Bodi and Zoe, for putting up with more than their fair share of "I know you're hungry, but I'm almost done!" and still loving me.

Sean, for telling me I don't write crap, even when I do.

My mom, who taught me to believe in soul mates and happily ever after.

My agent, Kim Whalen, and to Karin Tabke for pointing me in her direction.

And to my fabulous editor, Tara Gavin, for taking a chance on me and helping me make this book everything I dreamed it could be and more.

PROLOGUE

She made certain they didn't have bodies to bury.

Hatred and rage weighed down Declan Black's shoulders, already heavy from his newfound responsibility as King. Since the news of his parents' deaths hit the lair, the only thought in Declan's mind was that he had not been able to bring back their bodies for a proper burial. Every dragon in their flock had gathered around their mountain to say goodbye to the King and Queen and usher him in as their new ruler. But the vampire Queen had ensured their ancient order and traditions would not be upheld.

They didn't have bodies to bury.

That was the only thought running through Declan Black's mind.

That and revenge.

Declan stood at the lip of the cliff, staring through the darkness at the churning sea a hundred feet below. Moonlight and night winds caressed his bare chest, carrying a scent right to him. The salty ocean air masked the stench of death blanketing the beach. Most humans would not even take notice. But the animal within Declan sensed it lingering in the undertones of the sea air.

Blood.

Declan crouched low. The tip of his booted foot dangled over the ledge, sending a handful of pebbles tumbling to the water. Undaunted, he leaned farther and cocked his head.

She was down there. He could not see her, but he could smell her. Powerful. Evil.

His sharp eyes zeroed in on the ragged cliffs and caverns below, searching for an opening. He always thought it ironic that the warring clans both chose the comfort of caves as their dwellings. Vampires inhabited the ground beneath the earth, while the dragons lived high above to avoid the increasingly astute human population. The security and protection a cave offered also appealed to his species. Only one entrance meant that they would always know their foes were coming and could block them or guard the cave to keep out attacks.

Much like his dragon kin's lair, the vampire catacombs below no doubt were elaborate and full of surprises. He'd have to be careful.

Declan fingered the brown satchel in his hands and stood. Despite his reservations, he knew he must do what his parents had died trying to do.

What she had killed them for.

Someone yanked the bag from his grip. Declan whipped around. At the sight of a small female with violet eyes, the frown he'd worn all evening deepened.

"Tallon, get back to the lair," he said, swiping his arm out. She shifted her hold, keeping the bag just out of his reach. Declan rolled his eyes. They were not hatchlings playing keep-away anymore.

"I'm coming with you."

"Like hell you are," he seethed, easily snatching the satchel from her hands and turning his back to her. He slid the straps over his broad shoulders, making sure the bag hung low enough that his wings would not rip through the fabric when he shifted into dragon form.

"They were my parents, too, Declan."

At her words, he drew in a breath, releasing it slowly. "Tallon, please. I'm not getting into this again. You were there when I told the council. I'm going alone."

A firm hand cupped his shoulder, forcing him around.

"The Queen will capture and torture you like she did them, and then what? Then where will our flock be?"

"No closer to extinction than we already are."

Fire flickered behind her eyes. For a moment, he thought she might strike him. Hell, the dejection in his voice made him want to smack himself. However, she did not lash out. That was not her way. Instead, tenderness he neither earned nor deserved replaced her anger.

"We need you, Declan. Without you to lead us, all of our kind will be lost."

"No," he said through clenched teeth. "We will be lost if that bitch gets her hands on the Crystal of the Draco. You were there when Doc translated the scroll. *The power to rule all or destroy one,*" he quoted from memory. "You know what that means? If they harness the energy in that stone, the Queen will bend us all to her will and we will become slaves, like the auld days. Or worse, she will decimate us. And it's down there," he said, pointing to the caverns, "waiting for her to use it."

"The scroll's torn, Declan. We can't even be certain that's what it means…."

"They died getting that scroll to us," he shouted, his words clipped with emotion. "If Mom and Dad believed the prophecy enough to sacrifice themselves, that's good enough for me. As their successor, it is my duty to look after our kind. I'm flying down there to the horde's catacombs and retrieving that crystal."

"Fine. Then I'm going with you."

Declan released a frustrated groan and raked a hand through his hair. It was pointless to keep fighting. He knew Tallon. She was a warrior, a fighter. She would not give up until he granted her request. Not that he could blame her. He would have done the same thing.

"Do you swear to do what I say, when I say it, no questions asked?"

"Of course." Her lips quirked in a victorious smile before she launched into the air.

Declan watched her transform in a burst of iridescent pinks and purples and shook his head.

"Fools and dragons," he murmured, leaping after her.

CHAPTER ONE

DECLAN RAN UP THE narrow tunnel. Footfalls pounding the earth behind him told him they didn't have much time to escape. Straight ahead, the mouth of the cave yawned, the slight flicker of moonlight revealing their way out.

"Tallon!"

"I see it," she called over her shoulder, her legs kicking with each powerful stride.

"Fly," he shouted when they neared the ledge. Without slowing, Tallon leapt into the void. Her slight body fell for a split second before she shifted form and took to the sky. Declan made sure she was airborne before pushing off the cliff with a grunt. His long body soared through the cool air, transforming with seamless precision into a black dragon.

As he climbed upward, a glance back showed the vampire soldiers, armed and ready to kill for the treasure he'd carried out of their den.

Turning toward the heavens, Declan beat his wings to climb higher as a barrage of gunshots screamed from below.

"Faster," he shouted telepathically, seconds before bullets tattered the scales of his left wing. A hot spike of pain lanced between his shoulder blades. Slipping in his ascent, he paused to grab a breath.

"Declan. Come on!"

He ignored her. Instead, he stared at the vampire horde twenty feet below. Rage bubbled in his veins at the sight of them spilling out of their seaside catacomb like ants from a hill. A soldier lifted a bow gun to his shoulder and fired. Arrows cut through the sky. Declan swung into their path, taking in his arm the one meant for Tallon. The skewered flesh sizzled.

Silver-tipped arrows. He groaned.

Not good.

The fine metal acted like a poison on his kind, eating their flesh and siphoning their power from the inside out. Gritting his jaw against the pain, he slashed the knapsack from around his neck and tossed it at Tallon. She caught it in one clawed hand.

"Take it and go."

She looked up. The fear in her eyes eating at his soul. Tonight was not supposed to have gone down like this. They'd gotten what they came for. But he'd be damned if it ended with her getting hurt.

A second arrow ate through his thigh.

"Dammit, Tallon. You promised." He growled. *"Get out of here. Now!"*

A breath of relief sawed out of his lungs when she nodded. After she disappeared in the darkness, he turned his focus on the vamp with the bow gun. Snapping his wings wide, Declan arced into a kamikaze dive. Fire licked the back of his throat. Smoke curled out of his nostrils.

The vampire saw him coming and turned to run, but he was too late. Declan opened his jowls, raining a torrent of dragonfire on the soldier. Pale flesh melted off his face and hands, pooling on the stones below.

Before Declan could close his jaw, another blitz of gunshots saturated the sky. Blazing heat ripped through his veins with the same burning efficiency as the bullets had torn his flesh. His wings faltered and folded behind him. His elongated muzzle shrunk until cool night air whipped his human face, tossing strands of hair into his eyes.

"Shit," he muttered as he began plummeting toward the ground, human from the waist up. Unable to stop, he twisted in midair and tucked his chin, waiting for impact. His body smacked the dirt, bouncing and skidding, his flesh eating the small rocks and granules. He slid to a halt. A cloud of dust rose and then settled over him like a blanket, coating his lungs.

Coughing, he rolled to his stomach and opened his eyes to peek. Two soldiers were rushing him. Fast. Their black trench coats billowed behind them, showing off an assortment of weapons strapped to gun belts around their thick waists.

At least six more, all decked out like G.I. Joe on crack, were closing in not ten paces behind them.

Great.

The first two almost on him, Declan crouched and sideswiped his leg in an arc, knocking them down. Springing to his feet, he reared his tail. Blood splattered across his face and neck as he lodged the club-shaped ball at the end of it into the nearest vamp's chest. Spinning, he caught the second one by the throat. He snapped the soldier's thick neck around until a sickening crunch reverberated through his arms. Discarding the lifeless heap on the ground, Declan wrenched his tail out of what was left of the other vamp's torso, and turned to face the second wave of soldiers bearing down on him.

"Come on," he said, motioning to the approaching

horde. His blood-soaked tail lashed and bit like a whip behind him.

The pack stepped closer. Their teeth were bared and their black claws extended. Not caring if he died tonight as long he took a few of these bastards with him, Declan stepped forward to meet them head-on. He stumbled over heavy feet. Frowning, he looked down. The remaining armor scales on his lower body receded. Then his tail, the only weapon left in his arsenal, shrank back into his body.

The silver, he realized. Its poison was draining his dragon power.

As soon as the thought came, his body screamed in pain, his side and back burning as if someone held a blowtorch to his skin. Cupping the wound, he pulled back a bloody hand.

Another shot fired. Instead of more silver bullets, a heavy net collapsed atop him, dragging him to the ground. The instant his cheek hit the dirt, feet and fists rained down on him. With the net tying him up, all he could do was shield his head with his forearms and wait.

"Enough!" At a female's order, the soldiers backed up a step.

The Queen.

It had to be her. At the thought, an icy shiver passed

through him. A rational part of his brain had known she would come for him if he didn't kill her first. Knew she would take her vengeance against his kind out on his flesh—his soul.

Well, he thought, grabbing a fistful of net. He wasn't going without a fight.

With a roar, Declan looped the thick cord around his wrist and pulled, taking several of the horde to their knees. Jabbing a fist through the mesh, he seized the nearest soldier by the throat and squeezed.

"Dammit, Ivan. Hold him," a strong female voice ordered.

At her command, a boot rammed his jaw. Declan flew back, his chin kicking the ground in a teeth-shattering blow. Groaning, he spit out a mouthful of blood and pushed himself up, his head lolling in the direction he'd last heard the woman's voice.

The first thing he focused on were boots—spike-heeled, patent-leather, knee-high stripper boots, wrapped around a pair of slender legs that seemed to go for days. Declan lifted his chin and wrenched his swollen eye wider.

The female stood with one hand propped on black-leather-clad hips. The wind whipped thin blond hair around her—a delicately framed waist, bound in a leather corset that would have given any fetish kink an instant hard-on.

When his gaze finally reached her face, he noted she examined him with black eyes as cold and immortal as his soul. And that she was much too young to be the Queen.

"Where is the crystal?" Her smooth words held a faint trace of a Russian accent.

Not the Queen, but definitely of a noble caste. Declan grinned through bloodied lips.

At his smile, a dainty line furrowed her brow, and she cocked her head to the side. For a moment, she reminded Declan of a confused puppy. Until she raised a sawed-off 12 gauge and one black eye stared down the barrel at him.

"Tell me where it is and I might let you live, *Derkein.*"

"It's gone," he said with a chuckle. "You have nothing to take back to her. You're as dead as I am."

The vixen's onyx eyes flashed silver before she drove the butt of the gun down to his face. He was still smiling when she pistol-whipped his nose and the world plunged into darkness.

ALEXIA FEODOROVNA stood in the catacombs, staring into the stone cell. Although the beast lay sound asleep on the floor and chained to the wall, his size and strength still managed to unsettle her.

Big. Dark. Dangerous.

She had never seen anything like him. The dragon

lords never shifted into human form during battle, and were said to be all but extinct, or so she'd assumed until tonight. After seeing him fight, she wondered how she'd ever believed the lie.

He'd fought like a warrior of auld.

The way he'd protected that female of his kind, battled until he couldn't stand and yet met death with a smile on his face, affected her strangely. Not because she knew she would have met her own death like the coward her mother had called her. But because in the deepest part of her heart, she yearned to experience that kind of love, yet knew she would die without it.

The prisoner shifted. The metal cuffs around his wrists caught the moonlight filtering in through the rectangular window in his cell.

Alexia leaned her forehead on the cool iron bars and watched the play of light on the dark wall. Tipping her chin, she took in a breath of salty ocean air, wafting in the window, purifying the rancid odor of her horde's dungeon. Funny. She'd always thought that tiny window to be the cruelest torture in the cavern. The vibrant ocean, the alive taste of freedom danced on the tips of their prisoners' tongues, taunting their spirits from the other side of the dungeon wall. A small flavor of a salvation that for most never came.

At least they died having tasted hope.

Footsteps ascended the spiral staircase behind her. Sliding her eyes from the prisoner, she adjusted the tray in her arms and turned toward the guard.

"It's about time, soldier." She nodded into the cell. "Are you certain he sleeps?"

The guard stepped into the light from a wall sconce. Like every one of her mother's soldiers, he had crew-cut blond hair, a thick pit-bull-size head and dark sunglasses he wore even in the inky-black pits of their cavern dwelling.

"I drugged that *Derkein* myself," he said, unlocking the cell door and propping it open. "He'll be out for hours, if he wakes at all."

"Good. You may leave us."

A dark brow cocked over the rim of his shades. "But, Lotharus ordered—"

She hissed at the name, and stepped up to him. "Lotharus does not make the orders around here. I do. And I said, leave us."

Though disapproval radiated off the grunt, he clamped his lips together and bowed.

Alexia watched him leave under narrowed lids. She didn't trust those genetically enhanced soldiers. Sure, they were efficient, strong and practically unbeatable in combat. However, their increasing intolerance of showing her the respect befitting her station was troubling. Naturally, her mother blamed her for a lack of dominance over the horde.

Once the soldier disappeared around the corner, Alexia stepped through the iron threshold, slamming the door with more force than necessary.

Goddess! Just once she'd like to prove to her horde she was capable of leading them, capable of succeeding on the throne when her mother stepped down. Alexia knew if she retrieved the Crystal of the Draco, no one, not even Lotharus, would question her or the horde's centuries-old matriarchal way of life again.

She stopped beside the slumbering beast, realizing the only one who knew where the crystal might be lay bleeding to death on the floor by her feet.

With a sigh, Alexia settled on the ground, unwound a measure of coarse thread and nipped it with her fangs. Wetting the tip with her tongue, she threaded the needle and shifted onto her knees above the prisoner. Since he faced the outer wall, she decided to start by stitching the gash on his shoulder blade.

Alexia set her fingers to his flesh. At the contact, he moaned, rolled to his back and took a deep breath. Alexia held hers. Every dip, ridge and contour of his naked, bronzed body rose and flexed with the movement, beckoning her gaze.

What few noble men of her horde she'd seen unclothed had been tall and thin. Gaunt, when she compared them to this dragon lord. He was thick. Her gaze slid between his thighs. Everywhere. He had long muscled thighs and calves, solid arms and a broad, sculpted chest, not bones protruding beneath translucent skin like Lotharus.

Intrigued, she leaned closer.

Rich sable waves of shoulder-length hair curled around his neck. Her eyes fixed lower, on the pulse beating beneath his golden skin. A primal thrum tingled through her body. The air around her thickened, and her fangs burned.

Alexia sat back on her heels and gave herself a mental shake.

Just stitch him up and leave.

Bending, she set the needle to the torn flesh by his ribs. Before she could push it through his skin, long fingers dug into her wrists.

Her gasp stuck in her throat as the prisoner hauled her down. A pop, like sails unfurling, rent the air. One massive black wing tucked beneath her, cocooning her against his hard flesh and cushioning her fall to the floor. The cool scales glided against her shoulders, a contrast to the hot breath feathering against her face.

"Did you like what you saw, vixen?" he said in a smoky voice.

Embarrassment flooded her face. She wriggled beneath his hold on her and barely moved an inch. "Let me go."

The dragon propped himself up on an elbow. His electric-blue eyes slid from hers, to the flesh her leather bodice failed to conceal.

"No."

Her jaw slackened. "Release me or—"

"Or what?"

"Or—" She looked around, nodding to the needle and thread beside her. "I won't stitch up your wounds. Unless, of course, you'd rather bleed out in this dungeon."

A black brow arched. "If I'm in a dungeon, why bother healing me at all?"

"Would you rather die?"

His lips kicked up. "Do you always answer a question with a question, little vampire?"

Alexia shook her head, and tried to ignore that sinfully sexy curve of his mouth. "No."

"Then answer me."

She sighed. "We cannot torture you in the state you're in. You'd never last through questioning."

At her words, flames flickered behind his icy eyes. Soft tufts of smoke wafted out of his nostrils.

Dragonfire.

Her eyes widened, panic gripping her like a spiked glove to the throat.

"Don't tell me you're frightened of me now?" His thumb began to draw lazy circles over the pounding pulse in her wrist.

"I'm not frightened of you," she said, the words coming out in a breathy sigh.

His wing coiled tighter, crushing her breasts against the warm steel of his barrel chest.

"Then why are you trembling?" He dipped his head below hers. "I can hear your heart hammering. Right here." His hot, open mouth covered the pulse beating beneath her skin.

A tingle of pleasure shimmied along her spine. She sucked in a breath and held it as his soft lips caressed her neck. Alexia knew she should be fighting him. Knew she should beg for death by his hell-sent flame rather than allow him such liberties. But the excitement and fear of being handled so gently paralyzed her. Never had a man touched her so softly, held her so tenderly. When his lips hummed against her skin, her eyes fluttered and a little sound purred out of her throat.

His lips curved against her neck and then a low chuckle rumbled in his chest.

Was he laughing?

Heat flooded her face as anger surged, taking over her misplaced desire. Eyeing the vein throbbing in his neck, she focused on the steady rhythm of his pulse. A red haze flooded her vision. Two teeth stretched past her lips. Although feeding was forbidden between vampires, no such laws prevented taking the blood of an enemy. Opening her mouth, she snapped for his throat.

He dodged her attack and then leaned more of his delicious weight atop her, restricting her movements. "Easy, little one. Your teeth don't frighten me."

"No?" She lunged for him and, maddeningly, he diverted her again. Only this time when he parted his lips in a smile, fangs twice the size of hers hung from his mouth.

Her dead heart flipped over on itself.

"You're—" she stammered.

"Hungry. And you look tasty."

His dark head swooped.

Fear had her grabbing his arms, trying to push him off. No man, not even Lotharus, dared drink her blood. It meant instant death in their world. Then again, what would a dragon lord care of the horde's laws?

All thoughts melted away as his hot tongue licked her throat. Then, in a winding path, his fangs raked down, searching out the vein. A shiver passed through her when they stopped over her hammering pulse. She sucked in a breath and held it, waiting. Teeth pierced her flesh. Alexia gasped at the twinge of pain from his bite, even as her body arched into it.

A large hand speared through her hair, keeping her neck tilted. The other covered her side at her waist, fingers digging into her leather bodice. The skin beneath his grip tingled. The blood surging through her veins, rushing to feed him, burned.

He was a fire, spreading through her, consuming her from the inside out. Each long, sensual pull of his mouth crackled white heat to her core. Her center wept, aching for something more. As if he read her mind, the tapered edge of his powerful wing dug into her butt, pressing her against the long, hard length of him. Pinwheels of fire licked her lower belly at the contact. When he did it again, she moaned at the sheer pleasure of it.

Parting her legs, she allowed his wide hips to sink into the cradle of her body. Big, heavy, he fit against her perfectly. Even though she knew she should be pushing him away, her fingers curled around his large biceps, pulling him closer. Nothing she'd experienced in her hundred and twenty years felt this natural, this right. To think she'd been denied this for so long would have sent her into a blind rage had she not felt so blissfully contented.

When he finally tore away from her throat, she mewled a whimper of protest. Dazed, Alexia opened her eyes and drank in the impressive sight of him arched above her. Once limp and useless, his other wing stretched out like a cat after a long nap. Her eyes fell to the gaping flesh wound on his side and widened as she watched it close as if sewn by an invisible thread. It struck her then her threat not to heal him meant nothing. He never needed her tools. He only needed her.

Her blood.

Then what did that make him? Dragons didn't feed from one another.

Before she could form words, he grinned and dipped his head again. The flat of his tongue ran along her throat, soothing her torn flesh. She licked her lips, tucking the lower one between her fangs as he nibbled and licked his way across her jaw.

"I should have warned you," he whispered in her ear. His smoky voice snaked around her, tightening the knot of lust already sinking hard and heavy inside her. "Feeding makes me horny as hell."

Me, too, she thought as he fit his lips over hers. They melted beneath the heat of his mouth. The taste of him and the flavor of her own coppery blood on his lips sent hunger coiling tight around her spine. Or maybe that was his wing, she thought as his tongue swept between her lips in a languid lick.

Alexia opened for him, eagerly accepting his searching tongue. Needing him to fill her any way he could. He tilted his head and swept his tongue inside. Two large hands palmed the sides of her face as his lips moved over hers in a sliding kiss.

Alexia lost herself in the sensations and sank into the wing behind her, relishing the support. Her hand lifted, gripping his strong jaw in her palm. Feeling the powerful muscles beneath bunch and flex and he worked his mouth over hers. His deep groan vibrated down her throat, all the way to her toes. The sound empowered her. To know how much he desired her was intoxicating. Lotharus never kissed her with such passion, with such palpable need.

Goddess above, help her. But she loved it. Loved the feel of his rough cheeks against her palms, the heavy weight of him above her, even the brawny and rather useful wing caressing her back.

"What the hell?"

At the guard's voice, Alexia jolted.

CHAPTER TWO

IN A BLINDING MOVE she couldn't track, the dragon hauled her to her feet, ripped the iron chain free from the wall and coiled the links around her neck. His other hand snaked around her waist, keeping her back pinned to his front.

"Get back," he told the guard in a deep growl.

Gasping, Alexia brought both hands to her neck. "What are you doing?" she panted.

The arm around her waist tightened, forcing her farther against his hard, naked body. His head dipped in the crook of her neck, nuzzling into the hair behind her ear. Hot and warm, his breath fluttered against her raw skin.

"Pity, I know," he murmured. "We were just getting started, you and I."

"You wish," she bit, jabbing her elbow into his gut. She

had the satisfaction of hearing him grunt out a taxed breath before the chain tightened.

Damn, he was strong. Alexia winced as the chain bit into her skin. She had not expected his surge of power. Apparently, the guard hadn't either, for he looked from her to the dragon before finally reaching for the gun holstered on his hip.

"Don't do it," the dragon lord warned. "I'll kill her."

A deep hole scooped out of the center of her chest at his words. Never had she felt a bigger fool. The way he'd kissed her, touched her, had been no more than an act so he could heal himself with her blood and escape.

The click of a gun cocking echoed through the chamber. Alexia noticed the guard held his standard issue, pointed at them. The dragon's already hot skin seemed to ignite at the threat.

"I'm warning you, soldier," the dragon bit out, tightening his grip and taking another step back. Alexia hissed in an audible breath and the guard relaxed his weapon slightly.

"Go ahead, *Derkein*." A deep voice purred in the darkness.

Alexia's breath caught.

Lotharus.

The deliberate clicking of boots on the stone floor announced his arrival. Alexia's heart pounded with each one, waiting, watching for him. Slowly, he emerged from the darkness, almost as if he'd been born of it.

As always, Lotharus dressed in black finery from head to foot and carried himself every bit the ageless immortal he was. Although tall and lean, his body reeked of unspeakable power that caused most mortals and immortals alike to shrink in his presence. Tonight, he wore his blond hair pulled back in a severe ponytail at his nape, showing off the aristocratic line of his jaw. However, Alexia could not take her gaze off his black eyes. They bore into hers, anger and the promise of punishment sizzling in their bottomless depths.

"Kill her."

LIPS DRAWN TIGHT, Declan loosened the chain, holding the woman in a more protective way than before. Her pulse was racing, her body stiff as a board in his arms. A cold blackness crept inside the room that had not been there before this vampire had walked in. His soulless eyes spoke of untold evil, and it was all focused on her.

And she was terrified.

Declan's eyes narrowed in thinly veiled hatred. Vampire or no, any man who thought he owned another didn't deserve to live, much less enjoy power. His hold on the girl tightened while his grip on the chain loosened.

"Who are you to choose if she lives or dies?" Declan asked.

The vampire smiled with the corner of his mouth. "Let's just say we're…close."

At the small shudder that shook her body, a low growl vibrated in Declan's throat.

"But what I think won't matter," the vampire continued. "Once the Queen finds out her daughter has become a willing whore and blood thrall to one of her enemies, I'm quite certain she won't mourn the loss."

Caught up in the insane urge to protect her, Declan barely registered the vampire's monotone words. Then they hit him, each one like a blow to the chest. His brow tightened. The air he breathed dragged like sludge in his lungs.

The Queen. Daughter.

Disgusted, he released her. The chains rippled to the floor, clanking in a pile at his feet.

The instant his grip on her slackened, the iron cell wall creaked. Declan looked up, muttering a silent curse when he realized Lotharus's full attention was fixed on moving the wall with his mind force. The metal twisted and bowed beneath unseen hands. A second later it sprung free of its frame and jettisoned toward them.

Without a second thought, Declan grabbed the female

by the shoulders, tossing her out of the way. He barely saw her fall safely to her knees before the heavy iron crashed into him. The blow picked him up off his feet, slamming him three feet back and into the wall like nothing more than a rag doll. Stones crumbled and a cloud of dust plumed around him from the hole his back dented into the wall. His body ached and pinpricks of pain shot out in all directions. But strength flowed in his replenished veins, taking over any hurt he may have felt. With a heaving grunt, he pitched the heavy iron aside. In one fluid move, he stood alert, braced for whatever else was coming at him.

The vampire smiled approvingly. Bringing his hands up, he began clapping his palms together in hard, methodic slaps. Declan frowned. What the hell was wrong with this freak? He could have killed the girl had Declan not pushed her out of the way. Yet he looked as if he couldn't have been more pleased.

"Well done, *dragon lord*." He ceased clapping, resting his index finger on his lips. Declan's eyes flashed on the wide-set ruby stone eating up the width to his knuckle. "That is what my little test proved you to be, correct?" When Declan didn't answer, the vampire ran his gaze up and down his body. "Strange, but it seems you are completely healed. Let's see what we can do about that, hmm? Seize him."

The three guards did not move. Declan smiled and beckoned them to come inside. At the taunt, the first soldier scowled and ran forward. Declan pulled back his arm, landing a stiff jab on the vampire's nose. He fell to his back. The other two stepped over him, bearing down on Declan. He took one step toward them. His heavy footfall shook the earth with force no human could muster. At the sound, the soldiers looked down. Declan wiggled the toes of his black, clawed foot. When their gazes flew back up, Declan held up his fist, the one that had felled the guard, revealing a swollen club of black scales and talons.

"He's changing!" The guard in front skidded to a halt, but he was too late to escape. With his strength renewed, Declan transformed to his true state with blinding quickness. Shiny black scales rolled over his flesh. Talons pierced the tips of his fingers and toes and his nose elongated into a horny muzzle of encrusted armor. Dropping to all fours, he let out an earthshaking roar.

Lips curled back, baring his teeth, he stalked his prey like a lion. With a mental cue, he fired up his now healthy and recharged dragonfire glands. Heat billowed inside him. Tendrils of smoke curled out of his nostrils. All he had to do was barbecue this joint and he'd be gone. Without knowing why, he paused, his eyes searching for the female.

Seeing she was safe against the back wall, he turned back to the guards. Opening his jowls, he blasted a torrent of flame on the felled soldier, consuming him in the firestorm. The other two covered their faces with their arms and backed away. Keeping the fire torching, he started swinging his hip, banging the stones with the clubbed end of his tail. Rocks skated down the wall, peppering the floor. The salty sea air teased his nose. He was getting closer. Each blow of his tail brought him another inch to freedom.

Something hit Declan in the chest with the force of a jackhammer. He tipped his head back and roared as agonizing pain speared through him. Another invisible fist jabbed his gut. This time he heard the gunfire. Knew the following blast of pain was another bullet entering his body, followed by another.

Declan shifted back with the force of each slug. The silver bullets spread through him like mercury, melting his insides. The flames in his throat died as the fire within consumed him. He fell forward, bracing himself on his hands and knees. His arms shook, the muscles barely able to support his weight. Like withering vines, his scales curled back, leaving rivers of bloodied flesh in their wake. His mouth opened in a scream, but nothing came out.

The gun skated across the debris-coated floor, followed by the empty magazine. He heard what sounded like handcuffs being unchained from the smoking remains of the fallen guard. Then boots scuffled to a stop by his head. A dark shadow cast over him.

Gasping, Declan moved his knee, trying to stand. A heavy foot stepped square between his shoulder blades.

"Nuh-uh-uh," the vampire said, stepping down hard. At the pressure, Declan's arms buckled. He fell face-first into the floor, the foot keeping him there. Hands reached down, sliding something around his head. Declan offered no resistance as the vampire snapped a thick metal collar around his very human, very weak, neck.

"There's a good boy," Lotharus said, patting his head like a dog's and lifting his foot.

Instantly, the cold metal heated. The skin around his neck tingled in an icy burn. Panicked, Declan's fingers clawed at the device as the flesh beneath the apparatus sizzled. The scent of burnt flesh filled his nose. He recognized the reaction immediately.

Silver.

Declan's back arched as he fought to wrench the band free. Nostrils flaring, he gasped for breath as the collar sucked even the will to breathe from his labored body.

"It burns, does it not?" The vampire's deep voice cut

through the pain-induced fog. "Can you feel your strength ebb? I must admit, it is one of Alexia's more ingenious designs."

Alexia? Declan's eyes flashed to that female he had fed from. The one he could still taste on his tongue, feel on his lips—the one his body still wanted to ravish. She created this? But of course, she would. Her mother would surely expect no less of her. Well, neither would he.

Narrowing his eyes, he vowed the next time he had her beneath him, she would feel only the pain of his bite as he bled her dry.

LOTHARUS WATCHED THE DRAGON stare at Alexia.

Such hatred in those eyes.

He turned his head to the side, trying to figure out why. Although that dragon lord was now weakened by the collar and clip of silver bullets lodged in his abdomen, he'd somehow regained his strength between the time he was captured and when Lotharus came to check on him. Somehow, in that little bit of time, he had recovered enough strength to use the fiercest and most devastating weapon any dragon owned— *dragonfire*. But how?

Lotharus's gaze slid to Alexia. Her leather-clad body was flat against the wall. Crimson streaks and dirt stained her usually pristine blond hair. Under his perusal, her shoulders jumped and her eyes slid to the floor.

Ah, so his future stepdaughter had something to do with it.

Eyes narrowing, Lotharus reached her in two seconds. Curling his fingers around the soft skin of her biceps, he hauled her to him. The tips of those hooker boots she wore, only because he hated them, barely skimmed the floor as he held her up. Instantly, the fear he worked so hard to instill in her fired up her onyx eyes. Lotharus smiled, relishing every minute of it. Like a drug, taking her innocence, her trust, her joy was never enough. He always wanted more.

"Would you know how this dragon came to be fully healed, Alexia?"

When she didn't answer, he pinned her back against the nearest wall. Alexia gasped, the air bursting out of her with a woof. As he stared at her, resentment lingered in his throat like stale blood. Stupid females. How did anyone ever think this weak sex could lead their kind?

The horde had not always governed this way. Centuries ago, in what female leaders now called the dark times, males had ruled the horde. More precisely, one male. The first pureborn of their kind. A vicious warrior feared by mortals and immortals alike.

Stefan Strigoi, the dark prince.

Over the last few years, Lotharus had painstakingly collected every text he had ever written. Every private diary entry he'd ever penned. Granted, he had done so illegally. The holy women sequestered in the *samostan* temple had been the only ones with copies of the books. In a maneuver reminiscent of how the human kings of auld suppressed their serfs with the divine right of kings doctrine and their Holy Bible, the female monarchs of the past deceived the horde. The truth had been so far buried beneath their lies that even Lotharus had problems believing it all at first. Yet, the further he dug the more painfully obvious it became.

Their horde ran better under the dark prince's thumb. His rule had been total, his philosophies infallible and his political infrastructure flawless from conception to execution. Their army had been strong, efficient against other beings who might challenge them. Indeed, they'd won every battle set upon them. Until the war that claimed the dark prince's immortal soul. It was during that wandering and purposeless aftermath that his wife had stepped up to govern. The idea of a female leader had arisen as an interim arrangement, only to become permanent.

At the thought, a surge of heat rushed through his

veins. By the blood, not many things baffled Lotharus. Yet simply looking at Alexia now, quivering and wide-eyed before him, reaffirmed everything he'd come to believe in. Women were weak, pathetic, destined to be submissive to men, not rule them. Unlike other beings, female vampires held no prize in Lotharus's eyes for their reproductive capabilities. He'd realized years ago they did not need the weaker sex to breed. In fact, there were methodical biological ways of creating the soldiers one needed, and none of it involved the act of mating.

Lotharus smirked, recalling the one way he had managed to use the act. Remembering the heady thrill of power, the one he still felt vibrate through him every time he neared Alexia. He tilted his head and allowed his gaze to slide over her body, relishing her instinctive shudder.

Releasing one hand, he ran the flat of his palm down the side of her beautiful face, down her cheek, slowly inching toward her neck. When he got halfway down her throat, she visibly winced. Lotharus lifted a brow in question and tilted his head to inspect her neck.

At the sight of the mark, an obvious vampire bite, all the arrogant certainty drained out of him. Fury tackled him from behind, taking its place. The force blinded him, nearly making him black out.

It should be me at her vein. Will be me. No one else.

The words repeated a litany in his mind. He squeezed his eyes shut, hoping to quell the voices along with his vision. It didn't work.

Lips curling tight, he snatched her chin between his thumb and forefinger, forcing her to meet his gaze. "Have something you'd like to explain to me?"

The flesh beneath his finger trembled, but she did not answer. Again, his gaze fell to the two teeth marks on her throat. Using his forefinger, he slid his long black nail over the bite. At the twinge, she hissed in a breath. He smiled at the sound and brought his finger to his lips, slipping it between them. At the taste of her blood on his tongue, light burst behind his eyes and he instantly grew hard. Her power surged through him like a jolt of electricity. Sucking in a breath, he rode the wave, coming close to orgasm as it crested and lapped through every nerve ending in his body.

A low growl of dominance bubbled up from his chest.

None of his men would dare bite her. It was that beast. He had fed from her. Rage at that dragon thing and Alexia for allowing him to absorb her power, power that rightfully belonged to him, engulfed him. The wound on her pale neck mocked him, his power, his plan. He could almost hear the dark prince laughing at him from beyond the Fatum.

Quaking in anger, he wanted to rip Alexia's head off, but settled for shoving her back with a push instead.

"Hold him up," he shouted, turning back to the soldiers. The dragon groaned, his face a mask of pain as the men seized him under the armpits and forced him to his knees.

Lotharus stared down with disgust in his eyes at the filthy flying rat. These creatures were below his race. For centuries, vampires had lived amongst human civilizations, evolving alongside them. The dragons rejected change and kept to the shadows, clinging to their barbaric ways. Shameful beasts. They reeked of animal. He could smell this dragon's filth, taste it in his mouth, feel it smother and cling to him like a wet towel.

Squatting, he fisted the beast's hair, wrenching his head up to meet his gaze. With his other hand, he forced his jaw open to inspect his teeth. Two canines similar to those he'd looked at in the mirror all his life stared back at him. "Interesting."

The dragon growled in his throat and the two fangs lengthened, hanging over his lips. "Very interesting. It appears there is more to you than meets the eye, *Derkein.*"

He lowered his head even further, wanting to be sure his next words rang clear as a bell in the dragon's ears and only his ears. "Or should I call you Declan?"

A flash of fear passed over the dragon's face before his features twisted into a study of rage. Like a leashed pit bull, he lunged for Lotharus. The soldiers held him in check, as Lotharus knew they would. Slowly, he stood, giving a nod to the guards.

"Take him to the dungeon." Then he turned to Alexia who stood watchfully in the corner. "Let us see what he knows of our lost little bauble, hmm?"

A ripple of sickness folded over Alexia. She turned, heading toward her chamber, needing some free air, some space to think.

Lotharus's hand snaked out, his long fingers digging into her flesh. "Where are you going?"

"I don't feel well," Alexia muttered. The anger pouring off him was palpable and cold. She wanted nothing more than to get away from him. But his grip on her arm tightened.

"Perhaps it is because you let him feed from you?"

"I didn't let him," she snapped, tugging her arm free. "He attacked me."

Lotharus offered her a smile that didn't reach his onyx eyes. The next thing she knew, she was airborne, flying across the room. Her back slammed painfully against the far wall, and the side of her face went numb from the force of his blow. She cupped her cheek protectively, staring in shock as Lotharus straightened the cuffs of his suit jacket as though he'd merely swatted a fly.

"You will not lie to me again, Alexia. You know I do not approve."

"Lie?" she began, but the look he tossed her froze the words on her tongue.

With lightning-fast speed only ancients possessed, he crossed the room in a flash and stood in front of her. Dragging her to her feet, he pinned her between him and the wall at her back. At the feel of his erection digging into her hip, she sucked in a breath.

"Yes, *lie,*" he seethed. "I saw you kiss him."

Alexia swallowed down the acrid taste of bile rising in her throat and pressed back against the wall. He leaned closer. So close his nose brushed hers. "I saw your body writhing beneath his, begging for him to claim you." The hot breath of his words fanned against her neck before he swooped, licking the wound. His low groan vibrated against her throat and a shudder moved through his body. That male part of him grew harder, pressing more insistently against her.

"I watched you grab his face," he said against her neck, sliding his fingers through her hair. "Saw you pull his mouth closer." With a feral snarl, he dug his fingers into her scalp, pressing his mouth against her. Alexia's stomach rolled when he forced his tongue into her mouth, flopping it around with the finesse of a fish.

Thankfully, it was over almost as soon as it had started. He didn't enjoy kissing. Didn't do it with the dragon lord's passion.

Lotharus pulled back. His head cocked to the side as his bottomless eyes regarded her. "Thinking of him, are you?"

Alexia swallowed.

"So am I." He released her. She breathed deep, filling her lungs with the air she'd been depriving them of.

"I think I'll go and see if our soldiers have broken that bird yet."

Vivid images of the dragon fighting earlier flashed across her mind. He was so strong, so proud. He would not fall, would not go down on bended knee before Lotharus.

"You are coming with me, aren't you? After all, torture is your forte."

CHAPTER THREE

DETERMINED TO BREAK the dense fog that had clouded around her mind since the dragon's arrival, Alexia notched up her chin and fell into step behind Lotharus. After descending the spiral stair, they maneuvered down the narrow corridor to the dungeon. The dark walls on either side of them wept. Musty water and stale minerals filled the air. The scents comforted her like a reassuring security blanket would a child. She'd made this trip dozens of times. This was what she did, what she was good at. Although she never found the twisted pleasure Lotharus did in torture, she'd always successfully retrieved information she needed from her captives.

And she needed that crystal.

The sharp crack of a whip followed by a tensed, muffled groan pierced the quiet. She stopped, her heart pounding in her ears. The whip lashed again. At the answering grunt of pain, the bite mark on her neck burned. Alexia fingered the sensitive flesh, covering it with a curtain of her hair when Lotharus looked over his shoulder at her.

A moment later, they rounded the corner into the subterranean bowels of the catacomb. Lit only by torchlight, the dungeon boasted everything one might need to punish, maim or kill an enemy. An assortment of bloodied weapons hung on the flagstone walls and littered the tops of the scarred wood tables. A row of iron-barred cells lined the wall to the right, while a rack and other instruments of torture numerous rulers or their minions had collected over their centuries on earth occupied the space to the left.

Tonight, the soldiers had strung the dragon up against the center wall. His arms and legs were shackled to the sides. The silver collar was attached to a bar above him. His gorgeous body in complete human form was covered in a fine sheen of sweat. Every corded and ropelike muscle was taut like a bowstring. His hard, muscled abdomen, peppered with bullet holes, flexed under the next bite of the whip.

Unbidden, her body warmed, remembering his body pressed flush against hers. Her palms burned to skate over every smooth inch of him. The peaks of her nipples tightened beneath her leather corset.

What was wrong with her?

Again, the whip lashed his flesh. She flinched at the sound.

"Come, Alexia."

At her name, the dragon lifted his head. She stilled as striking blue eyes burned into her, watching her with unwavering intensity, even when a soldier rained another biting blow on his shoulder.

"Do you want the honors, or shall I?"

At the query, her mouth parched. Lotharus was known for his insatiable bloodlust. Somehow, although she had no idea how, she knew this dragon would not break easily. In anger, confusion and frustration she strode forward to the soldier doing the flogging. "Give it to me," she ordered, holding out her hand.

The soldier smiled and set the leather instrument in her hand. She palmed the handle, feeling its familiar smooth line and curves. After a deep breath, Alexia put it on the table. Instead she stepped up and smacked the dragon square across the face.

"Where is the crystal?"

He slowly turned his head to face her, a cold smile in his icy eyes. "I don't know."

She hit him harder and asked again. Spitting out a mouthful of blood, he let out a low laugh and locked his gaze on hers.

"I guess it's true what they say about blondes."

Alexia raked her palm across his flesh again. This time, her claws broke the skin of his handsome cheek. And this time when he stared at her, his smile held no trace of humor.

"The crystal?"

"I told you. I. Don't. Know," he said through clenched teeth.

"You're going to have to lie better than that."

"Lie? Where could I possibly be hiding it?" He nodded to his bare body.

Lotharus stepped up from behind her, offering her a spiked cat-o'-nine-tails, an instrument designed to peel flesh from bone. "Let's find out, shall we?"

Sickness rose up her throat at his words. She swallowed it down and took the whip. The burden of it hung like a lead weight in her arm. She did not want to do this. For the first time in all her years as a warrior for her people, she did not want to torture her enemy. And she couldn't explain why.

"Well, what are you waiting for?"

At Lotharus's prod, she knew if she didn't whip the dragon, not only would she be punished, but Lotharus would take over the interrogation. And none ever survived Lotharus's questioning. Ever. Although, some far corner of her mind whispered that if anyone could last more than a night in the horde dungeon, it would be this dragon lord before her.

Clamping down her jaw, Alexia stepped closer. Her eyes fixed on the dark nipples on his bloodied chest, the hard lines of his body. So different…

She stepped closer, so close that the heat from his body curled around her. She leaned forward and spoke so only he could hear. "Just tell me and end this."

The dragon stared down at her, faint creases lining his brow. Then he looked at Lotharus and back to her. Understanding finally lit up his eyes. She noticed they stared at her with less cold revulsion, less hate. He let out a sigh as if coming to some kind of decision. Then he inclined his head toward her.

"Do your worst, vixen," he whispered before leaning back again. "You'll get no answer from me." The latter he shouted loud enough for all ears to hear.

When she still did not move to strike him, the dragon smiled. "It is a shame we didn't have just a few more minutes together, you know. I could have made you sing with pleasure," he said with a wink.

Lotharus lurched forward, snatching the nine-tails

from her hand. Alexia barely had time to duck out of the way before he swung the weapon high, raining a blow across the dragon's golden chest.

IN ONE FLUID MOTION, Tallon landed at the causeway of the dragon's mountain lair and shifted form, moving seamlessly from the air to the ground.

As she walked into the darkness of the cave's mouth, the ancient stones that guarded the doorway to the inner city shifted open, allowing her passage. It had opened only a foot before she saw Falcon, Declan's second, waiting anxiously on the other side of the wall. Tallon noticed he was dressed from head to booted foot in black combat attire and wondered if he'd come close to trailing them—wondered briefly if the outcome would have been different if he had.

Pushing the thought down, she stepped inside. At the sight of her, his handsome face lit up in a smile.

"Good, you're back," he said, pushing his bare shoulder off the wall. His waist-length black hair trailed behind him like a sultry veil. Tallon blinked and looked ahead as he fell into step beside her.

"The council has been awaiting you…." His words trailed off. Out of the corner of her eye she saw his brow crease when he looked over her shoulder and saw the walls closing.

"Where is Lord Declan?"

At the name, Tallon's heart tightened and her legs almost buckled beneath her. Clutching the tattered brown satchel to her chest, she moved farther into the black outer tunnel. The air cooled with each step she took, water droplets plopping against slick stones the only sound other than her and Falcon's footsteps. Tallon kept walking until large hands gently covered the caps of her shoulders, forcing her to turn. Although she reluctantly spun, she kept her chin down, her eyes closed. She couldn't bring herself to say it. Couldn't acknowledge the truth her heart already knew. To say the words *Declan's gone* would make it real and right now she could still pretend it had all been a bad dream.

"Tallon." Falcon's soft voice wrapped around her like she knew his arms wanted to. But theirs was a warrior's society, a hard, fighting order. Weakness of any kind, especially love, was frowned upon, more than ever since the murder of their King and Queen. Her parents…Declan's parents.

A barely audible sob hiccupped in her chest.

"Oh, gods, no." Falcon's fingers squeezed into her flesh with such need it seemed he'd fall over if he let go. It was then that Tallon allowed herself to look into the face she'd known since she was born. A face etched with pain and loss that mirrored her own. Tears welled in her eyes and she shook her head, still unable to speak the words aloud. Falcon nodded, silently telling her he didn't want to hear her say them. He lifted a hand, smoothing a strand of hair from her eyes before resting his warm palm on her shoulder.

"Come, we must tell them," he said, nestling her under the crook of his arm.

Tallon wanted to push away from him, wanted to walk into council with her head held high with pride that she and Declan had succeeded in the job they had set out to do. But the warmth of Falcon's body filled a tiny hole in her now empty heart. Made the enormity of it all shrink away for just a brief moment. So instead, she closed her eyes, rested her head against his shoulder and allowed him to guide her.

Their mountaintop lair spilled into a network of tunnels and caverns of every size imaginable. Tallon knew every room by heart. Now Falcon led her through the hub of their inner city. She knew it with her eyes closed. The heat of too many bodies suffocated the normally cool temperature in the caves. Lights flickered behind her closed eyes. The hearty smell of spiced meats filled her nose and the hum of constant voices buzzed in her ears.

Falcon's arms tightened as they turned down the long

corridor leading to council headquarters. Once the sights and smells of the inner city faded behind her, Tallon eased from his protective grip and opened her eyes. After the briefest of pauses, Falcon released his hold on her.

"Thank you," she whispered.

Falcon said nothing. He didn't have to.

A few more steps brought them to a set of double doors. Guards stationed on either side nodded at their approach and opened the doors. Falcon and Tallon stepped inside the circular chamber. A lone chandelier hung above the table, lighting the ancient meeting room. All of the council members were present and seated. Tallon's breath hitched at the sight. Other than Hawk, Falcon and his older brother, Kestrel, there were no elders left. Young dragons now occupied the table where just months ago, her mother, father and brother used to sit.

This war had been costly and not only to the Blacks. It touched every family in every line without discrimination or remorse.

And now it's taken Declan.

Tallon slammed her eyes shut. The hands holding the satchel shook. The fatigue and fear she'd ignored crashed down, nearly choking her.

A deep voice sounded. "Where is your brother, Tallon?" Kestrel asked.

She lifted her chin, forcing herself to keep it together. "They caged him."

"Damnation," Kestrel breathed, as a collective gasp sounded in the small room.

"Was he wounded?" asked Hawk, the last surviving member of the original colony and oldest council member.

Tallon couldn't find her voice, so she nodded in reply. Someone cursed. Another let out a long sigh. After a moment's pause, Hawk rose, his chair scraping against the stone floor as he stood.

"And the crystal?"

The room fell silent. Eager eyes met hers. Wordlessly, Tallon held up the satchel. Rounding the table, Hawk took the bag from her, ripped it open and searched inside.

"He made me take it and leave. He wouldn't let me stay and fight…." Her stumbled words died when Hawk removed the contents.

A rock. A plain stone sat in the center of his palm.

Wide-eyed, Tallon snatched the bag, searching every nook and crevice before chucking the useless fabric across the room. "Dammit, brother," she shouted, slamming her palms on the table and hunching forward. Grabbing a breath, she blew it out slowly and tried to think. Only one thing came. "He must have it on him, hidden somehow. Somewhere."

"Then we go back and get it." Ash, a young dragon barely out of his shell, jumped to his feet. At his words, Tallon looked up, thinking he had a hard face for one so young.

"We *are* finished if they find it first," Kestrel agreed.

"If they haven't found it already." Hawk released a sigh and smoothed a hand over his bald head before rubbing the tips of his silver goatee in thought.

"Griffon," Tallon said. "What if we sent him in after the Queen?"

Hawk dropped his hand. "The hunter?"

"No way," Falcon interjected, rising up to stand, as well. "We'll not send Griffon. Not until we know what's going on. A lord he may be, but he's too dangerous, too reckless." He set worried eyes on her. "Declan might still be in there. Alive," he said through clenched teeth, his eyes wide as if telling her some silent message her desperate heart didn't already know. However, even the hatchlings of their flock knew the tales of Griffon the hunter—the lone scavenger who lived like a ghost among his kin and killed his enemies with unnatural meticulousness at any cost. Using him wasn't a terrific alternative, but neither was losing her brother.

"What other choice do we have?" she asked. When no one answered, Tallon's gaze whirled around the room, taking in each man's concentrated look. A spark of fear ignited at the plan she saw forming in their eyes. "The horde's numbers, I've seen them," she stammered. "We are too few to fight them." She looked at Ash with his wide, eager eyes, his shaggy brown hair still dangling around his shoulders, unlike the full-grown, pure-bred males, who had hair down their backs. "We're too young to ever hope to win."

"Which is why we need that stone," Hawk said with a growl, hurling the rock across the room. Tallon's shoulders flinched and she lowered her eyes.

"Tal, we have no choice," Falcon said, moving beside her.

"Yes, we do. We trust Declan. He knows what he's doing. He must have a plan…."

"A plan, I wager, that did not include getting captured," Kestrel said, finally pushing up to stand. His gray eyes fixed on her. The long strands of his straight hair, so like his brother Falcon's and yet almost white in color, swayed with each hobbled step he took toward her. "Especially not if he had the crystal on him." He narrowed his wary eyes on Tallon. "You're certain he had it when you two left the catacombs?"

She reached him in two steps. Tipping her head back, Tallon met his gaze, hoping he'd read the truth in hers. "I saw it. I saw the damn thing with my own eyes."

His massive body seemed to relax and the doubt she'd glimpsed in his silver eyes vanished at her answer. "All right," he breathed. "Then we go back and find it. We'll have a small group search the cliffs and forests around the catacombs in case he stowed it somehow." His gaze met Tallon's. "Another small recon group will attempt to see if he yet lives."

At his order, the group moved into action. All except Tallon.

"See if he yet lives," she repeated. "Are you mad? We have to get him out of there!"

Kestrel pointed to the corner where his mate and resident healer stood, her arms littered with scrolls. "Doc says the horde's ritual is taking place in two days. There is no time to wait for Declan or plan an escape. I'm sorry, but retrieving that crystal is more important. Even Declan would agree."

"But…"

"No *buts*, Tallon," he ordered. "We cannot afford any more needless losses."

"A needless loss?" Tallon bared her fangs. "Is that what my brother is to you now?" Before he could answer, she lunged forward. And before she managed a step, Falcon's thick arms wrapped around her waist, pinning her back to his front.

"Let it go, Tal," he whispered beside her temple. "And you," he snapped to his brother. "Ease off her, would you?"

Tallon wriggled her shoulders, fighting against Falcon's hold. "Put me down." Even though she was angry, she would never bite Kestrel, or the others, for that matter. They knew it, too. Most had served her parents since before she was born and were used to her mother's fang-baring tantrums, as well.

Declan was the only one who never lost his cool. No matter what, he always stayed calm and levelheaded.

Declan. Her heart pinched in her chest and she finally quit fighting.

"I can't lose everyone, Falcon," she said, sinking back into his chest. Tallon closed her eyes and heaved a sigh of helplessness, allowing herself to relish the feel of his arms around her, if only for a moment. "I knew the minute he told me to leave I'd never see him alive again."

"You don't know that."

But she did. Somewhere in her soul, darkness festered and grew. So much sorrow, so much pain and loss, she couldn't take any more. Wouldn't take any more.

Lips quivering with renewed anger, she pushed out of Falcon's embrace. "That blonde monster," she shouted.

Chest heaving, she turned back to Falcon, ignoring the concern in his green eyes.

"She is going to pay for this. They all are."

CHAPTER FOUR

DECLAN WINCED AS SPEARS of pain lanced through his flesh to the bone. The rivers of blood, long caked on his skin, itched like mad. But he didn't have the strength to lift a hand and attempt to ease them.

In what became a slow struggle, Declan opened his eyes. His breath seized to see a swirling gray mist clouded around him. And to see he was standing even though a shift of his shoulders proved he lay on the dungeon floor.

"What the…?"

He slammed his eyes closed. Even though his senses confirmed he still lay on the dungeon floor, he saw that freakish fog around him. Felt himself vertical. Holding his hands in front of him, he cautiously walked forward. His foot touched air and the earth fell out from under him.

Wind lapped his flesh as he fell into a void. On instinct, he called upon his dragon form, hoping to shift and fly out of this vortex.

Nothing happened.

Opening his eyes wide, he noticed a small circle of red shining like a beacon at the funnel's bottom. Each passing second brought him closer to the light. Closer to the ground. Declan only had time to shut his eyes in useless but instinctual defense before he hit thick carpet with a thwack.

Carpet?

Head spinning, Declan fanned his fingers through plush red fibers. His brow tightened as he tensed and pushed up to stand, his eyes darting about an empty room. Seeing no one, he closed his eyes and channeled his dragon senses. Again it proved he still lay caged in that cell.

"So, I'm dreaming," he said beneath his breath as he opened his eyes. Even though it was vivid, more crisp and unsettling than any dream he'd ever had. "But of what?"

With guarded steps, he moved through a large chamber. The relentless fog closed in with every step, until even the walls melted into its embrace. When the mist had nearly engulfed him, a set of elaborately carved French doors materialized before him. They opened without a sound and Declan stepped inside.

The mist swelled at his approach and then parted, as if the room itself had taken in a deep breath and blown it away.

Declan swallowed. Hard.

A woman stood before him. A gloriously naked woman.

His eyes drank in the violin curve of her back, sliding lower over the soft swell of her ass. Every inch of her milky-white skin glowed and shimmered in the soft amber light. His palms burned to caress her and spears of heat shot through him, barreling like a rocket to his tightening balls. Then she pivoted and he found himself holding his breath.

At the sight, his heart stuttered and then stopped completely.

It was her. The sexy blonde vamp who fired his lust and fueled his hate.

"Alexia," he whispered. The flavor of her name on his lips bled into the taste of her. Tangy and rich, her phantom essence coated his throat and burst on his tongue, making his mouth water. Never had he tasted anything like her. It had taken all the will he'd owned to pull away from her sweet neck and he would give anything to be there again now.

Breathtakingly beautiful, her wide black eyes, pale skin and lush lips filled his vision. He stepped closer.

Though part of him wanted to awaken and end this torture, another wanted to get closer, crawl inside her and never come out. Overcome, he reached for her. However, the hand that lifted and smoothed down her cheek did not belong to him. Declan frowned. His gaze fixed on the fingers closing around her neck, the wide, ruby ring on the index finger and long black claws extending from each tip.

Lotharus.

Even trapped in this hallucinogenic sleep, the countless wounds and cuts on his body ached at the memory of the torture he'd endured at that monster's hands. And now they were all over Alexia. Declan shot his gaze back to her face. The fear in her eyes nearly felled him and set protective rage simmering violently in his veins.

Declan shuddered in his sleep, helpless as the vampire spun her around, forcing her to bend over the rail at the bottom of the bed. Lotharus swiped the curtain of her blond hair over her shoulder, baring the back of her neck to his gaze. One finger trailed over the long line of her nape before his hand bit down atop her neck and he positioned himself behind her.

"No." Declan stepped forward to help her, to stop this, but his feet wouldn't move. It struck him then that he couldn't even turn around. Clenching his jaw and fists tight, he closed his eyes, unable to watch and not opening them until Lotharus roared out his pleasure in one word.

Mine.

Declan jerked awake. As he had realized sometime before the crazy dream began, he still lay on his back on the dungeon floor. Cold sweat covered his body. He flexed his stomach muscles, wincing at the ribbon of slight pain curling around his gut. Wrapping an arm around the ache, he dragged himself to sit up. Resting his back on the wall, he closed his eyes and sucked in a breath.

Images of the dream flashed through his mind with lucid clarity. It had been so real, vivid, like a memory. Holding his head in his hands, he pushed it back to the far recess of his mind, trying to ignore the most unsettling aspect of it all—the protective rage and palpable anger still quivering through every muscle of his body. A body still ready to leap to her defense and stop that terrible event from ever taking place. To save the little vampire who'd shot him out of the sky and caged him here.

A cross between a chuckle and a grunt bubbled out of him.

Gods, was he already losing his mind in this place?

ALEXIA BRACED HER HANDS on the rocky shower wall and stood beneath a constant stream of water, relishing the warm spray sluicing down her scalp and back. Head down, she watched the water wash away the night's blood and grime, wishing it could wash away the images of that dragon lord's flesh splitting open under Lotharus's whip. Of his golden body arched above her, his blue eyes, dark and smoldering, speaking volumes of what he wanted to do to her.

She tilted her head to the side, wincing when the needles of water pricked her neck.

His bite.

She lifted a hand to her throat, flinching from pain and the memory it provoked. Why hadn't it healed yet? She never went more than a few minutes without self-healing.

Then again, she'd never been bitten before. Was this perhaps normal?

The water automatically shut off when she moved toward the door. Pushing the beveled glass open, she took two granite steps to the main level. Stopping in front of the sink, she tucked her hair in a bun with a comb. After wrapping a towel around her, she pulled out one thin metal razor and laid it on the counter.

A film of haze coated the mirror. Alexia lifted both hands, wiping the flat of her palms on the cool glass until the condensation was gone.

The reflection staring back at her stopped her cold.

Although she couldn't stand to see, she couldn't look away. The woman in the mirror looked desperate, sad and empty. Emotions she always felt, always carried on the inside, showed plain as day on her face.

For a moment, she allowed the truth of those feelings to sweep over her, let them take her to a place where years ago she'd vowed not to go. Self-pity, sorrow, longing— they were all weak and selfishly indulgent emotions. Luxuries a future Queen could not afford to entertain. At the sound of her mother's voice in her ears, Alexia allowed the wave of emotions to crest, the swell of anger to rise.

Without taking her eyes off her reflection, she lifted the blade to the glass. She slid the razor across the reflection of her face, just below her eyes. Then she lowered her hand, slicing it across her mirrored neck. The hand holding the razor trembled. A small voice whispered through her, wishing she had the guts to do it for real.

Alexia gasped and tossed the metal on the floor. Pinching her eyes tightly shut, she set her hands on the cool stone and hunched over the sink. A burning pit opened behind her stomach even though she tried to breathe it away. She covered the dull ache with her palm, acknowledging the cause.

A shadowy space, always present inside of her, had grown over the years. The crawling darkness wound through her, digging its roots deeper, further into her soul. Although she knew it was wrong, she'd fed the shadow at first. Every act of torture, every soul she'd put in the ground, bred and nurtured it until now it threatened to swallow her, consume her. Worse, she'd begun to have the impression the reasons she'd been fighting all these years were not as black and white as they once had seemed.

By the time she looked back in the mirror, the haze had cleared from the glass. Crisp and clear, her reflection stared back at her. Again she regarded herself, only this time she looked fine, composed, as if a mask covered her features, betraying the emotions truly bubbling up within. She did not look miserable, frightened or desperate, despite the fact she'd felt nothing but a blended cocktail of all these feelings since that night Lotharus…

Alexia pushed off the counter, forcing the memories back. Striding to the closet, she pushed aside her leather combat gear with more force than necessary, selecting instead a powder-blue chiffon toga, befitting the presence of her mother. The fabric slid over her head, settling in no more than a whisper on her flesh. Smooth and light, the texture was shockingly airy, the antithesis of the confining gear she wore each day.

At once, the air started to close around her. She felt naked. Exposed. She couldn't seem to drag enough oxygen into her lungs. Hastily, she reached back into her closet, her hands burrowing beneath a neat stack of pants. Closing her hand over a short throwing knife, she secured the blade in a thigh holster beneath her gown. With each tightening of the strap, her hands, once unsteady, became more sure and confident. By the time she'd secured the latch and stood, the threadbare line she'd been grasping tightened and drew her to the surface.

Exhaling, she moved to her bedside vanity and began methodically smoothing her hair. For some reason, the normal emptiness in the air smothered her tonight. Though the lack of men, females and children was always palpable, Alexia did not know anything different. She hadn't seen but the occasional natural-born vampire in years. They dwelled in a different compound set farther within the cliff walls. A place she wasn't allowed to go. Even her personal attendants were comprised of Lotharus's soldiers, as it was his orders keeping her and her mother separate from the colony.

Though he claimed it to be the best for their station, Alexia believed he did it as a way to keep them under his control, under his ever-watchful eye. Either way, it made her miserable. Again, something she assumed Lotharus intended.

In truth, she was no different than the souls rotting in the dungeon. Granted, she wore no shackles and her cage was bigger, less filthy. But she was still a prisoner.

Like him.

Closing her eyes, she shut out the thought. Instead, she called to mind a more serene memory, one of the only ones she had. From back when her grandmother ruled. The long-ago, lilting sounds of laughter and children at play echoed in her mind. Images of her running barefoot through the compound flashed behind her eyes. She felt the beaming smile on her face. Saw her long hair trailing behind her like a kite. Another girl whose name she couldn't recall chased along behind her. A friend, she thought with a wistful smile. How long had it been since she'd had one of those? How long had it been since she'd smiled like that?

A knock sounded at the door, jerking Alexia out of her memory. Standing, she rounded the stool and crossed the chamber. Ivan, one of Lotharus's most trusted men, opened the door before she reached it. His broad shoulders barely fit in the doorway.

"The Queen's been waiting for you."

CHAPTER FIVE

DECLAN HEARD HEAVY footsteps progressing down the hall. The swaying of chain links rattled along the stones with each step.

Closer.

Each sound brought closer what he knew would be his death.

Too spent from the crazy dreams and damnable collar, Declan closed his eyes. The animal in him immediately picked up what his eyes could not see. Cool night air with a hint of rain. He tipped back his chin, sniffing the sky. Filling his lungs with a deep breath, he shut out the drumbeat of the footsteps and focused on the sporadic yet heavy pattering of rain.

His dragon spirit howled for freedom, roared to taste just one drop of fresh rain on his flesh, rolling down his back. Beneath his skin twitched the wings, begging for the sweet release of slicing night's air with their instrumental precision.

The rain picked up, tapping against the earth and stones like impatient fingertips. He cocked his head toward the tiny barred window. Fat droplets splashed on the cliffs and slapped against the ocean water, which churned louder with each howling wind gust.

The cell door swung open. Two soldiers filed in, hauling him to his feet. Declan lifted a fist to fight back, confused when he could barely raise it to his chest. The collar weakened him more than he'd thought.

And that dream...

They slung their arms under his and proceeded out the cell door. The beast within whimpered when they tore him away from the window. The lack of air wounded him more than any amount of torture they could devise.

The tips of his toes slid on the floor as they led him down the long, winding corridors. Declan tried to keep his head up so he might learn where they kept him and discern a way out, but he couldn't. His head seemed weighted down, as if someone had strung an anchor to his neck. Dropping his chin to his chest, he closed his eyes and tried to gather the strength that still lived inside him in preparation for whatever they planned.

ALEXIA BRISTLED AT IVAN'S bravado, but said nothing. From day one, Lotharus had worked hard to undermine her position in the horde, especially around *his* soldiers. Bit by bit she'd watched as he'd tipped the power scales in his favor. When she'd finally had enough and demanded he stop, he'd taken a more drastic step to ensure she'd always feel inferior around him.

Although she did her best to move on from that night, the damage was done. The soldiers could not only sense her weakness around him, they could see it. Hell, she thought with a twinge of shame, even their dragon captive saw it.

Pursing her lips, Alexia swept past Ivan and into the hall, glad he remained behind. Sconces flickered and hissed as she passed. Their auburn light danced on the damp cave walls, casting shadows against them. Used to the clicking of her boots on the stones, the quiet shuffle of her slippered feet unsettled her. She focused instead on the cool metal pressing into the flesh of her outer thigh with each step she took. That felt normal…familiar.

As she made her way to the Queen's chamber, she thought about what she was going to tell her mother about the crystal. An ancient horde relic, the Draco Crystal had been in the safekeeping of her family for years. Yet only recently did they understand its true power. An earthquake had fractured the cliff walls, revealing half a dozen catacombs and vaults no one had seen in over seven hundred years. Among many of the olden treasures and artifacts found within were scrolls long forgotten and thought destroyed. One such scroll spoke of the Draco Crystal, of its power to rule all or destroy one. Of the terrible wrath and damage it had caused in the auld days and the subsequent reason for the scroll being buried.

Everything in Alexia screamed to abide the olden horde's wishes and keep dead secrets hidden. But Lotharus and her mother had other plans. They wanted to harness the crystal's power and use it against their enemies to ensure victory.

When a group of dragons had attacked last month, stealing the scroll, the captured dragon King and Queen were tortured and murdered. Now, with the stakes so high and both sides on the hunt, the race was on. Alexia knew it would only be a matter of weeks, even days, until this war would be at its pinnacle. Although she knew she should do everything in her power to ensure her people would be the ones standing on top, something about the crystal, about Lotharus's rampant bloodlust to find it, unsettled her.

Alexia rounded the corner. Dismissing the guard with a wave, she pushed through the giant double doors. They pivoted wide, revealing the bright splendor of the Queen's hall. Queen Catija's quarter had no receiving room. Instead, it opened into a dome reminiscent of an archaic cathedral or sanctuary, complete with fresco ceilings. Soft artificial light beamed from the top of the cavernous space. Alexia's eye was drawn upward, following the flowing arcs and sculpted curves of the vaulted ceiling.

While the Queen was the mirror image of her predecessor in appearance, unlike her grandmother, who enjoyed the finer things and believed in reform and harmony, Alexia's mother had barbaric tastes and a penchant for gore. Or at least she had in the past. A decade ago, just the sound of the Queen's name would strike fear in dragons and vampires alike. However, ever since Lotharus had entered the picture, first as her advisor and now as her future husband, she'd changed. Slowly at first—most had not even noticed the drastic transformation. But Alexia had.

Lowering her gaze to the gardens, a relaxed smile passed her lips. Marble statues of Goddess stood beside white pillars wider than the boles of the large trees stretching upward, trying to reach any light they could, artificial or natural. Tendrils of lush ivy embraced the whitewashed walls and myriad birds flew freely around the underground garden. A lazy path wound through the space, forking into two passageways. One led to the conference quarter, the other toward the Queen's bedchamber door.

Alexia followed the footpath toward the meeting room, pausing at a fountain for the divine hunter, Diana. The ivory Goddess stared with wide, vacant eyes at the water pooled at her feet. She held one palm up, as if waiting for some sort of offering to be fitted atop it. The other slim hand extended forward, pouring a pitcher of endless water into the rectangular pond stretched out before her. Alexia followed her gaze to the pool. Beneath the shimmering water lay an intricate scaled replica of Davna Vremena, a land far beyond the mists of the Fatum, deep in the olden lands of their foremothers.

Although she could not see the model, she remembered vague images of it from childhood. Her grandmother used to bring her here, used to raise the small city from the bottom of the pond and tell her stories of a peaceful world where every creature of light and dark lived in harmony. Alexia suddenly yearned to see the monument again, if only to prove that such a place had once existed.

Taking one last look at the fountain, Alexia continued

down the path. A frown tugged her brow at the sound of voices lingering over the constant trickle of streaming water.

"I do not think she's ready," a male voice said.

"She has not yet ascended." Her mother's voice answered, weak but confident.

"Even then, I don't believe she will be ready for the throne."

"Lotharus, though you are an olden, you have not personally borne witness to a princess becoming a Queen. The power she'll gain when she ascends will rival the Goddess herself. Combined with the training you've given her, my daughter will have ten times the strength of any one of those soldiers you hold in such high esteem."

"It's not her strength I'm worried about," he said. "It is her will. Her ability to rule to the standard of our ancestors…."

Alexia stepped out from behind the foliage. "My *ability* should be none of your concern." Lotharus turned to face her. As usual, he wore tailored black clothes. Their starkness stood in striking contrast to his sallow skin tone, and noticeably different from her mother's Mediterranean complexion, pure white gown and raven-black hair.

Light and dark. Good and evil.

"Ah, Alexia dear, you're here." Catija stepped forward to greet her, but her footing faltered and she wobbled.

"Mother." Alexia hurried to her side. "Are you all right?"

"I'm fine," Catija dismissed with a wave. "Just a little dizzy."

Lotharus wound his arm around the Queen's waist, tucking her against him and pivoting her away from Alexia. "You need to feed, dear heart," Lotharus said, tightening his hold around her middle. "Come." He pivoted, walking them toward the council quarters.

Alexia trailed a few paces behind. Her gaze fixed on her mother's black hair, plaited down her back. The tip of her long mane brushed the spotless, shimmering floors like a broom, swaying side to side with each dip of her hips. She had such a youthful, vibrant body. No one could see that a silent yet threatening illness was plaguing her mind.

"The wedding and ascension are two days away, Alexia, and you have yet to select a gown," the Queen said over her shoulder.

Alexia opened her mouth, but promptly closed it. It was pointless to remind her mother they had selected the gown just last night. "I shall see to choosing a gown straight away," she replied instead.

"Good." Her mother smiled. "Lotharus tells me the

community is eager to attend your ceremony. We wouldn't want them to be disappointed."

Alexia nodded, wondering exactly how her mother thought she should react. A group of strangers were excited to have an excused day off from work or labor. To them, the occasion of such fortune mattered little if at all. They came for the free food and spirits the festivities offered, not to wish her or her mother well. After all, she knew none of them, so it stood to reason none of them knew her.

Keeping her opinions to herself, Alexia followed the two of them into the conference room. The circular seating area reminded her of those Jacuzzis she'd seen humans use. However, this one was ten times the size and empty. Instead of water, the center bore a white stone table. It had a pedestal in the center and looked rather like a mushroom had grown from the ground, flattened and hardened in place.

After descending two steps into the circle, the Queen took a seat on the plush velvet cushions pillowing the bench. Her flowing white toga gown fanned out around her. The thick braid now rested over her shoulder, curling around her breasts to rest on her lap like a hairy python.

Alexia lowered to the floor, resting her hands on the table. Lotharus sat behind her, the fabric of his pants brushing the bare skin of her lower back. Shifting, Alexia sat up straighter, trying to keep from touching him. She glanced back to see him sitting with his legs open in a relaxed V, his elbows resting on the floor up behind him. His eyes regarded her with an eager tinge that sent bile rising in her throat before they flitted to a soldier perched in the corner.

"First things first." Lotharus snapped his fingers.

The soldier stepped forward. With awkward alacrity, he poured vintage blood from the royal cellar into three silver goblets. The Queen leaned forward, eagerly accepting and drinking her offer. By the masculine sound behind her, she knew Lotharus had swilled his down, as well. However, Alexia could not tear her eyes away from the goblet and decanter long enough to pick hers up.

Silver.

They were made of silver. Like the collar on his neck, eating through precious layers of his golden flesh….

"Are you not hungry?"

Startled, Alexia looked up at her mother's query. "No. I—I mean, yes." Recalling her weakness in the shower, she knew she should feed. However, her stomach rolled in protest.

When another minute ticked by and Alexia still hadn't taken the cup in hand, the Queen huffed out a breath and placed her empty goblet on the table. "Alexia, I know you heard us in the garden. But do not worry. Many have ascended before you, and many will make the journey after." Swiping a dainty wrist over her bloodred lips, she nodded her head and pointed to the tapestry hanging from floor to ceiling against the wall. "Your ancestors have long lived through much harder times than these and succeeded. You will, as well."

Alexia looked up at the family tree—a sickening reminder of her evil lineage and her utter lacking to keep up with it. Stretching up farther than even her keen eyes could discern were symbols and names of those who had come before her. Women who had overcome, ascended and conquered their fears and dominated those around them.

"For centuries, each female leader has been given a one-hundred-year incumbency to rule, and then the line passes on," the Queen continued. "This is the way it's been done since the dark times. The way it must be to keep this horde together, keep us strong. It will soon be your time, Alexia. Your obligation is to not only see us all through the next hundred years, but to keep our horde intact and in the seat of power amongst the other vampire clans."

I don't want to rule. Alexia nearly let the words fall from her lips. However, she did want to govern. Just not the way her mother had and especially not how Lotharus expected.

"Now." The Queen held out her hand. "Have you brought my crystal back, as I asked?"

Alexia stared at her open palm before blinking up at her mother. The words of her failure froze on her lips before she forced them out in a rush. "No, my Queen. It was lost."

"Lost?"

"Yes. But I have found something else."

Catija took her hand back and shook her head. "Let me guess, another *Derkein*. Lotharus, what on earth and sky should we do with her? I gave her one, simple task…."

"You worry without cause, my love," Lotharus said, a smile in his voice. "She will find the crystal and return it to you."

Catija offered him a lazy grin. "Only because you'll be there to guide her."

"Stop speaking about me like I'm not here," Alexia snapped, rising up to stand. "I managed to catch that dragon lord without his help."

Her mother's eyes flashed, color flushing her usually sallow cheeks. "Yes. However, you have obviously yet to retrieve anything useful from it. I need that crystal. More importantly, you will need that crystal."

"Why? Because *he* says so," Alexia said, pointing to Lotharus. "Our foremothers ruled without fulfilling that scroll's prophecy. You ruled without it. I fail to see why I cannot do the same."

"Enough!" The Queen stood. "You ask what good is

the crystal, and I ask, what good is another dragon carcass stinking up my horde?"

"If I may," Lotharus said, easing up from his perch. The Queen nodded and placed a hand over her heaving chest in an attempt to catch her breath. "That dragon lord may be of use to us. He is not just any winged snake from the flock."

Catija's brow furrowed. "Go on."

With a knowing smile, Lotharus moved beside her.

"That *Derkein* your daughter captured is the only son of the dead King and Queen."

"What?" Alexia breathed.

The Queen's face instantly paled. "He wouldn't possibly have told you this. How do you know?"

"I saw something. Something I've only seen once before." His cold eyes settled on Alexia. Their heated focus slid to her neck, lingering there before he met her eyes again. "Would you care to tell her, or should I?"

Alexia thought about holding her tongue. If it was true, the ramifications, the possibilities overwhelmed her. But then she realized it mattered not what she said or didn't say. Lotharus would tell her mother if she didn't. She sighed. "The dragon lord has fangs, like us."

The Queen covered her mouth with her hand. "Goddess, then it *is* him."

Alexia's gaze fixed on the look of horror on her mother's face. Something was wrong. Her mother, the most vicious and bloodthirsty Queen of the horde in centuries, was not scared of anything. But right now, she was terrified.

"Lotharus, we must not harm him," she said, clutching his lapel tight. "We must set him free." Her mother's words came out in a whisper but Alexia heard them clear and true.

"Are you mad?" Lotharus asked. "We couldn't have asked for a better situation to fall in our lap. Think on it, my sweet. What better wedding gift to give our people than the head of their enemy? He is the last, the missing link that ensures our triumph. They have no other son, no other heir. He is the only remaining hope and now he is ours."

"Which is why we must set him loose," she said, her voice cracking.

"No." He nodded to the soldier, now standing next to the wall. The warrior stepped forward, filled the Queen's goblet to the rim and handed the chalice to Lotharus.

"You're weak, my love. If you were strong again, you would see." Lotharus settled the cup at her lips and urged her to drink. "Without this beast, the dragons will slip into nonexistence. You will go down as the most successful ruler of our time, and we will finally rule."

"*You* will rule," Alexia stated, although neither of them paid her any heed.

Catija took a deep swallow of blood before glancing up at him, a question in her eyes. "I don't know…."

"That is why you have me to think for you," he said into her ear before taking the shell between his lips. Her mother's eyes fluttered and a smile curved her lips as she took another drink.

Alexia didn't know what was going on. All she knew was if she didn't act fast, that dragon lord's fate was as good as sealed and, for some reason, her mother did not want it so.

"May I have a word, Mother?" She stared at Lotharus. "In private."

His coal eyes steadied on hers. For a moment Alexia thought he might refuse. However, he disengaged himself from her mother's side. "Go ahead with your girl talk, my dear. I have a prisoner to interrogate."

Alexia's heart thumped as she watched him walk away. "Why?" she called after him. "If he knew anything about the crystal, we would have uncovered it last night. I say he is telling the truth and we do as the Queen says. Let him go. Demonstrate our goodwill to the dragons. Use the beginning of this new era to show them we are willing to change."

He stopped, his back visibly tensing. A heartbeat later, he'd crossed the room in a plume of smoke and mist to stand before her. Cold fingers wrapped around the bare flesh of her arm, pulling her into him. "I grow so weary of your insolence, little Alexia," he spat, twisting his hand until her skin beneath it burned.

Grimacing, she pulled free of his hold. "I'm happy to disappoint you."

Again, he made a move for her. But he stopped short, as if he finally remembered he stood in the presence of the Queen. With a shift of his shoulders, Lotharus straightened and turned his focus to Catija. "That dragon knows the location of the crystal and will confess it in good time. He is too strong and willful for us to have broken him in one night." He looked back at Alexia. "And as for releasing him, that is something I will not do until I am confident he speaks the truth. Or he's dead."

Alexia watched him turn on his heel and again make for the door. "I will not let you destroy my entire reign before I even get there," she cried. "Do you hear me?" When Lotharus didn't reply, a wave of helpless annoyance rode through her. "You cannot deny my orders! I am the ruler here."

Finally, he stopped and looked over his shoulder, his lips twisting. "Not yet, you're not."

Alexia watched in stunned disbelief as he left the room. The moment he was gone, she rushed back to her mother. "Are you honestly going to let him get away with this? He's trying to start another war."

The Queen casually took up the bottle and refilled her goblet. "We are already at war. Lotharus is only trying to do what's best for our horde."

"You say the words as if you're trying to convince even yourself. What is best is to let the prisoner go. You said so yourself only moments ago."

Catija lifted her head and Alexia couldn't help but notice it loll slightly to the side, as if it were too much effort to hold it upright. "Why this fierce stance on the dragon's life?"

"Me? What about you? A minute ago you were begging Loth—"

"How many others like him have you killed for the good of this horde?"

Her question hit Alexia like a bucket of icewater. "Too many."

The Queen stood. "Perhaps you should be thinking, *not enough*." Chalice in hand, Catija lifted her skirt and turned toward the bedchamber door. "I'll see to it that Marguerite comes to get you fitted for your ascension gown."

"So that's it. Are you going to lie down and let him make all the decisions for you?" She exhaled. "Goddess, he has you totally delusional, doesn't he?"

The Queen spun around, her black eyes flashing. "I will not have you address me so. This is my horde to rule until you ascend, and by the Goddess, I will do what I see fit."

"I wish you would rule. But you have only two days left. And you better pray the dragon lasts that long." She sucked in a breath, hoping to drag some courage into her lungs along with air. "If not, when I become Queen, you and your lover will have to answer to me."

CHAPTER SIX

EVENTUALLY, THE SOLDIERS hauling Declan came to a brace of doors and burst inside without knocking. When they stopped, Declan forced his heavy head up. Bloodred velvet draped the back wall of a lush chamber. Gothic tapestries hung along another. However, he could not keep his eyes off the bed in the corner—off the intricate wooden bed frame at its foot.

The one from the dream.

Vivid images of Lotharus and Alexia flashed behind his eyes. Unbidden, a low growl vibrated in his chest.

Declan felt Lotharus's cold presence before he saw him emerge from the corner. Although the room did not seem overly masculine, Declan deduced right away that this must be Lotharus's room. Realized with the little grain of consciousness left to him that Lotharus would want to hold the memory of his murder within his private walls, keep it close, like some sick kind of security blanket.

When the vampire finally stepped fully into the room, Declan's lip curled into a snarl. Memories of the last time he'd seen that sneering face, of what he'd done to Alexia, clawed to the surface. The hate he'd channeled toward her shifted to Lotharus for reasons he couldn't explain and wouldn't explore.

With a primal instinct, Declan yanked his limbs away from the unsuspecting guards and lunged for Lotharus. However, the collar quickly pilfered the strength his fury had given him. Hands descended on his chest and legs, pushing him back until he slammed against a stone wall. At the impact, chains rattled beside him. Declan swallowed an uneasy lump in his throat as the soldiers strung him up, securing that unbearable collar around his neck to a hook on the wall, his wrists and ankles to connecting chains.

He noticed Lotharus had not flinched a muscle during the entire ordeal. He merely stood, watching.

And Declan did not take his eyes off him.

Satisfied with the bindings, the guards slipped back and stood along the walls. Lotharus stepped forward, his black eyes leveled on Declan, no emotion in their shadowed depths. Only blackness, nothingness.

"Now," Lotharus said, tugging up the sleeves of his black overcoat. "Are you ready to tell me where the crystal is?"

Declan smirked. "Three things I can't stand…Horde, Thai food and answering the same question over and over…."

Lotharus tucked his arm back, landing his fist on Declan's nose. Before he had time to recover, another hit blew against his temple. A third slammed against his eyebrow. One for each hate, he figured.

Throbbing pain began a low drumbeat in his skull. Declan gritted his teeth to keep from making a sound, determined not to give the bastard one ounce of satisfaction. He lifted his head to see Lotharus staring down at him. Slowly, he started undoing the buttons of his coat. Shrugging out of the garment, he laid it carefully over the side of the bed before stepping forward.

"You know," he said, rolling up the cuffs of his black shirt, a sardonic smile twisting his lips. "I don't think I properly thanked you last night."

Declan forced his lips into a smile. "For what? Showing your girlfriend how to kiss?"

An elbow slammed into his gut before the last word had fallen from his lips. Declan sucked in a breath, groaning when he repeated the action again.

"You may think you're funny now, but it will be I who is laughing last, *Derkein.* I assure you."

"Aw, come on," he said with a pained grunt as he stood upright again. "I thought that was a good one."

A booted heel slammed into his ribs, sending him back over, and a fist cracked across his face, followed by another and another. Declan coughed, spitting out the stream of blood flooding his mouth onto the pristine white floor by his feet.

As he watched the red flow between the tiles, a shadow darkened over him.

"That was for drinking from what's mine." Lotharus's knee kicked into his gut, once, twice. Usually, Declan could handle these simple hits. But the collar acted like some sort of muscle relaxer. He couldn't tighten his abs and block the blows. Instead, each one sank deep into his body, crushing his lung and perhaps a rib or two in the process.

As Declan fought against the bolts of agony wrenching his gut, Lotharus squatted in front of him. "And that is for trying to claim her," he said before standing and walking away.

Declan smiled through the pain. So that was what this was all about? The girl? His smile turned into a chuckle. The chuckle morphed into an outright laugh. The footfalls stopped. Lotharus held his hands twined at the base of his spine. His demeanor and poise looked calm, composed. However, his actions had already given him away. Something about Declan touching that girl made Lotharus livid, even more so than the notion that Declan had the crystal.

"What do you find so amusing this time?"

Declan laughed again, stretching the cut on his split lip. He ignored the twinge. "I don't know what's funnier. The fact that she came to me like a bee to honey, or the fact that you're jealous."

With blinding speed, the vampire stood in front of Declan. "I can't be jealous of what's already mine," he spat. "I think it's you who is jealous. You fed from her once. I can only imagine the rush of power that flowed through you at the taste of her."

Declan's smile fled. His fangs itched at the memory. Clamping down on his jaw, he fought the truth of the monster's words.

"She's beautiful and ripe for the taking. I imagine you'd like to feel her beneath you again. Like to have those soft lips of hers on your skin. Be able to feel the amazing heat of her body swallow you, as I can—and, believe me, I do."

Lotharus's words stabbed through him with irrational precision. Narrowing his eyes, he met the black ones staring down at him.

"At least when I had her beneath me," he said through clenched teeth, "I didn't have to force her there."

A feminine gasp rent the air. Declan snapped his focus over Lotharus's shoulder. His eyes immediately settled on Alexia. The pale blue, floor-length V-cut negligee and wrapper she wore set off the golden color of her hair. She looked ethereal, beautiful and shocked. And to see her standing beside that bed brought the dream vision back into glaring focus.

"What did you say?" Lotharus's growled words held the distinctive tone of a covetous male.

Declan switched his gaze back to him. "You heard me, you sick fuck. Are you so pathetic you have to rape to get laid, or do you just get off on terrifying innocent females?"

The anger in Lotharus's stare multiplied. Shaking with rage, he lunged for the fireplace, grabbing a silver poker from the stand.

Alexia rushed forward, taking his arm. "Lotharus, no—"

Without missing a step, he turned, backhanding her. Instinctively, Declan's entire body lunged to protect her. His muscles strained against the iron bindings. However, all thoughts of helping her fled when Lotharus swung back around, impaling the poker where he'd landed his fists moments before.

The sharp burst of pain in his gut momentarily debilitated Declan. He couldn't see, think or hear, but only focus on the blinding agony radiating through his midsection. Lotharus leaned forward, holding his face mere inches from Declan's. "I will answer to no one. Especially not some flying rat."

Lotharus heaved back, dragging the poker's jagged tip through Declan's flesh. He doubled over, hearing the silver rod rattle on the floor, discarded.

Blinking, he looked up. Lotharus brushed his palms together as if he'd done little more than squash a bug. "Get this *thing* out of my sight. He's bleeding all over my floor."

The soldiers quickly unhooked him and Declan fell limp in their arms. His eyes drifted to the corner of the room, searching for Alexia. He couldn't make her out. His vision gone foggy, he shut his eyes, not opening them until they had unceremoniously tossed him on the ground, shackled his wrist to the wall and shut the dungeon door.

Declan wrapped an arm around his middle and curled into a ball on his side. Clenching his teeth against the pain, he focused on breathing, on Tallon, on images of home. He knew coming here was a dead end, an e-ticket to hell. As the pain lashed and bit, threatening to choke him, Declan told himself that he would take this suffering and any more the horde could dish out to save his flock.

Just like his parents had.

He stared at the filthy walls of the dungeon with newfound wonder in his eyes, feeling them mist. The idea both his parents might have lain in this very spot—may have felt unbearable agony and loss and yet faced it as it was—brought comfort to Declan and he finally fell into the sleep his body so desperately needed.

THE QUEEN CLOSED THE MAIN doors leading to her hall. Ascending the few steps into the garden, she walked with purpose toward her chamber, her sanctuary. The only one left, she thought. Even the once safe haven of her mind was now lost to her.

Low-hanging leaves brushed against her face and arms as she wound her way through the foliage. When she came upon the statue of Diana, a cold fear seized her heart, tightening around it like a noose. Keeping her head down, unable to make contact with the Goddess's judging stare, Catija skirted around the fountain and hurried down the path leading to her bedchamber.

The moment the lock on her bedroom door clicked, Catija let out the deep breath she'd been holding. The frantic tempo of her heart slowed to a more manageable beat and the invisible fingers around her neck loosened. Rounding the massive bed commanding the center of the room, she headed toward the far wall at almost a run. An antique polished oak and mahogany trunk sat alongside the wall, its rectangular surface centered by a profile of a maiden. She sat within a bellflower wreath adorned with birds, goblets, riches and urns. Her long hair was braided atop her head in a tight coil, almost concealing the crown above her brow.

Catija stepped closer to the trunk, admiring the strong female. The profile was her family's crest and the heraldry of Queens past. When her fingers touched the wood, she closed her eyes.

At no other time had she felt the weight, the burden of her pledge and duty more than she had this past year. Although it had become nearly impossible for her to remember even the simplest of things these days, there was one task she would never forget.

Keep moving forward.

No matter the cost to self and sanity, no matter what happened. She had to continue playing, keep strategizing her next move. Life for her had become little more than a chess match. Her existence had no more value than the lowliest pawns on the game board. There had been a time, so long ago she could hardly remember, when she had believed it possible to succeed. Believed she could play this game, traverse her piece across Lotharus's perverse game board and, not only endure every step, but come out on top. Yet now Catija could barely find the will and strength to get through a single day, much less hope to win.

But it didn't matter. She had to keep playing.

"Have to keep them safe," she murmured, pivoting open the heavy wooden top. A golden disc sat in the center of the box atop an antique phonograph.

Play this when you feel lost or alone and know I will always be with you, a familiar male voice whispered through her mind.

Almost in a trance, Catija lifted the tone arm and set the needle on the disc. At once a low hum of music began to pulsate and fill the room. Velvety and subtle, the orchestral notes spoke to her, transported her. A sense of peace rolled through her body with each wave of melody and song.

In a heart-wrenching union of peaks and valleys, the music swelled to a crescendo. The hair on the back of her neck stood on end. A heartbeat later, a familiar and welcome presence seeped into the room. Heels clicked loud and firm on the marble floor behind her.

"Is he dead?" she asked without turning around. Part

of her dreaded the answer. When none came, she looked expectantly over her shoulder at her advisor and the only friend left in her corner. And she felt close to losing even him at times. "Did Lotharus kill the dragon prince?"

"Not yet," Yuri finally replied, moving away from the door and climbing the few steps toward her. Catija watched her brother cross the room with interest. Although she'd known him all her life, he never aged, his image never changing from the one she remembered so fondly in their youth. He still wore his midnight hair cut even to his shoulders. A perfectly shaped and trimmed goatee framed his lips. And although the style of his clothing may have changed over the centuries, she never saw him wear any color other than black from head to toe. Perhaps that was where Alexia got it from, she thought with a smile. One that faded once the dire consequence of her situation again weighed down her shoulders.

Yuri, however, appeared to carry no such burden. He moved with grace and confidence, his demeanor giving nothing away as he stood alongside her. Warm and firm and *real,* his hand covered hers. He smiled, giving her a reassuring squeeze, although his words were anything but encouraging. "The dragon may be alive for now. But you know Lotharus. This will be like before. It's only a matter of time."

Catija nodded and looked back at the revolving disc. Instead of a spinning blur of gold, images of the last time dragons had resided in her dungeon flashed behind her eyes. A visible shudder quaked through her body, cramping her stomach. Drawing her arms tight around her, she backed up, lowering herself to the edge of the bed.

"I don't know how much more I can take, Yuri."

A long, regret-filled sigh echoed in the stillness. The mattress dipped beneath Yuri's weight as he took a seat beside her. "Times are dark for all of us, dear sister. But you must be strong. This will all be over soon."

Although she heard her brother's words, tried to take them to heart, a tremor of helplessness and resentment vibrated deep inside her. "By the Goddess, I'm the Queen of this horde. I should be able to eradicate Lotharus with no more than a flick of my wrist. Yet we play this game of cloak-and-dagger and, at times, I feel I'm losing."

As he had when she was young, Yuri wrapped an arm around her, pulling her to his chest in a comforting embrace. Catija fell against him willingly. Slow and gentle, his fingers brushed her hair. The tender act calmed her nerves, a palpable dichotomy to the panic and fear pounding in her chest.

"Yuri, he cannot find that crystal first. Alexia must

possess it. I keep trying to push her, to goad her into getting her hands on that stone, but it's not working. I am at the end of my reign and care not what they do to me. But I don't want them to kill her."

"And I don't want them to kill you," he said, kissing the top of her head.

Catija opened her mouth to tell him she'd almost prefer death, but stopped herself. The words would do nothing except hurt him, and she'd done enough of that to last them both a lifetime. Instead, she stared straight ahead and struggled to concentrate on her next move. However, a dense fog swirled in her mind these days, making it hard to think and almost impossible to concentrate. Her vision blurred as she tried to focus on the next move Lotharus had planned, until Catija saw nothing but clouded fears for her daughter. But beneath the tide of worry, an undercurrent of pride flowed fast and strong.

"At least Alexia is not fooled by him," she said, mindlessly rubbing the velvety fabric of Yuri's lapel between her fingers.

"She is very intelligent," he murmured, a smile in his voice. "Like her mother."

"No," Catija replied. "She's smarter than I. Not once has Alexia been taken in by him, believed his lies." She shook her head, annoyed at her stupidity and weakness.

Admittedly, Catija had been reckless and brutal in her youth, spurred on by a wicked family and more than her fair share of demented lovers. Although she'd been too drunk on power, too blind to see it then, she knew now how foolish she'd been. Instead of laying the foundation for those who would follow her, she had spent her early days as ruler gorging on vices, flaunting her cruelty like a preening peacock and placating various men with what seemed like harmless ranks of power beneath her.

Catija could no longer remember many things. Yet she recalled the day she had realized her life was a finite thing. A predetermined cycle with, not only an end, but a specific day her life as she'd been living it would end.

On her daughter, Alexia's, ascension day.

She realized on that day that she would not be passing the proverbial torch or even a slim version of a legacy on to her child, but likely her demise. She may as well have clothed her in a burial shroud.

"Goddess, I hate what I've done. Hate the way I have to treat her. The way she looks at me. But if Lotharus ever suspected her, if she ever found out, he would…"

"Shh," Yuri murmured, his long fingers continuing their lazy glides through her hair. "That is not going to happen."

Disbelieving, Catija shook her head. "Between hurting

Alexia and Lotharus's draughts, it's killing me." Catija licked her lips, tasting the horrid truth upon them.

"Yuri, I…" She swallowed. "I think *he's* killing me. Slowly."

The hand in her hair stilled, his entire body tensing at her admission. Before Catija could blink, Yuri shifted to kneel before her. His hands gripped her upper arms, forcing her to look at him.

"Sister…"

"No, please. Just listen," she interrupted, knowing she didn't have the strength to argue. "The ascension is only days away. If something happens to me before then, you must promise you'll take care of Alexia."

Yuri sighed, pausing for only a heartbeat before he clasped her face, framing it in his grip. Dark and glistening, his eyes bored into hers. "With everything I am, I swear. I will keep her safe. I will look out for her as I always have you, no matter what happens."

At his fiercely whispered vow, a smile parted her lips.

"I believe you, brother."

And why wouldn't she? Yuri had already proved he'd do anything to help her. Already made the greatest sacrifice she could ever think of. Once more, Yuri took a seat next to her. Again, he let his fingers continue their lazy path through her hair. However, Catija could not relax this time. Instead, the prick of conscience's needle stabbed the center of her heart. The unspeakable truth of what she'd forced him to do those years ago bled out before her.

"I have so many wrongs to right, Yuri. I do not think I can ever fix them all."

Catija tilted her chin to look at him. His jaw set in a firm line, his pensive gaze focused somewhere straight ahead, every handsome feature of his face was taut with unspoken emotion.

"Especially not the unspeakable wrong I caused you."

Yuri blinked, his stern facade cracking at her words. "You're rectifying that now," he replied, dropping his focus to the ground.

"Yes. But is it too little, too late?"

His gaze snapped to hers, warmth and compassion glowing behind his dark eyes. "No, Cat. It's never too late to make amends."

Catija nodded and rested her head back on his shoulders, allowing herself one more moment in her big brother's arms. One more second of letting the pressure, the fear, the uncertainty fade away before she had to once again put on the persona she'd been destined to wear since birth.

The music in the background began to fade. A sense

of panic flared to life inside Catija. Her heart beat faster and a cloak of dread tightened around her. She gripped his shirt, clutching him tight as if he might disappear if she let go.

"You kept your promise. You kept them safe. All of them." Although she spoke plainly, she couldn't disguise the question in her voice, didn't mask it from him.

He offered a rueful smile that didn't quite reach his raven-hued eyes. And again part of her wondered how much her tasks had cost him.

"Yes, my Queen," he answered.

The music abruptly ended. Loud cracks and pops took its place as the needle repeatedly scratched across the golden surface at the center of the playing disc. Catija jumped at the sound. Blinking, she shook her tired and groggy head, as if she'd woken from an impenetrable slumber. For a moment, an overwhelming sense of loss ripped through her. Catija glanced to her left and then right, looking for Yuri, even though she knew she sat alone in her bedchamber.

Always alone.

Exhausted, she pushed off the bed, her legs shaky as she stepped to the trunk. Gingerly, she lifted the needle off the disc and set it in its cradle. The crackling noises stopped and once again a cold stillness blanketed her chamber. Catija reached down, her fingers grazing over the smooth top of the disc.

Play this when you feel lost or alone and know I will always be with you.

A wet tear slipped over her cheekbone and down her face. She hated how bone-weary and drained she'd become. Hated how she had no idea if Yuri actually visited her when she played his disc, or if she had gone mad and her addled brain fabricated their meetings. But most of all, she hated herself. Hated how the sins of her past came back to haunt her and, worse, affected those she most cherished and loved.

"Don't worry, brother," she said, wiping away the tear with the back of her hand. "I, too, shall keep my promise."

HE KNEW.

Those two words repeated in a disturbing cadence with each breath Alexia drew since she had left Lotharus's chamber. That dragon knew what Lotharus did to her. She'd seen it in those sapphire eyes of his, heard it in the veiled threat that fell from his mouth.

But how?

The answer to that question kept her up well past dawn. Had her changing into her combat gear when she should have been slipping into her nightclothes. Now it had her sneaking below to the dungeons long after everyone else in her compound had gone to bed for the day.

Although some part of her recognized it was illogical and absurd to head below at this hour, she didn't really have a choice. She couldn't sleep, couldn't think, at least not of anything other than the fact that the dragon knew something that she'd never told anyone. Not even her mother.

As she rounded the corner and began her descent into the bowels of the horde, her heart sped up. Ignoring it, she reached around to the small of her back, unsheathing her silver dagger. Although she hoped he'd tell her of his own volition, Alexia was prepared to do anything necessary to get an answer.

At least, that was what she told herself.

Sucking in a breath, she stepped through the threshold of the dungeon and glanced around. The chamber was quiet and pitch-black. Iron shutters blocked the windows and every torch and fire pit had been extinguished, leaving no spot of warmth, no flicker of light. Only the pungent odor of decaying flesh confirmed her location.

"Isn't it early for you to be awake, little vampire?"

She gasped at his voice, low and deep. In the quiet room, it vibrated through her, nearly knocking her off balance. By the sound of it, he sat in the far corner by the wall and not locked in a cell, where she'd assumed he'd be. Lotharus must have had confidence he'd wounded him badly enough to keep him from escaping. Alexia recalled the pure strength in him, the resolve in his eyes, and suddenly wasn't so certain.

She stepped forward. The loud sound of her boots on the stone reverberated through the empty room. Her pulse thumped with each step.

Finally, her vision began to discern shapes in the darkness, aided by the tiniest shaft of sunlight seeping in from a timeworn crack in a side wall. First his outline, then his broad shoulders, his hair and his eyes slowly sharpened into focus. He sat on the ground, his shackled arm resting on his bent knees. Alexia folded her arms across her chest, keeping the dagger in front of her forearm where he could see it. The moment she knew he had, she notched up her chin and summoned the courage to ask what she'd came down here to find out.

"You know what he's done to me." It came out more as a statement than a question. She noticed his eyes widen before they narrowed. "How?" she asked.

"Why should I tell you?"

"Because I want to know."

"Then set me free."

The question took her aback, as she'd fought for his freedom only hours ago. "No," she managed to answer, amazed at the icy composure in her voice.

"But that's what I want."

Alexia felt a smile tug her lips, but she contained it. Her fingertips tapped on the weapon's handle. As she'd hoped, the movement drew his gaze and he nodded to the blade.

"Are you going to use that?"

She took a deep breath and tried to remain convincingly hostile. "Only if you don't tell me what I came down here to hear."

At her words, he tipped his chin back, resting his head on the wall behind him. "I can tell you, but you won't believe me."

"Try me."

He set his gaze on hers, his blue eyes piercing the darkness like a beacon. "I saw it."

CHAPTER SEVEN

"THAT'S IMPOSSIBLE," Alexia said with an exhale.

What he'd said could not be true. She didn't believe it for a moment. But when his gaze leveled on hers again, what she thought didn't matter. He believed it. There was no doubt in his cerulean eyes.

"I told you that you wouldn't believe me," he replied, again resting his head back against the wall.

Alexia took in the masculine outline of his face, his jaw, the Adam's apple protruding from his bowed neck. She licked her lips. Her gaze slid lower, to the wounds on his bare torso. The injuries appeared raw and aching and she had to look away. Not for the first time, the idea of torture seemed to leave a bad taste in the back of her throat.

Alexia turned, bracing her back on the wall beside

him. The cool stones bit the flesh of her back and shoulders. Slumping down, she came to a squat and leaned her head on the dungeon wall, fingering the dagger in her hands.

Use it. Lotharus's voice whispered the order in her mind. She slammed the weapon on the ground beside her, holding it beneath her palm. Lotharus was not here calling the shots. Not today, not right now. This was her chance to do things her way. After all, the dragon didn't have to know she had no intention of using the blade on him. That in reality, she feared that returning him to his kin was her only hope of bringing peace to their clans. That she wanted to keep him alive for the next two days so she could set him free.

Two days.

"So, do you like torture? Is that why you won't answer me?" she asked in the firmest voice she could muster.

"Funny, I was about to ask you the same thing."

His voice rolled through her in a velvety wave and she fought the urge to sigh. "Does it seem that way?"

He turned to face her, a dark brow arched like a bird's wing over his amazing eyes. "You did seem quite comfortable with a flogger, Alexia."

Heat fired inside her at the sound of that rich, deep voice saying her name. "Well," she managed to say, "you dragons seem comfortable with your talons tearing through my kin's flesh."

"Touché," he said with a laugh. She almost mimicked him. But then her mind finally caught up with her body and registered that he had used her name. He knew her name. Yet she did not know his.

"Tell me, dragon. What do they call you?"

At her question, he tossed strands of midnight-black hair from his face, revealing a lopsided smile that looked completely out of place in the dismal surroundings.

"Declan." He lifted his chin an inch, his face sobering. "Declan Black."

Black.

Her eyes widened. Lotharus was right. "That means you are…"

"The new King, yes."

Goddess. Why would he risk telling her? His parents were not just murdered. They had been brutally beaten and tortured for days until they had both died from it.

"I won't tell anyone," she said with a whisper, wishing there was some way she could take away the knowledge from Lotharus and her mother.

When he didn't answer, she looked over at him. Although it was hard to make out every nuance of Declan's facial expression in the dark, if she read him right, he seemed as astonished by her words as she was to have said them. His brow tightened, then relaxed ever so slightly and his face softened.

"Thank you."

He said the words as if he'd take any compassion she would bestow on him. This made her wonder. Was he lonely, like her? Did he have friends, family, a wife or a child back home, waiting for him, missing him? She remembered that female he'd been with last night before they caged him. Was she longing for him and he for her?

For the first time Alexia felt wave after wave of remorse, guilt, sadness. Each one lapped as the other ebbed so she never had a moment's peace. It smothered her. Goddess, what was she doing down here?

"I have to go," she said, shifting her feet beneath her to stand.

"Alexia, wait." His hand covered hers. Fingers, long and smooth, slid up her arm before closing around it. She closed her eyes, savoring the tenderness for a split second before she swiveled back around to face him.

"What?"

"I know you think me crazy, and I know you have no reason to believe anything I say. But I swear to you, I *saw* what he did to you."

Alexia's breath hitched to think what he said was true.

She tried to pull away, to get away. But his grip on her hand didn't budge. If anything, it tightened.

"I can't explain it," he continued. "But I saw what he did to you with my own eyes."

"Stop," she asked before her throat constricted. She swallowed hard. The knot of embarrassment, guilt and shame was so thick in her throat she nearly choked on it.

Somewhere in her mind, it registered he was rubbing his thumb atop her hand in small, tight circles. She didn't remember when he'd started caressing her, and although she didn't want to admit it, the small gesture soothed her.

Releasing a groan, she slumped back down on the floor beside him, cradling her head in her hands. He didn't move, or speak. If not for the sound of his deep, even breaths she wouldn't have known he sat directly beside her.

"He should be dead for what he did to me," she finally said. "Would be if anyone knew about it."

Again, the silence stretched on between them.

"I won't tell anyone."

Alexia couldn't help but smile as he mimicked her promise to him. With a resigning sigh, she laid her head on her crossed arms and looked over at him. "So, why do they call you Declan?"

He glanced over at her, surprise evident in his eyes.

Then they softened slightly, the blue of them becoming sharper with his small grin. "You mean instead of the traditional dragon lord names?"

She nodded.

"My father was named after one of our human ancestors from the fourth century and my mother insisted they keep the tradition." He shrugged, his lower lip bowing down. Her eyes lingered on its smooth, full outline, her body tingled remembering how delicious it had felt pressed against hers. "Since I was not dragon born, they did not have a hard time passing it through council. My sister, however, was not so lucky to escape the dragon custom."

Alexia heard everything, but her mind snatched on one fact and held. "So, you are not dragon born, yet you are a dragon lord?"

"Aye."

"Even though you're only a half-breed?"

Anger flickered behind his eyes and she instantly regretted her choice of words. "I'm sorry... I didn't—" she said before taking a deep breath and releasing it. "It's just that you're so strong."

The corner of his lips curved. "The Black line is like that. If you think I'm strong, you should have met my father."

A sad laugh forced out of him before his face visibly hardened, pain and loss etching his handsome features.

"I never did, you know. Meet your parents," she heard herself saying. "Lotharus and my mother kept them a secret from me. They were gone before I even knew they were here."

Declan's nostrils flared. Even with the collar ebbing his strength, a surge of heat rippled off him. The air between them warmed and for a moment she feared his fire would lash out with dragonfire, charring her to a crisp.

"What did they do with them?"

Every muscle in his mighty body tensed. She knew he held on to his control by a thread, one that could snap at any minute…one that, when it did, would catch her in its ricochet. She swallowed.

"How do you mean?" she asked, hoping he wasn't going to make her recount the various and painful ways she'd learned Lotharus had tortured them.

"Their bodies. What did they do with their bodies?"

His voice cracked, allowing raw pain and emotion to seep out. The sound reached something deep down inside Alexia, pulling cruelly. The urge to wrap her arm around him, to comfort him any way she could besieged her. But, instead of solace, he wanted to hear words that, if she had to hazard a guess, would gut him.

"They were burned. Their ashes dumped into vats of heated silver and fashioned into weapons."

His jaw bunched, his hands fisted so tight she could discern his white knuckles even in the gloom. Alexia turned away and fixed her gaze on the hands in her lap. She knew about the dragon beliefs. All horde warriors did. Without their bodies, the dragons believed the gods could not grant them eternal life, which was why horde were always on orders to mutilate or burn the carcasses. Lotharus and her mother had dealt his people a devastating blow. As if molding the King and Queen into instruments now used to torture their kind wasn't enough, they had assured a son he would never again set eyes on his parents. Not in this life or the next.

He let out a long exhale, his chin falling to his chest. "Why are you telling me?"

"I—" She inhaled and then turned to look into his face. Although she couldn't place it, couldn't figure out why, for some reason the thought of him hating her, of thinking her no better than Lotharus, was intolerable. "I'm not like him."

"No?" He lifted his gaze to hers, his face hard and expressionless. A flicker of anger sparked behind his eyes. His lips formed a grim line before he forced them into a grin. "That wasn't you kicking my face in last night?"

She tried to smile back, but only shook her head. "I'm a soldier following orders. A future ruler who wants what's best for her people and, like you, I will die fighting for it."

Alexia shifted her gaze to the ground and tried to rationalize why she wasn't leaving. Why words she'd never said to anyone, especially a dragon, formed on the tip of her tongue.

"Declan, I'm sorry about that night. I'm sorry about your parents. And I'm sorry you're here." The admission breathed out of her in a rush before she could stop it. In the silence that followed, she slowly turned her head toward him.

For what felt like hours, he regarded her, faint lines creasing his brow as if he weighed the fate of the world in his mind. Alexia told herself to get up, to walk out, walk away. But she couldn't move.

His hooded eyes searched her face. Then they fell to her lips. Under his perusal her mouth warmed in remembrance of his kiss. The chains around his wrist rattled when he reached for her. Heat spread across her cheek as his fingers cradled her face. A slow curl of expectation tightened in her lower belly. She wasn't sure she even breathed as he slowly dipped his head.

Warm and soft, his mouth pressed against hers in a tender, almost reassuring kiss. As if his lips spoke the words of sympathy and understanding he couldn't bring his voice to say.

Then he pulled back. Too quickly, she thought. But he

kept his face inches from hers. Alexia lifted her hand, holding his chin in her fingertips, the small gesture her way of screaming out to him to stay, to kiss her again. Her way of telling him she didn't want this to end, didn't want his lips to leave hers. Not now, not yet.

Softly, his thumb rubbed her cheek. Intense and consuming, his eyes devoured her, seeing through her, into her, where no one else had ever bothered to look. A tide of panic swelled for a moment, but Alexia forced it down. A tiny flicker of hope took its place. Hope that maybe what had happened in his cell last night, whatever it was lingering between them right now, was real.

And then his mouth covered hers again and all thoughts scattered.

DECLAN KNEW THIS WAS INSANE. Knew this place had to be messing with his head. The minute he saw her enter the dungeon alone, he'd decided to say whatever he could to gain an ally in this hell. Knew it might be the only chance he had at ever seeing his flock again. He kept trying to tell himself this was all an act. That she'd created the collar around his neck. That she was the reason his parents had been murdered. That she was a means to an end.

Yet as his mouth slid against hers, he knew some part of his brain had completely abandoned his plan, which was crazy. *He* was going crazy. That had to be the reason he'd looked into her expressive eyes and seen driving need instead of the monster he'd been bred to see. Why he'd reached out and given the little vampire in front of him any measure of comfort he could, even though he was the one beaten and bloody.

On the outside.

Declan's hold on her face tightened as the thought whispered through his mind. As his lips opened and closed over hers, he realized that was what had spoken to him, reached inside and pulled him to her. She was more broken and beaten and, if possible, in more danger than he. True, he'd first touched her for the sole purpose of feeding off her to get his strength back and escape. Yet, ever since that dream, a frightening sense of possessiveness had strangled him like an ever tightening noose. He'd lived through her fear, her suffering, and wanted to shield her from experiencing any more.

Beneath his, her sweet mouth softened and moved, tentative yet eager. Although obviously not skilled or experienced, her kiss completely enthralled him and held him captive. Nothing, not even a pistol to his head, could have made him move. To think of one so beautiful left to wither and rot in this horrible place made his chest burn. An anguished sound rumbled from the back of his throat and he palmed the side of her face, smoothing her hair back and holding her closer, tighter, as he allowed his tongue to sweep between her lips.

ALEXIA FELT THE PASSIONATE change in his embrace and gave herself over to his kiss. Parting her lips for him, she wound her arm around his neck and held on to him for dear life, trusting him to guide her through the burgeoning storm of the unknown rising between them. Declan groaned and bound his shackled arm around her waist, pressing her body tighter against his. Hard metal cuffs dug into her back, but she didn't care. The heat of his mouth, the hungered urgency of his tongue, the fire burning within him, drew her in and kept her there. She felt warm and alive, as if she'd been dead, and his kiss, his touch, brought her into being. The urge to crawl inside him clawed at her, to have his energy, his warmth feed her until she never felt cold or lonely again.

Something tickled her ankle. Alexia ignored it at first. However, when what felt like a large snake wound around her thigh, she gasped and pulled back. Coiled loosely around her leg was a long, black…tail? Was that his tail? She lifted questioning eyes to his face. A boyish grin crossed his face and his eyes flitted back down to her leg.

This time when it slid high along her inner thigh, she jumped. "What are you doing?"

Clasping his hands around her hips, he pulled her back to him and shrugged. "Think of it as another hand."

When his mouth would have covered hers, she leaned back. Her eyes stretched wide. "Really? You mean, it…you can feel me?"

He smiled and sat back. A resigning sigh fell from his lips as he rested his weight on his hands by his hips. "Go ahead."

At first, Alexia wasn't sure what he meant. Then he nodded to her leg and she understood he meant for her to touch his tail. Realized he was giving her permission to explore him. A lick of desire curled through her.

Tentatively, Alexia ran a palm over the thick-muscled extension. She'd only seen them used as weapons and assumed they were little more than armor. Yet the tightly scaled skin felt cool and smooth beneath her fingers. And powerful. So powerful. A shiver danced up her spine as the tail reacted to her touch. The diamond-shaped head appeared almost animal-like, leaning into her palm as she caressed it. A dull tremor rolled through the length of it before the end retracted and shifted. Unwinding itself from her leg, the slender tip slid upward, curling around her wrist.

Alexia let out a quick gasp as the tail tugged sharply, dragging her into Declan's awaiting arms. The moment her cheek fell against his shoulder, he dipped his head, fitting his mouth over hers. Reckless and feral, his mouth caressed and tasted her. When his tongue ran against hers, slick and hungry, Alexia moaned and clutched his jaw, holding him closer. She knew this was wrong, so wrong, but she couldn't stop.

Her hands caressed the planes of his cheeks and jaw as his tongue stroked hers again and again until she was dizzy. Until an ache coiled tight and hard inside her belly, begging for release she knew only he could grant.

Chains jangled as the hand splayed on her side inched higher. Alexia's breath hitched in anticipation, and then, warm and strong, the heat of his palm covered her corseted breast. The swath of leather did nothing to shield her from the all-consuming intimacy of his touch. A shiver of pleasure shot out in all directions, tingling through every part of her body. Alexia arced into his hand, pressing herself deeper into his palm and inviting him to do more.

"Gods, Alexia," he breathed, dragging his mouth from hers. When he moved to pull away, she instinctively reached for him, drawing him back to her lips. He submitted with a groan, crushing his mouth against hers. One arm wrapped around her, holding her to him. The other fell back to her breast, handling her with more wild and intense abandon than before.

Her hands clutched his bare back. Hot and hard, she glided her palms over every inch, learning every contour, every hollow, dip and scar.

Scar.

The realization hit her then. They were both scarred, physically and emotionally, from this war. Goddess knew some part of her mind must be cracked and ruined to even be thinking the lascivious thoughts racing through her mind. But she'd never felt such a heady rush of desire in all her days. Though madness to even entertain, some part of her recognized that this act her body yearned for so badly would heal her in some way. Perhaps heal them both. Make the utterly unbearable existence of life tolerable.

Alexia shifted away from the wall and leaned backward. Wrapping her fingers around his biceps, she tugged, dragging him down with her. His lips stilled and a shiver swept through his body. But he gave in, allowing his weight to cover her. The taut line of his body pressed against hers and at once she remembered how right, how wonderful he felt above her. Hitching a leg over his naked butt, she dug her heel into one round cheek, pulling him closer. When his abdomen flattened against hers, he hissed in a breath. His mouth left hers, his head dipping to his chest.

Although stunned at first, she recalled with aching

clarity the agony Lotharus had inflicted on him earlier. "Oh, your wounds," she said with an exhale. Unwinding her leg, she moved to sit. However, her back barely made it off the ground before he pressed his hips against hers, stilling her hasty move.

"I'm fine," he said, with a sideways grin she barely saw before her eyes fluttered shut from the bliss. A large hand possessively ate the width of her thigh, pulling it back in place around his hip. "Now, where were we?"

DECLAN BENT OVER HER, nudging her head with his until it rested back on the dirt. On instinct, a hand came up, cradling the back of her skull, shielding its blond luster from the muck of the dungeon floor. The rough stones bit into his knuckles, grating the top layer of skin off the jagged bones with each slide of his mouth. But he barely felt a thing. In fact, pain was the last thing registering in his body. All his brain seemed capable of processing was the rush of erotic sensations throbbing through him.

Her small hands gripped the base of his neck, pulling him closer as her body undulated in an erotic black-leather wave beneath him. Declan propped one knee between her thighs, using it and his bent arm to hold himself above her. The muscles in his arms bulged and shook with the effort it took to keep from rolling on top of her completely and connecting them from tip to toe. The insistent desire to grind his hips against hers, to slip inside her welcoming body, became too urgent to ignore each second he lingered.

Yet, slowly, as if time was something he had more than mere hours of at his disposal, his lips trailed from her chin, across her collarbone and back again, savoring every intense reaction flicking through him with each new perusal of her velvety skin. How her warm body cushioned his with aching perfection. The sweet yet spicy perfume of her skin filled his nose and brought flashes of desire and warmth pulsing through his sore body.

With his eyes closed, his acute senses easily identified his scent on her. The silent yet potent brand of ownership lingering around her excited him on some primal level he never knew existed. Intrigued, he followed the lingering trace to the bite mark still healing on her neck. A shiver moved through her when his lips and then his tongue brushed it. Declan paused only for a moment to consider if she trembled at the memory of his bite or at the thought of him doing it again, before tasting his way back to her lips. If he allowed himself to go there, he'd be at her throat, her vein, once more. Gods knew his body needed it. But as mad and lost as he may be, some part of him knew if he ever wanted to be free from this place, from her, he could not afford to go there again. She'd already nettled her way under his skin after one sample. He wasn't sure if he'd survive another.

By the time he sealed his lips over hers, a harrowing notion—that the woman beneath him was the root cause, not only of his capture and perhaps even the death of his parents, but the inner turmoil and unrest deep within his soul—transmitted in only a mute echo in the far recess of his brain. Which made sense, since the driving need pulsing in his core signaled most of his cognitive brain cells had shot southward with a vengeance.

A hand clutched his shoulder, holding him in place and pulling him closer at the same time. One of her thighs lifted higher on his hip, the cool leather sweeping across his heated flesh and sending a shiver up his spine. Painfully hard, he finally allowed his weight to sink into her hips. The little vampire moaned in his mouth. He swallowed the sound, feeling it run straight to his tightening balls.

ALEXIA HEARD DECLAN'S GROAN, felt him harden against her inner thigh. For the first time, the prospect of what came next sent only white-hot need through her veins instead of icy fear.

Suddenly, the insistent beat of approaching footsteps

sounded down the hall. Alexia frowned. Footsteps meant sundown, which meant…

"Guards!" She hushed, pushing hard on his chest. A pained moan tore from him when her hand grazed his injury. Yet he still managed to haul himself upright and take her with him seconds before Ivan walked through the doors. Alexia ran a hand through her tousled hair and tried to calm her ragged breathing.

The soldier's sunglass-shielded gaze panned the room, instantly settling on them. Their thighs, just brushing one another, their shoulders, turned decidedly inward, and then their faces, no doubt a study in guilt.

Alexia sucked in a breath and scooted away from Declan's side. Flustered, she flexed the hand covering her dagger. Placing it in the holster at her lower back, she shoved off the floor. Brushing off her pants, she did not dare hazard a glance back down at Declan.

Declan.

His name repeated in her mind, causing an unwitting smile to tweak her lips. She knew his name now, knew his scent, his taste. Unconsciously, she lifted her fingertips to her mouth. Her lips burned with the searing memory of his kisses. Alexia didn't have to look back to know he was wearing a cat-that-ate-the-canary grin. That he looked too sexy by half, even covered in dried blood and filth.

"What were you doing?" Ivan's narrowed eyes looked from the cell to her face.

"Interrogating him, what do you think?"

A dark eyebrow lifted over the frame of his glasses. "Well, you're wanted above ground," he said, before turning to retrieve whatever he'd been sent down there for in the first place.

"Above ground?"

"Yes." He lifted two crossbows on his shoulder. "There is something going on out there you need to see."

CHAPTER EIGHT

ALEXIA STEPPED INTO the turbulent night. Crisp sea air purged her lungs of the stale scent of the compound. Now, if only it would purge her mind, she thought with a groan. Tightening her coat around her neck, she followed the dirt path around the cavern to the cliff's edge Ivan had told her about.

One hundred feet below, the riotous ocean beat against rocks and sand, drowning out any other sounds. Tucking an unruly lock behind her ear, Alexia stepped alongside the scouts, looming at the edge of the cliff.

"What is it, soldier?"

Without turning around, Markov reached back, holding something in his outstretched hand. Alexia grabbed binoculars and set the device to her eyes, pointing them in the direction he looked. The sophisticated display monitor flashed, the bright red bull's-eye locking on to targets moving alongside a cliff not a hundred feet away. Her blood gelled.

"Dragons," the soldier stated.

"I can see that."

"What do you think they are doing?"

"It's obvious they are looking for something," she said, trying to sound unconcerned as she tossed the binoculars back.

"Or someone."

Or both.

At the thought, Alexia tightened her arms around her. Goddess, what should she do? Her mind leapt from one possibility to the next. Most of the outcomes were brutal. She needed time to think. "Inform me when they either leave or move within range," she said, turning back around.

"You're leaving?" one scout said.

"Without doing anything?" said the other.

At their questions, Alexia looked over her shoulder. "Do we have a problem?"

Markov flexed his jaw. "Pardon, princess," he said through obviously clenched teeth. "But they are right there. If you'll but call a few of our best archers up here we can drop them like flies."

"Yes, we could," she said, pivoting to face them again.

"But without discovering their reason for being here. Without knowing if more will come in their place while we are not so ready," she shouted. "Perhaps they find the back stairs next time and it's our women and young they run into instead of you."

His massive head shook and a disgusted snort grunted out of him. "Lotharus is right about you."

An icy shiver ran up her spine. "What did you say?"

Markov turned to face her. Even with his dark sunglasses, humor lay evident on his meaty face. "You are too weak-minded and pathetic to rule."

Alexia snarled, her fangs sliding past her lips. "There is only one stop left on this road you're taking, soldier." Her claws lengthened and the gun at her hip suddenly magnified in weight. "I'll warn you now. You don't want to take it."

A wooden smile spread across his face and he bared his fangs. "Wanna bet?"

Alexia didn't wait for the second syllable to fall from his lips before her leg shot forward, driving the heel of her boot into Markov's nose. His head kicked back and a loud roar bellowed out of him. The second soldier made a move for her. Alexia swirled into a crouch and thrust out her leg, laying him flat on his back with her sweeper kick.

Without pause, she stood and reached out for the bleeding soldier. Snatching a dagger from his chest holster, she stabbed it into his chest. His arms dropped from his broken nose to the weapon's handle. The glasses slipped off his face, falling to the ground.

Alexia's mouth slackened. "Your eyes," she breathed.

His face contorted into a mask of rage and he shoved her backward. Although she stumbled, she regained her footing in time to see him charging toward her. Reflexively, Alexia shot out her leg, landing a side kick on the dagger, driving it deeper. Markov flew back. However, instead of landing on the ledge, he tumbled over it.

Panting, Alexia scooted toward the edge, wanting to make sure he didn't dangle from an outcropping below, she scooted toward the edge. Keeping her arms in front of her, fists tight, elbows tucked close to her body, she peeked over. Only blackness and the faint churning of the ocean lay below.

A rock trickled down the cliff wall behind her. The second soldier, she thought, pivoting about. Frantic, her gaze darted to where she'd laid him out on his back. He was gone. Panic and worry washed over her. Questions rolled over and over in her mind. Without stopping to work them out, she ran back into the catacomb. She had to warn her mother.

DECLAN DIDN'T EVEN TRY to catch himself when the
soldiers tossed him back in the cell and slammed the
door. Not that he felt his flesh and bone slamming the
ground anyway. His insides blistered and throbbed from
the liquid silver they'd pumped into his veins. Every
nucleus of every cell in his body vibrated in sharp pain.
Declan writhed on the floor before slumping upon it in
defeat, letting his cheek sink against the rough surface.
Blood rushed to his head and his throat closed. Grunting,
he sipped a breath between his lips, crying out at the flood
of anguish that washed through him anew.

Great, now even breathing hurt.

He choked, and almost blacked out, would have
blacked out if Lotharus's voice had not cut through the
pain-induced haze blanketing him.

"Did he crack?" Lotharus asked, his voice low and
commanding.

"No, sir," the soldier replied. "He's got a strong mind.
We've learned nothing from him."

"Then drag him out of there until we do."

"But sir, we used the silver injection on him."

At the memory, Declan's veins burned and a moan slid
past his lips.

"So?"

"Well, he's unconscious."

"He sounds awake to me," Lotharus countered.

"Awake, yes. Responsive, no."

The jangle of keys sounded in the room, followed by the shuffle of steps ushering closer to the cell door.

"With all due respect, if you want to kill him then string him up and continue to beat him. But if you want that crystal, you have to be patient."

"I do *not* need you to tell me how to do my job, Ivan. In case you've forgotten, you'd still be a mindless drone if not for me."

"I—I," the soldier floundered. "Yes, sir. I meant no offense. I'm only saying, breaking a mind such as his takes time."

"Well, time is something I don't have!" Lotharus let out a curse. "I need that stone. The ascension is tomorrow."

The soldier grunted words Declan couldn't decipher as a new spike of pain wedged between his eyes in a dull throb. He gritted his teeth against the pain, straining to hear the vampire's next words.

"…and the Queen's daughter? You know what happened at the cliff tonight." The tone of his voice rose as if he'd asked a question, and Declan fought hard to stay awake, stay conscious. To find out what had happened to Alexia.

"Of course," Lotharus spat. "I heard firsthand when the soldier came to me on his knees, begging for his life."

"And did you spare him?"

"Are you mad? Because of him, we now have no way of knowing what Alexia may have seen. What she might have learned from Markov before she killed him."

Declan groaned. Alexia killed a soldier tonight? At the thought, a new current of agony moved through him. Something big was going down, something bigger than anything Declan or his flock had anticipated. He had no idea what it could be yet. All he knew was Alexia was in danger.

"We must keep her cloistered until the ascension ceremony tomorrow. I can't afford her going after the crystal on her own. Or worse, telling the Queen anything."

"I'll keep my eye on her," the soldier stated.

"You?" Lotharus said with a laugh. "I think not. I will keep the princess…occupied until tomorrow."

Oh, gods. The blackness pulsing around Declan became nearly impossible to resist as Lotharus's dark words sunk in.

"You will stay here and keep working on finding me that stone." Again the sound of keys rattling against one another echoed in the darkness, followed by steps leading away from his cell.

"What if the dragon doesn't talk? What if I cannot break him?"

Lotharus's heavy footfalls quit thumping against the ground, vibrating the earth beneath Declan's ear. "If he doesn't divulge the crystal's location by dawn, he'll have outlived his usefulness. Kill him."

"Yes, sir."

"Oh, and Ivan," Lotharus said, "when you dispose of the beast, be sure to leave his body intact. I shall like to feast on dragon blood on my wedding day."

Declan finally let the darkness swallow him.

THE CHOCOLATE-COLORED satin-and-chiffon gown fell in slippery waves over Alexia's skin. Only the bodice hugged her tight. Still too long by a yard at least, the dress pooled over her toes and onto the floor of her mother's chamber. Strips of the soft fabric gathered at her shoulders, falling down her back in two parallel ribbons.

"What do you think of the brown? Do you like it?"

Alexia had to bite her tongue to keep from telling her mother to hell with the dress and inform her of what had happened on the cliffs instead. But she had to approach this carefully. She looked down to see the seamstress, Marguerite, her head bowed in concentration as she worked on the hemline. Alexia couldn't voice her opinion with a colony dweller in the room. If her suspicions about Lotharus leaked around the compound, he might get impulsive and do something rash.

"I'd prefer black," she finally replied.

The Queen fiddled with a swatch of cloth before tossing the square back in the basket. "I'm sure you would," she said, lifting her fingers to massage her temples. "It seems to be the only color you wear nowadays."

Alexia frowned, about to ask her mother if she was feeling all right, when the seamstress stood.

"My Queen," she said, "I'm sorry, but I need more pins."

Catija pursed her lips, making sure her displeasure was known, before giving the girl a flippant wave. "All right, go on and get them."

Seeing an opportunity to speak freely at last, Alexia's pulse quickened. She followed the woman's departure from the room out of the corner of her eye. The instant the door clicked shut she stepped down from the small podium. The Queen looked up, surprise on her face.

"Alexia, what are you doing? Get back up there."

"I have to tell you something."

"But you'll ruin the dress."

"Screw the dress, mother! Listen to me," she said,

dropping to her knees before her. "We must let that dragon lord go. Now."

Dark eyes gazed down at her, unfixed, unfocused. "What?"

Alexia pointed toward the sea. "His people are out there, looking for him. Right now, at the back stairs."

The Queen's eyes narrowed in thought. "Whose people?"

"Whose people…?" Alexia's words trailed off. She grabbed Catija's frail hands and squeezed. "The dragon, mother. The King and Queen's son. Remember?"

"King and Queen," Catija repeated in a low murmur. Her gaze distant, focused far away. Then she yanked her hands free and stood. "They were burned." Her eyes wide and frantic, she twined her fingers together and hustled toward the door.

"Mother, where are you going?" Alexia asked, lifting the overlong fabric of the dress and following after her.

"I burned them myself, I swear it," Catija called over her shoulder.

"Not them. Their son. Our prisoner."

"I knew I shouldn't have done it," Catija mumbled as she descended the small stairs and began to wind her way through the path to the gardens. "But the Goddess Diana spoke to me. She's so lovely, so much like your grand-mother. Do you remember her?"

"Of course." Alexia struggled to keep up, both with her ramblings and her quick pace. Unease and worry filled her heart with each step she took into the garden.

The Queen stopped at the water's edge. "She said they had to fly over the mountain, across the river and beyond the sea. See?" she asked, pointing to the farthest end of the fountain, to where the submerged model city of Davna Vremena lay shrouded in water. "Far away, where she couldn't touch them."

"She?" Alexia's stare moved from the small pond to the Queen and then back again. What did the auld lands her grandmother used to tell stories about have to do with Declan or his parents? "Mother, what are you talking about? You and Lotharus killed the dragons."

Catija spun around, her cold hands gripping Alexia's arms. "Daughter, listen to me. There is another part of the prophecy. One Lotharus does not know of. The torn part of the scroll," she whispered fiercely. "The crystal is the key, but he cannot be the one to open the door."

"Door?" Alexia struggled to understand, fought to piece together her mother's cryptic words. However, the Queen didn't stop to explain. She only squeezed her tighter, drawing her closer until her mother's eyes were all she could see. Clear and lucid, they bore into Alexia's.

"You must see them all cared for. You must see he lives."

"Who?" Alexia asked. Although she suspected that deep down she already knew.

"What is going on?"

Catija blinked at the sound of Lotharus's voice. Although Alexia heard his question, heard the rustle of leaves announcing his approach behind them, she didn't take her eyes off her mother. Something was wrong. Something she couldn't place.

"What about the torn scroll?" The Queen let go of her and turned back toward the fountain.

"That is enough," Lotharus's voice called from behind her. Alexia ignored him.

"Mother, what about the King and Queen?"

"I said, enough!"

Firm hands fisted her shoulders and yanked her back against Lotharus's front. Alexia winced as he tightened his grip and bent his head to her ear. "Do stop with your questions now, Alexia," he spit. Slowly, his hands encircled her throat. His fingertips danced around her neck in circles, light at first and then with more force, gripping tighter until she wondered if he was going to choke her.

"You don't want to worry your dear, sick mother. One wonders in her fragile state if she would recover."

The threat had her hackles rising. "What are you doing here?" she asked over her shoulder.

The hands on her neck stilled before falling away. He stepped around her and walked to the Queen's side. "I was going below to take care of our little…problem."

Declan, her mind screamed.

"You must see he lives."

Alexia's heart thudded.

"But when I heard voices, I decided to come and see what you were up to. Is everything all right?"

Alexia looked from her mother to Lotharus. She knew what she had to do and, for the first time, she found the courage to do it. "No, it's not." Alexia took a deep breath and raised her chin. "I'm going to summon the colony founders and petition for my succession to the throne a day early."

Although his features remained calm, the muscles of his jaw twitched. "Pardon?"

"In addition, I am going to request your removal as chief advisor and have my mother secluded in the *samostan* until she recovers from whatever madness you've set upon her."

Lotharus's eyes blazed and he stepped forward. "You think to send her to the women's temple," he scoffed. "You foolish girl, who do you think you are?"

For the first time, she felt a surge of power rush through her instead of fear. "I am the Queen of this horde. And you are nothing." With that, she gently touched her mother's shoulder. Dazed, the Queen turned, a glassy smile in her eyes. "Come, mother. Let's get you back to bed."

"Oh, Alexia, your dress." The Queen pointed to the sodden and wet hem. "What are we doing out here? Marguerite—" Her eyes searched the gardens for the seamstress. "We must have her fix this."

"Shh." Alexia patted her mother's hand and guided her down the path. "I'll make sure it's taken care of."

They had not managed two steps before Lotharus called after her.

"Do not think this is over, Alexia."

An icy chill swept up her back, but she shook it off and glanced over her shoulder at him. The malice and anger in his black eyes had a bubble of panic rising in her throat. She swallowed it down.

"And do not think you've won. For that crown you covet may just slip down and choke you one day."

CHAPTER NINE

THE FAINT SOUND OF METAL twisting and creaking sounded in the room. Declan expected to see that soldier, Ivan, sharpening his instruments of torture when he awoke. So, when he tried to open his eyes and quickly lost the struggle, he didn't mind. He didn't need to see what was coming next.

So weak, so tired.

Those words bounced in his brain, lulling him back to sleep. Then the scraping grew louder, more insistent, and again he tried to wedge his eyes wide. This time, they obeyed. He lay on his side in the dirt, facing the bars of his cell. But instead of Ivan on the other side of the rusty iron, the little vampire stood at the door. Her blond head bent over the thick padlock, her eyes intent.

"Alexia?" His throat burned, raw and dry, making his

voice crack. The faint taste of metal lingered on his tongue and scented his skin as his body secreted the liquid silver.

Flattening a palm on the floor, he pushed himself to sit up, hissing in a breath at the pain radiating along his side. He shoved to his knees and then to his feet, using the bars for leverage as he pulled himself up.

"What…are you…doing here?"

A low breath puffed out of her and she dropped the still-fastened padlock. "I'm trying to get you out of here."

His chest tightened. "Why?"

Shaking her head, she ran a hand over her eyes before digging into her back pocket for something. For the first time he saw how exhausted she looked. "Declan, listen to me. There is a way out of here. One you must take."

"What makes you think I would take an easy way out of this?"

"I never said it would be easy," she replied. "I said it would be a way out."

His gaze fell to her hands, fidgeting to unwrap a folded document. Although he tried not to, he couldn't help but notice they shook.

"Here." He snapped his attention to her index finger. She pointed to a map of the dungeon. To a space in the back of the cavernous room he'd never seen. "There is a gap, a hole back here you can climb out of. Although the cliff is a sheer drop-off and it would be madness for one of us to try it, you can fly once you're outside."

He wanted to tell her there was no way he was flying anywhere. The collar, the torture and not feeding for two days had weakened him to the point it had become nearly impossible to stand and hold a conversation, much less shift and fly for miles back to the mountain. In fact, the thought of climbing through some bloody catacomb to even get outside was unbearable. However, when he looked into her midnight eyes, he could only think of one thing to say. One thing to ask her. "Why are you doing this?"

A slight flush splashed her cheekbones and her gaze dipped to her toes. "I—I…" she stammered. And then her shoulders fell, almost indecipherably, but he noticed.

"I don't know what else to do."

Plaintive and soft, the sound of her whispered words twisted like a sharp object in his chest. How many times had he said those words himself since the death of his parents? How many times had he kept everything inside him, not wanting to worry others with his responsibilities, his obligations?

Inexplicably, he wanted to pull her into his arms, hold

her, give her any measure of comfort he could. Then, everything Lotharus had said earlier came flooding back. His fingers tightened their grip on the bars. "Tell me what's going on in the horde."

A frown cut across her dainty brow, but she didn't hesitate in her reply. "Lotharus is up to something. The soldiers, they're different." She shook her head. "They have always been disrespectful toward me. But it's gotten worse. Now they won't even follow my orders. And their eyes." She closed hers. "I'd never seen them before. They always shielded them with sunglasses." Her eyes opened, finding his in the darkness. "Goddess, there is something horribly wrong in all of this."

Declan's head spun as he tried to follow her incoherent thoughts. "Eyes? What do you mean?"

"They have eyes I have not seen, only read about in old texts. Elder eyes. All knowing, all seeing, even though they are milky and clouded. Lotharus has done something to those soldiers. I just have no idea what."

He slid a hand through the bars separating them. Hooking a finger beneath her chin, Declan lifted her gaze to his. The need to tell her she was in danger clawed at him. But first he had to see what she knew. "You do. Deep inside, you know. Tell me."

She sighed. "I have to lead this horde, but I have no idea how. I've tried to summon the colony founders, but none of them will reply. It's as if he has them living in fear, too…."

"Stop."

At his command, her lips sealed tight. Forcing his gaze away, he nodded his head toward her cheek. The dainty jawline beneath his hand was lined with black and blue. His tensed. He'd been here only two days and yet he'd seen her beaten at Lotharus's hand on each one. Seen that bastard do something else to her that he knew would haunt him for the rest of his days.

"What happened this time?"

"I don't know what you're talking about."

"Oh, I think you do." Ever so lightly, his finger grazed the perimeter of her beaten skin. A shudder moved through her and a knowing flicker danced behind her dark eyes before she shielded them from his sight.

"It is nothing to concern yourself with, I assure you, *Derkein.*"

To hear that word on her lips sent unreasonable rage through him. "You're not like him, remember? So don't speak like him." Declan captured her wrist with his other hand. He ignored how fragile the slight bones felt beneath his palm, ignored the tickling knowledge that he could crush them to dust with one flex of his fist. Instead, he focused on how his feelings for her gave him strength he did not have on his own.

"Alexia," he breathed, willing his anger away. "How can you live like this?"

"Do you think, even for a moment, that I have a choice?"

"We all have a choice."

Her nose crinkled and she tugged her arms free. He let her go without a fight. "So, you're telling me you choose to be shackled in a hovel of a dungeon? And for what? To die as some martyr to a cause no one will remember?"

"No. I sit, shackled in a dungeon, surrounded by the corpses of my kin, for the slight spark of hope that my sacrifice can make a difference. That our kind still has a place in this modern world." Her gaze softened and he made an effort to strip the harsh tone from his voice. "If I don't believe that, then the future of dragon, vampire, man alike will be different and perhaps wiped out forever. That is something I will not allow to take place as long as I draw breath on this earth."

"Well, you won't draw anything for much longer if I can't get you out of here," she said, renewing her fidgeting with the lock. "Lotharus is coming and he means to kill you."

She was right. His acute hearing picked up footfalls in

the corridors above. Each one reverberated through him. Closing his eyes, he took a deep breath, blowing out the exhale. "You better go. They will be here soon."

"I told you, I'm getting you out."

Metal clanked as again she worked on the padlock keeping him locked inside the cell. Declan opened his eyes, reached through the bars and covered her hands with his. They stilled.

"For what it's worth, I'm really glad I met you," he whispered.

A moment passed. Then her fingers twined in his. "Me, too."

She squeezed him tight and hard before letting go. The desperate contact, though fleeting, was the most soul-shattering touch he'd ever known. His heart thudded to know that, after tonight, he'd never again feel her skin, her lips or her hand on his.

He let out a pained breath and curled his fingers around the bars, resting his forehead on the cool iron. Resigning himself to the fate stepping closer with each second. Realizing for the first time in a long time, he didn't want to die. That he had a reason to live not connected to the fate of his people or his duty to them.

Gods, he couldn't afford to think that like. Especially right now.

"Get out of here, little vampire." His voice cracked on the last word. "Get out of here before it's too late for you."

"I can't just leave you here to die."

The click of footsteps on the floor grew louder, nearer.

"You don't have a choice," he whispered.

Alexia's gaze darted from the door to him. Then she moved to back up, back away. Declan shot his hand through the bars, grabbing her leather coat sleeve. Surprised, wide eyes met his and he stared into them, hoping she'd read the urgency in his own.

"Promise me you'll run far away from this place."

"What?"

The sounds coming from the guards intensified. They were right outside the door.

"Just promise me."

She shook her head and backed up a step. "I can't." The hands that so recently had embraced his covered her mouth. The dungeon door flew open, and Alexia slipped into the neighboring cell seconds before Lotharus and his soldiers entered the room.

"Get him out of there now," Lotharus barked, tossing the keys to one of the soldiers.

Declan let loose a curse and backed away from the bars, wishing she'd chosen somewhere else to hide. To know she was now going to be forced to watch Lotharus and his cronies beat and probably murder him sent a new kind of torture stabbing through him.

ALEXIA FLATTENED HER BACK against the wall, hugged the shadows and held her breath. Watching as Lotharus paced in front of the cage like a lion waiting to pounce on its prey.

"I'm done playing with you, *Derkein*. Tell me where the crystal is and I promise I'll kill your family and friends swiftly. Deny me, and I'll take my time playing with them."

Declan didn't fight back as the soldiers hoisted him out of the cell, dropping him at Lotharus's feet.

Alexia hadn't exhaled yet. Some part of her brain transmitted that fact, telling her to let the breath out, to drag another draught of air into her burning lungs. But she couldn't.

Lotharus bent and fisted Declan's scalp in his hand. With a firm tug, he wrenched his head back and up. "Did you not hear me?"

Alexia's heart twisted and a sob stuck in her throat. She couldn't bear having to watch what she knew must be coming, yet she couldn't look away either. Taking a much needed breath, she allowed herself to close her eyes for a split second. Opening them the moment she heard Declan's voice in the dark.

"You'll gut every dragon you meet from gullet to groin no matter what I say," he answered. "What you could do with that crystal is much worse. Does the Queen even know its true power? Does Alexia know?"

Through the fear and disbelief, she heard the emphasis on her name. Realized Declan was trying to gain her attention.

"Do they know the race who wields the crystal's power can enslave, control or destroy the other?"

"Of course, you half-breed scum," Lotharus said with a growl, kicking Declan's chin with the toe of his boot. The heavy crack reverberated through Alexia's skull as if she were the one taking the pounding. Declan fell to his stomach on the ground. Flattening his palms, he lifted himself up. Blood dribbled from his mouth onto the dirty floor. Anguish and defeat crossed over every line of his face. The muscles in his arms visibly shook as he tried to push to his knees and failed.

Then his eyes looked into the cell, toward her. The perfect blue orbs searched her dark hiding spot, settling on her for a heartbeat, before he snapped his focus back to Lotharus.

"But do they know you're planning to steal it out from under them? Use it against them?"

Alexia covered her mouth with her hands and held in

the gasp threatening to break free from her lungs. Lotharus did not answer. He only laughed and nodded to the soldiers. Each one grabbed an arm and hauled Declan to his feet.

This is it. The thought seeped into her mind and it nearly paralyzed her. She wasn't certain she could stand here and quietly watch Lotharus kill him. But she wasn't sure she had a choice either. She couldn't beat Lotharus in battle, much less him *and* four of his best soldiers.

Lotharus grabbed shears off the table, snapping the massive scissors as he stepped closer to Declan. Her legs trembled and tears pricked her eyes.

"One, last chance, *Derkein*," Lotharus said, aligning the tip at Declan's throat. The dragon leaned his head back as far as it would go, his Adam's apple bobbing with his swallow.

"Where is it?"

"Go to hell," Declan bit out.

Lotharus nodded and Ivan moved behind Declan. He swallowed again as Lotharus raised his arms and the shears with them. Alexia pinched her eyes shut, wincing at the howl of agony ripping through the air, tearing through her soul with the force of a thousand bullets. She covered her ears, but did not attempt to shield herself from the pain, the injustice, the hurt swallowing her. The dam had broken. Something inside her had broken. And rather than mourn the losses, she vowed to use the hurt, the pain and the anger to destroy Lotharus, to gain control of everything that was rightfully hers and crush him with it.

DECLAN HAD CLOSED HIS EYES, not wanting Lotharus's evil face to be the last thing he saw before death claimed him. Instead, he thought of Alexia in the cell, watching, and he waited. Waited for the razor-sharp pain of the shears, sandwiching the sides of his neck before they separated his head from his body.

"...*leave his body intact.*" Lotharus's words rang in his mind and he tried to force those away, too.

Then he heard the splicing of metal, the scissors cutting through something thick and resistant. It took him a moment to realize Lotharus had not cut off his head as he'd thought, took a moment for the pain exploding through him to register an exact location. And then the force of it nearly blinded him.

A wounded cry screamed out of his lungs. Legs buckling beneath him, his chin fell to his chest. If the soldiers hadn't held him upright, he would have collapsed.

Lotharus squatted in front of him and forced his head up.

"I'll make you wish you were in hell."

Despite the unbearable agony tearing through him, the curve of a smirk tugged Declan's mouth. "And I'll die… before I tell you anything."

A maniacal glow burned behind Lotharus's eyes. "Oh, you'll die. It's just the *how* you have control over."

He lifted the shears, the tips pointed down at Declan's face. He instinctively flinched and twisted his head to the side. The metal hit the ground with a thud. Shocked, Declan looked up to see Lotharus stand and turn to face the opposite wall. Declan's gaze fixed on the long ponytail hanging between the vampire's shoulder blades.

Lotharus mumbled a low curse beneath his breath before he spun in a lightning-fast move. His boot was the last thing Declan saw before the acute pain of it striking his jaw saturated his entire being.

UNSHEATHING HER DAGGER, Alexia dug the tip into the lock on the cell. For what felt like hours she fought with the keyhole, trying to pick the lock with everything from a meat hook to one of her claws. Nothing worked.

"Why are you…still here?"

Declan's words sounded like something between a gasp and a whisper, and the anguish in them made Alexia's throat tighten.

"I told you, I'm getting you out of here," she said.

Ignoring the panic mounting inside her, she focused again on the padlock. She'd been trying to open the thing forever. Sweat trickled down her brow. Swiping it out of her eyes, she slid the dagger's tip into the keyhole and twisted. It slipped, slicing her across the palm.

"Ow! Dammit," she cried in frustration, tossing the weapon to the other side of the room. The sound of it skidding across the floor echoed in the empty space, grating her nerves like nails on a chalkboard. A glance up showed the lock still in place. An overwhelming sense of helplessness shrouded her, suffocating her.

Cupping her wounded hand, she closed her eyes and suppressed the urge to scream. Goddess, she needed a second to breathe, a second to think. A second, she thought, realizing Declan might very well only have seconds left. At the thought of him dying on that floor, a surprisingly large wound lanced her chest. The abrupt and unexpected ache was almost enough to make her weep. Pursing her lips, she willed the sob back.

"Go."

Declan's gasped word came out as little more than a hoarse whisper with his exhale, but she heard it. The agony and surrender in his voice made it nearly impossible to hold her tears back this time. It didn't help that her damn hand throbbed and wouldn't quit bleeding.

Alexia's eyes flew open wide.

Bleeding.

"Of course," she breathed, moving in front of the bars with renewed purpose. "Declan, move over here," she commanded, punching her arm through the cell bars. "I can't reach you."

GROGGY AND WEAK, Declan turned his head toward the sound of her voice. Blood, hot and sticky, trickled across his lips. A jolt of energy shot through him at the taste of it. At the taste of her. For a split second, he tilted his head to what she offered. But for only a second. He turned away, releasing a resigned sigh.

"Declan, please."

"No." His voice was raspy and his protest weak, even to his own ears. He knew he'd die without it and yet, drinking from her, tasting her, was something he wasn't sure he could do and survive again, either. The dreams already plagued him every time he shut his eyes. What would happen if he fed from her again? Only one thing was certain…what would happen to him if he didn't.

"Please, take it," she said. "Feed from me and fly out of here."

"I'm not sure I can, even if I wanted to." Declan rolled toward her, lying on his side.

"Oh, Goddess," she breathed. Her eyes widened at the wing, mutilated, broken and hanging by a thread behind him. Then her eyes fixed on his, steadfast resolve in their black depths.

"Come here. Now," she ordered, and he found himself complying. His entire body strained, fire cracking through every nerve ending in his body. "Move to the left, I can't reach you—" Her words broke off into a sigh as his mouth found its target.

Hungrily, his hands encircled her arm, clutching her to him. Although his fangs itched to burrow into her flesh until they struck bone, he held the urge at bay. Using all the control he owned, he carefully ran his tongue along the seam of her cut. The sweet, spicy and unique flavor of her blossomed on his tongue. His mouth watered. His head spun. Digging his fingers into her arm, he repeated the action before he closed his lips around her wrist and opened his jaw.

Locked into the perfect position to feed, he heard her breath hitch in anticipation of his bite. A shudder trembled along her arm. Closing his eyes, he allowed his dragon senses to hone in on her, on his prey. It picked up the frantic pace of her heart, her steadily increasing body temperature and the slight hint of sweet arousal secreting out of her pores. When the pheromone hit his nose, his cock pulsed and a primitive groan bubbled up from his core.

Gods, he wanted this. He knew it was wrong, knew he shouldn't let her heal him again, but at the same time he couldn't stop himself, either. In fact, he became blinded by the knowledge that he would kill anyone who tried to take her away. For a split second he realized what he thought was near lunacy. But it was only for a second and his body could not deny what she offered any longer. Lips quivering, he placed a soft, open-mouthed kiss on her wrist before he bit down.

At his invasion, she let loose an erotic gasp. The muscles in her arm tensed, but she did not try to get away. He pictured her in his mind's eye. Her back arched, her dark eyes shuttered, her skin flushed and her lips parted, a look of pure and unbridled ecstasy on her face. Exactly how he imagined she'd look when he drove into her heat. A pulse of want coursed through his body and blood rushed from his mouth straight to his hardening cock.

Closing his eyes, he focused on feeding. Focused on how sweet her blood tasted sliding down his throat. Hot and thick and her. It spread through him, like liquid fire in his veins. His belly glowed, his entire body heated and for the first time in days he felt warm and alive.

When he finally forced himself to pull away, he kept ahold of her hand, breathing deep the unique scent that was hers and hers alone. An intoxicating fragrance he had not sampled often, but knew he would never forget.

Alexia.

Her name whispered through his soul, searing it like a brand. An unaccustomed glow burned bright and hot as a star in the center of his chest. If he hadn't been so high from feeding, he'd think himself mad.

He liked her. Hell, maybe even more than liked her. And the crazy thing was he'd never done more than kiss her. Not that he didn't want to. In fact, he'd grown stiff as the iron bar keeping her from him, achingly hard, his balls drawn up tight between his thighs. As he laved a trail up her vein, he imagined it was the soft skin of her belly, her inner thigh. Gods, what he wouldn't give to taste her there. Just once.

As if she could read his mind, she breathed out a tiny sigh. The erotic surrender was almost enough to make him explode. Using every ounce of control he owned, he released her wrist and scooted away from her. Letting out a shuddering moan, he lay on his back parallel to the bars, letting her strength flow through him. Covering his eyes with a forearm, he tried to channel all of his energy into healing his nearly fatal wounds.

That became impossible when a tiny hand closed around the hard length of him. Declan hissed in a breath, his hips bucking forward in a silent plea. One she answered. She began stroking him softly, her fingertips tickling his sensitive tip before smoothing the skin down the length of him. His back bowed off the floor and a shudder racked through him.

Biting his lower lip to keep from crying out, he looked out from beneath his arm.

Alexia's beautiful eyes were wide. Excitement, interest perhaps, but no fear. Again, her delicate fingers squeezed and pulled, teasing him. He fought the urge not to beg her to do it harder. Instead, he bit down so tightly his jaw muscles burned, and he let her caress him to near madness. Desire vibrated through him, pulsing in a low, dull throb in his groin.

Her other hand weaved between the bars, tentatively running her fingers along the clenching muscles of his torso. A low groan rolled out of his chest. Shifting, he vaguely realized that her hand roamed over the now perfectly smooth, healed flesh of his stomach.

Declan looked up to tell her thank you, but at the sight of her his breath caught. She watched him intently, her eyes flickering with something dark, something primal, something the male in him could no longer ignore.

Without taking his eyes off her, he rose to his knees in front of her. Her lips parted in a sigh, her chin tilting up slightly in silent invitation. Jabbing his hands through the bars, he cupped her face. She closed her eyes and leaned into his touch. Caressing her cheek against his palm, his mind pulled ten different directions all at once. Then she opened her eyes and he could only think of one thing.

"Come here," he growled, pulling her to him.

CHAPTER TEN

AT HIS THROATY COMMAND, Alexia eagerly leaned forward. However, he tightened his hold, keeping her scant inches from his lips. She glanced up from his mouth, the heated look in his eyes scorching her to the marrow.

Slowly, he tipped his head to the side, closing the distance between them. His breath warmed her lips. The scent of him, dark and spicy, curled around her, overpowering the metallic scent of the bars. The tips of her nipples crimped, hardening to painfully aching peaks. Every inch of her cried out for him to kiss her, to claim her.

Right now, she could only pray to the Goddess that he'd listen. For she didn't care if Lotharus beat her within an inch of her life, for once she wanted to feel passion, feel desired, feel alive.

Slowly, her tongue slid between her lips, wetting them. His eyes lowered. His thumb repeated the action, brushing back and forth over her mouth. A light tingle hummed across her lips and she nearly whimpered with need. Then his hand was gone, the pad of his finger only a whispered memory on her lips.

She leaned toward him, her forehead pressing against the cool metal. This time, he met her, coming so close their noses brushed.

"Alexia." He breathed her name against her lips before covering her mouth with his. The hands on her face slid to her nape, his long fingers curling around the back of her head, holding her to him in a tender embrace. Without taking his lips from hers, he tilted his head to the side, angling for a better position through the bars.

In an agonizingly slow glide, his tongue traced the outline of her lower lip, seeking entrance. Alexia yielded with a shudder and parted for him. He groaned, low and feral as he took what she offered. Unbelievably slick and hot, his tongue came into her mouth, tasting hers in a sensual move that made her head spin. She swayed slightly from the bliss, thankful he held her tightly, unsure if she could remain upright on her own.

His hands tangled in her hair, then moved lower as he devoured her lips with his expert mouth. Alexia whimpered a soft, relinquishing sound as she eagerly opened herself up to the feast.

Large and sure, his hands slid down her back. She arched into each exploratory perusal. Every nerve ending in her stood alert. Each brush of his fingers and lips caused a riotous hunger to rise in her, one she wasn't sure she could ever feed. His touch aroused her in ways she couldn't justify or prevent, so she gave in to them.

When his hands encircled her rib cage, pulling her tighter against the bars, against him, a wave of fire crashed over her. Hot, consuming, frantic. A rush of heat pooled between her legs. At the unaccustomed feeling, Alexia squirmed. The leather pants intensified the heat building between her thighs. She moaned, kicked a knee through the bar and wrapped her hand around his back, pulling him closer, tighter. She needed something. Needed…

The scent of him, deep and rich like a fine chocolate, tingled though her veins. Her fangs itched and stretched. Gods, she hadn't drunk in days and the thirst was almost unbearable. She tore her mouth from his, gasping as his lips fell to her throat. Saliva flooded her mouth as quivering hunger and need trembled through her in unison, although she couldn't explain why. She'd never fed from a person, and yet everything in her screamed to sink her teeth into him, to taste him as he had her.

His mouth found the space behind her ear, her neck, her collarbone and back up. Spearing her fingers through his hair, she held his mouth in place. A low groan of approval answered her seconds before fangs pierced her flesh. She cried out at the ecstasy of his playful nip, feeling a fiery shaft of desire jolt her core. Her hands wrapped around his wide shoulders, clutching him to her. Flesh afire, she wriggled her body as close as she could against his. Cold, unyielding iron pressed into her flesh, however, inches of skin meeting his was worth every second of discomfort.

He lifted his head and their gazes locked. Both of them were panting, trembling. Beneath her hands, his hard, hot body shuddered. She knew without asking that his body ached like hers. Everything about him, about them, felt familiar and yet new at the same time. Desperate and yet overwhelmingly calm.

Alexia reached up, palming a stubble-roughened cheek. His eyes dipped at her touch, a deep breath exhaling out of him. She rubbed her thumb over his lips, amazed at how smooth they were. A fierce desire to know how every inch of him felt beneath her hands clawed at her. Emboldened, she trailed her palm lower, over the ridge of his columned throat, eyeing the pulse leaping beneath the skin. Again her fangs twitched, begging for a taste of him.

Dipping her head to his neck, she let her lips follow the path her hand had made, feeling his body tense beneath her mouth. In expectation of her bite? she wondered. Slowly, she trailed the tip of her tongue along his throat.

Alexia closed her eyes and let her other senses take over, took in the salty, musky flavor of his flesh, the hard yet smooth feel of him beneath her hands. She flicked her tongue across one dark nipple before closing her mouth completely over the hard peak. A low groan rumbled deep in his chest and he wound a hand in her hair. Alexia smiled against his skin and did it again.

When her tongue swirled lower, skating over the ridges of his abdomen, the hand on her head flexed.

"Ah…gods…what are you…" he panted. His fingers tightened in strands of her hair, pinching her scalp. She winced, loving the way he clutched her, the fierce possessiveness of his embrace. It was born of nothing other than pure passion and want. The same want echoing through her aroused body. Unlike Lotharus, he did not desire to wield power over her, or establish dominance over her. He only wanted to pleasure her. And, Goddess, she wanted to let him.

Alexia ran her fingers over the flat plane of his abdomen, the hollow of his hips, which thrust forward.

Reaching lower, she danced her fingers around the impressive shaft jutting up to meet her, relishing his quick intake of breath.

"Feeding makes me horny as hell." She recalled his words from before and couldn't help but note the evidence of those words extending up to greet her. Beneath her lips, his chest heaved. The hard length of him pulsed with each kiss, no doubt knowing where it would take her.

On her knees before him, her eyes came level with the target she'd been kissing her way down to meet. A rush of liquid coated her mouth at the sight. She remembered the way he felt in her palm. Smooth yet hard, and so thick she could barely get her fingers around him.

Like everything about this dragon lord, he was opposite of all she'd known, been told or experienced before. Her womb clenched in arousal, feeling his phantom girth spreading her, moving inside her. A shudder skated along her spine. Although her body may want to take him inside her, it was impossible with him caged like this. However, there was another way she could have him.

Licking her lips, she reached for him again. He hissed in a breath when her fingers encircled him. Slowly, she stroked the length of him, marveling at the sheer size of his velvety hardness. Closing her eyes, she drew in the intoxicating scent of him. Lust, the forbidden and the smell of the sea rippled off him. Peeking out her tongue, she dipped the tip into the slit at the top of his engorged cock. A deep tremble started in his toes, quaked up his muscular legs and shook up his body.

"Alex," he murmured in a harsh groan.

Blood rushed to her face. No one had ever shortened her name in affection before. She dared not look up and let him see how much his simple endearment affected her.

Instead, she would show him.

But first, she would taste him.

DECLAN ALMOST CAME the instant her sweet fangs sank into his hip. His vision blacked out and a shudder quaked through his body. When she began to feed, to taste, to drink from him, he kicked back his head, biting his lip hard to keep from crying out.

He'd never had a woman feed from him before. Ever. For it to be Alexia rivaled any erotic fantasy he'd ever had. Jets of heat left his body with each pull of her mouth. The tip of her tongue laved flat on his skin, a satiny ribbon stoking the burn, the hunger inside him.

Although he could have fed her for hours, days, until the life flowed out of his body, she dislodged her fangs from his skin. A tremble rolled through him and his pulse thundered in his skull. As weak as he suddenly felt, he realized it was a good thing one of them had the sense to pull away.

He'd barely finished the thought when Alexia's hot, wet mouth perched over the tip of his erection. Declan gritted his teeth as, inch by inch, she took him inside. His legs trembled, his buttocks clenched. When the sensitive end of his cock brushed the back of her angled throat he finally let out the breath he'd been holding. Stars peppered his vision. His eyes rolled in the back of his head as she slowly eased herself back. Declan watched the erotic sight of her cheeks concaving as she sucked up his length.

"Gods," he said on an exhale, tilting his hips toward her. Tension gripped his muscles from his groin to his toes with each bob of her mouth. He had to make this last, had to stop himself from coming too fast. But he couldn't, not when her mouth was sucking him oh, so perfectly.

A low, shuddering gasp flew from his lips as his cock spasmed, jetting out the first wave of his orgasm. Declan clutched the bars, fighting vertigo as his seed exploded into her mouth, coating her throat. Pulsing blackness clouded his vision, but he wouldn't look away for the world. Nothing he'd ever seen compared to the sight of his cock buried between Alexia's beautiful lips. The pulses of her throat, sucking and contracting around him, drove a primal groan from his lips.

Tunneling his hands in her hair, he slid his fingers through the silken strands until he cupped her head. It hit him how vulnerable she had made herself. Right now, her life was literally in his hands. They shook with the realization. Three days ago, he would have crushed her skull without a second thought. Yet now the only thought racing through his sated brain was figuring a way to tear the iron bars from the walls. Not to escape. But to take her in his arms, bury himself inside her and never come out.

She released him, and cold air kissed the heated flesh of his cock. Declan sucked in a breath. Alexia fluttered her gaze up to him. She visibly swallowed, tongue sweeping over her lips. Gods, how he wanted to taste them, lose himself in them. Another shudder moved down his spine and he collapsed to his knees before her. Her black eyes blinked, fluttering when he slid his hands to cup her face.

Up close he realized her eyes weren't completely black as he'd first thought them to be, but two different shades of onyx. The inner ring was a fiery coal, reminding him of cut black stone, the outer as lush and dark as a crow's belly. Set against her pale skin, her eyes seemed enormous and their depth infinite. Under his perusal, they darkened even more than he thought possible.

Then they flickered to his lips and before he could process a coherent thought, his mouth claimed hers, kissing her with hungry, fierce abandon. She met his passion, returning it. At the notion, a heady swell of desire surged inside him. The passion between them seemed almost natural, which made no sense. He could handle it, though, used to it now where she was concerned. However, the wave of protectiveness and tenderness that followed close behind threatened to engulf him, to swallow him whole.

Instead of dwelling on it, he embraced it, rode it. Let it carry him away as he lost himself in her mouth, her taste. The experience of giving in to his emotions was both intensely satisfying and agonizingly painful. What he was doing went against everything he'd ever been taught, ever preached, ever believed, but it felt too right to ignore.

"Alexia," he said with an exhale when they parted. Words flitted through his mind. Words he must be mad to think, much less consider saying. Closing his eyes, he rested his forehead on hers. Her hands cupped his face, her breaths came in soft pants against his skin. A shiver danced up his spine. "I…"

She sucked in a breath. "Oh, no."

Declan barely registered her whispered words before he heard the footsteps, heard the door swing open and felt a familiar coldness leak into the room. His heart stopped a second before Lotharus stepped into the dungeon.

"Well, well," Lotharus said. "What do we have here?"

Although Lotharus appeared calm on the outside, the tight line of his jaw and drastically narrowed eyes, one slightly twitching, gave away his fury. The same four soldiers who'd helped Lotharus beat Declan fanned out from behind him, like some kind of sinister cloak.

"Come now, Alexia. Take your scolding like a good girl."

The small hands around his neck fidgeted before they fell away and slipped back through the bars. Alexia made a move to stand, to protect herself, but Declan wound his arms around hers through the bars and pulled, holding her as tight as he could. His tail snaked between the irons, coiling around her ankle. A growing sense of dread sank like a stone in his stomach, as two of the soldiers headed toward her.

Alexia turned to face him, her eyes wide. "Remember what I told you."

Declan's mind raced. What had she told him? Then he remembered the hastily sketched map, the opening in the back of the dungeon wall that led to freedom.

A booted foot crashed down on her ankle, knocking his tail loose and pinning the tip to the ground. As much as his tail throbbed, he ignored it. He tightened his grip on her arm, his heart worried for her. Let them hew the damn appendage off, as long as they left her alone.

Instead, he sat caged and helpless as the soldiers ripped her out of his arms and wrestled her to Lotharus. Fear tightened like a noose around his neck. He clenched his fists around the bars tight, wishing they were Lotharus's throat. "What are you going to do to her?"

"Well, I can't very well have her healing you every time I almost kill you, now can I?" His clawed hand closed around her neck.

"How does this crown feel, Alexia, hmm? Do you still think you can turn me in, turn me into nothing? Do you?"

Alexia gasped. Her eyes wide with fear as she brought her hands to the one tightened around her throat in an attempt to pry his fingers loose. Her chest rose and fell in a frenzied, staccato beat, the muscles in her arms quivering.

Declan saw her losing the battle, noted her face flush and then turn a deep purple. He drew in a breath, his nostrils flaring in rage. "If you harm her…"

Lotharus let go and spun to face Declan. Alexia crumpled to the ground by his feet, coughing and wheezing. "You'll do what, exactly?" he sneered.

Declan heard his breath coming in deep, hard pants. Felt the collar already begin to steal whatever strength he'd gained feeding from her. He bit down on his jaw and looked away.

"That's right, *Derkein*. You'll sit here and do nothing," he said, taking a step closer. "Just like your father sat there and did nothing while I defiled that half-breed mother of yours."

The words hit Declan with the force of a brick wall. All the air was knocked out of his body and his head spun. Gripping the bars to keep himself anchored, Declan slammed his eyes shut, forcing out the images Lotharus had created in his mind. "Shut up," he murmured.

"By the time I was through with her, your father was practically begging me to end his miserable life."

"Shut up!" Declan leveled murderous eyes on Lotharus.

The vampire grinned. "You see." He slid his finger along one bar and then the next as he paced the length of the cell. "I know how to inflict the most pain, derive the most agony out of my prisoners. Call it a gift. And I enjoy every moment of it."

Lotharus turned, setting his attention back on Alexia. All Declan could think of as he walked toward her was what that monster had done to his parents. What he was going to do to her.

Alert, Alexia's eyes flitted from Declan to the door and back up to Lotharus. Then she hopped up and held out her handgun, pointing the barrel at Lotharus's chest. Declan held his breath. She paused for a heartbeat before shifting the weapon. In a flash of metal and roar of bullets, she dropped the soldier closest to the door and ran for the exit as fast as she could.

A thin shiver of hope traveled up his spine.

Run.

He willed her faster, visualized her making it out that door and away from this place. In a whirl of dust and wind, Lotharus leapt in front of her, blocking her path.

"And where do you think you're going?" he snapped. Alexia gasped to see him in front of her and pivoted to avoid him. But he was too fast. The back of his hand connected with her face. She went flying back the way she had come. Her gun skidded across the floor, stopping right in front of one of the soldiers, who instantly bent to retrieve it. The other soldier fisted Alexia's hair, forcing her to her feet.

Already a darkening red mark had spread across her cheekbone. Although she had to be hurting, she wriggled and fought against the soldier's hold, testing it. She barely moved an inch.

The sound of a boot shuffling against the floor pulled

Declan's attention to the other side of the dungeon. Lotharus stared down at the fallen soldier, kicking him slightly with the toe of his boot. Dead, the soldier didn't move.

"You always were a nice shot, Alexia." Lotharus bent, took the coiled whip off the soldier's belt and slowly unraveled it. "Personally, I never cared for guns. It doesn't take much skill to point and shoot. I much prefer the intimacy of hand-to-hand combat. There is nothing quite like facing one's quarry in a duel, with sword, fist or a whip, is there, dragon lord?"

Before Declan could reply or even knew what Lotharus was doing, the snap of leather cut through the still air. Alexia whimpered and everything in Declan pulsed in time with his heart until it alone was all he could hear. Although he knew Lotharus spoke by the movement of his lips, and saw the whip slash and bite Alexia's flesh again and again, his world had gone completely silent. Everything before him continued, but it played out in a slow-motion haze.

Finally, low, murmured words seeped into his conscious mind.

"I said, what's the matter, *Derkein?*" Lotharus asked with a mocking chuckle. "Aren't you going to help her like she helped you?"

Those words rang crystal clear in his mind. The callous

precision and truth of them sent dread and self-loathing rolling along his spine. His utter inability to help her brought him to his knees.

Lotharus smiled. "That's what I thought."

CHAPTER ELEVEN

"ALEX!"

Declan shouted her name until his throat burned. But she didn't respond or even move. Worry clawed at him, brutal and unforgiving. Stabbing his hands through the bars, he worked on the padlock, trying to get it loose. Frustrated, he shoved against the rails, pulling and yanking on them frantically.

Lotharus had forced him to watch as he had strung Alexia to the wall and beat her mercilessly. At the memory, blistering rage swelled inside him. Guilt and revulsion followed close behind. As much as he'd wanted to look away, he hadn't. Not only had he not wanted to give Lotharus the satisfaction of seeing him upset, he'd tried to be strong for her. And she had fought with all she had. But feeding and healing Declan had weakened her, and Lotharus was just plain stronger. She hadn't had a chance. And worse, it was all because of him.

Cradling his skull in his palms, he fought the adrenaline pounding and roaring inside him. Flattening his hands over his temples, he pressed hard, hoping to silence the disconnected thoughts warring within. When that didn't work, he yanked his hands away and let loose a frustrated roar. The sound of something hard and heavy striking the floor by his feet sang in the still dungeon. It took a moment to register that whatever had fallen had come off his body. Puzzled, he looked down.

The collar.

Declan gasped and brought his hand to his now bare throat. His mind rolled through the past hours, stopping just before Lotharus had walked in on him and Alexia…her hands on his neck. His gaze flew to her, unconscious across the chamber. She must have unlocked the clasp when Lotharus had entered the room with the soldiers.

Closing his eyes, Declan channeled his anger, focused it all on firing up the energy stores already thrumming back to life inside him.

He focused on breathing, each inhalation fanning the flames, stoking the fire building inside him. Feeding the beast he would need to free himself.

In and out. In and out.

Anger wouldn't get him out of this box, wouldn't help her. But he knew something that would.

Skin humming with renewed energy, power coursing through his veins once more, Declan cocked his head and rolled his shoulders, shifting into his dragon self the instant he had the strength. Before the last scale rolled over his flesh, he opened his mouth, spraying a deluge of dragonfire on the bars.

The iron glowed, first red and then white, before it melted like wax from a candle beneath the white-hot flame. The metal dripped down, pooling in a blackened puddle at his feet.

Closing his eyes, he bent his head down and ran forward. Declan shouldered through what was left of the bars, feeling only a moment of discomfort as his armored body took the brunt of the impact.

The minute he stood upright in the center of the dungeon, his eyes sought her out. Part of his brain recognized he should be escaping, using the information she'd almost died giving him to free himself. The other part screamed that he could not in good conscious leave her here. For, no matter their past, their future, here and now he owed her his life. He knew Alexia was no more than a pawn in whatever jacked-up game Lotharus was playing.

The mighty black dragon released a shuddering groan and stepped toward her.

Alexia.

He couldn't vocalize her name while shifted, but it whispered through his thoughts.

Dipping his head, he nudged her cheek with the side of his muzzle, the tough skin warming at the feel of her silken flesh against it. She didn't wake. Narrowing his eyes, he gazed down at her. Faint sprinkles of moonlight cast shadows across her face, illuminating the sullen eyes, deep black circles and beaten skin. The urge to kill Lotharus very, very slowly flooded him.

He puffed out a breath. Smoke wafted out of his nostrils, curling around her, hazing his vision. Declan shook his head. Getting angry would do her no good; it would do him no good. He needed to calm down before his rage and hate had the animal inside him lashing out.

He let out a quivered exhale and again tipped his snout toward her, inhaling deeply. At first, the acrid and bitter smell of the dungeon pricked his sensitive nose. Then he caught a sniff of it—the slightly sweet, decidedly feminine scent of her. A low purr vibrated his throat. He concentrated on that scent, on her. The fire inside his throat burned out and the dragon receded with a resigning groan.

Human once more, Declan ran a hand over her bent

head before cupping her cheeks in his hands and lifting her closed eyes to his.

"Alexia," he said softly. "Alex, wake up."

ALEXIA HEARD SOMEONE CALLING her name. But it sounded so far away. A strange cloud enveloped her, preventing her from seeing anything. She groped her way through the smoke.

"Hello?" she called, feeling a bubble of panic rise in her throat when the haze wouldn't lessen despite all her efforts to swipe it away.

Spinning in circles, arms jutting out in front of her, she walked in shuffled steps. Then, the next thing she knew, she was falling face-first into a white void. Alexia barely had time to scream before her body jerked and she flattened out. Almost like someone had snapped a harness around her midsection and tightened a bungee cord. Heart still racing, she frowned. Currents of air breezed through her hair and slid past her skin, so she hadn't stopped falling. But she wasn't on the ground, either. Was she flying? She couldn't really be sure, as she had her eyes shut tight.

"Alexia."

A voice called to her again. Sucking in a breath of courage, she opened her eyes. Miles and miles of purple sky peppered with white, cottonball puffy clouds stretched before her. A laugh bubbled to the top of her throat, and a beaming grin crossed her face. Then she caught sight of a huge black dragon flying beside her. Her first instinct was to scream, but then she saw its sparkling blue eyes, its familiar black wing.

Declan?

A strange mist around her shimmered, each particle catching light until it shone so brightly it was like looking into the sun. She shrunk back, feeling a great weight slam upon her as the grains turned to sand. Mountains of sand poured on her, pulling her down, closing over her head. No matter how hard she struggled to get free, it piled higher and higher….

"Alex!"

She gasped for breath. Panting, her eyes wide with shock, she glanced wildly around, waiting for the wall of deathly sand to collapse on top of her again.

Only warm hands enveloped her face. They forced her head still, her gaze to lock on a face. A face she knew.

"Declan?"

His blue eyes smiled brighter and warmer than his sincere grin. "I thought I'd lost you there for a moment."

Alexia closed her eyes and shook her head, trying to dislodge the random and dizzying thoughts still bombarding it. When she opened her eyes, reality came back into glaring focus. Over his broad shoulder, she saw his cell. Noticed the bars were melted and gone. Remembered she'd used her fingerprint identification to unlock his collar the instant Lotharus had entered the dungeon. She moaned and recalled the brutal beating he'd given her afterward. She felt mortified that Declan had seen her at her weakest.

"Oh," she said, closing her eyes again, wishing she could forget again.

"Alex, stay with me."

His deep voice rang in her ears, commanding and yet concerned. A hand petted her cheek, rubbing lightly. Then a warm forehead met hers. The tip of a nose rubbed against hers, whisper soft.

When at last she seemed to breathe normally, seemed calm, he let out a sigh. His warm breath melted her lips and feathered against the skin of her neck.

"You," he said, the word a combination of a scold and a laugh. "Why did you do it?"

Alexia opened her eyes. "Do what?" Speaking, actually talking, brought a new kind of pain to her jaw. One she had not felt in Goddess knew how long. Every muscle in her body tensed, riding out the wave of pain.

"Why didn't you leave when I told you to?" he asked.

A warm hand floated across her throbbing flesh, taking away some of the ache. "Why did you try and save me?"

The answer, the truth, was too much to bare. But she couldn't deny it, couldn't fight it. Not anymore. In fact, she wasn't sure she had any fight left in her at all. Everything seemed too much, too overwhelming. The only thing that made any sense in her crazy world stood in front of her. And that made no sense at all.

Alexia stared into his eyes, feeling herself spiral into their depths, wanting to lose herself in them forever. She opened her mouth to answer his question, but what felt like an earthquake rocketed through the cavern. The catacomb walls quaked. Dust sprinkled from the ceiling, which crumbled beneath the weight of whatever had landed above.

Declan threw himself over her, shielding her with his body. Warm and hard, his bare chest brushed against her, his head falling into the crook of her neck and his palm covering the back of her head protectively.

A roar splintered through the night, vibrating through the air. She felt more than heard Declan's surprised gasp before he leaned off her, his gaze fixed on the ceiling.

"Dragons," he breathed.

She looked from him to the ceiling, frowning when she

saw lines of worry marring his handsome brow. She'd expected to see him smiling.

"What is it?"

He opened his mouth to answer. However, the cadence of marching footfalls pounding on the ground outside the dungeon door stopped him. Declan flattened himself against the wall beside her just as a mile-long line of soldiers rounded the corner. They held their weapons at the ready and moved so fast they did not even spare a glance inside the chamber or notice him loose, his cell bars melted.

Chest rising and falling sharply, Declan peered out the door. Once he was certain they were gone, he moved in front of her and began working on her bindings.

"The soldiers are mobilizing," she said, urgently twisting against her bonds.

"Yes. And by the sound of it, Kestrel has sent the entire legion to come free me," he said without looking up from this task. "And if I know my sister, she won't let them leave here alive without me."

"So? That sounds like pretty standard procedure for a rescue mission." Her voice cracked though she tried to steady it. Something about the tone in his, and the haste with which he tried to free her set her on edge.

As Declan tugged the last knot free, unwinding the

rope from her chafed wrists, she took a step forward. "If they succeed, they won't leave here without hunting down the Queen and her heir and killing them both. Not if I don't get to them first."

Alexia's footing faltered. She couldn't tell if it was from his remark or the weakness in her limbs, but told herself it was the latter. A hand gripped the side of her face, the other her hip, helping to steady her.

"Of course they wouldn't." Alexia swallowed and tried to suppress the abrupt sense of hurt. "And if they fail?" she asked, glad her years of training took over, hardening her voice.

His thumb lightly caressed her cheek before it fell away. The cold air that swept across her skin mirrored the emptiness growing inside her.

"Then we will all die." His answer intensified the hollow void in the pit of her stomach. "Those here are the last of our original line. If they perish, soon it will be as if dragons had never existed."

Alexia didn't hesitate. "Then you have to go. Now."

The fingers on her hip bit into her desperately. "I can't leave you here."

"You can't stay, either."

As if to further emphasize her point, another booming crash rained down from above. But now gunshots fired in answer. His broad shoulders jumped with each one. He didn't have to tell her his conflicted state of mind, one half telling him to go and the other to stay. She saw the war rage across his face clear as day.

"Go," she said again, this time giving his arms a push.

The hand that held her hip ripped free and he backed up a few steps. Alexia nearly whimpered at the loss, at the thought that this would be the last time she'd feel his touch, see him standing in front of her.

Declan's gaze searched her face.

More gunfire and screams pierced the air above.

"Go," she repeated.

"What about you?"

"I belong here, fighting for my people. Just as you belong out there fighting for yours."

"But Lotharus…"

"Will be nothing after tomorrow when I take the throne." She shook her head, unable to say aloud the truth of what that meant for them. What her becoming Queen made them. "Declan, I…"

He rushed forward, reaching her in two steps. His lips covered hers hard and fast. Whatever she had planned to say became lost in his kiss. Alexia gasped into his mouth as he swept her literally off her feet and into his powerful arms. Goddess, she sighed, melting into them. His dominance overwhelmed her. With no restraints, no collar keeping his strength in check, she found his sheer power and size intoxicating.

And she yielded instantly.

Wrapping a hand around his shoulders, her other palm cupped the back of his head. Warm and desperate, his mouth claimed hers, kissing her with fierce hunger. A minute passed and then another. More shrieks and gunfire blasted above them, but the only thing she could think of was the urgent, plying rhythm of his mouth on hers. After three and then four minutes he pressed her backward, pinning her between him and the wall.

The warmth of his body seeped into hers, consuming her. A knee wedged between her legs. Like lightning, lust crackled through her. Fire blossomed in her core, igniting the already burning desire eating away at her for this man…her enemy and the one person who knew the whereabouts of the crystal.

The thought crept in her mind, although she tried to suppress it. Some part of her knew this was good-bye, but she forced that thought back, as well. Forced herself to live in this moment, this instant, knowing the minute he left they would return to being rivals once more. Hunting each other for the one thing both of them needed.

Large hands framed her face and he pulled away,

leaning his forehead on hers. Eyes still closed, her lips tingled, wet and swollen from his kisses.

"Promise me you'll fight hard. That you won't go down easy, no matter what." Although he wasn't asking, she heard the entreating tone in his voice. It nearly undid her. Even he couldn't lie about their situation, their future. The fact he even stood here now, begging her to stay safe, had her heart twisting in her chest.

Unable to speak, Alexia nodded. Reaching out, she tightened her arms around his neck and closed her eyes. "I promise," she finally whispered.

Although it took more will than he thought he owned to pull away, Declan managed to release her. Taking a step back, he held her gaze. He knew he said too much with one look. Knew trying to comfort, plead, say goodbye and apologize in the seconds they had only made him fail miserably at all of them instead of succeed at one. He knew it, he felt it. But he couldn't help it, either.

He shook his head, unable to believe that those were the thoughts raging through him. Not revenge. Not hate. Not killing the vampires who were slaying his kin above ground. Only thoughts of her.

Declan spun and walked toward the back of the dungeon. He felt her eyes on him as he shifted tables and pushed debris out of the way, but he didn't turn around until he had one foot inside the crack in the wall. Taking a deep breath, he cast a regretful gaze over his shoulder, knowing the image of her standing alone in the dungeon would forever be burned into his mind.

"Thank you, Alexia. For everything," he said, before stepping through the gaping hole she'd told him about, not unlike the one through his heart.

LOTHARUS TURNED THE PAGE of the centuries-old text. Or more accurately, the loosely bound fragments of scrolls that comprised the dark prince's diary. What was left of it, anyway. Lotharus bit down on his jaw as his eyes roamed over the lines of text, one of the last entries in the collection. Even though he hated reading of the final days leading up to the Dark War, he studied them carefully. After all, if he wanted to rule, to bring back honor and dignity to the males of his race, he had to know how the dark one had failed.

Thoughtful of the aged and delicate parchment, Lotharus flipped to the final entry. The one he loathed reading most of all. Unlike the rest of the entries, eloquent in their precision and destruction, this final page seemed penned by a madman. At times Lotharus questioned its very validity. Doubted the possibility these final words had been penned by the same brilliant genius who had begun their race.

Lotharus released a disgusted snort out of his nose. The disbelieving voice was the weak part inside him speaking. The one who whispered doubts in the back of his mind, asking him, if the dark prince had failed, how could he ever hope to succeed? Reminding him that, while not desirable, the status quo was better than failure, was it not? Had his life not been above and beyond his sire's? Was not his station, reputation and daily life better than ninety-nine percent of his male counterparts'? Hadn't life behind the curtain, holding all the power yet none of the public blame or responsibility, been working for him?

As he had many times before, Lotharus allowed the cynical voice to run its course. Let his mind slide through the possibilities of the coming days if he chose to abandon his carefully laid plan. And as usual, his conclusion remained the same.

Lotharus found the mere thought of following Alexia's orders, of seeing her as leader and Queen of this horde, more abhorrent than death. Even the doubtful part of him agreed.

Pursing his lips, he slammed his hand atop the last page, wanting to crumple it in his palm. However, the sound of his study door opening pulled him back.

Lotharus glanced up to see the Queen sweep into the room. Her long black hair and billowing crimson gown trailed behind her as she walked. It did not take someone of his advanced age and intellect to discern the displeasure and anger etched across her beautiful features. Or for him to determine by the healthy glow in her eyes that she had not been drinking the carefully measured concoction he'd given her to keep her sedated.

"Catija," Lotharus said, stowing the book in a drawer and rising up from his perch behind his desk. "Darling, you look famished. Have you been feeding?"

"Where is my daughter?"

A frown tugged his brow. He'd barely stretched his legs before she'd issued a demand. "Sorry?"

"You heard me, Lotharus. Where is Alexia?"

"In the battle, I imagine," he said with a carefree smile. Inside his mind swarmed with possibilities and scenarios.

The Queen eyed him skeptically before notching up her chin. "I want to see her. Now."

"What is this vexation, my love? I told you," he said, moving alongside her. "She is doing what she does best."

"You mean what *you* trained her to do."

Resentment simmered inside him, rearing up from the lower regions of his mind and body. A dark place he worked tirelessly to keep hidden from the Queen lest his plan—this carefully choreographed masquerade he'd swept her into—would collapse. He would fail.

That couldn't happen.

Taking her hands in his, he plastered a smile on his face and forced himself to hold it firmly in place while he stared down at her. "Dearest, you and Alexia are the only family I have. Never would I do anything to jeopardize that, to harm either of you. This horde means everything to me." He bent, kissing the top of her hand. "But you mean more."

Like a bad aftertaste, the lies he'd just told stuck to the back of his mouth. However, they rolled easily off his tongue and Catija, poor, pathetic Catija, bought into every single one of them. First the anger left her black eyes. Then her face relaxed, resembling more the beauty their historians wrote about…or rather, used to write about. A smile spread across his face, one she mimicked, although he was quite certain she wouldn't if she knew the cause.

Lotharus opened his arms and she came willingly. Enveloping her, he leaned his chin on her shoulder, then bent down and kissed it. A soft moan slid past her lips and she clutched him tighter.

Females, he thought, were so easy to placate, so gullible in their foolish notion of love. It made his plan advance so easily, almost absurdly so. At times, his instincts told him to be wary, to be on alert and always look over his shoulder.

However, no one was ever there.

"Now, why don't the two of us sit and enjoy a meal." Lotharus lifted his head to gaze at the soldier standing guard beside the doorway. He angled his chin toward the open chamber door. Ivan nodded and slid through it, immediately heading toward the dungeon.

The Queen wasn't the only one looking for Alexia. After all, he needed both of them for his plan to work.

CHAPTER TWELVE

DECLAN HAD DIFFICULTY maneuvering through the small crawlspace at first. But then it opened up into a maze of low-ceilinged passageways where he could almost stand upright instead of scooting along hunched over. Four-legged creatures scurried in front of him and cobwebs stuck to the thin sheen of sweat covering his back and forehead. He pushed through them, forcing his mind to focus on what lay ahead and not behind.

But pictures of Alexia, thoughts of her sweet lips and even softer body, plagued him. At the forefront of it all lay the hope she would not find herself outside in the fight he was barreling toward. That he would not be forced to fight her. Or worse, watch one of his kin sink their talons into her flesh.

The thought sent him reeling. He didn't want to be

forced to harm one of his own to protect her. Didn't want to stop and consider what kind of a ruler that made him, or place a name on feelings he held in his heart for the vampire princess.

Declan turned sideways, sliding through a fissure in the cliff before finally stepping into the night. Ocean air and rain blanketed his flesh. Each pore screamed out in pleasure at the sense of freedom. He allowed himself one second to absorb the bliss before he maneuvered up the cliff. Once he crested the ledge, his jaw fell at the sight before him.

The plum- and gray-hued sky was bathed in flame. Ear-piercing shrieks of the dragons drowned out those echoing from the soldiers below.

It was as he'd feared. An all-out battle raged on the catacomb rooftop. Death hung heavy in the air; many had already died. The rocky shelf of the cavern roof was slick with rain and the blood of the fallen. He looked up to see at least half of the full force of his dragon legion flanking the sky. They circled the soldiers like vultures, taking turns swooping from the pack to snatch up a soldier in their claws or teeth.

Beneath his skin, the corded tendons of his back itched to shift, to transform and to join the battle.

One of the soldiers ran forward and crouched to his

knees. His dark leather trench coat fanned to the side as he whipped a crossbow from beneath it. Scores of arrows began to litter the sky, splinters of metal piercing the flesh of the dark night. As some found their marks, the cries of his kin filled his ears.

Declan balled his fists. The creatures of the night were in their element.

Out of the corner of his eye, Declan saw a pink female plunge out of formation from the pack of dragons. Before the vampire could switch his aim, she rained down an inferno, highlighting the rain-quenched rooftop of the rocky shelf above the catacombs. He'd know her anywhere.

Tallon.

Declan smiled, despite his anger at her for coming after him. Pride swelled to see his flock was in their element, as well. Resolving to get ahold of Falcon and stop this before any more lives were lost, he turned his concentration inward. Pinching his eyes, he focused not on the wings beneath his skin, burning for freedom, but the calm scent of rain. The droplets tapped against his shoulders, as if they eagerly awaited his foray into battle.

Pulling the clean night air into his lungs, he let it coat them, fill them. Empowered by the free air, Declan stretched his arms out to the sides and kicked back his head, embracing the fire inside him. In a flash, heat and flame ignited over his flesh, turning skin to scale. In one sinuous move, he shifted into his animal form. Declan arched his back and let loose a roar. The earth shook beneath his transformed foot, and again when he slammed his other beside it.

Before he had a chance to touch off, a green dragon appeared beside him.

"Tallon knew you were still alive."

Declan heard his friend's relieved words in his mind. Although dragons couldn't vocalize in animal form, they could speak with their minds if close enough to each other. He turned his head, feeling a smile tug his lips. *"Gods, Falcon. It's good to see you."*

"And you." Although the green dragon before him didn't smile, he heard the grin in his best friend's voice. One tugged at his mouth, as well, but it was short-lived. He had to get orders to Falcon, had to stop this mess he'd helped create.

"Falcon, you must listen to me closely. Gather everyone you can and retreat back to the mountain," Declan said before thrashing his wings in preparation to take off.

Falcon landed in front of him, his green eyes alight with fire. *"We risked everything to save you. So, with all respect, my lord, I'm not leaving your side until we are flying back home. Together."*

Declan's lips curled. *"Don't be a fool. I'm safe now."*

"How did you get free?"

Declan's heart pinched. *"I'll tell you later."*

"And the crystal..."

"It's secure. Now, alert who you can and go, quickly!"

"But..."

"Now!" With that, Declan shot upward.

Once he'd cleared Falcon, he veered toward the rocky shelf. Tallon was nowhere to be seen. However, his eyes fixed on a smaller dragon, yelping and flailing on the rooftop. The vampires circled the wounded creature. When it tried to stand, Declan recognized the youngling immediately.

Ash.

Declan cursed beneath his breath and vowed to punish the legionnaire who'd let him into battle. Horde surrounded the fledgling on all sides. If Declan didn't act, Ash wouldn't make it home. At the thought, heat churned from deep within him and coiled up his throat.

Opening his jowls, he screamed a war cry, hoping to take the soldiers' attention off Ash long enough for him to catch his footing.

It worked.

They spun around, aimed their weapons at Declan and fired. Slicing through the air, Declan somersaulted in a spiral, avoiding the bullets and arrows shooting at him. Although he knew the fireball he was working behind his throat would be enough to barbecue all of the vampires, he focused on one. The one his sister's carefully managed attack had failed to affect—the soldier with the crossbow and the itchy trigger finger.

Ready to spit enough dragonfire to melt the flesh off the lot of them, he parted his lips. The soldier saw him coming and switched his aim. Declan figured one, perhaps two arrows would spear his armored flesh before he managed to kill the son of a bitch, but he didn't slow his course. After all, he'd received much worse than silver-tipped arrows piercing his flesh over the past three days.

The vampire cocked his head down, sighting his scope at the same time Declan roared.

A shotgun blast rang out. The soldier's face whitened before he fell sideways, dead. Declan blinked the rain out of his eyes. Another deafening roar of gunfire echoed in the night, followed by the cries of his enemies. His keen eyes zeroed in on the soldier who'd collapsed on his back, a hole the size of Texas blown through his gut.

What the hell?

A flash of blond hair and polished black leather waved past his vision.

Alexia?

Declan closed his mouth in time to stop the flow of dragonfire from killing her and every other vamp on the roof, but he didn't have enough time to slow down.

He'd have to land in the thick of the fray. Jerking his shoulders, he managed to flatten out his dive and land on his hind legs.

The earth quaked and shuddered at his landing. Rocks shifted underfoot before the edge began to give way under his weight. The brittle rim wouldn't hold much longer.

Shit.

Launching forward into a dive roll, Declan sprung to his feet in half-human form, opting to keep only his wings and his tail. The second he stood, a soldier ran at him with a silver stake. Spinning to gain momentum, Declan wrenched his tail in a wide arc. When it should have struck the soldier's trunk, it hit air. Unprepared, he fell off balance, smacking to his knees on the slick granite.

Once he righted himself, he looked over his shoulder. Alexia held her shotgun in her hands like a stave, parrying and blocking the hulking soldier's stabbing weapon. Using his free hand, the soldier swung a wide right hook. Alexia bobbed, kicking her makeshift staff in a violent upper cut on his chin that sent him reeling backward. He landed on his ass, blood streaming out of his obviously broken nose. She widened her stance as he popped back to his feeet. First, he straightened his black sunglasses and then his shoulders, before circling his fat neck. Eyes on Alexia, he laved the trail of blood flowing out of his nose with the tip of his tongue and crooked his finger.

Without a moment's hesitation, Alexia stowed the shotgun in the holster on her back and ran toward him. However, it was Declan who knocked him to the ground.

When he turned, wide, black eyes met his.

"Declan." Her breathy voice sent lust vibrating though him, but he tamped it down.

"What are you doing out here?" he asked, hearing the dangerous quiver in his voice.

"What does it look like?" she shouted, roundhouse kicking a soldier in the gut before smashing his face with the heel of her hand.

Declan released a frustrated growl and bent at the waist, rolling an attacking vampire over his back before stabbing him through the heart with his tail. "You know what I meant! Why are you fighting the soldiers?"

Alexia aligned herself so they stood back-to-back, looping her arms around his. "Lotharus sicced his puppies on me," she said over her shoulder.

With a grunt, she pushed against him hard enough to make him double over. One second she was behind him and the next she flipped over his head, standing face-to-face with him. At the sight of her, his heart kicked against his ribs. Curtains of wet hair clung to her face. Her eyes flickered at the sight of him, and Declan was instantly drawn into their depths. Every emotion coursing through him was mirrored in her eyes.

Without hesitation, he snaked an arm about her, tucking her slim body against his. A groan hummed along his skin as she fell against him. The hard-boned corset and leather she wore was unyielding and cold against his bare chest. The exact opposite of the creamy, flawless perfection it protected.

She blinked. "He's ordered the soldiers to seize me by any means necessary," she said, clutching his arm and spinning out of his embrace. Keeping one hand on him, she shot the other hand to the gun at her hip. Her focus solely on the soldier closing in on her left, she skinned her Glock and fired.

Declan tucked his chin to his chest to shield his face from the blast. When he spun back around, he saw another soldier pop up behind her. He tugged on her arm to yank her out of harm's way, but she held him in a death grip, her attention still to her left.

"Alex, look out," he shouted.

Before she could turn around and raise her gun, Declan pulled her back to him forcefully. Drawing her into his body, he shielded her with one of his wings and spun his tail, smashing the end into the soldier's head. Hot liquid coated the tip, the blood dripping down the length of it. He yanked it free of the vamp's skull with little effort.

Chest heaving, he slowly stood upright, opening his wing and releasing his grip on her.

Wide eyes looked up at him. "I didn't see him," she said with a gasp.

His lips tilted in a smile. "Good thing I did."

Declan looked down at the beauty in his arms and felt the battle, the world, fade into oblivion. "Alexia, the horde is falling apart. You're in danger."

"No more than you."

"Exactly. I can't protect you out here," he shouted.

"I don't need your protection."

As if on cue, the sweet scent of her blood filled his nose. Frantic, his eyes scoured her body, settling on her waist. The black leather was shiny, slick with her blood. He narrowed his eyes more in fear than anger. "You're hurt."

Alexia barely spared a glance down before shrugging him off. "It's nothing. I'm fine."

"Fine?" he roared, recalling all too clearly the blinding

rage and panic he'd experienced as Lotharus had beat her. The helpless frustration he felt even now, knowing she was hurting yet again. "You're not fine."

She wouldn't look at him. Her gaze was suddenly fixed on something over his shoulder.

"Alexia, look at me…." His words faded when she unsheathed the shotgun from her back and pressed the stock to her shoulder, aiming the muzzle right at him. One eye closed, she cocked the weapon, loading the barrel.

"Duck!"

Declan bent and covered his ears before she'd even finished the order. The shotgun exploded, rattling his brain with numbing force. A body smacked the ground behind him a millisecond later. Heart racing, he lowered his hands and looked up.

Alexia propped the shotgun on her shoulder and shrugged, looking like a cross between a dominatrix and Annie Oakley. An unwitting smile crossed his lips for a moment before a shrill dragon's cry pierced the night. Declan whirled around, his eyes confirming what his heart already knew.

"Tallon," he called in disbelief.

ALEXIA'S HEART KICKED against her rib cage at hearing that name on Declan's lips. A flood of memories poured over her like ice water, and she recalled the female dragon he'd helped escape.

She sucked in a breath and let her gaze follow his to a pink female fighting and losing to a band of Lotharus's soldiers. Three of them had her pinned to the ground on her back. She'd shifted to her dragon form, but still couldn't fend them off. A look back at Declan showed him embroiled in a battle of his own and unable to reach her.

Turning back toward the female, Alexia dropped the shotgun to the stones. Her claws lengthened. Without a second thought, she ran forward, swiping, hacking and slicing Lotharus's soldiers to get to her. Blood, hot and thick, coated her hands, but she managed to grip her pistol with a sure hand. Jumping between the soldiers and the felled dragon, Alexia fired rounds into their skulls one by one before they even knew what had hit them.

Inhaling, she pivoted around, expecting to see the dragon on the ground. Instead, what she saw made her heart seem to thud louder than the myriad of gunshots discharging all around her.

The female stood, towering a good ten feet over her, its pink lips quivering with anger, its violet eyes narrow.

"OH, GODS," DECLAN SAID beneath his breath. "Tallon, no!"

Declan watched in horror as Tallon opened her serrated

jowls and roared. Alexia's blond hair fanned out behind her from the force of air. She lifted her hands to shield herself, but Tallon's hammerfisted claw backhanded her hard. Alexia sailed across the shelf, smacking the rock wall.

Tallon pushed off with powerful hind legs, bounding in a huge leap. She landed directly over the dazed Alexia, straddling her.

"Die, you bitch."

Although it sounded like no more than a violent roar to the soldiers and Alexia, Declan heard his sister's words like a gong in his mind. Panicked, he clamped down his jaw and ran as Tallon's clawed hand snatched Alexia's throat, hauling her off her feet. Alexia dropped her handgun, bringing both hands up to her neck, her legs flailing and kicking the air.

With a roar, Declan swung his tail, punching Tallon in the gut. She dropped Alexia and flew back, landing on the ground so hard a cloud of dust kicked up around her. Hustling to his feet, Declan spun to Alexia. He had to make certain she was okay. Coughing and sputtering, Alexia rolled to her stomach, keeping one hand on her throat as she pushed up to her hands and knees.

Satisfied, he looked back to his sister. She stared from him to Alexia and back at him, abject confusion and disbelief in her eyes.

"You blood-traitor bastard!"

Declan barely had time to register the words before a very human Tallon jumped on his back. Her legs wrapped around his waist. Slim hands circled his neck and pulled.

"How could you side with her after what she did to you?"

Although she tried to choke him, their skin was slick from the rain and she couldn't get a tight grip. Still, with what hold she had, she held tight. Declan did not want to hurt her, but she wasn't being rational and this wasn't exactly the place to sit her down and have a heart-to-heart.

With a heaving grunt, he pitched her off his back. She landed on her bottom, bouncing and skidding across the gravel. Declan immediately straightened and faced her.

"Tal, remember Mom," he said over the roar of the fight. "I would never betray you, sister. Think!"

Tallon pushed on her shoulders and arms, flipping from her back to her feet in a flash. "Dad saved her from one of the Queen's soldiers. She was never one of them."

Murder in her eyes, she charged him again. This time instead of trying to fight or evade her, Declan dropped to his knees and set his arms to his sides. Tossing the sodden hair out of his eyes, he took deep pulls of wet air and waited for whatever wrath she would unleash upon him. The sign of submission had her halting in her tracks.

"What are you doing? Get up and fight me."

He shook his head and closed his eyes. "No," he said with an exhale. "I won't fight you."

A stinging slap knocked the side of his face. Declan clenched his jaw at the abrupt pain—not so much across his face, but ripping through his heart. He took a deep breath before looking up at her again.

"Fight me, damn you!" she shouted. Rain streamed down her face, but it could not mask her tears.

"Why?"

At first, his question caught her off guard. Then renewed anger and hate lit up her violet eyes, making them glow and burn. "You chose her over me."

Declan could have thought of a dozen things to say to her, but only the truth would come. "I care for her, Tallon."

The hurt and shock on her face would have brought him to his knees if he hadn't already been there.

"What did they do to you? You went mad in there!"

"Nothing, Tallon, listen to me...."

A piercing dragon wail vibrated the air around them, cutting off his words. Declan winced at the earsplitting war call and instantly looked up. A flash of lightning ripped through night's veil, illuminating the sky and the massive grayback dragon flying through it.

Hawk.

His eyes followed the dragon's flight over the catacomb shelf and beyond. Near the edge, Alexia stood in close combat with a sword-wielding soldier. Like all of the vampire soldiers, he was twice her size and bearing down hard. She parried his slashing broadsword with a stick before it snapped and she tossed it aside. Her hand went to her hip. However, her gun was gone. Declan saw the look on her face at the moment when the memory dawned on her that her pistol had dropped to the ground.

Defenseless, she dodged out of the way of the soldier's next stabbing blow. Heart thundering, Declan stood and ran toward her. Diving past fights, hurdling over dead bodies, he was only a few feet away from her when an arm shot out of nowhere, striking him across the throat. The force of the hit sent his feet sailing upward. He crashed to the muddy ground, landing flat on his back. Any air he'd managed to regain was knocked free, and pulsing stars peppered his vision. Declan barely looked up in time to see a sword falling toward his chest. He rolled to the side, hearing the blade sink into the soft earth where his body had lain moments ago.

By the time he turned back over, the soldier had raised his sword overhead again. Letting loose a grunt, Declan kicked out his leg, his heel colliding with the soldier's kneecap. It inverted on impact, bowing backward. The vampire howled and fell to the ground. Declan easily pinned him down and twisted his fat head, snapping his neck before turning back to find Alexia.

He noticed her hair first. The radiant veil fluttered in the wind, every golden strand illuminated by the moonlight. With the glittering sea rolling behind her and the starlit sky above, Declan couldn't recall ever seeing anything so serene, so visually arresting, in all his days.

Somehow she'd manage to defeat the soldier. His dead body lay on the ground by her feet. Declan watched as her hand clutched over her midsection. His eyes zeroed in on the wound he'd seen earlier, to the blood seeping between her fingers. Thinking of nothing but getting to her, he stepped forward. A gigantic shadow darkened the sky above her. Declan paused midstep and looked up. Dark fear swallowed him whole at the sight of Hawk circling above her like a bird over its prey.

"Oh, no. Alex!" She looked up at his call, confusion in her black eyes.

Declan watched what seemed like slow motion as Hawk swooped and kicked out his massive claws. She had no time to duck. No time to dodge. Hawk's meaty fists slammed into her.

Alexia fought for balance, her arms windmilling as her feet slipped out from under her.

She's not going to make it.

The moment the thought came, she tumbled over the lip of the cliff, disappearing into the void.

Declan's heart jerked. Without a second thought, he charged toward the cliff in a blind run. His eyes fixed on the space he had seen her last. *Alexia!* At his heart's scream his legs raced harder. Each fall of his feet pounded against the stone canopy in a frantic tempo of hope, even though his brain was already conscious of the truth his heart flat out refused to accept.

There is no way she could survive that fall.

No way.

Not if he didn't get to her first.

His mind screamed the words his heart didn't want to hear. However, his body was not listening, either. He rocketed toward her, driven by fear and something else he couldn't label. Already his wings had popped free, primed to fly after her. His feet struck the stones mere inches from the edge where he'd seen her fall not seconds before.

With a roar, he leapt over the side, falling into a head-first dive after her.

Icy jets of wind spliced over his human skin like white-hot razor blades. Immediately his eyes narrowed, adjusting to the constant airstream and inky darkness. At his will, scales coated his body, sealing his skin from the cold, cutting wind. At first he couldn't see anything. But then he saw her. For a heartbeat the flutter of golden hair glowed in the darkness, shining like a far-off star.

And he knew he wasn't going to reach her in time.

CHAPTER THIRTEEN

No, HE SILENTLY VOWED. Not catching her wasn't an option. Declan shifted, his bones stretching, lengthening. His wings folded tight together between his shoulder blades, streamlining him to go faster, ripping him through the sky.

Rain struck him like a thousand needles, nearly stealing his breath. But he disregarded the pain. He was finally closing the distance. Close enough to see the delicate curves of her unconscious face. Close enough to see the breaking foam of the ocean rising up fast below her.

Grunting, he dipped his long neck against the wind and arched his tail, angling to slide beneath her. He had one chance to grab her before gravity won and the water swallowed them both.

Thrusting his wings hard, he lowered his head and stretched out a clawed hand. The moment something brushed his fingertips, his talons closed tight, sinking into what he thought was her arm. Pulling her to his chest, he wound the other claw around her leather-clad waist and pivoted toward the sky.

Holding her firmly, Declan pounded his wings, hard and fast, vaulting up with all his might. A strangled roar cried out of him with the effort. Cool sprays of turbulent seawater sprinkled his back. For a moment, he thought they wouldn't make it. He saw in his mind's eye his back crashing through the water, felt the water's pressure closing in around them. But only cool night air met his cutting wings as he pulled them higher into the night.

Without slowing, he climbed until the fear of the water subsided.

Although he didn't want to, he looked down at the woman lying limply in his claw. A burning sense of fear and loss sluiced through him. Panicked, he circled a deserted beach, setting her down on the first bank he saw.

After laying her on the sand, Declan faced the wooded area surrounding them, sniffing for threats before he shifted back into a defenseless human. Only the smell of nature and the sea filled his nose. However, a remnant of blood, of vampires, hung in the undertones. His eyes scanned the area for the source. Steps of rocks, covered in a carpet of moss, stretched upward along the cliff. Huge trees stood like giants' legs planted between the steps.

This place must be some kind of back entrance into the horde's cavern. But he didn't have time to worry about that now. Shaking off like a dog, he hovered over Alexia. As he shifted, rainwater dripped off him, stinging the various cuts on his flesh. He swiped them away with a flat palm and bent over Alexia.

Laying his ear above her mouth, he held his breath, listening, waiting.

Not breathing.

Panicked, Declan tilted her chin with two fingers, lowered his lips to hers and huffed a breath into her mouth. He repeated the move twice before pumping the heel of his hand against her sternum.

"Alexia, don't you leave me."

Again he blew air into her lungs. This time her lips seemed warmer. At least, that's what he told himself as he continued to try and feed her life.

Feed.

The errant thought snuck up from the back of his mind.

There's another way to save her.

Declan forced the idea back. He didn't want to go

there. Couldn't go there. Gritting his teeth, he pumped his hand against her chest again and again. This time when he blew air into her lungs, her back arched and a burst of air escaped with the force of her cough.

With a sigh of relief, he rolled her to her side. Rubbing his palm on her back, he whispered assuring words in her ear as she fought for air. Fierce trembles racked her wet body. Instinctively, she curled in a fetal position, trying to warm herself. After a moment, her eyes slid closed and her breathing slowed.

"Alex?" He grabbed her shoulder and shook her slightly. She didn't wake. The sand beneath her darkened, soaking up the blood seeping from her wounds. Again that cloying sense of panic seized him. If he didn't get her to someplace warm, someplace he could ensure she'd receive any care she needed, she would either bleed or freeze to death.

The thought of returning her to Lotharus's care made him violent. He'd have to take her home. Gods. He stabbed a hand through his hair. That thought didn't fill him with the warm fuzzies, either.

Releasing a breath, he stared down at the very fragile vampire curled up beside him. Three days ago, he would have let her die without a second thought. Now, not only had he just saved her life, he was actually thinking about taking her home and laying her in his bed.

His parents' bed.

The cold, harsh truth of Tallon's words swished through his mind, threatening to swell and crack the wall of resolve he'd felt was so solid and sure before. Had that place gotten to him? Was he a blood traitor?

Shadows moved above, cutting out the moonlight shining down on her in strobelike pulses. Declan frowned and looked up. Winged silhouettes skated across the darkness. Dragons. The entire legion, by the looks of it. Flying in the direction of the lair.

Either Falcon got word to them or they must have seen him leave. Must believe he had the crystal and was headed for safety.

Declan let his gaze fall back to the woman lying defenseless in the sand. His enemy, his obsession. Although everything in him screamed to take her, everything he'd ever been taught ordered him to abandon the vampire. Declan held his forehead in his palm and closed his eyes tight. He didn't have time. He had to act now.

Leave her or take her.

CATIJA PUSHED OPEN the doors of the dungeon and winced. The repulsive odor nearly felled her. Reflexively, she turned her head to the side and closed her eyes. Every instinct within her immortal body shouted for her to turn and run. Instead, she stepped inside and secured her torch on the wall sconce beside the doorway. Like skeletal fingers, strips of firelight slowly highlighted the cavernous space. First lighting up the door and tables around her in an orange glow, until the light crept farther, illuminating even the darkest corners of the dungeon.

Each inch that came into view highlighted memories of her last visit down there. Catija blinked rapidly. Images of the dragon King and Queen, covered in grime and blood, passed behind her eyes. Their naked limbs entwined in an embrace so tight and desperate she couldn't tell where one of them ended and the other began. As it had that night, her heart constricted. Never had she felt more a monster than she had the eve she'd come down here with Lotharus and seen them together.

Covering her nose with the back of one hand, she lifted her skirts with the other, trying to avoid the various and questionable puddles, even though she was soaked to the marrow from her trip to the catacomb roof. Frantic, she hustled from cell to cell, disappointed to find each one empty. The ring of keys she'd stolen from Lotharus's study clanked in her pocket with each step she took.

Although Lotharus had told her the prisoner had

escaped, Catija wanted to be certain he had not lied. The moment the opportunity had arisen, she'd emptied her stomach of the vile contents he'd made her imbibe and followed the driving need to come below and see with her own lucid eyes the truth her confused heart and addled mind didn't want to recognize.

She could not recall at what stage of their little game her onetime lover had begun spiking her feedings with a mind-altering agent. As she had then, Catija saw no other choice but to drink them. First so Lotharus would not suspect her, and second so she might discover why he wanted her to be complacent. At the final reason a solid mass of shame formed in the center of her throat. She swallowed it down, acknowledging the truth. Some deep, dark part of her had enjoyed drinking his draughts. Preferred being numb to the cloying guilt and shame she felt when sober. After all, she had brought Lotharus into their lives, made him general of their army, given him free rein over the horde, over her own daughter.

By the Goddess, why had she ever listened to that man? Why had she let her selfish desires and his evil words cloud her judgment and put her horde at risk? Her daughter at risk? Her baby, she thought with a choked sob. Alexia was now Goddess knew where, and all because her mother had failed to listen to her.

As Catija scoured the empty dungeon, she knew she'd been a pure and utter fool to think she could atone for what she'd done over her long life. A fool to think by saving the dragon King and Queen, or even their son, she could ever hope to save herself. She'd done too many horrible things, caused too much pain and suffering to ever balance the scales and make it right. Yet it did not mean she had to leave this plane of existence without trying.

Something on the ground flickered in the light bouncing off the wall torch. The object had a familiar shape. Catija squinted, trying to make it out. When she couldn't, she stepped forward. The hair on the back of her neck bristled and a wave of sickness knotted her gut. Bending, she reached down with trembling hands, knowing what it was the instant cool metal touched her fingers.

One of Alexia's daggers.

But why was it on the bloodstained dirt by the wall chains?

"Dearest."

Catija gasped at the voice and spun around, clutching the dagger tight behind her back. "Oh, Lotharus. You gave me fright."

He cocked his head, an unsettling smile passing over his handsome face. "I can't imagine why." The heel of his boot clicked against the floor with his slow step forward. He held a torch in his hand. The light flickered against his pale skin, illuminated the protruding bones of his face, making him look almost skeletal.

Like death come to claim her.

"What are you doing down here?"

"I was looking for Alexia."

"But I told you that dragon escaped and took her with him."

"I had to see with my own eyes," she said, gazing around the dismal surroundings with uncertainty. She'd so blindly let Lotharus school Alexia in the ways of the soldier, in warfare. Suddenly, she wondered if she hadn't done so with rash detriment.

"Is something wrong?"

At Lotharus's words, she gasped, looking up. He stood, closer now, mere feet away, regarding her intently, his eyes seeing more than she wanted him to.

"Lotharus, I—I think," she stammered, curling her fingers tighter around the weapon, feeling its cold indifference penetrate through her to the marrow.

"Yes," he prodded, a brow rising in question like a dark wing over his vacant eyes.

Catija swallowed. "I think we should postpone the wedding until my daughter is safely returned. The people wouldn't understand how I could celebrate, with her…in the hands of such dangerous monsters."

"Of course," he said without hesitation. "I understand completely." He opened his arms for her to walk into them. Fearful he knew she wasn't quite as drugged as she should be, Catija forced herself to smile and comply. However, this time as his arms wrapped around her they felt like a prison instead of a sanctuary. The lips on her neck sent a quiver of fear rather than lust down her spine.

The dagger seemed to grow heavier in her hand, the metal warming against her flesh. Catija blinked with realization. In that moment, she knew what she had to do. Knew her seemingly endless path across Lotharus's sick game board was at long last coming to an end.

As if she stood outside her own body watching events transpire, she saw her hand rise up to the sky. The dagger's jagged tip pointed downward, hovering over Lotharus's back like a sharp-toothed demon.

"I'm sorry," she heard herself say. "You would have made a great King, Lotharus."

The lips on her skin stilled. His mouth brushed the side of her face, his hot breath warming the skin beneath her ear.

"I still will."

Her upraised arm shook, the bloodstained blade vibrating in the flickering firelight. "What did you say?"

Lotharus leaned back, his body unfolding before hers like a massive snake rising for a strike. Satisfaction lit up his eyes as he caught sight of what must have been shock in hers. He smiled, his fangs hanging long and fearsome. "Checkmate."

Game over.

Catija's heart stuttered to a dead stop. For the space of a heartbeat, they stood still and silent. Then he lunged. Screaming, Catija stabbed downward hard and fast, meeting little resistance as she sunk the metal into his shoulder blade. However, it did not deter him. Razor-sharp fangs sunk into her neck, hard and deep. Catija opened up her mouth to scream again, but nothing came.

The force, the pain of his bite, brought tears to her eyes and stole the air from her lungs. Blindly, her hands pulled on the handle of the dagger, trying to dislodge it so she could strike him again. When it didn't move, she tugged at the fabric of his coat, pushed at his shoulders and his head in an attempt to break free. He clasped a wrist, forcing her arm behind her where he'd wound his around her. Panicked, feeling her life force seeping out of her, Catija raised her free hand, raking her nails over his face, clawing for freedom. However, he easily restrained that hand, as well.

The band of his arm tightened around her waist with each pull of blood he drew from her body. Slowly, a soft blue light rose like vapor from her skin. Her power. Again, Catija tried to fight, tried to squirm away. But the arm around her only tightened like a constrictor with each effort, until she couldn't get any more air into her lungs.

As he drained the life and energy from her body, the only coherent thoughts streaming through what was left of her conscious mind were of Alexia. Images of her as a small child, vibrant and happy, passed in front of her eyes. Of her long, bright hair, her chubby cheeks, dark eyes shining with glee from behind long, graceful lashes. A sob stuck in her throat.

Lotharus finally pulled back, his grip on her relaxing. Unable to move or hold herself up, she hung bent over his arm, boneless and weak. Panting in small, quick breaths, Catija used her last vestiges of strength to meet Lotharus's gaze. He grinned and she instantly wished his heinous smile would not be the last thing she saw on this earth.

Summoning the last of her strength, she narrowed her eyes on his face, proud of the gashes her nails had rent on his once pristine features. Knowing how deeply that would upset him. "Go ahead," she breathed. "Finish it."

He smiled and ran his hand over her mauled throat. The Queen hissed in a breath as he dug his claws into the wound, nearly making her black out from mind-numbing agony. "All in good time, my love."

ALEXIA RAN HER FINGERS through Declan's thick hair, down the nape of his neck, over the broad bridge of his shoulders. Slick and hot, his mouth claimed hers. On contact, she felt something inside her bend and snap. Winding her arms around his neck once more, she pulled on the back of his head, dragging him closer, harder, against her. The delicious weight of him on her sent a familiar jolt of vertigo splintering through her aroused body. Every time he touched her, swept his tongue in her mouth, tangled it with hers, her head spun and the world fell away beneath her.

Her fingertips grazed his columned throat at the same time he glided his hands down hers. A trail of goose bumps followed in his wake. Again, his wing lifted her up to meet him, rubbing that deliciously hard length of him against her. A lightning crack of pleasure soared through her body. Warmth flooded her core. The skintight leather pants she wore proved to be a thin barrier, the only barrier between them. And she wanted it gone.

As if he'd read her mind, he slid the pants down her legs, replacing them with the heat of his body. She yearned for his touch, his blood, and arched her hips in invitation. Something smooth and cool wound around her back, pressing her flush against his naked body. Entranced, she allowed the wing to cup her in its embrace, allowed the dragon to wedge that very potent and intoxicating male part of him inside her. Without a moment's hesitation, she took him in.

Her hands roamed over his smooth skin, almost hot to the touch, as he moved gracefully above her, moved skillfully inside her. The heat of her desire threatened to scorch her, engulf her. And she didn't care. Everything felt right. More right than she'd ever imagined being with another person could be. She trusted it, trusted the fire between them, almost as if it were fated, meant to be. They were meant to be….

Alexia moaned, the deep, primal sound awakening her from sleep. As she slipped into consciousness, the first thing she noticed was how utterly warm she was—from the tips of her toes to her ears. Unwitting, a drowsy smile curved her lips and she nestled deeper into the mattress. A frown tightened her brow. The bed felt…different, silky.

Her eyes shot open wide. Some cognizant part of her brain struggled to discover which of the many unfamiliar sensations she was experiencing had woken her. The silken expanse of the sheets sliding beneath her arms and face. The thin air, crisp and pure and with no hint of saltwater lingering in it. The long, solid mass of warmth radiating from the body lying beside her. Or the possessive hand splayed across her abdomen.

Declan.

She took a breath and held it. Where was she? What had happened? She couldn't recall anything past the fight with the horde and dragons. Closing her eyes, she fought to remember, fought to sift through the thick fog in her mind.

Cloud.

Sky.

Falling.

Her stomach lurched at the memory. She'd fallen.

Had he caught her?

A low groan rumbled by her ear and the body beside her shifted. His front curved tight against her back in a move that sent even more heat through her. The arm around her tightened, pulling her against him, and the potent, masculine scent of him curled around her. A clean and spicy smell, different and yet still Declan. He held her for a minute or more before he woke. She could tell the moment he did. The hand on her belly stiffened, as if shocked to find itself there, before it fell away.

"Sorry," he mumbled, rolling to his back.

A wave of bereft cold seeped across her. Some part of her wanted to reach back and tuck him against her, if only to experience one moment of waking up in his arms.

Then she was. Her hand reached back before her mind could stop it, landing on his bare chest. An electric jolt shot through her arm at the contact. Ignoring it, she slid her hand farther to his side and pulled. His body came without fight. The delicious weight of his arm fell back around her.

"Just hold me. Please."

She heard him pull in a breath at her plea. Not wanting to force him to do anything, she tucked her hands beneath her cheek and waited for what he'd do. At first, he didn't move. Then fingers brushed her collarbone. His hand swept her hair aside, exposing her neck and shoulder to his view. His stubble-roughened chin nuzzled into the crook of her neck. Then his mouth, those soft, warm lips she'd dreamt about, covered the side of her throat. Alexia's eyes fluttered shut and a tremor of lust skated along her spine.

On a primal urge, she arched back, grinding her bottom against him. Long and impossibly hard, his erection nestled in the curve of her hip. His mouth opened, sealing against her neck in a searing, open-mouthed kiss. Instantly, desire hummed along her skin and razor blade–sharp need clawed through her abdomen. She gasped, amazed how her body responded to the stark want and longing in his touch.

One large hand covered her hip bone, pulling her to him as he rocked forward. Alexia reached out, twisting her fingers in the satiny sheets in front of her at the force of the next wave of passion coursing through her. He didn't relent. His hungry mouth blazed a trail to her ear, taking the shell in his mouth. On fire for him, she tried to turn to her back, to see him, to touch him, but his grip on her tightened, keeping her in place. Alexia closed her eyes, a tremble unfurled down her spine, as his mouth continued its hot, sweet assault on her sensitive neck.

Strong and firm, his other hand slid upward, skating over her bare abdomen. Only then did she realize her corset was gone, replaced by a cotton bandage wrapped around her middle. Declan's hand skirted the wound, reaching up instead to cup her breast. His hand enveloped her flesh, kneading it. His long fingers twisted the tip of her achingly erect nipple, rolling it between them.

When she again pressed back against the hard length of him, a shiver raked his massive body and he exhaled an expletive into the tangle of her hair by her ear. At the raw need in his voice, Alexia whimpered, feeling alive and on fire, yet somehow still hollow and incomplete on the inside. As if only he held the key to her sanity, her body and her soul. Only he could bring her into being, bring her back from the precipice where the scales of her existence teetered.

"Declan," she said in a voice not her own.

He stilled and lifted his head from her neck. "What do you want?" he panted. His fingers ran along her cheek, down the curve of her neck he'd just sampled. "Tell me, little vampire."

Alexia turned toward him. This time he let her fall onto her back, let her come into his arms. Her breath caught at the sight of him hovering above her, the handsome features, the deep indigo of his eyes and the delectable curve of his mouth. Yes, that's what she wanted.

"Kiss me."

His eyes moved over her face, as if trying to read her mind. Then he swooped, his mouth covering hers. Alexia sighed at the contact and parted her lips, eagerly allowing him inside. Slick and hot, his tongue ran along the seam of her lips before stealing between them in a sampling lick.

Alexia lifted her hand, cupping the side of his face. The muscles beneath her palm flexed, his powerful jaw working hers open with each demanding spear of his tongue. When he finally pulled back, Alexia was breathless and quivering. She threaded her fingers into the hair at his nape, unwilling to let him get even an inch away from her. The soft curls slipped through her fingers. His panting breath feathered against her lips, warming her mouth.

"Now, what do you want?" He breathed the question against her lips. She arched her back, squirming beneath him.

"Touch me."

At her request, he moaned and tilted his head slightly, angling over her. But instead of touching his lips to her mouth, he rocked forward, his hips grinding against hers. Long and iron hard, his erection nestled between her thighs. She let her knees fall wider and he collapsed into the frame of her willing body. One large hand wrapped around her, flattening on her tailbone. The back of her mind yearned for his wings to unfold and aid them as they had in her dream. However, his next move proved he didn't need the help. With a dark groan, he forced her hips up harder to meet his next dry thrust. A gasp fell from her lips, her fingers curled into his biceps.

Still, his mouth hovered over hers. His heated gaze watched her reaction to his every touch. It was maddening, erotic and driving her insane.

DECLAN RAN HIS HAND along the flat of her abdomen and back up, his knuckles skimming her breasts. Miles and miles of smooth skin met his perusing hands and he couldn't keep them off her. Although her wound had already begun healing, he avoided that section of bandaged flesh, allowing his fingertips to barely brush the velvety soft skin on either side of it.

He bent, his lips pressing against the flesh of her cheek, her jaw. A shuddered moan slid from her, and her body undulated beneath his mouth in a delicious wave. Lust, hard and rampant, stampeded through him. The blood in his body drained from his light head to his throbbing erection. Damping it down, he focused on pleasing Alexia.

His mouth traveled down the slim column of her neck, tracing the line of her collarbone and back again. Paying special attention to the soft hollow at the base of her neck where, each time his tongue flicked out, a kittenish purr would hum out of her.

Slowly, his hand slid past her rib cage, lifting to palm one breast as his mouth fell to the sensitive skin between them. Alexia arched into his hand, driving the hard nipple into the center of his palm. His head spun and his mouth watered. Feeling the weight of her in his hand, he kissed his way to her breast, placing an open-mouthed kissed on the soft skin before taking the erect tip between his lips.

Long fingers curled around the back of his head. He closed his mouth over her tight, raised nipple, twirling his tongue around the tip while mimicking the move with his fingers on her other. The hands in his hair tightened and a gasp flew from her lips.

Smiling, Declan continued his path down her body. He brushed his lips lower, grazing her ribs, her belly, her hip bones. Slowly, he slid his flattened palm into her leather pants. A little voice told him he was moving too fast, so he shifted his hand to slip back out. Her palm covered his, stopping him.

"Don't stop," she said with a sigh. Heat and arousal softened her eyes and her usually fair skin was flushed a delicate pink. Although she looked every bit like she was enjoying their love-making, he had to be certain.

"Are you…" The words stuck in his throat when she gripped his hand and pressed it under the leather for him. His heart stuttered and a low growl vibrated in his throat at the feel of her. Beneath his hand, her flesh was blistering hot and utterly bare. Not a strand of hair blocked his probing fingers from feeling the velvety softness of her sex.

"Gods," he breathed against her neck as his fingers slid between her moist folds. "You're already so wet for me."

ALEXIA HAD NO IDEA what he was talking about, but she didn't care. All she knew was she had never felt like this before. She needed him, needed his kiss, his touch, and she needed them all right now. More than blood, more than the damned crystal, more than her next breath.

"I've got to..." he murmured.

The bed shifted beneath his weight as he moved lower. Cool air blew across the heated flesh of her side where he'd lain. Firm hands gripped her waistband, shrugging her out of her pants. The fabric swooshed off her legs with the strength of his pull. A bubble of apprehension rose within her at being laid so naked, so bare, before him. She ignored it.

When he positioned himself above her thighs and forced them wide, her eyes shot open. Edging his body between her legs, he hooked one of her knees over his broad shoulder and sank down. She couldn't help the bubble from forming this time and propped herself up on one elbow to look at him.

"Declan, what..." Her words turned into a gasping sigh as the flat of his tongue laved up the seam of her sex in a languid lick.

"Declan," she cried out, a trace of uncertainty evident in her voice.

His dark head lifted. "Just relax, Alex. I would never hurt you."

Alexia chewed her bottom lip and held her breath, waiting. His piercing blue eyes never left hers as he opened his mouth, his tongue lapping up the length of her again. Alexia's thighs trembled and her arms shook as the aftershock of bliss rippled through her body from head to toe. Hot and wet, she'd never felt anything more delightfully wicked in her life.

He cocked a brow at her. Those sea-blue eyes of his danced in a way that made her racing heart trip over itself. "Do you trust me?"

At her wordless nod, he wrapped his arms tighter around her thighs, bringing her closer to his mouth. The playful tug had Alexia's bottom slipping against the sheets. She fell back against the bed with a giddy laugh that died in her throat the moment she felt his head between her thighs.

Fingers parted her folds, exposing her heated flesh to his gaze. Her stomach clenched, waiting, anticipating and craving the next pass of his mouth. She didn't have to wait long.

Blistering hot, his mouth pressed against her. She bit the inside of her cheek to keep from crying out. Declan slid his tongue against her again and again, groaning as if she were the sweetest delectable he'd ever tasted. Fevered, hungry, he devoured her, consuming her in a maelstrom of desire. Alexia clawed at the bed, the cool sheets slipping through her fingers.

With aching precision, he swirled his tongue against the apex of where she ached. The sensitive button seemed to pulse and thicken with every pull of his lips, growing more responsive with each flickering pass. When he fastened his mouth around the nub, drawing it between his teeth, balls of light peppered her vision. Every muscle in her body tightened and then melted until she was rigid and yet boneless at the same time.

Trembling, she pressed against him. He moaned, his tongue entering her channel, spearing her. Alexia gasped, her back bowing off the bed. A large hand flattened over her belly, holding her in place while his other joined his mouth between her legs. He focused the attention of his tongue back on her clit, letting his finger slip into its place.

"Declan." She almost screamed his name as another wave of pleasure swelled inside her, lapping her insides like a tongue of fire. Her cry seemed to spur him, for he began pumping his finger in and out of her in rhythmic pulses. Her body bucked with each one. Greedy, her channel clenched around his finger, hugging and sucking him into her body. He slipped another in on his next pass, stretching her deliciously while his wicked tongue kept swirling over her clit.

In that instant, she couldn't think, couldn't see. Every muscle in her body stiffened. Her lungs seized so she was unable to breathe and her fangs stretched painfully long. The constant hum of a thousand wings in her lower belly increased. They began beating frantically against her inner walls, as if trying to break free. Then, in a moment of blinding ecstasy, the pressure surged and she exploded. She couldn't keep back her cry this time. It sang out of her. Without Declan's strong arms keeping her grounded, she was sure she would have floated to the heavens.

Shaking, gasping for air, Alexia lay limp atop the bed, unable to move. She registered Declan untwining his body from her legs. Felt the smooth brush of his warm lips upon her belly, on each rib, her breasts, her collarbone, behind her ear. The mattress dipped as he finally lay next to her, a heavy arm wound protectively around her waist.

As she floated back to awareness, the steady drumbeat throbbing inside her began to ebb. The heady wings of passion she'd flown upon slowly released her back to earth and at once she felt taken over by both wonder and vulnerability.

"I never…I never…" She looked over at him, lying beside her, and frowned. "What did you do to me?"

The corner of his lip did that curvy thing and another flutter tremored through her belly. His warm palm covered her stomach and began making small, flat circles on it as if he'd sensed the riot he caused within her.

"I hope I just pleasured you." His voice was deep, thick and confident. But his eyes held the unmistakable hint of doubt. Alexia's heart ballooned and a shy smile passed her lips. She'd never felt womanly, or much like blushing, but knew she was doing both.

"Oh, you did. I just never knew it could be like that."

His face grew serious and she knew right away where his mind had gone. A hand cupped the back of her head, pulling her to him. He scooted closer, taking her in his arms. From shoulders to toes their bodies pressed together, his hard to her soft.

"Alex," he murmured, tucking her head to his chest. "It will only ever be like that with me."

She quivered. His words were not an empty promise, but a fierce conviction. A vow she knew he would never let go of. Alexia closed her eyes.

"I wish I could take it back," she whispered.

"Take what back?"

"Your memories of that night. Only one of us should have to live with that."

Hands cupped her cheeks, forcing her up to meet his gaze. "I'm glad I know. Not only does it help me understand you, it will make it all the more gratifying when I kill him."

The thought of him fighting an olden as evil and wicked as Lotharus was almost too much to physically bear. Alexia swallowed down the fear and focused on the second emotion coursing through her.

"Tell me again, how can you know what he did?"

Declan closed his eyes. "What I told you that night in the dungeon was true. I saw it."

Before she could speak to refute his claim, he ran his fingers through the soft hair framing her face and hushed her with his words. "I have been dreaming of you, Alexia. Every night, no, every time I close my eyes," he answered, gliding a hand through the silken yellow strands. "But these aren't like regular dreams." He frowned. "They are more like—"

"Memories," she finished for him.

He opened his mouth to reply, but didn't get out the words before she spoke again.

"I've dreamt of you, too."

Declan's heart stilled, gripped with sudden fear. He could only imagine what horrible truths she'd seen buried somewhere in his past. "You have?"

"Yes. Just now and before in the dungeon." She nodded, a confused look on her face. "But, it couldn't have been real. I mean, I didn't think it was until you…"

A flush crept across her cheeks and she dipped her chin

to her chest. The weight crushing his spirit lifted. Smiling, he licked his lips. The honeyed flavor of her lingered on his mouth and his cock twitched at the taste. Forcing back his need, he tilted her head up, compelling her to look at him.

"What did you see in your dream?"

Every inch of her skin, from cleavage to chin, flushed an enticing pink and he knew the answer. Instantly, he was besieged with incredible desire for the woman lying beside him. The woman he could still taste on his tongue. He wondered if that tempting color would rush over her skin and face as he rocked inside her. If that was how she would look the moment her pleasure peaked and his body had wrung every last drop of pleasure from hers.

"I saw us together."

Oh, Gods. At her admission, his pulse pounded in his ears. Clearing his throat, he focused on speaking, on making sure they were both on the same page and he wasn't completely lost in his lust for her.

"You saw us together, like we are now?" he asked.

She shook her head and another wave of color spread across her cheeks, followed quickly by a frown. "Not like this. But it didn't make sense."

Declan couldn't help but smile. "What didn't make sense?"

"Well, for one, you had a wound." She lifted her hand,

running her finger alongside his cheek. "Right here. And I don't see a scar." A shudder moved through him at her simplest touch. Declan laid more of his weight atop her, letting loose a groan at the exquisite feel of her skin on his. A fine sheen of perspiration coated her, warming every inch of her flesh. Their eyes locked, palpable heat building between them.

"And two?" he asked, his voice deep and thick. Bending, he brushed his lips against hers, whisper soft. Hers parted beneath his, her mouth eager and willing. Heady exhilaration hummed through him at the knowledge she was as affected as he by their closeness.

"I was flying," she breathed against his lips. "I had wings, like yours."

The hair on the back of his neck stood on end and goose bumps peppered his flesh, even though his body was anything but cold. Declan pulled back. Slowly, her eyes opened, a lazy smile curving her lips. Although he still ached for her, confusion and awe took the place of his desire. He sat upright, dragging the sheet with him. Alexia quickly captured the edge, clutching it to her bare chest self-consciously.

"Declan, what is it?"

"Nothing." He tried to smile through the unease building in his gut. "Are you hungry?"

CHAPTER FOURTEEN

BOISTEROUS VOICES AND music filled the grand hall. Alexia shifted her shoulders, fidgeting under the coarse layers of heavy clothing Declan had given her to wear. Although scratchy and anything but comfortable, she understood right away why the dragons wore such garments. Their enormous lair stood high in the snow-covered mountains. Even in this huge room, filled with bodies and roaring braziers, the temperature felt below freezing. She wasn't used to anything under fifty degrees.

Hunkering down farther into the sweater and skins, Alexia's gaze roamed around the space. Their hall reminded her of the keep of medieval legends and tales of auld. Barbaric even, and nothing like the refined gardens of her mother's chamber. Massive wood tables lined the available floor space. The four large fire pits dug into the floor around them burned bright, and large animals she could not discern rotated on spits atop each one. The hearty smell of stew and baking bread perfumed the air, making her tummy growl.

Antlers, skins of animals they'd hunted and eaten littered the walls and floors of the cavernous room. From what Declan told her, they used every bit of the animals they killed. If the rustic jewelry hanging around their necks, the candelabra of antlers and animal heads mounted on the walls were any indication, she believed him.

A riotous laugh rent the air, followed by a loud bang. Alexia gasped, her gaze darting to a nearby table. A man had obviously drunk too much and fallen off his stool. Alexia tensed, wondering if the bigger man leaning over him was going to punish him. However, he only reached out a hand and helped him to his feet.

She took a deep breath, relaxing slightly. This group was boisterous and lively, warm and full of vibrant life. The complete antithesis of what she was used to. Another shudder racked her. She tugged the skin tighter around her shoulders, ignoring the lingering smell of animal as she sucked in a breath.

Casting another quick glance about the room, she saw that everyone wore heavy sweaters, mostly in earth tones and some in better condition than others. Black combat boots seemed to be the footwear of choice and overall a masculine and gritty feel permeated everything from decor to clothing to personalities. Even the few women she could discern had well-defined muscles, firm bodies—warrior bodies. Such a hard people. She vaguely wondered how hers would compare. Were they just as rough, resilient, hardy and severe? Did they have grand feasts such as this?

At the thoughts swimming through her, a hole of wonder and doubt grew bigger, wider inside her. Her whole life she'd fought for people she did not even know. Yet Declan knew what he fought for, what was at stake.

Again her eyes sought him out. He stood beside a roaring fire pit, his lips pulled back in a relaxed smile. Flames accentuated the golden hue of his skin and dark blue of his eyes. He wore a huge woolen pullover, so white she wondered if the fur came from a polar bear. The massive cuffs rolled up thickly but still hung around his wrists. She briefly wondered if it had once been his father's. Declan had said he was a large man, and if this sweater had fit him, she could only imagine his size.

Dark pants clung to his well-muscled legs. The ends tucked into calf-high combat boots, the laces loosely tied. Strange, but it was odd to see him with clothes on. To not have every inch of his perfect body uncovered and exposed to her gaze.

He reached up, fitting the mug to his lips. She noted he wore a pair of black fingerless gloves. Right away, her eyes caught, transfixed on his hands. So strong and sleek. Even sitting half a hall away from him, she could feel their phantom caress on her skin.

A feeling of contentment laced through the constant pressure and doubts weighing down her chest. Wearing a tiny grin, she looked away just as a dark-haired woman walked past, a youngling by her side. Alexia offered a smile, but the female clutched her child protectively under the wing of her arm, as if shielding her young from a monster.

The smile fell from her face. The woman strode to a group of men. She didn't need to hear their words to know they spoke about her. The hate in their eyes spoke volumes. Alexia swallowed and turned her focus to her lap, feeling a cold stab of reality pierce her heart.

She was the monster.

DECLAN GAZED AT ALEXIA and frowned. She'd been nervous from the first moment they'd stepped inside the hall. He'd sensed it immediately and, although he understood the cause, it surprised him. She was so in command of herself and her soldiers. After all, she had managed to catch him when no one else had.

At the memory a faint smile curved the corner of his

lips. It amazed him how they moved from one extreme to the next without him realizing when or how it happened. One minute he hated her. The next, he couldn't stand to be away from her. And, gods, if seeing her sitting in his hall hadn't brought a smile to his lips then nothing would. He'd lived in fear for so many hours the past days, to see her safe, where Lotharus's evil machinations couldn't hurt her warmed his heart.

A shadow passed over his thoughts.

"I had wings, like yours."

Declan tensed his brow at the memory. A nagging suspicion of what that meant crept into his mind.

"You dare bring her here. In our hall. Our home."

All his thoughts faded at Falcon's voice. Declan turned to face him. The flames from a nearby brazier flickered across his face. Ire he wasn't quite certain he deserved lit up his friend's emerald eyes. Declan bit down on his jaw and turned back to the festivities. Rocking back on his heels, he tightened his arms around his chest and brought the tankard of warmed mead to his lips.

The sharp smell of alcohol filled his nose a second before the sweet flavor hit his lips. Their potent home brew rolled hot and smooth down his throat. The urge to slam the entire cup back, to feel its warmth sliding down his gullet, giving him the courage to continue this conversation, was almost too much to bear. He set the cup back to rest on his arm.

"Even you cannot bring yourself to justify it aloud, can you?"

"Falcon, I'm not having this discussion with you."

"This *discussion* started the moment you stepped through that gateway with her in your arms. Everyone is talking about it, about how their King is a traitor."

"Remember who you're speaking to," Kestrel said, clapping his brother on the shoulder.

Falcon shouldered out of his hold. "That's just it. I don't know who this man is. The Declan I knew hated the vampires who murdered his parents. By flaunting your vampire whore around for all to see, you mock the deaths of those children's fathers," he said, pointing into the crowd. "Your parents."

Gods, was he? "You don't know what you're talking about," he murmured, annoyed by the question in his own voice.

"Don't I? Then explain it to me," Falcon said, throwing his arms to the sides. Declan looked around, thankful no one paid heed to their verbal sparring.

"You can't rationalize it, any of it, and you know why? She killed them."

Defensive anger reared its head, only this time he

didn't hold it back. "And how many of her kin have I slaughtered?" he asked. "How many have I butchered like the animals we thought they were?"

Falcon opened his mouth to speak, but closed it again.

"Those animals have wives, young," Declan continued. "They live, like us. Love, like us. Who are we to judge who's worthy of life on this earth? Who deserves to die? When does all of this killing and hate end?"

Falcon blinked, understanding lighting up his eyes. With a loud sigh, he moved to step closer. Declan lifted a hand before turning and walking away, heading for Alexia, finding her chair empty.

ALEXIA REACHED BACK, tugging the woolen hood over her head. Keeping her eyes lowered, she rounded a table and moved toward the massive double doors. Without looking behind her, she stepped through the threshold and started back the way Declan and she had come. She'd gone to him, hearing most of the fight he'd had with Falcon. Guilt tore through her. Instead of being the adhesive holding her home, Declan's home, together, she tore everything apart and she didn't know how to mend any of it. She felt alone, lost in more ways than one.

"Are you lost, vampire?"

Alexia inhaled at the low voice and spun to face

whoever had snuck up behind her. She only made it halfway before a large male body pressed hers back against the nearest wall. Alexia slammed into the wall, the hood falling back to her shoulders. A gasp tore from her lips, more from shock than the force, for the man in front of her was huge. At least six foot four and all of it thick, corded muscle that was visible beneath his filthy brown tunic. Tattoos wound around his mountainous biceps, another across the skin beneath the V of his shirt.

A dragon lord. He had to be.

She swallowed and forced her chin up, unwilling to show fear even though it coursed heavy and thick through her limbs. He tilted his head to the side, regarding her. Dark hair fell against his jaw, his lips were thinned tight. A scar split the skin above and beneath one indigo eye. Deep and puckered, its raised white line stood in contrast to his dark complexion.

Alexia's entire body tensed, adrenaline coursed through her veins, telling her to run or fight. And she couldn't help but notice how he seemed completely relaxed, at ease with his tenseness, as if he were used to living life on an adrenaline rush.

"Are you deaf, vampire? Or do you not speak anything other than that heathen tongue of your kind?"

Alexia frowned. She could have sworn he'd said the last sentence in their ancient language, but shook it off.

"No. I'm going back to Declan's room," she said, finally answering his first question.

"*Lord* Declan's room. Our *King*." He bared a row of white teeth and leaned closer. He smelled of ale, dark spices and death.

She shuddered. "Yes, that's the one."

The dragon grunted. "I've fought you before, you know. You should be in our dungeon, not our hall. Not our lord's bed." Lips curled back, he smacked a flat palm on the wall beside her. Alexia jumped, and his eyes fell to her chest, then lower. She felt his gaze rake over her appreciatively and she suddenly wondered if the brute harbored some resentment toward Declan for not sharing the spoils of their recent battle.

"Well, your King has found other uses for me."

"Oh, I bet he has," he said, dragging a thumb across his lower lip before stretching his hand toward her.

"Griffon," a low voice stated.

They both turned their heads. Declan stood in the middle of the corridor, mug in hand. His expression was taut, his blue eyes blazing.

"Back off her. Now."

The dragon looked at her once more and Alexia found

herself holding her breath. A lazy smile tweaked his lips. Casually, he pushed off the wall and faced Declan.

"I was just saying hello to your new girlfriend," he said, almost brushing his shoulder against Declan's as he pushed by him and back into the hall.

Declan's body lunged as if he meant to go after him and his mouth opened, but whatever words had formed in his mind, he kept them to himself. Alexia saw his jaw flex in the low light, saw the struggle, the weariness on his face. He closed his eyes. Then his long lashes fluttered open, revealing a steel-blue gaze, burning with an anger that made her breath catch.

DECLAN SAW THE LOOK on Alexia's face and knew she'd misread his anger. She thought it was directed at her. So, he closed his eyes again. Counting to ten, he willed control, knowing he had none where she was concerned. He never had. Still, he repeated in his mind that he would not slaughter Griffon tonight. That the hunter had not said or done anything that would permanently destroy any chance the rogue had at remaining part of his flock. He tried to forget how his heart had stuttered to a stop when he'd seen him looming over Alexia.

Fear he had never felt before had flooded his body, numbing his brain. The raw truth kept flashing like a neon sign in his mind. The hunter could have ripped her limbs from her body and gutted her in the seconds it would have taken Declan to reach her.

"Are you all right?"

Her words caught him off guard. He'd thought Alexia would still be frozen by the wall, so when a hand brushed his, he nearly jumped.

"I should be saying that to you."

A weak smile passed her lips. She brought her hands together, rubbing her palms as if cold. "I'm just tired. Can we go?"

Declan frowned, feeling she wasn't telling him everything. But he didn't voice his thoughts. Instead, he placed the mug down on a small table beside her and took both her hands in his. They were cold. Her fingers threaded through his, gripping him tight. A low shiver ran down his spine. *From the cold or her touch?*

Shaking off the thought, he tugged her hand, pulling her into the crook of his shoulder.

"Come on," he said, motioning down the hall.

They didn't speak on the way back to Declan's chamber, but he didn't let go of her hand. It was odd, to walk hand in hand with someone, especially in his mountain home. Declan had been with women before, had even had a serious girlfriend or two. However, he'd thought about none as much as he did about this woman. It seemed his mind was consumed with Alexia. How he could make her happy, make her smile, make her comfortable. The revelation terrified and yet excited him at the same time. Like the first time he jumped free from his mother's arms and took to the sky on his own.

"I'm sorry about leaving before," she said once they'd stepped inside. "It's just that I'm not used to so much excitement."

Her words took Declan by surprise. When they finally registered, he laughed. "Really? But you have a huge horde."

"Of soldiers," she replied, slipping the heavy fur off her shoulders and tossing it across his bed. The gray sweater he'd given her to wear fell almost to her knees. He watched the slight dip and sway of her hips as she moved to stand in front of the roaring fireplace. The highlights of her blond hair caught the light, making it look like early spring honey.

"I've not been around my people since I was a girl."

The smile left his face. He realized with stark clarity that, while he cared for her much more than he should, he really didn't know her. Grabbing the back of his neckline, he tugged the heavy garment over his head. Tossing it on the ground, he moved closer, stepping behind her.

"Why?" he asked. When she didn't reply, he reached

out, slowly stroking his hands up and down her arms, his fingertips barely grazing her skin each time he reached her forearm. Even that light touch made his stomach clench, his heart beat faster.

She let out a sigh and spun in his arms. After a pause, she tipped her chin up. Declan didn't speak, but he urged her to talk with his eyes.

"Lotharus," she said, closing hers as if it pained her to even say his name. "He advised my mother to separate ourselves from the compound. He said it would be in our best interest if we were apart. Not only would it keep harm from us if we were surrounded by him and his men, but it would elevate us. Keep us untouchable and supreme in our people's eyes."

"Do you believe that is the way to rule?"

She shook her head. "No. I never did. I believe he only wanted to isolate us. Keep us to himself."

Yeah, I bet. Rage boiled in his veins and he fought to control it. He needed to be here for her now. In the present. Not trapped in some hate for a vampire who had left scars he could only kiss and soothe. Even if he killed the bastard, she would still bear them, always bear them. He could only help her ease the burden.

"In my lifetime, our horde has changed so dramatically. Our mission is nothing like it used to be."

Declan's brow tightened. "Go on."

"My grandmother wanted peace, worked toward developing a better world. But my mother's mind was twisted in those early days. She demolished and destroyed anything civil and created what was the first of our soldiers with Lotharus and her equally warped brother."

"Uthen." Declan growled the vampire's name. The very one who had attacked and almost killed his mother that night his father had saved her. *Turned her.*

"Yes. When she banished Uthen from the horde, Lotharus dug his claws into her. She hasn't been the same since." A small sigh deflated her lungs. "He's cut from the same cloth as Uthen, although he's better at hiding his maniacal genes. I don't think she knew until it was too late."

Declan rested his chin on her head, running his hands up and down the curve of her spine. "You don't ever have to go back there."

"I don't look forward to going back there."

They both said the words simultaneously. Declan jerked back, looking into Alexia's eyes, nearly as wide and confused as his own.

"But, you can't possibly go back," he said.

The slim column of her throat shifted with her swallow. "I'm not scared of him."

Declan wanted to laugh, but contained it. He reached out, smoothing a hand down the side of her face. "You don't have to pretend with me, Alexia."

"But I'm not…"

He tightened his grip, forcing her to look into his eyes. "And you can't lie to me, either."

A low sigh breathed out of her. "He frightens me at times. But I've never feared for my life. While my mother lives, he can't touch me. Not to mention he would be signing his death warrant if he hurt me. The *vanators,* the blood hunters, would be dispatched by council and he would be forced to live in exile or face death if they found him."

"But he's already hurt you once and gotten away with it."

"I told you, no one knows about that," she answered in a small voice.

"And why not?" he asked, hoping she would admit her fear, admit the lunacy of the idea of returning to that horrid place. "Why did you not tell your mother and have him exiled then?"

"You don't know what it's like to live under her shadow, to live with her turning to him for her touchstone, for everything, while berating me as a disgrace. At that time, my ascension was so close. I knew it would only be a matter of time before I became Queen and the two of them would retreat to the colony. I thought if I could just hold out until then…" Her words trailed off.

Declan covered his hip bones with his hands and sighed. "Do you believe he'll simply step aside and let you rule?"

"What other choice does he have? He may have delusions of grandeur now. But our horde is run by females, not men. That is the way it is." She exhaled and tightened her arms around herself. "And as of tomorrow, I'll be the new Queen. The new ruler. I'll be in charge of ensuring his tyranny ends."

She gazed up at him with a look that told him he would not like what she said next. "And now you know why I'm going back."

Damn. He couldn't swallow, couldn't speak. Not at the thought of her walking out of his life, walking back into the role of his enemy. Taking in a breath, he forced his throat to open, forced the words to come.

"Alex." He took her hands in his, licking his suddenly parched lips. "I hope you know, you don't *have* to go back."

Alexia looked up, her gaze meeting his. Goddess, he believed that. Although his eyes had darkened, appearing indigo in the low light of his chamber, she could still read them plain as day. He believed she could stay here, with him.

"We both know that isn't possible."

"Why not?"

Alexia let out a mirthless chuckle. "Aside from all I just named?"

He shrugged and her mouth slackened.

"For one, everyone here hates me. Not that I can blame them."

"No one hates you. No one knows you," he said as he stepped up to wrap his arms around her waist. "If it makes you feel any better, I used to hate you."

Alexia smiled at his attempt to make her feel better, but it quickly faded when the truth settled thick and heavy around her once more. His smile fled, too. A large hand cupped her cheek, brushing across her cheekbone.

"They don't know you, Alex. Once they do, I'm certain all will work out."

Alexia shook her head, her cheek rubbing against his palm. "Even if any of that mattered, even if I could stay, I'm a vampire, not a dragon. I don't belong here," she said.

Hands gripped her upper arms, forcefully but not hard enough to hurt, just to get her attention. "Yes, you do. You belong with me."

The heart that had blossomed in her chest only a few days ago now withered in pain. Didn't he understand that no matter how her heart longed to stay with him, she had to go? A strangled gasp hurdled out of her before she could keep it in. He bent down and quickly caught it with his lips. Took it inside himself as if he wanted to take all her pain, all her suffering into him. As his lips caressed hers, she could all but taste how much he wanted her.

"Stay," he said against her lips when they pulled away, even though she'd read the message loud and clear without words. "Stay with me."

"Declan, I—" She wanted to stay, she really did. The thought of spending the remainder of her days, alone and isolated in the catacomb walls, made her heartsick. But it was her destiny. "I can't."

The expression on his face took the strength from her legs, so she turned away and looked into the fire. "Goddess, why is this so hard? I know what I have to do. But my world has turned upside down since you came into it. I feel off balance, like I'm teetering on an edge that any minute will shift and slip out from under me."

Hands covered hers, squeezing. Instantly, she recalled the last time he'd held her so, before Lotharus had come into the dungeon and clipped his wing. The suffocating agony and pain of those horrific moments washed over her anew. The thought of losing him then had nearly killed her, yet here she was living the moment all over again.

"It's the same for me." The deep timbre of his voice cut through her dark thoughts. Alexia lifted her gaze to his. Hope, emotion and anxiety swam in his eyes. "But I hear that's what's supposed to happen when…" He swallowed and lowered his gaze to the floor.

Tears stung her eyes. Ashamed at her weakness, at her utter inability to know what to do, what to say, she closed her eyes and moved to turn away. However, his hands covered her shoulders, stilling her movements. They slid up her neck, his long fingers curling around her nape before he cupped her cheeks, tilting her up to his face. Although frightened of what she'd see, she opened her eyes. The look of utter misery in his eyes mirrored every emotion raging through her.

The tears that had been threatening finally fell free. Not wanting him to see, Alexia leaned forward, burying her face against his warm chest. His arms instantly closed around her, his chin resting on her head.

At the realization she was crying, actually crying, and in front of him, deeper, harder sobs racked her body. She'd always held her emotions inside her, guarded and hidden where no one could see them. Now Declan could see everything. Even the deepest secrets she held close to her soul. The enormity of it only made the dam crack open wider, the tears flow harder, faster.

His body shifted as he bent his head to hers. Warm lips brushed her temple before pressing against it. And then his voice, low and strong, began whispering words she couldn't hear over the sound of her sobs. But the soothing tone comforted her nonetheless. The rhythmic feel of his hands sliding up and down her back in a reassuring glide caused the shaky muscles to calm.

Soon, the tears quit falling. Air once again flowed into her lungs and with a final shuddering sigh, she stopped.

Declan did not make a move to release her, though. If anything, he held her tighter. For the first time in her life, she didn't try to push someone away. Instead, she clung to him and burrowed her head against his chest, praying he'd never let her go.

That she wouldn't let him.

TALLON STEPPED into the chamber, lit by only the faint glow of embers from the fireplace. Crossing her arms over her chest, she walked to the bed and cocked her head. She regarded the blond vampire lying so carefree and peaceful in her brother's bed. What used to be her parents' bed. Parents this fanged demon no doubt helped kill.

Folding the tattered, calf-length brown sweater in front of her chest, Tallon squatted. Digging into the only pocket without a hole in it, she pulled out a dime-size silver disc. She set it in her palm, warming it between her hands before peeling off the backing and placing it behind the blond bitch's ear.

"Try walking out of here with his heart now, vampire."

"Tallon, what are you doing in here?"

At Declan's voice, she stood and whipped around. "I came to see you."

He looked like he didn't believe her, but resumed walking toward his desk. A towel was slung low over his hips and his hair hung in wet strands around his shoulders, dripping rivers of water down his bare chest. A chest that bore more scars and welts than it had four days ago.

"About what?" he said, bringing a steaming coffee mug to his lips.

Tallon nodded over her shoulder, toward the sleeping Alexia. "As if I need to say it aloud."

"Falcon's already chewed my ass. Are you here for the other cheek?"

"How can you joke about this?"

His eyes fell to the floor. The evidence of guilt on his face was enough to send her storming up to stand toe-to-toe with him. "What you're doing is putting this flock at risk. Huge risk."

He set the cup down. "I know."

"Obviously you don't, else you wouldn't have brought her here."

"She was injured."

Tallon tossed her arms to the side. "So? Let her die. She's the Queen's daughter, next in line for the throne. As we speak, the council is talking about going back to defeat them, and to plan her death."

His head snapped up. The sharp rage in his eyes took her by surprise. "You'll all leave her out of this."

Tallon frowned. "What is with you? What don't you get? She's next in line. She's knee-deep, Dec."

"Tallon, I know what you're going to say…."

"Like the rest of them, she wants to exterminate us."

"No, she doesn't. She's been following orders, nothing more."

"Um, yeah," Tallon sassed. "Orders from her mother."

He bit down so hard his jaw muscles visibly clenched. Nostrils flaring, he ran a hand over the top of his wet scalp. Tallon took in his body language with interest. He was nervous, irritated. She flicked her gaze to the bed and he instinctively moved his body to block the vampire from her view. *Protective.* A sudden ball of dread sank in her gut.

"The covenant our ancestors wrote, Declan. What you're thinking about, if not what you've already done, is forbidden. You can't mate with her."

"I know that."

"She's a vampire."

"I know."

"Then why bother entertaining this infatuation? I mean, I realize you had to pretend to cozy up to the bitch to stay alive in there, act like you liked her, but come off it. You're home now—"

"It wasn't an act," he shouted, cutting her off. He closed his eyes and tipped his head back to the ceiling as if asking for strength from above. "I love her, all right. Is that what you wanted to hear?" He lowered his gaze back to her. "Does that make you happy?"

The air whooshed out of Tallon. Every cocky, righteous and noble idea in her fled. Her brother, her King, had pulled a Romeo and fallen in love with the enemy. She stared at him with what she knew was a blank, wordless look. At the heartache in his eyes, the sister in her came out and took over. "Declan, you can't be serious. It's this mission, the stress of your capture and torture at the hands of the same people who killed Mom and Dad. You can't really *love* that monster."

"She's no more a monster than you or I," he said in a low, even voice. "We are all killers. That is what this war has done to us."

Tallon placed a hand on her forehead, searching her

mind for something, anything to make this madness end, to get her brother back. "Send her home and rest, then. Give yourself time, space to get your thoughts back."

Placing his hands on his hips, he took a deep breath and set a resolute gaze on her. "The vampires, Lotharus, he sent terms. What are they?"

"Brother, rest. I beg you…."

He stepped up to her, his face contorted in anger. "Damn you, you'll tell me. As your King, I demand it!"

Tallon battled back the hurt, the disbelief, and swallowed it down. "They will descend upon us in the thousands by sundown unless we give them the crystal."

"And Alexia?"

Tallon rolled her eyes. "For the love of…"

"Tal, what did they say about her?"

"What do you think? They want her to bring it back, of course." Crossing her arms tightly in front of her, she eyed her brother skeptically. "Where is it, anyway?"

He chewed on his thumb, barely sparing her a glance. "Safe."

"Enough with these puzzles and secrets, Dec," she said, shaking her head. "After that stunt you pulled with the bag, I need to see it."

Declan looked like a wounded puppy, effectively making her feel like she'd been mean enough to kick one.

Without another word, he stormed to his desk. Tallon watched in dismay as he lifted a small dagger from the top drawer and pointed it at his side, just under his ribs. Again that damned *Romeo and Juliet* tale sprang to her mind. "Declan, no," she shouted as he drove the weapon into his stomach.

Forgetting her anger, she ran to his side. "Gods, brother," she said on an exhale, wrapping her arm about his back. He shouldered her away, almost with enough force to send her to the ground. Tallon's jaw dropped as she watched him slam the bloodied blade on his desk and shove two fingers into the fresh wound.

Low, pained grunts gurgled out of him. Tallon fought the urge to be sick as she watched him probe deep. A curtain of sweat broke out on his skin and his face paled. Then, with a loud exhale, Declan yanked something from his body. Bracing a hand on his desk, he hung his head and took two deep breaths before standing upright once more.

Tallon's eyes narrowed, widening when he lifted the blood-smeared crystal in his hand. "Satisfied?"

Regret and self-loathing ate at her in equal measure. "Oh, gods," she sighed. "Declan, I'm…"

"Just get out," he said with an exhale. "Get out and tell everyone to prepare for battle."

THE RHYTHMIC SOUND of Declan's breathing echoed in the room. Alexia lay on her side, her gaze following every shadowed ridge, dip and curve of his powerful back, as if instilling them into her memory. Sighing, she closed her eyes and realized part of her was doing just that.

Words and images flashed behind her closed lids, making it impossible to keep them closed. Try as she might, she couldn't stop thinking...about every word she'd heard pass between Declan and his sister, about the scroll, the crystal, her mother and, most of all, Lotharus's plan.

Declan may be the King, he may be smart and brave and strong, but she'd trained with Lotharus, knew his strategy, knew he would never risk mounting an attack on the dragon mountain. With weather and sun complications, the mission was too risky to undertake. And Lotharus did not like to take risks. He liked things to go smoothly and easily and pre-dictably. He never liked to get his hands dirty. Nothing was adding up; none of what Tallon said made sense.

"Okay, Alexia, think," she whispered. Lotharus wanted the crystal, needed it. But wouldn't he need the scroll, as well, or had he had it transcribed before the dragons had stolen it? What did it even say? Her gaze flitted to Declan's desk.

Easing the heavy fur coverlet off her legs, Alexia slid

off the bed and padded to the other side of the room. Even with the heavy flannel shirt Declan had given her, the frigid air sent a chill down her spine. She wrapped her arms around herself and stepped closer to the desk. On top of it lay the scroll he'd spoken about with his sister. Beside it was the crystal.

Her heart thudded. Vividly, she recalled watching Declan pull it from his body. Recalled back further still to the night she'd met him. The night he'd first fed from her. She closed her eyes, seeing him arched above her. Remembered watching the wound close with her own eyes that night she'd caged him. He had hidden it within his body then. It had been her blood that had healed the wound, kept the crystal safe and undetected inside him.

Although she'd intended to read the scroll, the crystal called to her the moment she opened her eyes. She reached out, her hand closing around the cold ball. No larger than an apple, the stone weighed less than a pound, but its weight balanced her. Cupping it in her open palm, she stared at the rainbow beams of kaleidoscopic colors inside the crystal. Three circles surrounded one bright ring in its center. The power center. So clear in this low light the inside looked liquid. It amazed her that something so beautiful could cause such ugliness.

At the thought of Lotharus, anger and frustration

seethed inside her. She curled her fingers over the crystal and brought her fist to her forehead. Her entire arm shook. Grabbing a breath, she pulled it deep, willing the anger to abate. However, the only thought running through her mind was to destroy the stone. Alexia pulled back her fist, wanting to pitch the thing against the mountain wall and shatter it and the tyranny it promised to a million pieces. But she stopped midswing.

Lotharus would never believe she'd destroyed it. A battle would happen anyway and their only bargaining chip would be lost.

Lowering her hand, she let her gaze slide to the bed. Declan still slept. His handsome face looked relaxed and peaceful. Waves of dark hair curled around the golden skin of his neck. The sheet slid past his hips, one leg slung out of the fabric, revealing every inch of his toned body. A body she knew she could never forget, never close her eyes late at night alone in her chamber and not see his image burning behind them.

Alone in the Queen's chamber.

A sob stuck in her throat at the thought of returning to the catacombs, to her duty. She swallowed it down. Yet, she'd mourned their relationship last night when she'd tried to tell Declan she had to return to her horde, her people. After all, it was her home, her future, her destiny. He may have chased away all coherent thought and reasoning last night with his kisses, but the fact remained the same.

She could not stay here. She couldn't abandon those who trusted her to Lotharus and whatever evil plan he had in store. No. In less than twenty-four hours she would ascend the throne and be Queen of the horde, the highest rank in command of the dragons' enemies. At least now she could hope the relationship Declan and she had forged offered a chance for a future filled with peace. She had to believe that. Had to believe they wouldn't end up on that catacomb rooftop again, only this time facing each other in a fight to the death.

"I love her."

Declan's words echoed in her ears. Each one wrapped around her heart before piercing it with barbed magnificence. The pure and utter sweetness of his admission turned sour before she had time to truly savor it. They had no future. Not in this world. No matter how much she wanted it. No matter how hard he tried to convince her otherwise. But perhaps if they worked together from their opposing thrones, as painful as it may be, they could create a future. A place where dragon and vampire coexisted. A world where her family wouldn't destroy the lives of those she loved and who loved her.

Goddess, did such a place even exist?

At once she thought of Davna Vremena, the utopian society that once existed and now lay immortalized in the pool of her grandmother's garden. She looked down at the crystal cupped in her hand. An image of the fountain of Diana, her palm open, waiting for something to be placed in it, flitted across her vision. Then her mother's words whispered through her mind.

"They had to fly over the mountain, across the river and beyond the sea. Far away where she couldn't touch them."

"Oh. My. Goddess." Alexia blinked down at the crystal in her hand. Although not the way Lotharus or the scrolls intended, she realized she just might hold in her hand the key to peace with the dragons. But there was only one person who knew for certain.

CHAPTER FIFTEEN

A SLOW SMILE SPREAD across Declan's lips the instant he woke. Thoughts of Alexia, her soft sighs and even softer flesh, flicked through his mind. A low growl rumbled in his chest.

"Mmm, Alex," he murmured, his voice groggy. Stretching a hand behind him, he reached for her, hoping to have another sweet taste of her before the day began.

The flat of his palm hit cold sheets.

"Alexia?" Frowning, he slid his hand up and down the mattress, finding only expanse after expanse of bedding. Declan jackknifed up. Flipping to his hands and knees, his gaze frantically scoured the sheets.

Empty.

The first thought blazing through his mind was that someone had taken her from him. Blinding fury quaked so hard through his entire body that his arms and legs shook. Tossing the blanket off, he stormed to his closet. Snatching the first article of clothing his hand hit, he pulled an ashen wool sweater over his head, followed by a pair of crumpled-up jeans from off the floor. Barefoot, he strode to the desk, taking up the scroll.

It was then reality slapped him like the coldhearted bitch she was.

The crystal.

Disbelieving, he put the scroll back down, his eyes flitting over the desk and floor.

It was gone.

She was gone.

It didn't take a genius to figure out where they both were. Declan's legs buckled, so he bent, bracing his hands on either side of the splintered wood desk. His chest blazed in pain so sharp and deep he almost couldn't breathe. Dropping his chin, he deeply inhaled and froze.

Although a mug half-full of day-old coffee, his bloody dagger, quills and inks lay spread out atop his desk, all his eyes could focus on were the hastily scratched words scrawled across the uppermost corner of the scroll.

"I love you, too...."

All the air left him in a whoosh. Disbelieving, he grasped the fragile paper in his hands, tearing the part with her handwritten message free. He pondered only for a moment that it was the first time he'd seen her handwriting. It was as delicate and lovely as her face.

That chasm opened up a well of possibilities, of how many things, nuances he had yet to discover about her. Things he wasn't certain he'd ever get the chance to know. Declan forced the thoughts back. Holding the paper in front of him, he read and reread until the words blurred.

She loved him.

She left him.

A howling sense of loneliness ripped through him. Part of his soul shredded, torn to bits like the fragments of the scroll littering his desk. Fisting the paper in his hands, he held his knuckles to his forehead and closed his eyes. At once images of Alexia bombarded his mind. Declan gritted his teeth and pinched his eyes, trying to ignore the warm elation spreading through his chest as the impact of her written words hit him. Instead, he focused on the hollow pit of worry burrowing in his gut over her. On the driving need to get her back.

Opening his eyes, he again held the small paper out in front of him.

"I love you, too…."

Over and over he read those four words, trying to make sense of it all. Trying to figure out why she would say something so significant on paper and why now? Declan's eyes widened and worry plunged down his body.

It was a goodbye.

Declan ran a hand over his face, his heart and mind warring with his reason. She had heard him last night. Had Alexia heard him and then proceeded to take the crystal and run back to a man trying to kill her? Wait, it didn't make sense. None of this made sense. Declan may not know her handwriting or other mundane things, but goddammit, he *knew* her. She would not just leave him, not unless…

Oh, gods.

The air sucked out of his lungs so hard and fast he had to grasp the back of his chair to keep upright. The Alexia he knew would do something rash in an attempt to save him, save the dragons. She'd risked her life before for him. Hearing him profess his love might have been the catalyst she needed to try and stop Lotharus on her own. By the gods, it would be just like her to do something so rash, so foolish.

Declan shoved papers and quills aside until he found what he needed. Slamming his hand on the walkie-talkie on his desk, he switched it on as he brought it to his lips.

He pushed the button down to talk, only to release it. Emotion had lodged in his throat, strangling his words until he was unsure if he could speak. Clearing his throat, Declan took a breath and tried again.

"Kestrel, do you copy?" he bit out.

Static hissed through the small speaker.

He gave only a fleeting thought to the early-morning hour before impatient anger overrode any worry he had about being rude. "Kestrel, this is Declan, do you…"

"Yes, yes. I'm here."

By the time Kestrel had replied, his voice thick with sleep, Declan was already in the corridor, taking the steps three at a time to the main chamber. "I need you to call an emergency council meeting."

"A meeting? But half the council is…"

"Now!"

ALEXIA STEPPED THROUGH the catacombs, trying to ignore the aching void spreading in her gut. Trying to ignore the small voice telling her the revelation she'd had in Declan's chamber was a fool's hope.

Declan.

Thoughts of him sliced through her like a knife. Clasping a hand in front of her stomach, Alexia braced the other against the wall, using it to prop herself up. Closing her eyes, she fought for each breath, fought to remember why she'd dragged herself out of that bed.

Their future. A peaceful future.

Pushing off the stones, she repeated that mantra with every step down the silent halls.

When she rounded the corner to her mother's chambers, Alexia hung back. No soldiers guarded the door. Without pausing to find out why, she palmed her Glock, holding it cocked and by her head. Bracing her back to the wall, she slid sideways until she reached the door to her mother's chambers. Wrapping her fingers around the door handle, she pushed it down, opening the door wide. Pausing for the space of a heartbeat, she pivoted, pointing the gun into the chambers.

She didn't expect anyone to be there, so she wasn't disappointed when only the birds greeted her. Descending the stairs, she started down the trail through the gardens, for the first time cursing the narrow pathway for harboring so many hiding places. Bending at the waist, she swept her gun under the brush in a full arc, repeating the act toward the trees above before again quickening her pace to her mother's bedroom.

Finally close to the meeting rooms, Alexia rounded the bole of a large oak, taking the stone path toward the upper level, and stopped short. Even from here she could see her mother's room lay in complete and utter darkness.

Back hugging the wall, Alexia skimmed along the

smooth marble and began slowly climbing the stairs. After the third step, her gaze flitted down and held. Her breath caught. Streaks of ruddy brown and red stained the usually pristine stones.

Blood.

At the sight of it, a heavy stone of fear sank cold and hard in her gut, bubbling up panic in its wake. Alexia took a deep breath and another step. Her heart hammered against her ribs, the sound of her breath echoing in the silent room. Whirling her focus over her shoulder, she checked the gardens one last time before pivoting through the bedchamber door.

Holding her gun out in front of her, Alexia quickly checked the corners to her left and right before allowing her focus to settle on the massive platform bed commanding the center of the room.

In the low light, she could only make out the foot of the bed. But it was enough.

The gun in her hands visibly shook. Alexia blinked, her mind unable or unwilling to process the image before her. Dried blood smeared the white bedding as if something heavy and lifeless had been dragged across it. Her heart dropped to think of who that person might be.

"Mother?"

Alexia didn't wait for a reply. She stepped to the side

of the bed, more of the scene before her revealing each second as her eyes grew accustomed to the darkness.

"Mother," she repeated, trying to ignore the frantic tempo of her heart. She transferred the gun to one hand, fumbling with the other where she knew the bedside table lamp was. Her heart jumped in both shock and relief when her fingertips grazed the cold metal chain dangling in the darkness. Twining her fingers around it, she held her breath and pulled.

Blinding yellow light blanketed the room. Reflexively, Alexia closed her eyes. Blinking rapidly as her eyes fought to adjust, she turned her focus to the bed, to the bloody form lying motionless atop it.

"Oh, no," she breathed, dropping to her knees. The Queen lay on her stomach, her head turned to the side and her arms stretched out in front of her as if she were reaching for the something. Alexia scanned the room, seeing only a large wooden box with a gold disc in the center of it.

Placing her gun on the floor beside her foot, Alexia turned her attention back to her mother. Carefully, she smoothed the heavy curtain of dark hair aside, revealing Catija's beautiful face. Her eyes were closed, a dreamy, almost serene look on her ethereal features. Alexia's heart constricted. The queen appeared at peace, more so than Alexia could ever recall seeing her. If not for the copious amounts of blood and the pallid color of her skin, Alexia would have thought her walking through a glorious dream.

Narrowing her eyes, she ran her hands over her mother's prone body, searching for a wound. Nothing. Where was all the blood coming from? Grasping the Queen's shoulders, she rolled her on her back. Almost immediately, the heady scent of fresh blood pricked Alexia's nose.

Without warning, a red haze flooded her vision. Unbidden, her fangs stretched past her lips, as the hunter within focused on the scent. Zeroing in on her mother's delicate neck, she sucked in a breath and held it. Two angry and swollen bite marks oozed a steady stream of blood with each fading pulse of her mother's heart.

"By the Goddess," Alexia said on an exhale, her stomach convulsing at the sight. Without pause, she brought one hand up, pushing against the wound to try and staunch the bleeding. The other she threaded through her mother's fingers, trying not to notice how cold her palm felt pressed into hers. A nauseating wave of helplessness rolled through her. The truth of what had transpired nearly topped her with its force.

The Queen of the horde had been bitten. Been fed from, although not drained enough to kill her fast, but agonizingly slowly, as she bled out little by little.

"Why?" Alexia gasped out a sob, realizing she was on

the verge of tears. "Who could do such a thing?" she cried aloud, although she didn't need a reply. Only one man would dare break horde law so flagrantly. Like the tip of a match igniting into flame, her fear and sadness swiftly erupted into hate.

Lotharus would die for this.

"Alexia?"

At the sound of her name, the hate and revenge left her eyes. When she saw her mother's were still shut, Alexia reflexively tightened her grip on the Queen's hand, affirming her presence. "I'm here."

The Queen tilted her head toward the sound of her voice. Her eyes fluttered open. Tired and waxen, her black gaze fixed on Alexia's.

"There you are," the Queen breathed, a tiny smile curving her lips. "My darling daughter. My lovely one," she wheezed.

"Yes." Alexia nodded, bringing her mother's knuckles to her lips. "I'm here."

"Come closer. Let me see you."

Alexia leaned down, so close the tips of her blond hair brushed against her mother's shoulder. "Mother, listen to me. We have to get out of here."

The Queen shook her head. "You and I both know that is not possible."

"But we can't stay. It's not safe." Alexia's mind reeled. "I have to get you somewhere safe."

Where, where, where? her thoughts chanted in a never-ending litany. There had to be a place within the horde to find sanctuary. However, even if she could think of such a place, her mother wouldn't make it alive out of the gardens, much less out of the caves. Alexia's mind frantically pored over every possibility, every way to save the Queen. Her gaze flitted down to the blood-soaked fingers pressed against the Queen's neck, to the hand clutching her mother's. She remembered Declan, how she had healed him with her blood.

Without hesitating, she released her mother's hand and pushed up her sleeve. Twisting her arm behind her, she removed a switchblade from her back pocket. The metal sang as she snapped it open.

"Alexia, what are you doing?"

"You need strength," she said, bringing the blade to her wrist, about to open a vein.

"Stop."

The command in her mother's voice made her halt. However, Alexia did not remove the knife from her skin. "I know what you're thinking, Mother. But you need to feed. You must get your strength back so I can get you away from this place."

"And go where? This is my home. Your home."

"But…"

"It's too late, Alexia. I'm diminishing."

Alexia shook her head, disbelieving.

"Now, you must listen to me and do as I say. There isn't enough time for me to tell you everything. You must drink from me instead." Slowly, her mother turned her forearm up.

"What?" Alexia blinked at the request. When she saw her mother's upturned wrist, she recoiled. "You can't be serious?"

"My time here is over."

"That's not true."

"Alexia, please…" she wheezed in a breath "…it's the only way my death will matter."

Heat welled behind Alexia's eyes, stinging them to the point of tears. "You can't ask me to kill you."

"I'm dying with or without your help. Lotharus saw to that," she said, her pallid face pinching in an obvious twinge of pain. "Drinking from me is the only way you'll be able to see."

"I don't understand."

"Alexia, there is a reason feedings were outlawed after the Dark War. Reasons we now drink from synthetically aged stores instead of humans or other vampires."

"Yes, the proclamation from the dark council after the war," she said, nodding her head. However, the Queen shook hers in disagreement.

"No," she said with a gasp. "When vampires feed off one another, or even humans, the memories we imbibe along with the blood are too much for most to deal with and stay sane. Your dreams become haunted, your past, future and memories bleed together into one not entirely your own."

Alexia's thoughts immediately shot to Declan. They had fed from each other. Was that what all of this was? Why his presence in her life knocked her off her feet?

"It's why some say the dark prince went mad. He became addicted to the taste, the rush that followed the feedings. He abused it, eventually becoming paranoid, suspicious of even his most trusted associates and supporters."

"I don't understand."

"I think you do."

Alexia stared in mute horror as her mother again lifted her wrist, offering it to her.

"Quickly, there isn't much time."

Alexia licked her lips, willing her fangs to lengthen. Doubt, fear and the cloying scent of betrayal filled her lungs. "I can't," she whispered, closing her eyes.

"You can and you must. Before I'm dry and cannot help you."

Alexia forced herself to reach out. Her hands trembled as they cradled her mother's slim forearm, her skin ice-cold against Alexia's warm palms. Lowering her head, Alexia brought her mother's wrist to her mouth. Parting her jaws, she positioned her bite along the veins visible beneath the nearly translucent skin.

"Hurry," the Queen urged. "I'll try to focus in on what I want you to see."

Alexia nodded, again feeling the burn of unshed tears behind her eyes. Yet it wasn't until her fangs punctured the smooth flesh of her mother's skin that the tears fell.

The moment the metallic flavor of blood hit her tongue, a jolt cracked through Alexia's body. Dense and heavy, a gray fog swirled over her irises, blanketing her vision in a haze until it was all she could see. Unlike the time she had fed from Declan, it all happened so fast. She couldn't have stopped it, couldn't have pulled back from her mother's arm if she'd tried. The fog held her now. Its pillowy mist filling her lungs with each intake of breath. So thick she could taste it, smell it, feel it throbbing through her skin, down her arms and legs in a powerful tremble that rocked her. Part of her realized the energy rush came from her mother's blood ripping through her veins. Realized she now tasted the madness that Lotharus sought his whole life and the addiction that had changed the history of her people forever.

Sudden shapes began to form in the swirling, colorless matter floating around her. First merely dark outlines, indistinguishable shadows moving behind a curtain. Then slowly layers began to peel away and fold back, revealing bits and pieces. The shapes became people. The constant roar of blood behind her ears became voices. Sounds, once muffled as if she were underwater, began to prick her ears in distinct consonants and tones. One recognizable voice lifted above the others.

The Queen's voice, low and hushed, filled the room along with two others, a male and a female. Alexia squinted, willing the images, the memories clearer. As if the thought begot the act, the fog lifted completely, unveiling a picture before her.

The dungeon. Alexia would know it anywhere. However, at the sight of the other two people whose voices she'd heard, Alexia reeled back, almost tipping off the bed.

The dragon King and Queen!

Her heart kick-started in her chest, racing at a breakneck tempo. She had been right. Her mother did have something to do with all of this. Pinching her eyes tighter, Alexia willed herself to focus, to listen, to hear.

The three of them stood in the corner of the dungeon, not far from where Declan's wing had been clipped. The King and Queen, much like their son, were bloody, filthy from their time spent in the horde's version of hell. Alexia stared at them with curiosity and wonder. Goddess, Declan was right. His father was huge. His broad back and shoulders ate up the vision, commanding nearly all of it. Bulges and valleys of thick corded muscle rolled over his back, his powerful arms. Intricate tattoos wound around each biceps, and ancient lettering had been penned with a delicate hand up his spine.

Slowly, Alexia let her gaze drift to the small female the dragon King shielded protectively under one massive limb. Her delicate shape appeared so fragile and small next to his mighty dragon form. There was no mistaking she'd been born a human.

Alexia recalled how Declan had spoken of them both, the sadness in his soul over their deaths, and her heart swelled with pride and grief. The emotions were so over-whelming, she nearly choked on them. Swallowing down another mouthful of the Queen's tart, hot blood, Alexia focused on what the memory was showing her. What her mother was trying to show her.

"Why should we trust you?" Declan's father spoke, his voice firm and determined. The inflection and tone of it instantly called Declan to mind.

"You don't have any other choice," her mother answered. "You stay, you die."

"But I don't understand," the dragon Queen said. "Why are you helping us?"

"My reasons are my own. All you need for them to succeed is to live."

Another silhouette emerged from behind the Queen. A fourth person Alexia had not seen until now stepped from the shadows and into the low light of the dungeon. When he stepped fully into the light, Alexia gasped in shock.

"Yuri?" she breathed. The uncle she thought had died alongside her father stood beside the Queen. Tall, handsome, with dark hair framing his face and mouth, he looked at the dragons with neither contempt nor empathy.

"This is my brother," the Queen said, motioning to Yuri. "He will take you where I cannot."

They must have sensed the same palpable indifference emanating off Yuri as Alexia had, as neither of the dragons seemed pleased with the plan.

"Why can we not simply return home?" Declan's father asked.

Alexia saw the pulse increase in the carotid on her mother's neck, anger ignite in her usually serene gaze. "This is not a game, *Derkein,* and time is a commodity you do not have. If you live, it's by my hand, by my rules. Do you understand?"

Without waiting for their reply, Yuri shouldered around the Queen and stepped forward. His intense onyx gaze fixed on the two dragons. Declan's father shifted, putting his body in front of his female, shielding her in a protective move. However, Yuri stopped a few feet away and made no attempt to physically touch either of them.

Alexia looked on in awe as her uncle's pupils sparked to dazzling white as if someone had flipped on a light switch inside his head. By fractions, the light expanded, eating up the black iris and beyond until both of his eyes shone like headlights.

It all happened so fast, it took a moment for Alexia to realize what she was seeing. Took another moment for her to realize what her uncle was doing. What he was.

A Medij, her mind whispered.

Vampire Medij were rare and feared by almost everyone for their invasive abilities. Alexia had only heard stories of his kind and the amazing psychic skills they possessed. But it was said they could occupy a mind with a look. Read thoughts or even place their own in yours. Touch your psyche from miles away with their powerful telepathic force. Some even had the gift of divination, the power of precognition to tell the future or possible futures. Others had been said to be able to move things with their minds. Goddess knew what else a true

Medij of her uncle's age and station could accomplish. The possibilities astounded her.

Blinking, Alexia looked back to the scene before her. Under Yuri's Medij stare, all signs of tension left the dragon King and Queen's bodies. Their muscles and posture relaxed. Their defensive walls dropped. For all intents and purposes, the two became mindless slaves to Yuri's will.

Alexia inhaled sharply. To think, if power like Yuri's fell into the hands of someone like Lotharus, if he knew her uncle still lived... A shudder passed through her.

Bit by bit the light faded from Yuri's eyes until they were once again a dark onyx. Without uttering a single word, he pivoted back to the Queen. He paused beside her, their shoulders almost touching. After a moment's hesitation, he looked over at her. His black eyes glittered with commitment and resolve.

"My daughter must be found and brought back to me."

The Queen swallowed and licked her lips. "I swear it."

"Do you? Do you vow to keep your promise to me, sister? That after we are free of his yoke, you'll go down the mountain and find her? You'll right your wrong."

Catija nodded in agreement. Yuri's shoulders dropped slightly, followed by his chin. Although his accusatory words came out smooth and powerful, Alexia saw nothing but guilt in his posture.

After a few hushed words Alexia could not distinguish, the siblings acknowledged one another with a nod. Yuri took a folded piece of paper from the Queen's hand and started walking toward the dungeon doors. The two dragons followed behind him in mute and mindless acquiescence. Their stance and carriage indicating they knew they had to be not only stealthy but quiet.

Alexia marveled at his mind control over them, realizing he must have put them in a powerful hypnotic trance so they could all flee to wherever he was taking them without resistance. Although she had never thought of it until now, such a mental state explained why no one had seen the dragon King and Queen. Why they had not tried to return home since being set free. They were still being controlled by him, which meant that in order to find the dragons she had to find Yuri.

But where had he taken them?

The edges of the memory began to blur. The heavy mist closed in again. Wind whipped around her, pulling her hair around her head like a sack. Fear seized Alexia. She hadn't seen enough, hadn't learned enough. But she was powerless to stop the vision from fading. First Alexia could not make out distinct background images. Then, after a few more moments, the entire picture began to lose clarity until everything faded into a whitewash.

Broken and faint, her mother's heartbeat once again thudded in her ears, commanding attention. The pungent taste of quickly chilling blood settled in Alexia's mouth. With the vision gone, reality snapped back upon her like a bucket of ice water. Alexia pulled away from her mother's wrist, gasping for air.

Reality smacked her hard and fast. The force of it tipped her world sideways. Off balance, she rocked backward, her hip slamming on the floor beside the bed. Propping herself up, Alexia leaned her back against the bedside table. She was trying to recover from the physical and mental onslaught she'd just endured, to tame the stampede of powerful blood jolting through her body. An unbearable gnawing sensation clawed at her insides. Icy hot skewers of pain lanced through her skull in a driving headache that nearly made her vomit. But she had to combat them all. Had to get off her ass and get back to her mother's side.

"It's…my time," Catija said between gasps. "The burden…on my shoulders…lifted."

Although undeniably weak, her mother's voice sounded emboldened with strength at the same time, and waved warning flags in Alexia's heart. She rolled to her knees.

"No. Wait," she breathed, a flash of white lights bursting behind her eyes. Clasping the edge of the bed, she moved to pull herself up, struggled to get vertical. When that failed, she rested her head on the bed and closed her eyes. Listening to the rhythmic pull and push of her mother's breathing, she tried to get hers under control.

A hand clasped hers and squeezed. Alexia lifted her head, thankful it did not throb in protest. "Promise you'll be the Queen I see in you, Alexia. Search your heart and decide who she must lead, who she must be," Catija said in one long breath, as though she was trying to force the message out of her mouth before it was too late.

"But I don't know what to do," Alexia said. "I don't know where any of them are."

"Do you…have…crystal?"

"Yes."

The Queen smiled. "Take it…Diana…show you…the way."

"But I can't just leave you here."

"You must." A lone tear rolled down the Queen's face. "Now…go."

CHAPTER SIXTEEN

CATIJA LAY ON THE BED with her eyes closed. Unmoving, she listened to the steady rhythm of music. Each melodic note of the song throbbed through her, replacing the long numbing pain. Although she recalled asking Alexia to put her disc on before she left, she couldn't remember how long it had been since she'd left her side. She could only breathe in the music. Feel it encompass every inch of her. Each breath came shallower, the time between them prolonged until she thought they might cease altogether.

The bed sunk beneath someone's weight. Long legs stretched alongside hers. At the brush of fingers in her hair, a smile curved her lips.

"Yuri?"

"Yes, Cat. I'm here," he replied. "As here as I can be, anyway."

His voice seemed remorseful, tight with emotion.

Something she hardly ever heard from her stoic older brother. Catija wanted to comfort him, reassure him she understood his exile and held no ill will toward him at all. While part of her grieved along with him for mistakes made and all of the time they had lost, right now she did not care about any of that. None of the past mattered anymore. None of the things said or done seemed relevant...except one. One regret, one promise she'd made and would not get to complete.

"I'm sorry..." she whispered, "...failed you."

"Shh." The arms around her tightened and soft lips brushed her temple by her hairline. "You did not fail anyone."

"But..." she swallowed "...the dragons..."

"Will be found," he replied, his palm smoothing down her cheek in a reassuring glide. "As will my daughter. At long last she will be returned to me."

"How?" The moment the question left her lips, understanding pricked what was left of her conscious mind. A glimmer of hope sparked through her dying body. "You've..." she began, but she could no longer get her lips to function. Her tongue felt fat and heavy and stuck to the roof of her dry mouth.

"Yes, Cat. I've seen it. Seen the future," Yuri answered for her.

Those words released the heavy chains shackled

around her heart. For the first time in as long as she could remember, she felt free.

"I did it," she breathed, a smile on her lips.

Yuri nodded, his powerful chest trembling, and she briefly wondered if he was crying. "You did. And I thank you, dear sister."

Warmth Catija had not felt since childhood spread through her like an absolving bath of light. It filled her, shooting out from her core through her limbs in all directions. So bright at first, so all encompassing, she did not register the menacing shadow lurking nearby until it blocked out the light.

Someone else was in her chamber. His cold hate and age-old anger tried to leach the positive energy and remaining power from her. But it was too late. Catija had her release from Lotharus and her past. Death was no longer feared, but a salvation.

Yuri screamed. The heart-wrenching sound a warning, protest and a threat all at once. Catija felt his corporeal being dissipate. His body and limbs shifted into a cloud of energy in an attempt to blanket her. Helpless and raw, Yuri's bellow filled her ears, nearly breaking her heart. While his sadness and loss upset her, she could not find it in herself to feel regret. Even when Lotharus drove the pointed tip of his staff through her heart, absorbing what was left of her power into himself, Catija was still smiling.

"LORD DECLAN!"

At the sound of his name, Declan spun around. A familiar figure was running full bore down the passage to him. When he neared, the flames from a wall sconce illuminated the young fledgling legionnaire.

"Ash?" Declan handed Doc the parchment he'd been reading and started toward the young dragon. At his approach, Ash stopped running and leaned over. Resting his hands on his knees, he tried to catch his breath in heaving gasps.

"They need you...council."

The last word had barely fallen from the youth's lips before Declan took off at a blind run. A thousand thoughts flitted through his mind, but he only hoped and prayed on one. Combat boots pounding on the stones, he took the turns and passageways at breakneck speed, barreling past the guards posted outside the council room without so much as a glance.

The room was empty. Panting, he swept his hand through his hair and paced. He was just about to head back out the door when it opened.

"Did you find her?" Declan asked the first person who stepped through the threshold.

Tallon's brow tensed at his remark. "No. But we found someone else."

Behind her, Griffon entered the room, followed closely by a scowling Falcon. Declan cocked a brow at the sight of Griffon wrestling one of Lotharus's soldiers into a chair, securing his hands and feet with duct tape. If his face were any indication, the vampire had not come easily. A gash split across his forehead, spilling blood along the sides of his face. The purple flesh had already swollen around one eye to the point it was nothing but a sliver. The other one, milky white, fought to remain open as he visibly warred to stay conscious.

Elder eyes.

Alexia's words floated through Declan's mind, making his heart pinch. When he'd awakened to find her gone, the truth of how much she meant to him, every emotion he'd been too frightened to label, had slammed into him with aching clarity. It didn't matter that the crystal was missing. Nothing mattered to him except Alexia. God's truth, he wanted her in his arms, in his bed. But right now, he'd settle for just knowing she was safe. He could worry about the rest later.

Declan settled his gaze on Griffon, who stood, his arms crossed tight about his wide chest. Declan didn't need to ask who had taken the vampire down. Didn't need to see Griffon's gloved hands to know they were blood-stained. Disgust rolled through him at the realization that one of his flock had beaten this soldier. To think they were no better than the vampires who'd tortured him for information sickened him endlessly.

"Now, tell him what you told us," Tallon ordered, bringing Declan back from his thoughts. The soldier sucked in a breath and rested his head back on the edge of the chair.

"Lotharus has a secret society…of vampires," he said on the exhale. "An army of soldiers he's built and per-fected over the past few years." The soldier closed his eyes, wincing as he took in another deep draught of air.

"What do you mean, 'perfected'?" Griffon asked, his face showing distaste at being in such close proximity to a soldier that wasn't dead. When the soldier failed to answer right away, Griffon cracked a meaty fist across the vampire's face. The soldier fell sideways, nearly toppling the chair.

Declan winced as the soldier struggled to sit back upright in the chair. Enduring this was like some form of exposure therapy he wasn't yet ready to undergo. The raw pain of being beaten and tortured still vibrated in the forefront of his mind.

"Olden blood," the vampire finally panted. "He found

blood of the true ancients in the lower catacomb vaults after a quake tore through the caves. Pure blood."

"So, he found a bottle of blood. What's the big deal?" Falcon chimed in.

The vampire leveled his good eye on him. "Like any species, our blood had become diluted over the centuries. The lines did not remain as true and strong as they should have. At first, Lotharus tried to use the blood to convert himself. When that didn't work, he made us. But then the scroll that spoke of the Draco Crystal, the ritual, fell into his lap and he abandoned everything he'd worked on to find it and prepare."

"And what's so special about you?" Griffon said with a grunt. "Other than those freaky eyes, you all look and die the same to me."

"It is said the true oldens possessed memory blockers."

"Memory blockers?" Tallon asked.

Griffon leaned over her. "It means they could feed off their prey without conscious," he replied under his breath. "Feed off humans again without the threat of going mad."

Falcon pushed his way back to the soldier, his hands fisting the vampire's bloodstained collar, nearly yanking him off the chair. "Anything else?"

"Yes," the soldier snapped. "It's also said they could walk in the sun."

A collective gasp filled the room. Falcon released his hold of the soldier and took a shaky step back.

"Can you?" he asked.

"Haven't tried," the soldier replied, sulking back into the chair.

"As interesting as all of this is," Declan said, "it doesn't help me find Alexia."

"Alexia?" The soldier arched a brow and turned toward Declan. "Lotharus plans to kill her at midnight when she ascends and steal her power. With the ruler's force harnessed in the crystal, he can overthrow the order and become the first man to rule our horde in centuries."

The vampire's face showed no feelings, his voice held no inflection of emotion, which amazed Declan as he stood in speechless disbelief.

"But the Queen…" Tallon finally said, staring at each of them with shocked incredulity before turning back to the soldier. "He can't do that, can he? Won't she stop him?"

The soldier shook his head. "He's already killed her."

Declan's heart stopped. Without a word, he spun, heading for the door.

"Dec, wait."

When he didn't slow, Tallon's hand grabbed his bicep, turning him around.

"I'm going for her, Tallon. You're not stopping me."

Her pink lips twisted and she reached beneath the tattered hem of her sweater to dig something out of her pant pocket. "Then you're going to need this."

Declan glanced down. She held one of their black tracing sticks in her hand. The red light at the top blinked in a steady rhythm, meaning not only was it turned on, it was tracking something. *Someone.* Frowning, he reached for it.

Tallon dipped her chin. "I put a tracer on her last night."

His frown tightened into a scowl.

"I won't apologize, so don't ask me to. You're my family and I'll do what I think is best to look after you, no matter what."

Declan took the device from her hand, unable to utter the thanks on his lips.

"For the record," she continued, "I don't agree with this. You shouldn't go there. It's too dangerous."

"She's right." At Falcon's voice, Declan glanced up. "You need a plan. If Lotharus has already killed the Queen, he will be even stronger now than before."

Declan closed his eyes and took a deep breath, forcing himself to calm down. "All right. Griffon and Falcon, head back out to the catacombs and see if you can spot any activity that might tip us off to Lotharus's whereabouts." Opening his eyes, he set what he knew was a worried gaze on his sister. "Tallon, go and get me Doc. Tell her to bring every bit of parchment, every book and scrap of paper regarding the vampires and their histories with her and meet me in my chamber. Make it quick."

"Right," Tallon said. "I'm on it."

ALEXIA RAN INTO THE HEART of the garden, stopping at the fountain. As always, Diana stood with one palm up, the other offering water to the sunken city. Panting, Alexia carefully pulled the crystal from underneath her heavy sweater. It seemed to grow heavier in her hand, as if it knew what she was about to do. Wanted her to do it.

"Mother, I hope this works," she whispered, placing the ball in Diana's hand. Slowly, Alexia released the stone, pulled her hand back and held her breath.

Nothing happened.

Alexia sighed and muttered a curse. She was about to reach for the crystal when a soft hiss, like air escaping a balloon, whispered through the garden. Alexia froze, watching wide-eyed as the statue began sinking into the earth. The fountain turned off until only small droplets of water fell from the lip of the pitcher. The bottom of the pond fell away and water streamed out, revealing the secret hidden beneath.

It was then she saw what she'd come here to see. Davna Vremena. And on the far side of the pool, farthest away from Diana, it sat, alone and forgotten. An island shrouded in myth and Myst.

Dragon Island.

Alexia quickly scribbled a rough map of the island, stowing the paper in her boot before staring once again at the wonder before her.

"Over the Boginja Mountains, across the Uklet River and beyond the Zavodnica Sea." She repeated her mother's words, adding in the landmarks before her. "Far away where *she* couldn't touch them." She looked over her shoulder at the statue of Diana, who stood at the farthest possible point from the tiny island.

There. That was where mother had hidden them.

"So, you brought it."

Alexia instantly spun, clutching the crystal with one hand, training her gun on his chest with the other. "Brought what?"

"Don't play with me." Lotharus stepped out from behind a tree, his shadowed face a study in rage as he examined the slowly filling pool of water. "Did you really think I didn't know what your mother had done? I allowed her to keep her pets alive, knowing I'd learn their location the minute I tasted her blood."

Despite the sweat breaking out on her brow, hair rose on the back of her neck. "Then why did you kill her?" Alexia seethed, shaking the hand holding the gun on the last syllable.

"I assure you, killing her was not the plan. I needed her very much alive in order to harvest her at peak power. But now I suppose yours will have to do. I do hope it's as potent as the auld texts say." He took another step into the faint light of the garden.

Narrowing her eyes, Alexia tilted her head and looked closer. Four bloody scratches ran in parallel lines down his cheek. Not scratches, claw marks. Someone had run their nails over his face in what looked like a last-ditch attempt to save themselves from a fate horrible enough to warrant such panicked recklessness. At the thought it had been her mother, fighting for her life, bile tickled the base of her throat.

"You'll be slaughtered by the vanators for what you've done!"

"Perhaps in *your* world the blood hunters would come for me. But not the one I'm creating. The one I rule."

Alexia shook her head, unable to believe the sheer lunacy in his eyes. "You're mad."

"No. It's evolution, Alexia. Think about it. The dragons have male leaders, do they not? Even the humans know better. It is only us, the bees and the elephants that have not yet realized our mistake, moved on and evolved."

"What you're saying is treason," she said. "You'll be exiled."

"By whom?" He cocked a brow and prowled closer. "You? *My* soldiers?"

Alexia swallowed down her fear and trained her gun between his eyes. "I'll shoot you where you stand."

Lotharus grinned and stood with his hands stretched to the side. "Give it your best shot." The malice and madness in his eyes had her pulling the trigger without hesitation. However, before the bullet left the chamber, he appeared beside her. A moment later, a shattering pain ripped through her wrist and the gun was wrenched free.

"Not good enough," he said, dangling her gun from his fingertips before tossing it aside. On reflex, Alexia shot her arm out, catching his chin with a jab. When she tried to follow with another, Lotharus snatched her arm and hauled her to him.

"You smell like him. Every filthy inch of you," he snarled, swinging his arm in a wide arc. Alexia twisted her arms free and dove to the side. Tucking into a ball, she rolled back up to stand two feet away, missing the blow by seconds.

"You fed me lies," she panted. "About the war, about the dragons, about everything."

"Of course I did. Why whip the mule into action when it will work twice as hard for a carrot?"

Alexia's blood boiled. Narrowing her eyes, she reached behind her back, curling her fingers around her dagger's hilt. "Dangle that carrot too long, your mule will get hungry and bite you instead." Grunting, she flung the weapon toward his heart. The blade sank into its mark, protruding from the center of his chest. She released a breath and stood, watching as blood oozed from the wound, staining his shirt. Lotharus looked down, curled his long fingers around the hilt and pulled. Alexia stared in disbelief as the flesh healed within seconds.

"No." She shook her head. "That's not possible."

Lotharus glanced up, his lips curved before he vanished in a plume of smoke.

Gasping, Alexia turned to see if he'd materialized behind her. Something smacked her across the face so hard, so fast, she fell back. A small cry of pain hummed from her lips as she sensed a welt already forming above her jaw.

She rested the wounded cheek on the stone pathway for only a moment before shifting to her hands and knees, about to stand. Something wrapped around her, yanking her up hard. She spun and saw Lotharus standing a good five feet away. He was using mind power against her, pulling her to him. Alexia twisted and fought with everything she had, but it was useless.

Goddess, he was fast and so strong.

When she stood before him, his hands took the place of his will. He clamped her body tightly against his until it felt like iron manacles encircled her wrists.

"Too bad for you—I'm not scared of your bite," he drawled. Tilting his head to the side, his black eyes traveled the length of her body. "But I am interested in something else."

"You really are pathetic, you know that?" she said, keeping the fear out of her voice.

He blinked but didn't lift his eyes from her bodice. "And why is that?"

"It's like Declan said, you have to force someone to lie with you to get any at all."

His gaze snapped to her face, but instead of anger, bloodlust lit up his eyes. Slowly, his fangs lengthened to hang over his lower lips. Fear, thick and debilitating, slid down her spine.

"Who says I want you, Alexia? You never did anything more than lie there like a petrified tree. But this…"

A whimper escaped her as he wrenched her neck back, exposing her throat.

"This I've wanted to do for nearly a century." He swooped. Brutal and with no regard to pain or thoughts of pleasure, Lotharus plunged his teeth into her throat.

Alexia's eyes watered as he twisted his head, sinking his fangs deeper into her flesh, increasing the flow of blood to his mouth. She slammed her eyes shut. Thoughts of Declan, images of him burned behind her closed eyes with Technicolor clarity. *Fight,* a voice screamed in her head. It was his voice, deep and smoky and ordering her not to die here. Not now. Not like this.

Lotharus let out a low groan. The hand on her wrist slipped an inch. Using the advantage, Alexia tugged her arm free, jabbing her fist against his ear. Bones crunched beneath her knuckles. Lotharus howled and fell back, clutching his head as he stumbled back from her. Alexia fell, her back smacking the jagged stepping stones. Wincing, she flipped over. Blackness swallowed her vision. Grabbing a breath, she began crawling down the path, using her arms and fingers to pull her.

A hand seized the waistband of her pants, tugging them and her backward. "If you would have just drunk out of the goblets I served you, like your mother did, this wouldn't be so hard." Through a hazy film, she saw her gun and reached for it.

"I tried to keep you both complacent. Tried to make this easy for all of us." Knees dug into her back, pinning her to the floor, as his fingers bit into her scalp and pulled hard. Alexia gasped when his teeth clamped down hard on the back of her neck. A low groan of triumph, of domination, filled her ears. Using her last reserve of strength, Alexia bucked him off and threw herself forward, toward the gun, frowning when her limbs wouldn't move. She tried again and could barely lift them an inch.

Lotharus clutched her shoulder, easily flipping her over. His hands dug into her pocket, retrieving the crystal. "But you, Alexia, chose the hard way," he said, studying the ball. "And I still win." His bloodied lips were the last things she saw before he lowered his head and bit down hard. His mouth covered the column of her throat, his teeth piercing deep, constricting her windpipe. The fresco ceiling above swirled as she felt her consciousness slowly fading. Heavy and weak, every muscle in her body drooped limp until she thought she might sink into the ground, into her grave.

CHAPTER SEVENTEEN

DECLAN SAT AT HIS DESK, poring over every line, every word and every implied nuance of the old texts Doc had given him until his vision blurred. There had to be something they'd missed, something they weren't seeing. Declan would not believe they were helpless against a simple stone. There had to be a way to use it against the vampires, had to be a way to fight back. The power in that crystal couldn't only go one way. But how? Why? He stared down at the book in front of him. The answer was right there before him, but he couldn't read the language.

Swiping a hand over his burning eyes, he flipped over another page of the ancient book. Particles of dust flew into the air, landing behind his eyelids like sandpaper. With a frustrated growl, he shoved the useless book to the floor. The sound of it thudding against the ground drowned out the faint knock on his door.

"My lord?"

Declan spun in his chair at the voice. A small female stood in the doorway. "Doc, you're back. Have you found something else?" Declan felt his heart race in anticipation of her positive answer.

"I hope so," she replied, wedging the door open with her shoulder. The white lapels of her lab coat flared to the sides as she stepped inside. Hands full, she kicked the door closed, barely managing to balance the copious amount of books and scrolls piled in her arms.

"Here, let me help you." Declan walked forward, taking a few of the heavier books from her stack.

"Thank you," she replied, her gaze flitting up only briefly before settling somewhere near the floorboards once more. Declan couldn't help but notice that even after she'd gained an appointed seat on the council, even after all he'd done to help her, she still had trouble making eye contact with him. It was the same story for all the other dragon lords. Declan chuckled to himself, thinking it amusing that someone as small and timid as the Doc had his mighty dragon captain, Kestrel, wrapped around her frail little finger.

Carefully, Doc laid the scrolls on the floor. Rising

back up to stand, she took one of the parchments off the top, unrolling and flattening it on the desk before him.

"I ran some specs on the ceremony off what we managed to translate from these scrolls and the soldier's testimony. Now, nothing seemed out of the ordinary and none of it connected to the Queen or her daughter until you mentioned the word *ascension,* and the fact that Lotharus had already killed the Queen."

Doc pushed her glasses up her nose and bent over the desk, her thin, blond ponytail skating over her shoulder, concealing the protruding collarbone poking beneath her delicate form.

"Now." She tapped her finger on the paper, drawing Declan's attention. "I did some digging and put two and two together. I believe Lotharus means to take over the horde."

"Yes. We gathered as much from the soldier Griffon brought in."

She turned her face to his, her light brows drawn together in concentration. "He told you Lotharus is over-throwing their society and creating a new one? Reverting them back to the dark times when men ruled the horde?"

Declan nodded. "But what does that have to do with the crystal? With Alexia?"

"Uhh, well," she said, bending to the scrolls and books

she'd laid on the floor. "As an olden, he is powerful enough in his own right. A fact I'm sure you can attest to if you've faced him and lived through it," she said, flipping through the stacks of paper. "However, his ability now is nothing compared to an ascended Queen's at the height of her youth, like Alexia would be after tonight. That is where the crystal comes in. Ah, here we are." Selecting one of the parchments, she stood, placing it on his desk. Unraveling it carefully, she pointed to what looked like a sketch of a long staff with the crystal set atop it. "If he can harness the energy in the crystal, contain it within the power center here, he could wield her force from outside his corporeal form."

"In other words, he could turn the crystal into a weapon?"

"Exactly."

Declan fell back against his desk chair. "But in order to gain Alexia's power and harness it within the crystal…"

"He has to kill her."

Declan swallowed down the urge to be sick. "How do I stop him?"

He heard the desperate panic in his own voice. Knew the minute Doc leveled her unsettling gaze on him, she'd heard it, too. Declan ran a hand through his hair, wishing he could punch his fist through a wall instead.

Doc squatted down until her eyes were level with his. A sudden rush of energy and heat charged the air between them. The hair on Declan's forearms and neck stood on end as if static energy pulsed through his pores.

"Doc, what are you…?"

Without a word, she moved closer, closing the distance between them. His gaze locked with hers and he realized at once what was happening.

Declan knew Doc used her empath powers when she healed wounded legionnaires in the infirmary, himself included. However, her patients had always been knocked out cold when she'd worked on them, and no one ever witnessed her powers firsthand. He had no idea what to do, or how she wanted him to react. So, he did nothing. He only stared at her, hoping he wouldn't have to do anything for Doc's magick to take effect.

Excitement and fear pumped through him, the twin emotions both exhilarating and frightening. Soft and small, her hands cupped his face. Declan sizzled in a breath, the flesh beneath her fingers burning on contact, only to feel freezing cold a second later. He swallowed hard and stared into her eyes.

Beneath her glasses, her eyes widened. The black eating up the blue until she almost appeared more a vampire with onyx eyes than a dragon. Declan stilled as her stare tore through him like a flesh-eating wind. Realized it let her see things, memories and feelings he kept buried deep, perhaps even from himself. Doc saw it all. He knew it. He felt it.

She continued to stare and every muscle in Declan's body, from his face to his toes, tensed in reply. His body literally vibrated with the demanding impulse to withdraw, to shut his eyes and disconnect from her.

Now!

Instead, Declan forced his anxiety to subside. Pulling in a breath, he gripped the arms of his chair and fought against his instincts. Forced himself to open up to her. Willing to do anything, let her see everything, if it might help him save Alexia.

Before he could exhale, Doc was careening backward, her hands grasping the edge of his desk for balance. "Sorry," she murmured, lifting a hand to adjust her glasses. "I didn't mean to do that. Kestrel and I have been working on my control. But sometimes it slips."

"It's fine, Doc," Declan reassured her, even as his heart beat a frenzied tempo in his chest. He closed his eyes and took a deep breath. "Did you see…did you see how to help her?"

At her silence, Declan opened his eyes, focusing at once on her cobalt gaze. At the fear swirling in their depths, icy fingers coiled around his spine before fisting his gut in their piercing grip. "Please," he whispered. "I need to know."

"I—I…" Doc's eyes softened and she shook her head. "I'm sorry."

"Why? What did you see?"

"Nothing," she said, her fingers nervously fidgeting with the hem of her lab coat. "I mean, I don't know what I saw. It doesn't work like that. I feel what you feel. See what you see. Not the future."

An odd combination of relief and disappointment sliced through him. He sighed. A defeated lump sank in his chest, dragging his heart down with it. He knew he should be focused on getting the Draco Crystal back, on fighting to save his flock from certain annihilation. Yet he couldn't get his mind off saving Alexia.

Right now his only plan was to fight Lotharus and his soldiers on their ground. Hope that, like the last time he'd battled the soldiers, he'd be given the chance to save Alexia. He'd have to spend time unraveling the mystery of the damned crystal and how to destroy it once and for all after he knew she was safe. He frowned, thinking about her note. Found himself wondering if perhaps Alexia didn't already have the answer to that question.

As if sensing his despair, Doc leaned over him,

grabbing a book off his desk. "But you're right to look to the crystal. That is the key. So, this crystal has the power to rule all or destroy one, right?" she asked, thumbing through the pages. "Well, that could mean a couple of things…."

"Doc, please," he said.

"…our two races, naturally."

"Doc."

"But it could also…"

"Sparrow." He said her given name and spoke firmly enough this time that she listened. Mindful of how delicate Doc could be in demeanor and frame, Declan gently placed his hand atop hers, stilling her frantic movements and speech. "Listen. I need you to go to Kestrel. Tell him I need everyone, and I mean everyone, to ready for battle, and fast."

She blinked over at him, not only meeting but holding his gaze. "But we can do this. I can help you," she said in a small voice. "I want to help you."

Declan smiled up at her as best he could. He had always adored Doc and would never be able to thank her enough for healing his warrior captain and friend, Kestrel, after the battle that had taken his parents. But he knew what he had to do and he didn't need her here to do it. "You have."

After a moment, Doc nodded and stood upright. "I'll come back if I find anything new," she said, heading for the door.

"Thank you," he said, before turning back to his desk, to this impossible task before him.

Propping his elbows on the table, he rested his forehead in his hands. Beneath him, the blueprints of the horde's catacombs stared up at him, mocking him. Even with the locator, he wasn't sure he could find Alexia in that maze. The dragons only had on file this makeshift design of the horde's home. It wasn't complete by any stretch of the imagination. And by the sound of it, the vampires themselves didn't know what lay in the bowels of their dwellings.

"...plans to kill her at midnight when she ascends and steal her power."

Declan peeked up from under his arms. It was nearly ten. Two hours. Two hours and she'd be gone. Somewhere he couldn't bring her back.

Gods, he couldn't think like that. Not now. Helpless anger rose inside him. Images of her flashed in his mind, and the scent of her filled his nose. Collapsing, he laid his head on his crossed arms. Hoping he was tired enough for sleep to blanket him. Consumed enough to once again dream of Alexia.

It seemed he'd barely shut his eyes and Declan had his answer. As it had before, that damn thick fog he'd become so familiar with the past few days collected and then parted in a whoosh like a stage curtain, revealing whatever it wanted him to see.

Unnatural darkness, cold and wet, hit him first. Having lived amongst the stones all his life, he knew the sensation well. However, it was the rest of the surroundings he had trouble comprehending. Frowning, he tried to take in as much of the scene as he could. Candles, hundreds of them, lit up every nook and cranny of the cave. Dozens of dark, hooded figures swayed, but there was no music. The low murmur of male voices thrummed in a constant drone.

What was he seeing? Where was the rest of the horde? This second thought snowballed on top of the first and Declan almost willed himself awake. And then he saw Alexia.

Oh, gods, he saw her.

"Alex." Her name tore from him in a sob. She stood on the raised dais, beside a large stone table. Her arms shackled over her head on the wooden pillar she was bound to. Even from this distance, he could tell she was injured. Dark blood stained her neck and chest, soaking her exquisite brown evening gown and soiling her light hair.

When her head lifted, the look of cornered desperation

and agony on her face was enough to send him running for her. However, he barely got five steps before his entire body slammed into an invisible wall. Knocked off his feet from the force, he collapsed backward with an unforgiving thud. Pain shot up his spine, but he didn't feel it. He didn't feel anything except fear, sending wave after wave of terror through his veins.

Lotharus emerged and the hooded figures began cheering. Declan scrambled to his feet. The crowd began a low chant that grew louder with each word. Lotharus spoke but Declan could not hear over the now deafening mantra. Frantic, Declan glanced from one corner of the room to the next, looking for something, someone to help.

A soft blue light began emanating from Alexia, coiling around her, engulfing her. At first, Declan thought his vision had failed, or the low light of the cave was playing tricks on him. But Lotharus smiled, and his chant grew louder. Alexia's body jerked, fighting against whatever force ripped through her. Sweat dotted her brow and her body writhed in pain.

Declan pounded his fists against the invisible wall keeping her from him, shouting a warning when Lotharus unsheathed a gleaming silver broadsword. Her black eyes flew wide open, but she made no struggle to fight the undeniable fate looming over her. The notion she'd given up lingered for only a moment before all thought fled completely. Lotharus jabbed, skewering the weapon through her middle. The blue light shot through the weapon like a current of lightning, buzzing straight to the crystal he now held in his outstretched hand. After the last pulsing stream left her body, she fell limp in the rope bindings. Lotharus bent, ducking a goblet in the bucket beneath her. He hoisted the crystal in one hand and the chalice of her blood in the other before downing its contents.

Declan took a step back, refusing to believe any of this could be happening. The visual proof before him refused to register in his breaking heart.

Alexia's dead.

The truth struck him like a death blow, hard and strong. Although he knew he'd find no physical evidence of the pain tearing through him, he looked down, half expecting to see a sword sticking out of his chest. Instead, the image of her hung and slaughtered burned behind his retinas.

Collapsing to his knees, he cradled his head in his hands and allowed the darkness, the sorrow, the loss to swallow him.

He awoke with a start, sending papers flying off his desk. His hand unconsciously went to cover the pain still radiating in his chest.

"Alex," he gasped, his eyes scouring the scattered desk for his clock.

The flashing red numbers nearly made him weep.

Twelve-thirty.

He was too late.

CHAPTER EIGHTEEN

TALLON PULLED THE WOOL sweater over her bent knees, wrapping her arms around them. Tilting her head, she took in the sweeping view of the jagged, snow-capped mountains stabbing through the blanket of dark clouds before her. Bursts of icy wind shot through the various holes in the worn knit, blowing freezing air over her body. She was numb, and not from the cold. The hollow nothingness born the night her parents had been caged seeped from within until it consumed everything, even her will to care if she would one day be able to pull herself out of the black hole her life seemed to be spiraling into. She had nowhere to go, no one to turn to and the utterly pathetic truth of her situation infuriated her.

While Declan's feelings for the vampire shouldn't affect her, they did. Call her childish. Call her selfish. She wanted her life back, wanted her mom and dad, wanted her brother back. A long sigh escaped her and she closed her eyes.

Not ten minutes ago, Declan had left the lair like a man crazed. She'd pleaded with him to let her help him, to let her go with him. Although she may not care if that vampire lived or died, he did. And both of them had suffered so much these past weeks, part of her was willing to do whatever it took to keep him from feeling any more pain.

But he had shut down, closed her out. When she'd stood right here on this very spot and held his face, forcing him to stare at her, his eyes seemed void, resolute in the task he'd set upon himself. She saw the look of a haunted, desperate man and feared what he would do if he found the princess dead as prophesied.

If she were honest with herself, that burning question was the reason she sat out in the cold in the middle of the night. She was scared. Scared she'd never see her brother again. After all, she'd only just gotten him back. Now, she feared, even if he did return, nothing would be the same. A wall had grown between them since that night they'd stolen the crystal, and she couldn't figure out how to knock it down.

The view before her blurred, her vision swimming in unshed tears. Her chin quivered, and it had nothing to do with the cold. Giving up the fight, she let the tears fall. Her cheeks stung as the cold night air froze the liquid to her face.

Gods, why did she let him leave? The answer came at once. He'd asked her to let him go alone, and she'd obeyed. For the second time in her life, she'd yielded and granted his request without a fight. And now she was regretting it. Last time she'd given in to his demand to take care of things alone, all hell had broken loose and she'd nearly lost him. Something in her soul told her this time they would not fare any better.

A snowflake landed on her nose. Tallon sniffled and tilted her chin to the sky to shake it off. In the distance, a glinting purple mass caught her eye. It hovered just above the lower ridge, swirling in and out of the white snowfall in an almost circle-eight pattern. At first, Tallon tried to ignore it. Yet, as it continued its lazy dance around the mountain, she found her gaze drifting in its general direction. Or more precisely, *his* direction. It was Griffon, the hunter. It had to be. He was the only purple-hued dragon of such size who would dare brave this horrid weather for a flight.

At the thought of him, undeniable warmth shimmied up her spine. She shuddered and hunkered farther into her worn-out clothes. Although she could not explain it, Tallon found herself wondering more and more about the hunter. Where he came from, why he left, why he never spoke of his past and, most of all, why he was so haunted and alone. The answers to those questions burned hotter in recent days, and like a moth to flame she flew closer and closer to his light.

Tallon could not place or explain it, but she felt a connection to him somehow. As if he and he alone not only saw but recognized the blackness inside her. As if he knew soul-shattering loss, viscerally and bone deep, and yet unlike her had the ability to mend the pieces.

As Tallon watched him spin and arc in the sky with the deftness of an eagle and the beauty of an angel, for just a moment she forgot how miserable she was.

"There you are."

Tallon started at the voice, hastily sliding her fingers over her damp cheeks. She glanced up, annoyed to see Falcon rounding the cliff wall toward her. Normally, his presence would be a balm, a security blanket and pacifier when nothing else soothed her. But something inside her churned, wild and enraged. The fact that his handsome face appeared calm, his nerves weren't frayed to pieces and his heart wasn't blackened with loss nettled her.

"You shouldn't be out here at this hour."

"I can handle myself, thanks," she said, loathing the sarcasm evident in her voice.

A frown creased his brow and his smile fled. "I know you can. That's not what I meant. It's freezing out here. You could catch your death."

She opened her mouth, about to say she didn't care if she died out here of pneumonia or not, but thought better of it. Falcon had always been her touchstone, her rock. She wanted to upset him about as much as she wanted Declan to love that vampire.

When seconds and then minutes ticked past and she made no attempt to move, a loud male sigh sounded over the wind howling in her ears. "Why don't you come back inside with me?"

Tallon glanced up. She stared at the calloused hand reaching down for her. Thought about what he offered. Take his hand and walk inside. Move forward. Go on with life as normal. Without Declan.

A tide of anger and resentment swelled inside her. "Why don't *you* leave me alone," she snapped, pushing up to stand on her own.

He instantly turned, reaching for her. "Tal, I know you're hurting…."

She shooed his arm away, keeping distance between them. "You don't know anything about how I feel right now, so don't try to comfort me."

For a moment, Falcon didn't move. Then his outstretched hand fell to his side and his jaw tightened. The howling wind picked up strands of his dark hair, dancing the long strands along his handsome face. "You're scared of losing someone you love." His eyes bored into hers, too all-seeing, too beautiful. "Right now, I know *exactly* how that feels."

Her heart seized and all the air left her in a whoosh. Oh, gods. Not this again, not now. "Falcon, don't do this," she began, but he took a step toward her, and then another, the bare emotion in his eyes silencing her.

"Do what? Tell the woman I love how I feel? Tell her that it's killing me to sit idly by and watch her in pain? Tell her how impotent I feel to not be able to help, when everything inside me is screaming to do whatever I can to ease your ache?"

"Stop," she whispered. Knowing how much he sacrificed by voicing his feelings aloud cut her to the bone as effectively as his words. To realize with brutal agony that not long ago she would have been overjoyed to hear those very words fall from his lips devastated her.

More guilt, more pain.

Two emotions she did not need to feel any more of at the moment. In fact, she wished she didn't feel anything at all. Wished her body looked as broken as she felt. Briefly, she wondered if that was why she sat out here in the subzero temperatures, hoping to numb her outsides along with her insides.

"You don't want to hear me say it," Falcon continued, his calm voice deceptively masking the barely veiled pain etched on his face. "You don't think you deserve my love or anyone else's." Hands curled around her upper arms, pulling her into his. "But you do," he said, shaking her slightly on the last syllable as if the act could jar her into believing him. "And if it takes forever for you to realize that, then I'm willing to wait that long."

"Stop." Tallon closed her eyes and shook her head. She couldn't breathe, couldn't think….

"I'll wait for *you* forever."

"Stop!" Tallon shouted, her chest heaving. "You don't love me, Falcon. You don't even know me. And you sure as hell can't fix me."

Pushing against his chest, she backed out of his hold. Falcon let her arms go without a fight. The hurt and confusion in his green eyes made her hate herself even more. To realize he offered everything that the unbroken and happy Tallon wanted yet this new Tallon could not fathom, shredded her soul.

Wrapping her arms around her chest, she shook her head and took one step back.

"Do yourself a favor and don't wait that long," she

said, the soles of her worn boots sinking into the snow and the image of Falcon burning behind her eyes. "I don't love you, Falcon. Not now. Not ever."

The moment the last word fell from her lips, Tallon turned and ran back inside the mountain. Unsure if she'd said those words for Falcon's benefit or hers.

IN DRAGON FORM, Declan sank his talons into the same sandy beach where he'd taken Alexia that night she'd fallen off the cliff. Turning, he tipped his head and sniffed. Again, only faint traces of blood filled the air. Shaking his powerful shoulders, Declan shifted form. He closed his hand around the tracer dangling from his neck, snapping it free with one swift tug.

No matter what he thought he saw, he refused to yield to a dream. He had to believe she yet lived. Following the faint but steady beat of red on the tracer, Declan took the hidden stairs he'd spotted the last time he'd stood on this beach. A soft breeze sent a slight scent of the horde to his nose. Once at the top of the stairs, the rock leveled off and the moss fell away to sand. A secret beach with a crystal pool of water filled by a nearby waterfall stood before him, nothing more. Frantic, Declan held the tracer out before him and swept his arm in a wide arc. Squinting, he stared down at the device in his hand in defeat.

It indicated Alexia was in the rock beneath the pool.

Chest heaving, he looked around the quiet night. The moon reflected off the still water, so it appeared more like a sheet of glass than liquid. He stood for only a moment before dropping the tracer in a small plastic bag he'd stowed in his pants. Shoving it in his back pocket, Declan dove headfirst into the pool. The dark water enveloped him, but only for a moment. As if led by a string, he burst through the surface, coming up on the other side inside a cave.

An underwater cave on the other side of the mountain.

Reaching forward, he arched his arm through the water, pulling himself to shore. Shiny black pebbles dug into his feet as he padded up the hidden beach. Bending at the waist, he covered his knees with his hands and looked around. It took a moment, but his eyes adjusted to the pitch-blackness of the cave. Outlines and shadows formed until he could see the fissure opening in the walls in front of him, but no soldiers, no guards.

Standing, he tossed wet hair off his face and reached in his back pocket, pulling out the plastic bag. He ripped it open, flipping on the device as he stepped inside the crevice. The tracker's constant red blinking flashed quicker with each step he took.

He was close.

Hope and worry sent him into a jog. Darting his eyes to the left and right, he ran down the narrow passageway. The air ahead warmed by degrees and the scent of blood grew stronger. Panic rose inside him. Declan ignored it. Panic wouldn't get him there. Panic wouldn't help her.

He turned a corner. Soft light shone down the tunnel where an opening yawned in the passageway. The tracer began flashing so fast it was almost constantly red. Declan slowed to a cautious walk once he was a few feet from the light. When he heard nothing, he poked his head out. The passage opened into a massive grotto. Hundreds of candles burned, illuminating the darkness. Chairs faced a stone dais to the left. A gory tapestry depicting the dark times, the times when vampire warlords reigned instead of female monarchs, took up the back of the stone stage, like a painted curtain.

The cavern from the dream.

Images from the dreadful nightmare seized him, gripping him like a hand about the throat. He drew in violently for breath. "Alexia," he said on the exhale.

The tracking stick slipped from his fingers as his wings snapped wide and he took to the air. Hovering twenty feet above, he stared at the exact picture he'd dreamt of less than an hour ago. His heart almost seized at the carnage below him—the rows of chairs, the massive wood pillar smeared with blood and…

"No." Two bodies lay twisted and broken on the grisly stage below. One had hair the color of spun gold.

Declan torpedoed to the ground. Tucking his wings back, he ran for the altar, hurdling over broken furniture and boulders to get to her. His heart pounded in a savage beat against his ribs. Each strident thud hammered with such force he expected it to break free of his chest.

Skidding on his knees, he slid through what must have been pints of blood coating the stone floor beneath her. Reaching out, he tugged on the ropes binding her ankles. It wasn't until he moved to his knees and began unwinding her wrists that he noticed the thick broadsword speared through her middle.

The pounding of his pulse stopped and all the air left him.

No. He thought the word this time, but couldn't say it. Couldn't find enough breath to speak it.

With his mind, body and fingers numb, he worked methodically on freeing her. First he yanked out the sword and then used it to cut her bonds.

When she fell, Declan clutched her limp body to his chest. It wasn't until he felt the weight of her against him that the truth hit. He sucked in a deep, ragged breath.

"No, no, no." He held her tight, repeating in a mindless litany the one word he'd been thinking since he'd awoken from that awful vision. As the truth that this was no longer a dream but reality sank in, his legs shook and then gave out completely. He collapsed on the hard ground.

Cradling her against him, he gazed down, smoothing her stained hair out of her face. Her skin was blue, nearly translucent. Dirty yellow bruises covered her cheek and temple, evidence of Lotharus's cruel and brutal feed at her mauled neck.

Everything he'd seen in that horrifying nightmare had come to pass.

Gods, the way she'd suffered.

The memory of how she died, how she'd been murdered splintered through him. He beat his fist against the ground, relishing the dull ache vibrating into his hand. Hoping it might take away some of the agony, the anger, the helpless fury threatening to suffocate him.

It didn't.

He stared down at her. "I'm so sorry," he whispered. Bending his head to hers, he shut his eyes and bit down hard on his jaw to keep the soul-shattering sobs from sounding.

He felt a slight thud move against him. Declan bolted upright. Alert, his eyes darted around for a cause. He could see nothing. Hear nothing. Frowning, he looked back down at Alexia. He felt the vibration again, only this time his eyes zeroed in, catching the faint pulse fluttering beneath her skin.

"Alex?" Hope sucked his tears dry. Cupping the side of her face, Declan gave her a shake. "Alex!"

When she didn't move, he bent his head to her chest. Closing his eyes, he whispered what could only be a prayer, and held his breath. Waiting. His ears picked up the faint thump of her heartbeat again. When he doubted it and lingered, another one followed, only softer this time. His mind reeled, backpedaling to believe the truth before him.

She's alive!

Frantic, he darted his eyes around for something, anything that could save her. But he was alone. Only a halo of blood circled her body.

Blood.

The air stuck in his lungs. He held it in as the lunacy of his plan raced through his mind. Gods forgive him, but he knew what he had to do. Grabbing her under the arms, Declan yanked her closer onto his lap, propping her head on his hip.

Her head lolled to the side when he released it and brought his wrist to his mouth. Baring his fangs, he bit down hard, tearing the top layer of skin from his wrist.

Blood gushed in his mouth, the coppery flavor smothering him and sparking the vampire within him to life. He suppressed it and focused on her.

Tilting her chin, he suspended the flow of blood over her lips. The droplets splattered on her unmoving mouth. Faster, quicker they fell, the crimson blood collecting in a pool against her lips instead of sliding inside them. Panic swelled, nearly strangling him. Swallowing down despair, he bent over her and closed his eyes.

"Stop fighting it, Alex," he said against her temple before placing a kiss upon it. "Drink for me. Live for me. Please."

The side of her face and neck felt like ice where she touched him and he could no longer make out the beat of her heart. Still, he could not pull away his arm, couldn't give up on her. "Please live," he repeated in a fierce whisper. "Please. Please."

For a moment he thought perhaps the gods knew that what he attempted was wrong. But he lived, did he not? Tallon lived. Aberrations they may be, but they lived. As Alexia needed to live. Rage, helplessness, resentment uncoiled inside him to think she would not. To think the spark of hope he'd just experienced had been a cruel lie.

"Drink, damn you!"

At his shout, teeth, sharp and long, drilled into his flesh. Declan gasped at the shock only to smile in relief.

Alexia whimpered and lifted her hands to his wrist, keeping him imprisoned. The immortal life inside her must have sensed death, for she now fought for life with a vengeance. Declan wasn't fighting back. In fact, he willed his blood faster as it rushed into her.

"Yes. That's it. Take it. Take what you need," he murmured.

Closing his eyes, he focused on offering his life to her. For the second time in as many minutes, words that could only be likened to prayers repeated over and over in his mind until coherent words failed him.

As she fed, Declan placed all his attention on her. Her eyes were closed. Her cheeks, once an icy shade of blue, became flushed, warm and rosy. Her body, once rigid with death near, now pulsed and throbbed with vibrant life.

A wave of dizziness struck him. He closed his eyes and nearly passed out from the vertigo. Light-headed and weak, he felt the elbow supporting him buckle. Declan fought to remain upright, but without his arms to buoy him, his abs gave out. He collapsed back, the dirt floor pillowing his head.

At the movement, her fangs dislodged. Declan rolled his head to the side so he could see her. After she slid her mouth from his wrist, a smile crossed his to see her moving, to see her alive. However, when her face pinched, her mouth opening in a silent scream, he frowned and sat up, worried. Forgetting his weakness, he cupped the back of her head, supporting her weight as her slim body convulsed in his arms.

"Alex." His shout came out with a low croak. She didn't respond. "Alex."

Her back bowed with such force he nearly dropped her. Small and frantic, her fists beat against his chest as she visibly fought some invisible war raging within her body. Declan could do little more than hold on to her and wait. Doubt and fear ate at him. It killed him to think he'd caused her any pain.

However, within seconds, her skin became hot to the touch. This time when she opened her mouth, a sharp cry pierced the air and faint wisps of smoke curled out of her mouth.

At the sight, relief flooded Declan. "Shh," he hummed, whispering soothing reassurances in her ear. After a few moments, her body calmed. Smoothing his palm over her head, he kept his head to her ear, his cheek against hers. Eventually her breathing slowed, became less of a struggle. Straightening wisps of hair away from her face, Declan tilted his head to look into her face.

When he pulled back, his breath caught.

He gazed down into two of the most beautiful amethyst eyes he'd ever seen.

Dragon eyes.

CHAPTER NINETEEN

ALEXIA KNEW SHE STARED up at Declan and immediately thought she was either dreaming or dead. A low throb pounded behind her temples. And her eyes weren't working right. Everything seemed so bright and colorful, almost as if she stared through a kaleidoscope.

"Declan?"

His face beamed before he swooped down, covering her mouth with his in a tender kiss that stole her breath. He kissed her like a man starved for the taste of her. As if she were blood and he'd gone for days without feeding. As if he thought he'd never see her again.

When he pulled back, she reached up and touched his face. "Where am I? What happened?"

His smile faded and he swallowed hard. "Lotharus."

A frown tightened her brow as she tried to wade

through the fuzzy memories seeping through her mind. Bold images pricked her thoughts. The crystal…Dragon Island…the ascension…Lotharus's sword.

A lance of pain sliced through her body as that memory bombarded her, sharp and lifelike. Warm hands cupped her face, holding on to her like an anchor as she rode out the storm of dying for a second time. When she finally pulled to shore, Declan's face was all she saw.

"Where did he go, Alex? Where is Lotharus now?"

Alexia tried to focus, tried to pluck some memory out of the foggy haze that engulfed her. And then it all came rushing back. "He's gone," she said through gritted teeth. "Gathering horde to…fight the dragons…but doesn't make sense…too risky with the sun…"

"Shh, it's all right." He cradled her in his arms, rocking her as one would a child. "We are ready for them."

The pain increased, nearly blinding her with the strength of the next convulsion. She gasped and clutched a hand to her stomach, forcing down a need to vomit. Sweat dotted her forehead and an acrid taste burned the back of her throat. What had she done the hours before her ascension?

Ascension. She groaned. "He has my power. The crystal. Aghhhhh!" The sharp, stabbing pain had her crying out. "Wh-what's happening to me?"

"You'll be fine, I promise." Soft lips kissed her damp temple. Her skin absorbed his scent, his essence and it instantly calmed the burning pain inside her.

"How did you find me?"

A large hand flattened on her back and slowly began rubbing up and down. "I dreamt of you, of this place."

The vibrations of his voice soothed her. As if her body were made of water, each tone sent a ripple of relief pulsing through her.

"Don't stop talking. Please," she begged.

He laughed a low male chuckle that made her womb clench. "All right," he said. And then he began telling her the story of them. How this beautiful, sexy woman, this little vampire, had managed to cage him when no one else could. How the first time he'd seen her, his body had reacted with a want his mind told him repeatedly he could not recognize. But that every time she came near him it became harder and harder to resist the pull, resist the urge to kiss her lovely lips, even though it went against everything he had ever been taught, ever believed. Even more amazing, he knew that every conflicting emotion, every spark of infatuation coursing through him echoed through her.

"When I awoke to find you gone, all I could think of was making sure you were all right. After the soldier told us of Lotharus's plan, I couldn't formulate my own fast enough. And when I woke from that dream of your ascension, my heart was screaming you were gone and I thought I'd never breathe again."

A knot twisted in Alexia's throat. She wanted to tell him it had nearly killed her to leave his bed that night. That thoughts of him and only him were the last ones streaming through her conscious mind as the life had drained from her body. But the words wouldn't come. So she listened, his voice helping to fight the unbearable agony slicing through her body.

"Since the night I met you, first tasted you," he said in a low rumble by her ear, "I've been dreaming about you. Only, as you said, they aren't just dreams. They are memories. We are connected, little vampire. I believe we were meant to be connected. And now we are one."

Alexia frowned at his cryptic words, but a fresh spike of agony lanced through her. It felt like her insides were on fire. Even his voice no longer helped. Alexia chewed her lip and scissored her thighs. Unable to take it any longer, she released the sob she'd been stoically holding in. Curling her fingers into his biceps, she buried her face in his chest, resting her forehead on his body. The contact made the ache inside her worse.

"Declan." She cried his name in a whimper, making

his heart rip. He wished he could take the pain for her. However, he knew there was only one thing that would ease the endless ripple of agony eating through her body.

But he couldn't claim her here. Not in this place. Not like this.

Declan hooked his arms beneath her knees and tucked her against his chest. His gaze shot left and then right, looking for a way out of this place. His breath soughed in and out of his lungs, each one coating them with the scent of her anguish.

Forcing himself to calm down, he closed his eyes and focused on memories of her, on something that might help him get her somewhere safe and private for what he was about to do. Blinding and vivid, images flipped behind his eyes. Declan shot them open and took off at a jog for the back of the cavern.

A door.

A hallway.

Another door.

He moved through the underground tunnels and passageways as if he'd been here before, as if he knew these walls like his own.

The air all around him felt still, eerie. No voices, no footfalls. Only the constant beat of his heart thrumming in his ears.

Her room. There.

Declan kicked the door open, repeating the action to close it before he strode inside. He ignored every detail of her massive chamber save for the one thing he needed.

The bed.

She whimpered when he laid her down, her long body writhing against the sheets in an instinctive invitation. His body tightened knowing he would soon have the one thing he'd been craving since he'd first seen her those nights ago.

Dropping down to her, he froze. He knew what he needed to do, but wasn't sure he could. Not without telling her what he'd done, why she felt his urgent need for him, why she felt different.

"Alex," he breathed.

She pinched her eyes, her head tossing back and forth. Hooking a finger under her chin, he forced her eyes to his. "Alexia, look at me." She complied. But at the pure agony and torture on her face, he decided he could tell her later and pulled her to her feet. Once she was steady, he removed the dirty gown and tossed it aside. The intoxicating scent of her arousal perfumed the air around him. His mouth watered and his cock throbbed with need. When he pulled back, the sight of her sent his heart kicking against his ribs.

So beautiful. So delicate. The beast within him roared to dominate her, to pound into her hard and fast and claim her as his own. The urge so intense and overpowering he didn't know if he could hold it at bay. Tremors raked his body and blood roared behind his ears. Granite-hard, his shaft stood out from his body, reaching for her heat. The stories he'd heard about all his life finally rang true with a vengeance.

Dragons were fiercely violent when they mated.

Mated.

An intense wave pulsed between them, beckoning him to her. His fingers bit into her hips, holding her an arm's length from him. "Alex," he panted, his voice as shaky as the rest of him. "I can't do this without telling you."

Small hands grabbed his face, hard, yanking him to her lips. Claws scored his cheeks as her warm tongue speared between his lips. Declan groaned at the sweet pain and wound his arms around her waist, pinning her against him.

ALEXIA CRIED into his mouth. The friction of his skin on hers was more powerful and intoxicating than she had expected. It was like she was freezing cold and only he could warm her. Frantic, desperate, their bodies, mouths, souls did all they could do to get closer. Yet, it was never close enough. An unquenchable burning smoldered inside her. An itch she could not reach, much less scratch and soothe. But she knew Declan could. Knew only he could tame the wild inferno raging inside her.

"Please," she begged, tearing her mouth from his. "I can't wait anymore."

Turning, she rested her hands on the bed frame and bent forward, offering herself to him. Anticipation thrummed through her. Her sex pulsed, greedy, hungry, waiting for him to ease the ache. Seconds melted into minutes. She looked over her shoulder to see what kept him and her breath stuck in her throat.

He stood, fists swollen, face drawn tight in a mask of rage. In a flash, he reached out, seizing her shoulders in a firm grip, spinning her around.

"You never do that with me," he bit out, his face inches from hers. "Ever. Do you understand? Not with me."

Shocked, she could little more than nod. The flames of rage died in his eyes. It was after that she saw the sorrow and affection burning behind them. Then he closed his eyes and enveloped her in his embrace.

"I'm sorry," he whispered fiercely. Wet and hot, his kisses scored her throat, easing the wounds she'd already forgotten about. Shivers danced along her skin. She tipped back her head and wrapped her arms around his neck. "For everything," he said in a dark, seductive voice as he lifted her in his powerful arms and set her back on the edge of the bed.

DECLAN'S HEART SPLINTERED into a thousand fragments when she turned, submitting to him the way he'd seen Lotharus take her. He'd barely been able to control his fury. It had been her eyes that had brought him back from the edge. Those beautiful pink eyes, blinking up at him with awe and complete surrender. In that moment, he realized she'd given herself to him. That she trusted him enough to go through something that had never been pleasurable for her, to please him.

He could not change the past, but he could take control of the future.

Inclining his head, he bent his lips to hers, his eyes never leaving her face. When their mouths would have touched, he held back, hovering over her. Their breath mingled. The delicate, feminine scent of her crackling through him like lightning, summoning him to her. His shoulders shook and tension coiled his insides, but he did not move. He wanted her to come to him, wanted her to have all the control, all the power for once. She already wielded it over his heart, but he wanted to give her power over his body.

A hand cupped his cheek and he jumped at the contact. The demand to mate tackled him. His hands gripped the edge of the bed frame in a white-knuckled grip, holding himself back, fighting a nature inherent to his kind since creation.

"Declan, please. I need you."

She did. He could see it on her face. Dots of sweat covered her brow and dark circles lay under her sallow eyes. If he didn't claim her soon, she would wither. Her newfound strength would ebb and she would slip back into the untimely death his blood had saved her from. Yet, it still wasn't enough for him to let go of the reins and give in to the dragon.

"Don't want to…hurt you," he panted.

"You can't hurt me. I'm burning already."

He shook his head. "Don't understand." Every muscle in his arms shook. The tendons burned, feeling like he held an avalanche away from her.

Long and smooth, her legs wound around his waist, pulling him close where he tried to keep back. His body tensed as she scooted forward so her butt rested on the edge of the bed. Her breasts jostled with the movement, heavy and perfect. The nipples puckered so tight it looked painful. His mouth watered to taste them. An unseen force pressed on his head, trying to fulfill his silent desire.

He yanked back only to have another pull of her emerging dragoness pheromones beckon him back to her. His hips bucked forward and showers of light burst in front of his eyes. This time she felt it, too. Her body answered back, arching toward him. A visible shudder trembled over her skin and her eyes widened in understanding.

"I think I do."

Sitting up tall, a sense of wonder in her eyes, she tangled her fingers in his hair and pulled herself up to his mouth. His bones melted at the feel of her warm lips sliding against his. A low purr hummed out of her and she did it again.

ALEXIA KNEW HIS RESTRAINT hung by a thread. Knew only a thin fiber of control stood between the gentle, caring lover before her and the beast that would ravish and claim her. Heat pooled between her legs at the thought. Although she recognized and admired what he tried to do, whatever happened had changed her. She needed him as badly as he needed her.

"Please," she murmured, brushing the tips of her sensitive nipples against his chest. "Let go." Another spike of need pulsed through their bodies. They both tensed and held their breath. Alexia clung to his back, her open mouth covering the apple of his shoulder.

"Mating is the…" he groaned as another jolt wrapped around them, drawing them together "…only way to stop this. It's what you need. Me inside you."

Alexia leaned back and gazed into his face. His eyes were completely black, the pupils dilated, covering up the blue. Without taking her gaze from his, she reached down to his hand. It took more force than she imagined to yank him free from the bed frame. She wouldn't be surprised if the wood bore the indent of his fingers.

"Touch me," she said, placing his hand over her naked breast.

His chest heaved and his nostrils flared. And then, whatever leash held him back snapped. He lunged for her and she met him, accepting the full brunt of his assault with contented relief. Ravenous, his mouth covered her lips. Alexia captured his kiss, claiming him in return with equal lust and fervor. A primal sound rumbled through his chest. The desire she heard in his groan made made her yearn to be claimed.

Heavy and thick, he covered her. She cried out in bliss at the feel of their bodies clashing together, clawing to get closer. The hand on her breast flexed, squeezing and kneading her flesh. Declan bent, taking the aching tip in his mouth, sucking, curling his tongue around it and nipping the sensitive peak with his teeth.

Liquid heat shot through her veins, pooling between her legs. "Declan," she whimpered.

He released her nipple. Cool air kissed the damp skin, making it crimp tighter, reach up for the heat of his mouth. But his head lifted, his gaze settling on her face. Eyes dark with passion, he kept his gaze on hers as the hand on her waist slid lower. Alexia let her knees fall open. The move had his heavy body sinking into the cradle of her hips. Her eyes fluttered shut at the delicious contact. So close. Soon.

DECLAN REACHED BETWEEN her legs, his hand covering her sex. A low groan tore from his throat at the feel of her. Gods, she was fire, burning, slick against his fingers. His cock pulsed, begging to plunge inside her heat. Feeling like he'd desired nothing but this for so long.

"Please," she panted, her hips arching into his hand. "I don't know what's wrong with me. I'm burning."

He knew. Gods, he knew.

"Declan, I need…"

"I know."

Her body was telling him what she needed, as if she hadn't spoken it eloquently enough already. The exotic fluid of her need bathed her skin. His fingers slipped between her pink folds with ease. Blood rushed to the tip of his already stiff cock, engorging it even further. Hard and heavy, his balls throbbed with the need to come, to give her what she longed for. Instead he glided a finger inside her heat. Her tight walls gripped him, greedily hugging his finger and sucking it deeper. Gods, he couldn't breathe, couldn't think of anything other than how amazing she was going to feel wrapped around him.

He wanted to dive down and taste her, wanted to worship every inch of her. But he knew now what she required to live was not his tongue but his seed coating her womb. She whimpered when his hand left her, sighing when he positioned the swollen head of his cock at the heart of her.

ALEXIA PIVOTED HER HIPS, trying to ease him inside, but he held back. Bending over her, he set his mouth to hers, his tongue slipping between her lips, sampling the moist recess of her mouth. Alexia's head spun, her body vibrated on the edge of madness. Her core contracted, trying to pull the tip of him farther into her body, while she sucked his tongue deeper into her mouth.

Then he pulled back. The flat of his palm skated down her face, a look of awe and wonder filled his eyes before he bent to her once more.

"I love you, Alex," he whispered against her lips before entering her in one plunging stroke, joining them. Alexia cried out as the delicious size of him spread her, stretched her, filled her.

DECLAN HELD HIMSELF INSIDE HER, his face buried in the sweet place between her neck and shoulder. The overwhelming sensation of her wrapped around him was almost too much to bear. Declan wasn't sure he could stand to move. Wasn't sure he could move. But then he was. On primal instinct his body began the dance both of them had been moving toward since he had first fed from her days ago.

At the vibrating pleasure quaking through him, he hissed in a breath and eased inside her an inch, and then two. And each time he did, she took him in, took him deeper. Alexia moaned and tipped her hips. Every gasping sigh and breathy moan spurred him on and reined him in.

Declan stared down at the beauty beneath him. Her blond hair fanned out across the bed, her flushed skin and beautiful eyes. Suddenly, the sight of her was one sense too many, so he closed his. The hot slide of her walls hugging his cock intensified. So warm. So tight. He pressed in and out of her in a deep rocking rhythm, faster, deeper, harder. Each stroke declaring the litany repeating in his mind—*Mine. Mine. Mine.*

Alexia was his, now and forever.

WATCHING DECLAN'S BODY loom above her, his golden skin slick with desire and hot to the touch, nearly sent her over the edge. Alexia clung hard to his shoulders, her fingernails burrowing into his skin as her body crested. At first she tried to hold on, tried to keep the pleasure from taking over her. But Declan wrapped a wing around her back and dipped his mouth to her throat. That amazing voice of his, deep and thick, told her he wanted her to let go, wanted to feel her contract and pulse around him, wanted to hear the sounds she made as she came.

As it had when his mouth tasted her, the muscles of her core burned, knotting tight and hard before melting in a pool of fire. His low, satisfied groan rumbled against her throat, his body shaking as hers quivered to a mind-blowing release. Declan's palm flattened against her thigh, hitching her knee up to his shoulder.

"One more time," he coaxed, grinding his hips and pistoning into her with excruciating perfection. At the feel of his strong, assertive strokes, her back arced and a cry gasped from her throat. Before the first wave of bliss had even receded, another blasted her, overpowering and overwhelming.

This time, he followed her into oblivion. His body tensed and a shuddering groan fell from his lips. The sound of his wings snapping wide echoed in the chamber.

Alexia opened her eyes, marveled at the sight of him above her. His body strained, his wings flared out to the sides, quivering with the force of his orgasm. She'd never seen anything more vibrantly arresting in her life than Declan releasing deep into the sanctuary of her body. Her heart surged, filling her chest until she thought it would burst free.

The raging need for this man, this dragon, to claim her having been fulfilled, her need morphed into the primal urge for his blood. A curtain of red shrouded her eyes and her otherwise replete body begged for something more. The tips of her fangs itched, burning to burrow into his gorgeous flesh. They lengthened, stretching out toward him.

As if sensing what she needed, he leaned his head, offering his neck. Alexia flitted her gaze from his throat to his face, looking for the approval she knew was already there.

"Please," he hushed.

At his verbal cue, she tipped her head to his neck, kissing the skin before plunging her teeth deep in his flesh. Another surge of pleasure raked her womb as the taste of him burst on her tongue. Potent and male, his essence coated her throat. She closed her eyes, savoring every drop of him.

The heat of his mouth covered her shoulder. Alexia

shuddered in anticipation, groaning against his neck when his fangs punctured her skin. Her insides burned, her belly heated from his blood. Sated, she released him and fell back. His arm cradled her head, easing her down and pillowing her head against the bed.

Alexia smiled and turned her head, allowing him access to keep feeding from her. She wanted to be anything and everything he needed. Wanted him to feel complete and satisfied in every way possible, as if her love were food and enough to sustain his very life.

THE MOMENT DECLAN dislodged his fangs, his arms gave out. He didn't fight the respite. Instead, he rested his forehead on hers, placing a kiss on her lips before dipping his head in the crook of her neck. Long and slender, her arms enveloped him, holding him to her.

Declan didn't want to leave her, but he rocked his hips back and up, slipping out of her body. A female whimper sounded in his ears and then the next thing he knew, she pushed on his chest. He fell back willingly, groaning when she sat astride him, her palms resting on his chest. Declan lifted a hand, sweeping aside the long curtain of hair to see her face. She met his gaze with a shy smile, one that made his heart melt.

"Are you feeling better now?" he panted.

Alexia dipped her chin, a blush creeping across her cheeks before her hair fell forward, covering her face again. "Do I look better?"

Although a laugh rumbled through his chest, the sight of her naked perfection above him was anything but funny. His gaze settled on the pink bite mark on her neck, the curve of her breasts, her hips. His head was reeling from the feel of her hands on his body, her perfect butt resting on his thighs and the enticing warmth settled oh-so-sweetly above him.

The weight of her atop him transferred as her hands lifted to push away the mass of unruly hair hanging all around him like a sultry veil. Declan reached out, grasping her wrist in his hand. She stilled the other arm, her body frozen in question above him. Slowly, he pulled her palm to his mouth, brushing his lips in the center of her warm hand.

He felt more than heard her shuddered inhale and it went straight to his already tightening groin. Releasing her hand, he lifted both of his to the edges of her hair, running its silky smoothness between his fingers before bringing it to his lips and kissing it.

She looked down at him with those amazing eyes and suddenly kissing anything but her lips was not enough. Tightening his abdomen, he curled up to sit, cradling her jaw in his palm. He kissed her mouth again, deep and slow. After a few unhurried strokes, Alexia's lips on his became demanding, hungrier. A sound between a moan and whimper hummed in the back of her throat and his body responded to it immediately.

Arms wrapped around his neck, and her hips rocked against his in rhythm with their tongues tangling in each other's mouths. And then with one pivot, Alexia worked him inside her again. Impossibly warm, her body took him in, consumed him. Now it was his turn to groan as she started to ride him.

Declan's entire body vibrated on the edge of bliss, about to fall over it again. Making sure she followed, he wound his tail between them. The tip found the place their bodies were joined, massaging the sweet little button he couldn't quite reach with his hands. A gasp tore from her lips and a shudder raked the muscles beneath Declan's palms. His victorious smile faded as her inner walls clenched and flexed, hugging him tight and sending him over that precipice with her.

TALLON PACED THE LENGTH of her chamber, her mind reeling. Declan had been gone for hours with no word and still the council would not act, would not go after him. She vibrated with anger, hate and confusion. She wanted to pull her hair out. Scream until she lost her voice. Smash something to pieces to match her fracturing soul.

Blindly, Tallon reached out, snatching a vase of half-dead flowers someone had given her at her parents' burial ceremony. With a howl, she pitched it across the room. The sound of the container shattering did nothing to ease the empty ache inside her, so she picked up another object and another until she'd broken every piece of glass in her chamber.

Chest heaving, she stared at the pieces of glass strewn on the floor, feeling every bit as broken, every bit as scattered. Tears threatened. She nearly couldn't keep them back. But she managed to swallow them down. Instead, she let the weakness, the helplessness she felt stoke and feed her anger. Pivoting, she grabbed the back of the nearest chair and sent it sailing across the room. She turned over furniture, tossed books from their shelves, decorations off their tables until there was nothing left standing.

The empty hole pulsing inside her didn't abate. Tallon braced her palms against the granite wall and closed her eyes. The strident pounding of her heart and her gasping breath was the only sound in the room. Desperation and misery suffocated her. Its claws were digging into her, dragging her down. Yet, the faint desire to not lose herself bubbled up from somewhere inside her. A desperate need tried to surface, to reach out and grasp any anchor that might keep her from floating down the dark path her heart had started down. She held her breath, letting it out in a low cry when her hope sank back into the abyss.

It was too late.

She didn't care anymore.

About anything.

With a choked cry, she pulled back her fist, smashing her knuckles against the jagged stone wall as hard as she could. A lightning bolt of pain shot up her arm, momentarily silencing the storm raging inside her. She gasped at the sensation. Finally, she felt something other than hopelessness. Grimacing, she jabbed the wall harder this time. Again and again she struck the hard surface. Until her hand bled, until her bones felt shattered to powder, until a broad arm wrapped around her, pulling her away from the wall and pinning her back against a very hard, very male frame.

"Whoa, there, little one," a deep voice spoke in her ear.

Tallon bent forward, taking him with her before kicking back her elbow, lodging it in his side.

He grunted. "Ease up," he said, his voice calm, his hold on her tightening.

Ignoring him, she began to repeat the move. But his leg

kicked out, swiping across hers, knocking them out from under her. Tallon let out a cry as she fell to the floor. However, she didn't hit the ground. Strong arms shifted their hold on her, spinning her almost three hundred and sixty degrees before slamming her up back against the wall.

Tallon gasped at the force, blinking once, twice before her vision cleared. At the sight of the hunter looming large and dark in front of her, carnal heat crackled through her. But her anger overrode it.

"You," she gasped. "Let me go." She squirmed beneath his hold.

"So you can punch walls again? I don't think so."

"This is *my* room. I can punch whatever I want to."

"Sorry, little one," Griffon said, his muscles bulging as he held her back with infuriating ease. "But if you want to hit something, it's going to have to be me."

Tallon stopped fighting to get away. Instead, she tilted her chin to meet his slanted gaze. "I'll do it," she panted. "Don't think I won't."

He regarded her for a moment before releasing her and stepping back, a slight smile tweaking his lips. "Go ahead," he said, opening his arms to the sides. "Take your best shot."

Without stopping to think, Tallon swung out her arm, landing a right hook on the side of his face. Although he didn't budge, her hand throbbed in agony at the contact. She realized she should have used her left hand instead of the one she'd used to punch the wall. Angered at the pain, at life and, most of all right now, at him, she swung again. This time her uppercut punch landed on his chin. Bone hit bone. His head kicked back, but straightened almost right away. Again, his lips curved.

"Feel better now?"

"No," she breathed.

His smiled widened. "Good. Then I guess it's safe to tell you that you hit like a fledgling."

A haze of red blanketed her vision, and her fangs dropped. Griffon's eyes flashed and he widened his stance, as if this was what he'd been waiting for. "Here we go," he said under his breath, preparing for her attack.

Tallon made sure not to disappoint. Snarling, she lunged, sending her arm out in a wide arc. He blocked the move with ease, his big body scooting agilely out of the way. At her startled reaction, he let out a chuckle, his eyes taunting her. Tallon narrowed hers and dove forward, and again, he deflected her. Only this time, a hand clamped around her wrist and pulled. The offensive move took her by surprise and she slipped into his arms. In a fluid move, he curved her back over his forearm and bent over her. His face hovered inches above hers.

"Do you want to dance or fight?"

For the first time in her life, Tallon snapped her teeth toward another dragon's throat with the intention to harm, perhaps even kill.

"Ah, finally a challenge," his smooth voice hummed as his grip tightened on her waist.

He leaned back just far enough to where she could not reach him. Tallon brought her leg up fast and hard. The ball of her knee crushed his side. Griffon let loose a grunt, his body instantly curling in on itself to protect the wounded area from another attack. Tallon used the advantage to push out of his hold.

For a moment, she thought she'd gotten clear of him. But in a quick move, he grabbed her, spun and released her. She landed on her stomach on the ground. Hands clutched hers behind her back, not painfully tight, but firm. A shadow darkened above her, the warmth of his big body covering her like a blanket as he settled in a squat above her, his knee at the small of her back.

"Do you yield?" he asked, his breathing short and taxed.

"No." She wriggled her shoulders, trying to break free of his hold. A deep male chuckle filled her ears and his grip tightened. Then he bent, his mouth hovering beside her temple.

"Come on, little fledgling," he said in a low voice, honey smooth against her ear, his words warming her skin. "Do… You… Yield?"

Frustrated and exhausted, Tallon rested her forehead against the cool stones, letting her body relax into the floor. Closing her eyes, she shook her head. At her surrender, Griffon released his hold and eased off her. Tallon exhaled and brought her arms forward, sliding her hands under her shoulders. Flattening her palms on the ground, she pressed her upper body off the floor. Sore and weak, her biceps shook with the effort and a small cry rent from her throat.

Arms wrapped around her, gently helping her to her feet. Griffon settled her in front of him, and after a heartbeat, he let her go. Unsteady, she stumbled to the side.

"Whoa," he said, gripping her again, ensuring she'd stay vertical. "Are you okay?"

At the genuine concern in his voice, Tallon looked up, blinking at the tiny knot furrowing his brow. For a split second it appeared he was almost afraid he'd hurt her. Tallon's breath hitched at the random thought. It was then she realized with a start that she actually *saw* Griffon. Not the rogue dragon who had mysteriously turned up at their mountain lair one day. Not the feared and violent hunter with a past murkier than the darkest cave.

Just Griffon.

Tiny beads of sweat formed along his dark hairline, his tan skin flushed from their sparring match. True, his face was scarred and she had thought it imposing. Yet right now she found the marks running down his face undeniably sexy. In fact, it appeared that every cut line of his muscular jaw, even the raised line of the scar itself, seemed etched by an artist.

Utterly black, his hair reminded her of a starless night. Like all dragon lords, it fell in dark waves over his shoulders and down his back, the thick strands framing the masculine structure of his neck and shoulders.

He cleared his throat and Tallon flitted her gaze to his. Deep lavender eyes, edged with thick black lashes, stared down at her, a spark of challenge behind them. One the female in her recognized and instantly rose up to meet. She sighed aloud, her body relaxing, warming.

The grin faded from Griffon's lips. His nostrils flared slightly and something she couldn't quite name sparked in his gaze. Before she could blink, he stalked forward. His heavy body leaned into hers, crushing her breasts against the warm wall of his chest and forcing her back against the wall. A wave of acute pain shifted down her spine as the jagged stones jut against her flesh. He didn't notice, and as his hands closed over her wrists, pinning her arms up by her ears on either side, she no longer cared. The dominating strength and size of him fired her blood and had her purring behind her throat.

He groaned and dipped his head to her neck. Tallon closed her eyes and waited for his lips or his tongue to brush over her sensitive skin. A hum of anticipation vibrated through her, and she felt herself melting against the wall. Instead, he inhaled her scent in a deep, strong pull. Erotic and slow, he rose up, following the arc of her neck. The tips of his hair brushed against her skin, sending a shiver down her spine.

When he leveled his gaze on her again, Tallon noticed his eyes had darkened, only the barest hint of indigo evident now in their shadowed depths. She swallowed again for what felt like the hundredth time since he had come into the room, and his gaze slid to her throat. The air between them charged by degrees, heat rising. The heavy pullover clinging to her skin felt leaden.

One of his hands shifted from her wrist, grasping her hip bone. Her body reacted to his touch, her hips bucking toward him. He dropped his gaze to his hand as if in awe of his power over her. His fingers bit into her flesh, gripping her hard and yet not hard enough. Still, she whimpered at the contact. A shudder quaked through his massive body, mirroring the tremors buzzing through her.

And then it happened. A slow burn she could only liken to fire ignited inside her, soft and warm. Liquid, the heat poured through her tired and aching muscles, spreading out in all directions. A mewling sound hummed out of her, and her hips again instinctively rocked into his. Griffon's head snapped up, his gaze roamed her face, passing through shock, to anger, to surrender.

He felt it, too, she thought, this undeniable, clawing need, like lust on steroids.

"Tallon," he breathed her name. The sound both a question and an answer that tightened the knot of desire already twisting low and hard in her belly. He released her wrist, curving his fingers around her face. Large and warm, his hand caressed her cheek, his thumb sliding across her lips, her cheekbone, before he lowered his head. And, *oh, gods,* he was going to kiss her. And she couldn't wait.

Tallon had never felt feminine and demure, but as his mouth lowered, she could have sworn her eyelids actually fluttered closed. Then, soft and tentative, his lips brushed against hers and all thought drained away. All she could focus on was the feel of him. Tallon's heart stuttered in her chest, her sex clenching. Without taking the time to process the hows or whys, she kissed him back, pressing her mouth to his harder, more urgent lips. The taste of him, rich and masculine, made her want more. His scent, earthy with hints of leather and man, overwhelmed her senses and blurred her reason.

Tallon reached out, fisting the front of his tunic, pulling him closer. His body leaned aggressively into her, every rock-hard line molding against her softer ones with aching precision. His mouth covered hers, kissing her deeper. Each slide of his lips, each angle she made to meet his demanding mouth, scraped her skull against the stones behind her, but she didn't care. A low moan rumbled out of him, and his other hand came up to cradle her face with a gentleness she hadn't known he possessed.

When his tongue swept across her lips, Tallon eagerly parted her lips for him. In a velvety arc, his tongue stroked, sampled and tasted her until her head spun from the blissful storm of emotions pounding through her. Caught up in the maelstrom, Tallon lifted her hands to his face, gripping his jaw. She ran her fingers through his hair, smiling against his lips. His midnight hair was soft and smooth, a dichotomy to the hard man towering over her. She loved the way it felt between her fingers. Loved the way he felt in her arms. The way his back rippled with hard muscles. How his warm skin felt, so slick and firm beneath her fingers.

Reckless, wild, Griffon began tugging at the collar of her shirt, as if desperate to touch her in return. The sound of yielding fabric ripped through the room as he tore at her clothes, unveiling the skin beneath. All the while, his scorching and wicked mouth tasted her lips, trailed lower to kiss her throat. Once he had her bare, his hands framed her ribs, moving upward. Tallon sucked in an expectant breath when his palms cupped her breasts, testing their weight in his hands, kneading and teasing each raised nipple. Pleasure shot out in all directions. Her head slipped back involuntarily, a sigh escaping her from the bliss.

Then his lips found hers again. His tongue was in her mouth, his hands all over her. Without breaking the kiss, he leaned back. But only long enough to unbutton and discard his tunic. Then he was back against her, his fevered skin blanketing her body. Tallon immediately wrapped her hands beneath his arms, clutching his broad back to her, flattening her sensitive breasts against his chest. The skin-to-skin contact sent a heady tremble through her, fueling the insatiable fire burning between them.

Skating her palms down every ridge and contour of his back, Tallon lowered them to the swell of his leather-covered ass, pulling him tightly against her as she opened her legs wider to accommodate him. He fell against her and groaned, the sound deep and dark. *Anguished,* she wondered? Before she could process coherent thought, he leaned away from her again. Air pricked her heated flesh, causing her nipples to crimp, tight, aching. She yearned for his hands, his mouth. Yet this time he stepped back far enough to see her, and for her to really see him.

Tallon's body hummed at the sight.

He was big, gorgeous and panting as hard as she was. And she craved him like nothing she could remember.

"Tell me to stop," he breathed. "Tell me to walk out that door and forget this ever happened."

Tallon blinked at his thick voice, surprised at what he said. Then her eyes fell to his broad, muscular shoulders, following the lines to his narrow waist. Tattoos hugged his belly button, another wound around his shoulder and pec, and a hunter's intrinsic designs covered both forearms. However, her eyes fixed on the low-slung leathers embracing his hips, the scant dusting of dark hair peeking out from beneath the zippered seam. A steady throb beat in her core, nearly making her knees buckle. Her tongue darted out, moistening her already kiss-bruised lips.

Realizing she stood ogling him, she forced her gaze to his face and gasped. Griffon's dark eyes were not on her breasts, where she'd assumed they'd be. Instead, he stood watching her drink in the sight of him. His dark eyes hooded, his face taut with desire.

"Don't keep looking at me like that unless you mean it."

Heat fired her cheeks. She shifted her gaze to the floor for a heartbeat before lifting it back up again. "Mean what?"

Instead of telling her, he showed her. Slowly, his heated gaze slid languidly over her body. Each pass made her skin react as if he'd brushed his lips across her flesh. She whimpered and sagged against the wall. At the sound, his focus lifted to her face and a slow grin teased his mouth. He stepped forward, one step, two. Slowly his fingers moved to his pants, unzipping the only barrier keeping her from him as he closed the space between them.

"What about Falcon?" he asked.

"What about him?" she panted, holding her breath as he eased the pants off his sculpted legs and kicked them out of the way.

"You two…" he bit down, his jaw muscles bunching "…care for each other."

Tallon nodded. Falcon cared for her and she cared for him. However, something had snapped inside her since her parents' deaths. She'd meant what she'd told Falcon earlier. He couldn't fix her. But she had a feeling Griffon could wrestle the ugliness inside her and maybe even win. She swallowed. The truth, as ugly and cold as it might sound, fell from her lips.

"I don't want him. Not tonight," she said, reaching her fingers out to trace the outline of the tattoo on his shoulder. His eyes closed and he tipped his chin back. Fixing her gaze on his chest, she stared at the contrast of her small hand on his tanned and tattooed body, feeling a sharp spike of longing through her heart.

"Make me feel something besides the pain."

She wasn't sure she spoke the small plea aloud until a finger tucked beneath her chin, forcing her gaze up.

"So beautiful," he said, caressing her cheek. Her chest rising and falling in small excited pants, she stared up at him with complete surrender. Like any predator, he sensed it immediately. His hands roamed over her shoulders, her breasts, down her body, finally curving around her butt. With an abrupt pull, he tugged her off her feet.

Tallon opened her legs, wrapping her thighs tight around his hips while her arms surrounded his neck. Her breath caught at the feel of him, hard and insistent, at the feel of herself, warm, wet and ready against him. Leaning into her, he positioned her so the wall supported most of her weight. The toothed surface dug into her shoulder blades and the small of her back, but she didn't care.

Just sex, what was left of her conscious mind intoned. *This is just sex.*

Nothing more.

And then he shifted his hips and, with one swift move, pushed himself inside her. Long and impossibly thick, he filled her perfectly. A strangled gasp tore from her lips, at the same time he murmured an expletive against the hollow of her throat. Griffon held himself hilted inside her, his massive body trembling as he fought not to move. Tallon locked her ankles, ensuring he wouldn't.

Then, slowly, he shifted his hips, sliding the hot length of him out almost to the tip before slamming back inside her welcoming body. At the thrust, stars danced behind her closed eyes and her body vibrated with pure hunger. A hunger she sensed in him, as well.

As he pistoned his hips, moving inside her, his hot mouth tasted her neck, his tongue laving and sampling her dampening skin. The muscles in her legs burned, the stones at her back dug deep into her flesh, firing her pain sensors into overload. But the currents of pleasure tearing through her dominated them all. And the rush of sensations made her cry out.

She'd gone from feeling nothing to feeling everything. The solid thickness of him inside her, against her, the pool of fire building and gathering in her core, even the granite scratching her shoulders, they overwhelmed her, bombarding her from every direction, inside and out.

Then, the knot inside her snapped free. She came hard, her body pulsing and throbbing around him. Raw and feral, Griffon groaned, his hips bucking once, twice, before his entire body tensed. Burrowing into the crook of her neck, he gripped her tightly as he released inside her body.

He held himself like that for what felt like both eternity and a second before he shifted his hold on her thighs. Tallon kept her eyes closed as he set her legs back to the floor, easing the pressure off her back. However, Griffon did not let go of her right away, and Tallon found it more difficult than she imagined to finally unwind her arms from his neck. And when he slipped free from her body and released his hold on her, all the emotions she'd been feeling accumulated in her heart.

Tallon put her hand on her chest, realizing that having *just sex* with *just Griffon* may *just* have been the biggest mistake of her life.

CHAPTER TWENTY

ALEXIA STEPPED OUT from behind the closet wall. Her long hair was still damp from her shower. The soft scent of her, clean and feminine, tweaked Declan's nose and made his cock stir. Gritting his teeth, Declan crossed his arms over his chest and turned. Hoping that if he couldn't see her he would be able to control this new level of lust coursing through him since they'd mated. However, he came face-to-face with her bed. The bed where they'd just…

Releasing a groan, he turned back around.

He watched her hitch a booted foot on the counter. With practiced precision, she began securing gun holster straps around her thigh. A flood of saliva washed his mouth at the sight of her creamy legs. Legs he could still feel wrapped around his waist as he'd bucked inside her heat.

The black miniskirt she wore barely grazed the sumptuous curve of her bottom. The calf-high boots sported what had to be at least five-inch heels. Despite her usual preference for leather and constricting corsets, tonight she wore nothing but a simple, long-sleeved black cardigan that draped in a low-cut V to the single clasp at her cleavage, revealing what looked like miles and miles of pale flesh.

"You're going to fight Lotharus," he said, lifting a brow, "in that?"

The corner of her lips curved briefly before they thinned. She smacked a cartridge of rounds into her Glock and slid the pistol in the holder alongside her outer thigh. "I don't plan on getting close enough to get dirty."

Declan took a deep breath and stared at the floor. The abject pain he'd felt when he'd thought her dead, the overwhelming sense of loss, pricked his conscious again at just the idea of anything happening to her. Gods, he knew with absolute conviction he would not survive losing her again.

"Don't think I can do it?"

At her question, he looked up and forced a smile. "No." He uncrossed his arms and stepped to her, taking both of her hands in his. "I know you can. But it's going to be dangerous, Alex. I've only read about what that crystal is capable of. There are so many variables."

Alexia squeezed his hand tight. "All we have to do is get the crystal from Lotharus and destroy it. Together we can do this. I know it."

"But you're still weak, not fully changed, not as strong as you will be."

Alexia pulled back, her eyes wide. "What do you mean, changed?"

"Alexia, you were nearly dead when I found you." He swallowed. "I was too late."

A tiny disbelieving laugh bubbled out of her. "That's absurd. I'm here. Now."

"Only because I fed you my blood."

Her blond brows drew closer. "But I've drank from you before."

The statement sounded more like a question and Declan dreaded giving her the answer. This was what his father had told him about, the clawing guilt and agony of playing a god when you were just a man. He'd given her life, yes. But was it one she wanted? Did she want to be by his side? Did she want to be Queen of the dragons instead of the horde?

"This is different," he said on an exhale.

Seconds felt like minutes until she finally spoke. "What are you trying to tell me?"

"Alexia, you're…changing. It's already begun."

A flame of panic fired behind her eyes, morphing their newfound color to a deep ruby.

"Into what?"

Oh, gods. "One of us."

THE MINUTE ALEXIA heard the words fall from his lips she knew them to be true. Although she couldn't pinpoint it before, she felt different inside. As if that always present, always gnawing darkness that lived inside her for so long had been filled with light.

She glanced back at Declan and her heart throbbed painfully. He looked stricken, like he hung on her words, waiting for the hatchet to fall. Waiting for her to scream at him, and for what? Saving her life?

Alexia walked into his arms and wrapped hers around his neck, pulling him tight. Placing her lips to his ear, she took a deep breath, drawing in the unique and intoxicating essence that was all him.

"Thank you for saving me," she whispered.

A shudder moved through his body. His big shoulders tensed. And then his arms slid around her waist, strong and firm, and her head buried in the crook of his neck. He released a breath, as if he'd been holding it in since he'd told her what he'd done.

At the feel of his embrace, a tremor of joy, of happiness, of completeness rushed through her, making her smile and hug him tighter. His palm cupped the back of her head and her body bowed into him, arcing into the space between their bodies, filling it. The heat from his other hand radiated through her cardigan, seeping across her lower belly.

Goddess, this was what she'd craved. What she'd wished for all her life and only experienced now. Contact, utter, true and uncontrollable. And now there was nothing to keep them away from each other. Instead of destined to be apart, they now had every reason to be together. They could be together. Alexia smiled, her gaze catching on her reflection in the vanity mirror across the room. At first, she hardly recognized herself. No longer did she appear depressed, lonely or sad. Instead the woman staring back her glowed with confidence, life and love.

Love.

It hit her then that she'd never told him. Never said the words aloud.

"Declan," she said, pulling back slightly. His head lifted, his cobalt eyes staring into hers with intensity that nearly stole her breath. "I—" she began.

"Shh." A finger on her lips silenced her. Although a frown tightened her brow, he did nothing but smile. Then his hand moved to her cheek and his lips replaced his finger. Slow and sensual, his mouth slid against hers, their mouths mating as their bodies just had.

"Promise you'll tell me later," he said when they parted.

Alexia smiled. "I promise."

DECLAN FOLLOWED ALEXIA through the maze of the catacomb, even though somewhere in the back of his mind he knew which way to go. All dragons could use mind speak when in animal form. But their connection was a melding of two hybrids and grew stronger with each passing day, making him wonder if one day he'd be able to read her thoughts.

Alexia led them to a wide cavern, much like the one where Lotharus had held the ascension ceremony. At the memory, fire burned behind Declan's throat. He damped it down. He'd be able to use it soon enough. They bent at the waist, hiding behind a shelf of rocks. Peering out the windowless stone opening, Declan realized they were in some sort of crude amphitheater. On the ground below, there appeared to be a stage with seating all around. The level where he and Alexia hid resembled balcony boxes, each one a pocketful of armed soldiers.

"There are a hundred of them at least," he heard himself say aloud.

"All we have to do is stop one," Alexia replied, nodding toward the lower level.

Tipping his gaze back to the stage, he noticed Lotharus sat on what Declan assumed to be the Queen's throne, addressing his soldiers. Although he wore no crown to proclaim his new position in the horde, the staff propped at his side caught Declan's eye. It looked similar to one he'd seen in an auld text. More specifically, the scroll Doc had showed him that contained their knowledge of the dark age. Atop the polished wood staff sat the stone. Its multifaceted surface reflected the candlelight illuminating the cavern. The normally transparent crystal now burned a soft orange and blue. While delicate, the center appeared dark and angry, as if forged of fire, glinting like an opal when bowed to the light.

"He has the crystal with him."

Alexia tilted her head, trying to get a look at him from over the lip of the rock. "How can you be sure?"

"It's there, on top of the staff." He motioned toward it.

A woman passed in front of Lotharus, a tray of goblets in her hands. Declan's gaze followed her, his eyes zeroing in on a strange mark on the side of her throat.

"What is that symbol?"

Alexia looked at him, following his line of sight to the

female. "It's a symbol of our horde. Each pureborn colonist comes into this world with one."

He cocked a brow. "You don't have one."

The corner of her lips twisted in a coy smile. "The royal bloodline has a different kind of mark."

She lifted a hand, sweeping her long curtain of hair over her shoulder, revealing her long neck. When she turned her back to him and put her chin on her chest, he saw it.

"A Lunel," he said. Four crescent moons faced each other, their points hung like fangs. The mark was so intricate he couldn't believe it was natural and not a tattoo.

Pictures flipped in his mind of Lotharus over her, taking her. Declan clamped down his jaw, slamming down the violent, blinding urge to kill and focusing on what the vision was showing him. The Lunel. He saw the mark, had seen it the first time he had the dream, only he was too blindsided by his anger to notice.

It struck him why Lotharus had taken her the way he did. It was never about her. It was about the throne, about power.

Tunneling his hand in her hair, Declan bent, searing his lips on the mark. She sighed and relaxed back against him.

"Only the women born of the royal bloodline have this mark," she said with a sigh. "Everyone else bears two crescent moons to show they are part of our horde."

"On their neck?"

She shook her head. "It can be anywhere."

"Has a child ever been born without a mark?"

Alexia shrugged. "If they were, I would imagine they would be kept hidden or sent away. Lotharus is unwavering in his mission to keep our kind pure. I shudder to think of what he may have done." She paused, her eyes narrowing. "In fact, there was talk years ago about a child. A female heir to the throne born of my uncle, Yuri…"

She paused, her eyes widening before she clutched his forearm. "Declan, the vision."

"What vision."

"There was a child born to the royal family, *my* royal family. A female child, daughter to my uncle and descent of the Queen's line. Declan, I have to—"

A great uproar shook the cavern walls, cutting her words short. Peering over the ledge, Declan swept his gaze across the room, trying to discover the source of the sudden mayhem. It didn't take long.

"What is it?"

"More women."

Alexia scooted close enough to look down at the scene. Shackled women of various ages were being led into the den. They wore what looked like burlap sacks, some frayed and split at the bottom. Each carried a tray of food in toward the unruly soldiers.

"That bastard."

Declan looked over at her. The smooth line of her jaw tensed in anger and her hands bit into the stone.

"Do your women not serve the men?"

Her eyes met his and his breath caught. He wasn't sure if he'd ever get used to those breathtaking eyes. A frown tensed his brow when he realized he hadn't even told her they were a different color, and he wondered briefly if she even knew.

"Women are revered. Women rule. They do not serve, especially not the men. Pureborns know this," she said on a strained breath. "This barbaric depravity is all Lotharus's doing. Only *his* soldiers dare degrade the women like this," she said with a nod, sliding her gaze back to Lotharus.

Declan reached out, his hand covering hers. "You sound ready to stop him."

She turned back to face him, a small smile curving her mouth. "I'm ready to try."

CHAPTER TWENTY-ONE

"MY BROTHERS," LOTHARUS SHOUTED, standing from his throne. Curling his fingers around his staff, he tapped the end on the ground like a mallet. The excited voices quieted at once. A surge of power vibrated through him as he began the speech he'd practiced for a century.

"At last, a new era is upon us. An era we vampires once embraced and accepted, yet let slip away. An age where men hold the seat of power. Where a King, not a *Queen*, rules the horde."

"Not if I have anything to say about it."

Lotharus whipped his head about to see who was speaking, though he already knew. Alexia stepped out from behind an outcropping.

"My dearest Alexia." Casually, he stepped down the short flight of stairs to greet her, a wide smile on his face.

"What a wonderful surprise. I thought you'd passed during your ascension."

The women gasped, whispering praises to the Goddess that the Queen's daughter yet lived, and immediately fell to their knees before her. However, the soldiers tensed their massive bodies, coiled and ready to spring at his order.

Alexia moved her hand to the front of her sweater. In a confident move, she swept the curtain of black fabric to the side, revealing her midsection. "More like you thought you'd killed me."

Lotharus's gaze dipped. At the sight of perfectly smooth skin where a plunging broadsword scar should have been, his smile faltered briefly. However, he recalled the crystal in his hand, remembered he now held all the power and felt his confidence renew.

"A mistake I shall not make again." He nodded toward the crowd. At once his soldiers sprung toward Alexia, following his silent order.

A screaming roar echoed in the catacomb chamber seconds before a gush of flame sprayed down, eating the soldiers in its violent stream. Waves of heat swept across the room, rolling over the chairs and nearly overtaking the stage.

"Get back to the compound," Alexia shouted to the women, who quickly stood and scurried away.

However, Lotharus was focused on the dragon now

turning toward him, its eyes alert, its lips curling back in a snarl. Lotharus knew it was about to strike again. He lifted the hand holding the staff, blocking his face just as flames poured from the dragon's mouth. The hot jets of fire hit his invisible force shield, curving over it, leaving him unscathed. After a moment, the dragon ceased the blast.

Lowering his hand, Lotharus felt a victorious smile curve his lips, and snapped his gaze to Alexia. Her eyes widened as he shot the crystal toward her. Her body tensed, awaiting whatever blow might strike her. However, the earth quaked underfoot as the dragon lord landed in front of her, blocking Lotharus's aim. Massive and black, the dragon paced in front of her like a rabid guard dog. Its jowls snapped and lips quivered as it watched Lotharus. He trained the staff on the *Derkein,* waving the crystal in front of him as if it were made of flame, trying to ward it off or at least back it up. The dragon only gnashed its teeth and took another step forward.

Frustrated, Lotharus lowered his staff and turned to his men.

"Don't just stand there," Lotharus yelled to the soldiers. "Kill it!"

The dragon's blue eyes twinkled with an intelligence no animal possessed before it pushed up, launching twenty feet in the air.

"I'LL FEND THEM OFF, Alex. You have to get that crystal."

Alexia heard Declan's voice in her mind and smiled. "With pleasure," she answered beneath her breath.

Dropping her arms, she clenched a dagger in each hand. Circling him, stalking him, she waited for him to make the first move.

"What do you think to do, Alexia? I taught you everything you know."

A bubble of doubt floated into her mind. She smashed it. She couldn't afford to entertain the notion of failure.

"I have your mother's power. I have your power, right here." He held up the staff. The Draco Crystal glowed, throbbing red like a beating heart. Her eyes narrowed on it for a second before she grunted, tossing the first and then the second dagger at the staff. Lotharus spun with the speed of a tornado, easily evading the weapons as they clanked against the wall behind him.

"Damn," she muttered.

Lotharus cocked his head, his usually immaculate hair falling over his face. "Did you want this?" He twirled the staff in a taunting fashion before releasing a snarl. "You're going to have to come and get it."

Alexia slapped a hand to her thigh, reaching for her Glock. Before her hand touched the holster, Lotharus appeared by her side. "I don't think so, lover." Fingers dug into her scalp and tugged. The next thing she knew she was airborne, flying backward at highway speed. Although she'd braced herself, the crash into the cavern wall sent stars bursting behind her eyes and shot rockets of pain through her body. Limp, she fell forward, landing face-first in the dirt.

"Alex!" Declan screamed her name in a roar. The heavy beat of wings pounded the air above her, followed by the tortured cry of a soldier. Slipping her fingers through the loose earth, she flattened her palms and tested her weight. She winced at the stab of pain lancing between her shoulder blades.

Again, the dragon bellowed, as if her pain were his own.

"I'm okay," she said in an attempt to reassure him. Arms trembling, she pushed herself up to her knees. A boot kicked her stomach. Woofing out a breath, Alexia fell to her side and rolled. Cradling the ache with one hand, she patted her leg with the other.

"Looking for this?"

Lotharus stood over her, dangling her Glock in his fingers. A cloying sense of dread filled her, suffocated her. He was so fast. So strong. Their last battle rolled in her mind and for the first time tonight, she wasn't sure she could beat him.

"You're stronger."

At the voice, Alexia looked up. Declan loomed above her, black and beautiful. He held a soldier in his massive talons. His sapphire eyes fixed on her. Snarling, he tossed the soldier against the far wall with a pitch of his arm.

Suddenly, a rapid cadence of gunfire exploded. The dragon howled, the sound twisting Alexia's heart with an intense ache she'd never experienced before. Steadily, the gun beats continued to ricochet off the walls in earsplitting pings.

A machine gun.

Alexia's eyes instantly zeroed in on the soldier with the weapon.

Gaze scouring the ground, she saw a fallen dagger in the dirt and lunged for it, her body sliding against the rocky ground. Anticipating her move, Lotharus stabbed his staff toward her legs, the sharpened end aiming for one bare thigh. Alexia dodged it and hoisted the blade. Grunting in effort, she arced out her arm, sending the weapon flying across the room.

Without watching to see the knife hit, she rolled, popping to her feet. The machine gun's rattle slowed to a stop. The soldier's dead corpse thudded to the ground an instant later.

Alexia faced Lotharus, ignoring the fact she stood on rubbery legs, ignoring the sensation of her quad muscles literally shaking beneath the cool fabric of her skirt.

"Come on, *lover*," she spat, mocking his words to her earlier. "You know you want it."

His lips curled at the corner. "I already have everything I wanted from you."

Lotharus shot the crystal-tipped staff at her. Sizzling jolts of lightning crackled through her body. The powerful shock wave blasted her off her feet, tossing her in a circle before dropping her on the ground with a thud. The back of her head struck the dirt, making her head throb in a skull-splitting ache. She brought the heel of her hand to her forehead and shut her eyes, hoping to stop the pain.

"Alexia, if you cease this folly, bow to me and declare me King before the horde, I might let you live." Lotharus's voice sounded close. Too close. Alexia forced her eyes open, forced them to focus and immediately saw him above her.

Pursing her lips, Alexia did a backward somersault, rolling up to her feet. "Bite me."

He bared his fangs. "Love to." With that, he launched toward her. His body torpedoed in a spiral, making it impossible to track his moves. Alexia did the only thing she could and braced herself for impact.

DECLAN TENSED, feeling Alexia's pain shoot through him as if he had taken the blow. Daring a look down, his heart thudded. Lotharus had her pinned to her back, his fangs hanging, ready to sink into her flesh.

Something stabbed through his left wing. The tissue sizzled and burned. Declan kicked back his head and roared as silver bullets burned and scorched his flesh. Swirling his tail in a circle, he let it fly toward his attacker. The tip pierced the vampire in the head. Ripped from the body, the head rolled like a bowling ball across the floor.

When Declan glanced back up, two more soldiers had taken that one's place. He huffed out his nostrils. They wouldn't last long like this. Either of them. He glanced down, seeing that Alexia had managed to wrestle free of Lotharus's hold. His eyes zeroed in on the crystal, the staff, and a bubble of frustration rose up inside him. It was as if he knew what they had to do, as if he had the answer buried inside him but couldn't bring it to the surface.

"Declan, look out!" At Alexia's warning, his gaze frantically scoured the ground below him and the balconies at eye level.

Too late.

A brilliant glint of metal caught his eye. Declan turned his head, cursing when he realized that not one but a volley of silver arrows were bearing down on him. Fast. Before he could pivot, the first one struck his shoulder.

Another slammed into his collarbone and a third appeared poised to strike him between the eyes.

Declan roared, absorbing the blistering pain from the first two arrows, and prepared to roll to the side in a last-ditch attempt to escape the final one. Knowing the instant his wings faltered in their arcing sweep that he wouldn't be able to escape the blow entirely. Gods be damned! He'd been too caught up in his thoughts, he'd let his concentration waver from the fight. A mistake, he realized, which might prove fatal.

Life turned into a series of seconds. Everything happened in an eerie sort of slow motion: his wing slipping, keeping him in place instead of pulling him to safety. His heartbeat thudding behind his ribs. The arrow inching closer, so close he could see a fine crack in its brilliant surface. His name screamed from Alexia's lips, echoing in his ears.

A gunshot blasted from his right, snapping everything back to real time.

Great, now I'm going to be skewered and shot.

However, the bullet never hit him. Neither did the arrow. Instead, seconds before the arrow would have struck his face, a bullet slammed into the side of the arrow, sending it flying off course. It lodged in the stone wall to his left with a thud.

Panting at the near miss, Declan rolled his head to the right.

A figure, clad in black from head to toe, stood in one of the upper balconies. Tendrils of smoke curled out of the barrel of a gun still pointed at Declan, shrouding the person from view. Slowly, the gunman lowered his arm. He had shoulder-length black hair and a goatee. However, Declan did not recognize him, and he'd definitely never fought him before. It wasn't until the gunman flashed his fangs in a smirk that Declan realized a vampire had just saved his life.

"Watch your ass, *Derkein,* or there will be no one to watch hers," he said, giving an abrupt nod downward.

Declan sucked in a breath and shot his gaze below. Alexia still fought Lotharus, still managed to keep him at bay. Assured of her temporary safety, Declan looked back to the vampire, wanting to ask why he had saved him, who he was, what he wanted. But he was gone. Vanished.

"Declan!"

Alexia's cry brought his attention back to the fight. However, instead of a crushing sense of certain failure, Declan saw in a brief flash of clarity how they could win.

"Alex, do you trust me?"

Alexia pinched her eyes and focused on speaking to him with her mind. *"You know I do."*

His smile beamed through her like sunshine. *"Good girl. Now, when I give the signal, do exactly as I say."*

She frowned, but did not argue. She didn't have time.

"You should have just stayed dead." Lotharus's hands clamped down on her shoulders, hauling her to him. "A woman's place is not in the seat of power. Just ask your dearly departed mother."

Something primal and raw inside her sparked at his words. Something she'd never felt before. Ash coated her tongue and the walls of her throat thickened and warmed. Waves of energy pulsed out of her, through her, around her. She drew it in. A fist crashed against her nose, but she didn't feel it. Another slammed her ear. However, it was Lotharus's howl of pain that she heard.

She dodged the swipe of his staff with an ease that surprised even her. And when he released a frustrated bellow and tried to hit her again, she caught the wood stick in her hands.

Lotharus's mouth opened, but no words came. His face grimaced, twisting in pain as she wrenched his arm back and kicked him with such force he burst through the cavern wall, spilling onto the sandy beach outside.

Alexia curled her fingers around the staff and stepped out after him. A rush of salty ocean air shot over her, and the heels of her boots dug into the sand with each step she took. When she rounded the cavern, her gaze immediately shot to her left. The first fingers of dawn's light traced the sky over the horizon.

Minutes. They had minutes before the sun came up, scorching them all to dust. Lotharus sensed it, too. Frantic, his dark eyes scoured the beach for aid. A shifted Declan stepped through the hole in the cliff wall. His bare chest was riddled with cuts and bruises. By the looks of it, he had laid waste to most of the soldiers. The few others who remained stood on the beach, their gazes on the crystal in Alexia's possession.

Lotharus scurried to his feet, clutching only the hem of his black robe in his hands. "What are you all standing there for? Kill them," he shouted. When the soldiers didn't move, Lotharus shot eyes filled with dread of the approaching daylight to Declan. "You. Dragon lord. Stop her," he pleaded, actually dropping to his knees in front of him. "Stop her and I'll give you anything you desire."

"I don't think so, you son of a bitch." Declan bent down, hauling Lotharus up by the front of his coat. "You tortured me and raped Alexia. You're done."

With a growl, he tossed the ancient against the rocky cliff.

"Alex," Declan shouted. "Shove it in his heart. Now!"

At his call, Alexia snapped the staff over her knee.

Grabbing the baseball-size stone, she tore it free from its mount. The crystal warmed in her palm and Alexia got the distinct feeling the rock wanted the fate she was about to hand it.

She stepped up to Lotharus, hatred surging in her veins as for once she looked into *his* petrified eyes instead of the other way around. "You want power? Take it," she said, jabbing her fist into his chest as hard as she could. Lotharus's perplexed look was the last thing she saw before an unseen force slammed her backward, leaving the crystal embedded in his heart. Lotharus's black eyes widened, his hands closing over the wound. Bright and pulsing light strobed out of the hole in his chest, threading between his fingers.

Large hands covered her shoulders from behind. Alexia allowed them to guide her behind a boulder and force her to the ground. Declan's strong arms shielded her head in a canopy.

A heartbeat later, blinding white light ate up her vision. A jet of heat blasted hard against them. Declan tightened his body against her, pressing them against the rock wall as Lotharus's scream pierced her ears. She covered them, keeping her hands over them until the cloud of energy ebbed and settled.

Breathing hard, Alexia lifted her head, peeking over the

rock. Sparking embers, charred ash and a glowing red ring were all that remained of Lotharus. Releasing a shaky breath, she swept her gaze around. Soldiers lay sprawled on the ground beside them like broken dolls. Brilliant shards of glass, the remnants of the crystal, coated their bodies and sprinkled the sand. Each piece flickered, catching the bright rays of the early morning light.

"Are you okay?" Declan panted in her ear.

Light.

Alexia looked toward the ocean and froze, unable to speak. The sun, the bright ginger sun, danced in front of her vision, blanketing the sea in intense orange, purples and reds. Its radiance and heat hit her like a wave. Pure and absolute warmth such as she'd never felt before flooded her skin.

She swallowed, waiting for the incredible burn to tear through her body before she, too, disappeared in a breath of ash like Lotharus. She supposed if she had to see anything before she died, the majestic beauty of the sunrise over her ocean home wasn't the worst thing she could imagine.

"Alex." Declan's voice sounded like it came from underwater or miles off. *It must already be happening.* Slamming her eyes closed, she burrowed into his chest, trying to hide from the fate sliding over her skin with each passing second.

Strong hands forced her head up, tilting her face toward him. At the sight of him, a pang of longing ripped through her. "I love you," she breathed, twining his arms around her neck and holding him tight. His arms met her, a hand coming to palm the back of her head, the other on her lower back.

"I love you, too, Alexia."

The panic of impending death fled from her soul the minute he whispered those words against her ear. She closed her eyes.

At least they died having tasted hope.

Her memory recalled that random thought from the day she'd met Declan, and a smile spread across her tear-coated lips. She'd tasted hope, tasted love, and that was all she'd ever wanted, even though she'd like to hold on to all of it a bit longer.

"Alex, you're choking me," Declan said with a laugh, unwrapping himself from her embrace. When she frantically tried to keep him in her arms, he cupped her cheeks, his eyes locking on hers with blazing intensity. "What is it, what's wrong?"

She nodded toward the water. "The sun," she said in a low voice, as if, if the star heard her, it would find her and strike her down.

Declan's expression knotted in confusion before it

relaxed in understanding. Taking her hand in his, he brought her fingers to his lips, kissing the tip of each one. The motion drew her gaze. He'd reached her pinky before she noticed delicate fingernails had taken the place of her black claws.

"But…" She lifted her gaze to his.

"You're changing," he said. "Remember?"

The truth settled over her, hazy at first and then purging in its clarity. Of course. That's why Declan hadn't seemed concerned that they were outside the catacombs at sunrise. He'd known.

A smile tweaked her lips and she blinked in wonderment. The sun had risen in the sky, its heat coated her face in a warm glow she'd only read about. So bright she had to squint to see Declan's face clearly. It was full of concern and love and completely covered in filth. A laugh tickled her throat, but she contained it to a smile. His lips mimicked hers before he swooped, covering her mouth with his. She opened unquestionably for him and his tongue ran along her lip and then deeper. Moaning into his mouth, she ran her hands under his arms to clutch his wide back, pressing him closer against her. Although she never wanted to let him go, Alexia slowly pulled back.

Again the warmth of the sun washed over her. A soft wind rolled off the ocean, breathing over her kiss-dampened lips. She licked them, tasting the sweet salt air on her tongue. The primitive sensations pulled her back to reality. Forced her to face how very much her life had changed in just the few short hours since she'd left Declan's bed. In truth, Alexia couldn't believe she was still alive. Realizing others had not been so fortunate, she bit her lip and looked up at Declan. "Lotharus?" she asked.

"Gone," he replied, nodding his head toward the cliff where they had last seen him.

Alexia tilted her head, finally truly taking in the site, the brevity of what had happened. "How did you know to destroy the crystal that way?" Eyes still fixed on the spot, Alexia moved to stand.

"Doc," he said, taking her by the arm and helping her up. "She said the crystal had the power to rule all or destroy one. We always took that to mean races. However, as I watched Lotharus fight, I realized the crystal gave one person the power to rule and held the power to destroy the ruler."

She nodded at the logic, but couldn't stop a questioning frown from tensing her brow. "But you carried the crystal inside you and didn't implode."

Declan smiled, placing his hands on her rib cage as he helped her maneuver down the bank of sand. "Alone, the crystal was a worthless paperweight. He needed it to harness your power, your mother's power.

Lotharus could only hold on to them for so long without it."

Alexia stared at the blanket of ash on the sand. That was all that was left of Lotharus and the horrible yoke he'd put on her and her mother. Bending, she picked up the heavy garnet ring. The one Lotharus always wore on his forefinger. Something caught her eye as she moved to stow it in her pocket. Alexia held the ring up, noticing two capital *S*'s had been carved in delicate script into the stone. They flowed with almost serpentine curves, the tail end of each letter coiling around the other. She frowned. Certain she'd seen such lettering before, but unsure where or what it meant.

"Like a perfume, the power Lotharus absorbed would leak and evaporate until none of it remained with him," Declan continued. "But with the crystal, he could channel and control the power indefinitely."

Alexia pressed the ring into a fold in her sweater and smiled up at Declan. "Okay, well, what about the whole dragons aren't allergic to the sun thing?" she joked. "When were you planning on telling me about that?"

Declan turned and Alexia's heart expanded painfully in her chest at the handsome smile that crossed his face.

"In my defense, there wasn't a lot of time."

"You could have warned me," she said, reaching out and pinching him. "I thought I was dying."

"I'm sorry," he said with a laugh, dodging her next attempt to squeeze him. Instead, warm arms encircled her, one cupping her under the knee and another around her back. He lifted her as if she were a feather, tucking her against his chest. "But I promise to spend all night making it up to you."

His blue eyes settled on her with an intense force she had already learned to recognize, but wasn't sure she'd ever get used to. Desire, heavy and raw, wrapped around her in a silken ribbon and she was glad he held her, for she was certain she couldn't have stood on her own. Then a wicked smile curved his lips and he bent his forehead to hers.

"So, don't you have something you're supposed to tell me?"

Alexia felt a beaming smile pass her lips and she tightened her arms around his neck. An urge to tease him reared its head, but quickly vanished. Instead, she tipped her lips to his ear. "I love you, too, Declan Black," she whispered.

The hands on her waist and legs tightened and she heard his smile in his low voice. "Does that mean you are ready to be my mate, my love, my Queen?"

Alexia leaned back to look at him, but before she could reply, his final word sunk in.

Queen.

"Declan." She grasped his face, forcing him to look at her. "I don't think I *can* be your Queen."

"Why not?"

She tried to keep back her smile. "I know this is going to sound crazy, but I think your parents are still alive. And I think I know how to find them."

CHAPTER TWENY-TWO

DECLAN RELEASED HIS hold of Alexia at the mouth of the cavern, shifting back into his human form. His eyes quickly scanned her body, gauging her state of well-being.

"I'm fine," she said with a smile.

The stones shifted, undulating in that familiar rolling pattern until an opening formed. As he watched them move, his thoughts strayed to what Alexia had told him on the beach. How she believed her mother had not murdered the King and Queen, but hid them away on an island that until now he'd believed to exist only in myth. Declan struggled to wrap his mind around the idea his parents might not be lost to him. That he may one day walk through these doors and see their smiling faces again.

Instead, someone who looked a little like both his

parents emerged from behind the wall the moment it opened.

"Tallon," he breathed.

Rushing forward, he took her in his arms. Gods, he couldn't remember the last time he'd hugged her, truly showed her affection. By her shocked gasp and hesitancy to embrace him back, it had been much too long. But her arms did come around him, and the instant he felt her squeeze him tight, he knew they would be able to cross whatever distance had spread between them the past days.

When he leaned back, Tallon's delicate face lit up in a genuine smile. One that he noticed faded the moment she looked over his shoulder and saw Alex.

"What is she doing here?"

ALEXIA LOOKED FROM TALLON to Declan, hoping to convey the thoughts and ideas running through her mind to him effectively. When he smiled and nodded, Alexia turned toward his sister. Tallon's dainty brows drew together as she neared. She scrutinized Alexia from the toes up, taking in each bloody mark, each wound on her battle-weary body. Then she fixed her eyes on Alexia's and her jaw dropped.

"What the hell is going on?" She turned to Declan. "How is she one of us?"

"Tallon." Alexia closed the distance between them. "I have a gift for you. One I hope will perhaps one day mend the gap between us."

Tallon shifted uncomfortably, her eyes guarded. As if dealing with a skittish animal, Alexia used slow movements to remove a soiled scrap of paper from inside her boot. Holding it flat in her outstretched palm, she offered it to Tallon. However, she only stared at it.

"Take it, Tal."

At her brother's prod, she grasped the parchment.

"Do you know of Dragon Island?" Alexia asked as Tallon unfolded the paper.

"The one off New Zealand?"

"No. The one beyond the Fatum, shrouded in Myst and protected by the Goddess. The one only visible to vampires." Alexia paused for a heartbeat, a smile turning up her lips. "It's the place I believe your parents are hidden."

Tallon's pink eyes widened. "What?" she breathed, twisting and inspecting the paper in her hands for some kind of answer or clue before shooting her gaze to her brother. "What is she talking about?"

When Declan walked forward, Alexia took a few steps back to give them space. "Tal, Alexia thinks they are still alive."

"How? I mean, this doesn't make any sense. Why

would they keep them alive? Why go through all the trouble to hide them?"

Declan stepped up, placing his hands on her shoulders. "Right now, I don't care about any of that. I just want you to find out if it's true or not."

Tallon sucked in a breath. "Me?"

"Yes, you." He motioned to the three of them. "We are the only dragons who can find that island, Tal, the only ones with vampire blood in our veins. As compelled as I am to go, I cannot bear to wait until I am strong enough for the journey. And Alexia cannot shift yet." He sighed. "It's up to you to find them."

Tallon shook her head. "Oh, gods, Dec. What if it isn't true? What if…?" Her eyes lowered and a small sigh fell from her lips.

Declan hooked a finger beneath her chin, forcing her gaze to his.

"What if I can't find them?" she finally asked.

"You're strong, Tallon. You are one of the fastest and bravest on the council. I know you can do this."

"Alone?"

He paused. "No. I want you take the hunter along."

"Griffon?" Tallon's voice cracked. She cleared her throat, a slight flush peppering her cheeks. "Are you certain? Why can't I go with Falcon?"

"Tallon, Griffon is the only one of our flock who's been beyond the Mysts. The only one who knows his way around both the place and its inhabitants."

"But…"

"No *buts,* Tallon. I need to ensure you'll be safe."

Alexia saw Tallon's brow furrow, saw the unease written all over the young woman's face. After meeting Griffon she could understand her trepidation. However, there was something else, something decidedly feminine and familiar in her body language. Before Alexia could put her finger on it, Tallon nodded her consent. "All right. I'll ready to leave at once."

"Fly fast and safe," he said, giving her shoulders a reassuring squeeze before she turned. "And, Tallon," Declan called after her. "Speak of this to no one else until we are certain. That includes Falcon."

She opened her mouth as if to speak, but then closed it. "I won't, brother." Then her gaze slipped to Alexia, and she found herself holding her breath.

"Thank you," Tallon said.

Alexia smiled. "Good luck."

Once Tallon disappeared into the lair, Alexia turned back to Declan. "So, now we find Falcon?"

Declan nodded and let out a sigh. "And then Griffon."

"Need something from me, boss?"

DECLAN STARTED at the voice and whirled around, looking for where it might be coming from. The sound of rocks skipping down the side of the mountain clued him in on a location. He peered over the side. Griffon sat on a short outcropping, his weight precariously balanced on only the tips of his toes. The violent and cold winds picked up the long black mane of his hair, flying it wildly about his shoulders.

Declan propped his hands on his hips and hung his head before leveling it again. "Yes, as a matter of fact. I need you to accompany Tallon on a mission."

Griffon's gaze fell to his fingerless-gloved hands, his jaw flexed. "Why me? You heard her yourself. She'd rather go with *Falcon*."

Declan frowned at the sarcasm dripping from his words, but shrugged it off.

"If you heard that, then you heard me tell her you are the only dragon of this flock who knows what lies beyond the Fatum, in the land of the Myst and myth. The only one of us who's been there…"

"And what makes you think I'd be willing to go back?" Griffon bit out.

The harsh tone more than the comment itself took Declan aback. Squaring his stance, he placed his hands on his hip bones. "I don't pretend to know what happened to you. To know about your past or the life you once led.

You've made it quite clear that topic is off the map and I've never asked to go exploring. But if you aided the return of the King and Queen, there would be no more questions, no more doubts of your loyalty here. To this flock or this council." He stepped forward. "I thought that's what you wanted."

Griffon didn't move, didn't speak at that offer. So Declan took another step toward the cliff's ledge to present another one. "And what you didn't hear me tell my sister is that you're the only one I trust to protect her."

The hunter slid his gaze across the stones and stared Declan down with heated purple eyes. However, instead of glowing with irritation or anger, emotion swirled through Griffon's usually steely gaze. Respect?

Declan bowed his head and exhaled, saying the last thing he thought might make a difference. "I trust you with her life out there, hunter. And I will forever owe you mine if you keep an eye on hers."

Again met by silence, Declan tentatively glanced up. Griffon's massive body lengthened as he stood. Balancing on the tiny foothold with unbelievable stability for his size, he shifted his leather baldric across his chest and nodded.

"I'll do it," Griffon murmured, before jumping to the sky. Declan watched the hunter shift in a blast of purple and black, stared as he flew in a graceful spiral through the clouds until he could no longer see him.

"Where is he going?"

Declan turned, surprised and yet not to see Falcon grabbing a leather trench coat from the other wall and shrugging into it. Reaching back, he pulled his long curtain of black hair out of the collar before buttoning the front.

"Nowhere," Declan replied, noticing Falcon's combat gear and flying attire. "What about you?"

"Tallon's leaving. Although she wouldn't say where, I'm preparing to go with her."

Declan stepped to block him. "Falcon, you can't accompany her. I need you for something else."

Falcon paused, his green eyes searching Declan's face until he found the answer. "You sent Tallon on a mission without me? Why?"

Declan knew he had to broach this carefully. Although Falcon acted rational and level-headed at all times, this was Tallon they were discussing. Falcon always held a special part of his heart for her—had always protected and looked out for her.

"Remember that solider?" Declan asked. "The one who told us about Lotharus's plan."

His friend clenched his teeth and nodded. Obviously

wanting to run away but needing to hear what Declan had to say.

"Well, he was right. The soldiers can walk in the sun."

Falcon's eyes widened. "Gods, how do you know?"

"When the crystal exploded, it killed anyone in its path. Alexia and I were guarded behind a boulder, but the soldiers were killed by the shards. When the sun came up, Lotharus's body disintegrated. Theirs did not. Now," he continued, "if another head grows on the body Lotharus created, if those soldiers find out about their new power, this war could get worse before it gets better. The horde is scattered and leaderless without her right now," Declan said, nodding over his shoulder. "We can both sit around and hope the right person steps forward to fill her shoes…"

"Or?"

Declan paused. "Or we fill it ourselves."

An angry line tensed on Falcon's brow. "What are you saying?"

Declan sucked in a breath, letting it out slowly. "I need you to go down the mountain."

"To the humans? Are you nuts?"

"Alexia thinks a child, the next woman in line for the throne, was hidden amongst them."

"She *thinks*," he said, running a palm over his face.

"Yes, she doesn't know for certain. Lotharus could have discovered and killed the child. But if he hasn't, then this human female is the one we need to bring peace, once and for all, to our clans."

"Why can't she stay the Queen?" he asked, motioning to Alexia.

Declan followed Falcon's gaze. A sharp pain splintered through him at the truth he was about to tell Falcon. "They won't accept her. Not now that she's one of us."

Falcon's eyes closed, but not before Declan saw a familiar flash of agony lingering in their green depths. "But Tallon…"

Exhaling, Declan took a step closer to his friend, clapping him on the shoulder. "She's fine, I promise. I sent someone with her."

"Who?" Falcon's eyes narrowed as he put two and two together. "Griffon? Declan, no. Why don't you send that ox to find this human person and let me go after Tal?"

"You know as well as I, Griffon would never fit in down the mountain. He's five times the size of a normal human and scarred to boot. The female he needs to find would likely run in the opposite direction the instant she saw him." Declan shook his head, hoping the regret he felt showed in his eyes. "No, I need you to do this. Only you. Kestrel is not yet used to his prosthetic, Ash is too young and Hawk too old."

Falcon's face twisted in fury before he turned and roared his frustration to the sky. By the time he'd spun around, his chest rose and fell sharply and his eyes held sorrow, longing and a tint of madness Declan had never before seen in his friend.

"I'll do this for you," he said through clenched teeth. "But know this. Tallon is the only thing that matters to me." He held up one finger as if to further prove his point. "The only thing. And if you, her brother, her blood, cannot protect her while I'm gone, then gods help me, what I'll do when I return."

"Falcon, you're overreacting, plea—" He didn't get the word out before his friend turned heel, shrugged out of his coat and strode back into the lair.

Declan ran his hands through his hair and turned to face the majestic view of his mountain home stretched out before him. He wasn't sure how long he stood there, feeling the icy winds lap his face, before Alexia came up behind him. Sliding one arm under his, she wrapped it around his chest, resting her chin on his shoulder. The contact relaxed him instantly, bringing a happy smile to his otherwise worried body.

Turning, he took her in his arms. At the sight of her, all the doubt and uncertainty faded until he saw only her.

"Come," he said, tugging on her hand. "After we have Doc take a look at your wounds, I have something I want to show you."

CHAPTER TWENTY-THREE

"ARE YOU READY?"

Alexia nodded.

Strong arms braced around her middle, clutching her to his chest. The long, smooth length of his tail wound around it, too. The dusk wind spiraled up from the ocean below, causing riotous curls to dance across his handsome face. He began beating his wings, lifting them off the ground. Her heart hammered behind her ribs. Being near him, being in his arms had always been a heady thrill. But ever since the night of her ascension, the effect had increased tenfold. Butterflies fluttered in her stomach at just a look. At a touch, lust rolled through her like a steam train at full pressure. Pressed flush against him now, she felt longing she had never known.

"Now I've got you. Don't worry. Just focus, as I told you."

Again, Alexia nodded. She closed her eyes and focused on the butterfly tingle glowing in her belly. Focused on Declan, on her love for him.

Nothing happened.

"I can't do it," she said with a groan, opening her eyes to stare into his. "It's not working."

Slow and knowing, his lips curved in a smile.

"What?"

"Look behind you." He nodded.

A glance over her shoulder showed large, scaled wings like his, but of a delicate lilac color. Awe and then sheer panic gripped her. She clutched her arms around his neck, holding him tight. He flattened his palm to her back and clutched her to him, his laughter ringing in her ears.

"Don't laugh at me," she said with a smile. He leaned back to look at her and a squeal of panic tore from her lips. "Don't lemme go, either."

Panting hard, Alexia forced herself to look down, to will the fear at bay. "Goddess, we're so high up!"

They hovered far above the ocean now. Above the cliff, she realized, where not too long ago she'd captured Declan, the mighty dragon lord and King. A smile tweaked her lips at the memory, before they parted in wonder. The sun had set, casting the sky in layers of yellow, reds and purples. She didn't think she'd ever become accustomed to the majestic beauty of the sun.

"You best get used to heights, if you want to fly. You do want to fly, don't you?"

"I did," she said, leaning back to look in his face. "I do."

He smiled. "Good. Then give me your hand. I won't let you fall."

They flew hand in hand over the coastline. An intense wave of déjà vu floated over her and she realized she'd seen this before. It was just like in her dream. Sure enough, when she looked at Declan, the wound she'd seen on his cheek in the dream was there.

Laughing, she rolled into his arms and once again they embraced her readily.

"I still can't believe this. How did you know?"

A dark brow arched. "Know what?"

"That turning me would work."

His grin faded. "I didn't. I hoped. My father turned my mother after she was bitten during a vampire attack and she became both vampire and dragon."

Alexia nodded, recalling the story he'd told her before, and then she frowned. "I am still part…"

"Vampire, yes," he finished for her. "But like me, you are more dragon."

A large hand palmed her bottom and a wicked glint lit up his eyes. Undeniable, magnetic desire pulled her to him. Alexia dipped her head, kissing the side of his throat, the space behind his ear, tasting the sweat on his skin, tangy and salty. She ran her hands down his back, over the swell of his butt, feeling the muscles beneath tense.

"I'm learning dragonesses are more sexual, are they not?"

"Gods, yes," he breathed before pressing his lips to her throat. That slight contact made her heart rate spike and Alexia wondered if he knew how easily he could affect her. Moaning, she wrapped her legs around his hips, locking her ankles at his lower back to keep them in place.

"They are fiercely loyal to one another," she panted, threading her hands through his windblown hair. "And aggressive when they mate."

It was Declan's turn to groan as Alexia's fangs pierced the flesh of his neck. The dark sound of his lust sent heat spreading from her belly to her toes. She took a small pull of his blood, savoring the delicious taste of him before running her tongue up his neck, planting open-mouthed kisses across his jaw to his lips. His mouth met hers, coming down hard and fast, and she relished every second of it.

Alexia lost herself in his kiss until she forgot where

they were. The instant she remembered they flew a thousand feet above ground, she pulled back. Her breath caught to see Declan staring down at her with dark, hungry eyes. Grinning, she clutched his back for support as she pressed her hips against his. She found him, rock hard and urgent. The smile fled from her lips and a pool of heat liquefied her lower belly. Flames licked her inner walls in an unquenchable burn only he could sate.

"What it's like to mate when you're flying?"

A low groan rumbled in his chest and he pressed her tight, molding her small body against his. One large hand covered her thigh, hitching it higher on his waist, while his other cupped her butt, pressing her harder against the insistent length of him.

"Little vampire, you're about to find out."

* * * * *

NOCTURNE™

Coming next month

MOON KISSED
by Michele Hauf

Escaping from bloodthirsty vampires, Belladonna ran straight into the arms of a werewolf. As a man, Severo drew her in with his dark good looks; as a beast, he astounded her with his insatiable sensual appetite!

LAST OF THE RAVENS
by Linda Winstead Jones

Bren suspects that his lineage will end with him – as the last of his kind, a raven shape-shifter, he knows there is only one woman in the world who is meant for him. Yet he's stunned when Miranda visits his mountain and awakens his desire.

On sale 20th August 2010

TOUCH OF SURRENDER
by Rhyannon Byrd

Werewolf Kierland is haunted by Morgan. Not because of her beauty, but because of her long-ago betrayal. Now they must team up to rescue Kierland's brother. And completing their mission could mean surrendering to their suppressed passion…

On sale 3rd September 2010

Available at WHSmith, Tesco, ASDA, Eason and all good bookshops.
For full Mills & Boon range including eBooks visit
www.millsandboon.co.uk

/11/MB299

Heart-racing, pulse-pounding suspense from three *New York Times* bestselling authors

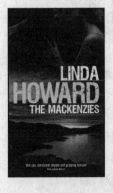

The Mackenzies
by Linda Howard

Men with the courage to protect and defend their own…

Available 16th July 2010

The Protectors
by Beverly Barton

Keeping her safe from harm…

Available 20th August 2010

Alpha Squad
by Suzanne Brockmann

Tall, dark and dangerous…

Available 17th September 2010

www.millsandboon.co.uk

New Voices

Do you dream of being a romance writer?

Mills & Boon are looking for fresh
writing talent in our biggest
ever search!

And this time…our readers have
a say in who wins!

For information on how to enter
or get involved go to

www.romanceisnotdead.com

Discover Pure Reading Pleasure with

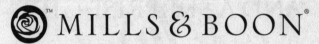

MILLS & BOON®

**Visit the Mills & Boon website for all
the latest in romance**

- **Buy** all the latest releases, backlist and eBooks

- **Find out** more about our authors and their books

- **Join** our community and chat to authors and other readers

- **Free** online reads from your favourite authors

- **Win** with our fantastic online competitions

- **Sign** up for our free monthly eNewsletter

- **Tell us** what you think by signing up to our reader panel

- **Rate** and review books with our star system

www.millsandboon.co.uk

 Follow us at twitter.com/millsandboonuk

 Become a fan at facebook.com/romancehq

FREE BOOK
AND A SURPRISE GIFT

We would like to take this opportunity to thank you for reading this Mills & Boon® book by offering you the chance to take A specially selected book from the Nocturne series absolutely FREE! We're also making this offer to introduce you to the benefits of the Mills & Boon® Book Club™—

- **FREE home delivery**
- **FREE gifts and competitions**
- **FREE monthly Newsletter**
- **Exclusive Mills & Boon Book Club offers**
- **Books available before they're in the shops**

Accepting this FREE book and gift places you under no obligation to buy, you may cancel at any time, even after receiving your free book. Simply complete your details below and return the entire page to the address below. You don't even need a stamp!

YES Please send me a free Nocturne book and a surprise gift. I understand that unless you hear from me, I will receive 3 superb new stories every month, two priced at £4.99 and a third larger version priced at £6.99, postage and packing free. I am under no obligation to purchase any books and may cancel my subscription at any time. The free book and gift will be mine to keep in any case.

Ms/Mrs/Miss/Mr _____ Initials _____

Surname _____

Address _____

_____

_____ Postcode _____

E-mail _____

Send this whole page to: Mills & Boon Book Club, Free Book Offer, FREEPOST NAT 10298, Richmond, TW9 1BR

Offer valid in UK only and is not available to current Mills & Boon Book Club subscribers to this series. Overseas and Eire please write for details.. We reserve the right to refuse an application and applicants must be aged 18 years or over. Only one application per household. Terms and prices subject to change without notice. Offer expires 31st October 2010. As a result of this application, you may receive offers from Harlequin Mills & Boon and other carefully selected companies. If you would prefer not to share in this opportunity please write to The Data Manager, PO Box 676, Richmond, TW9 1WU.

Mills & Boon® is a registered trademark owned by Harlequin Mills & Boon Limited.
Nocturne™ is being used as a trademark. The Mills & Boon® Book Club™ is being used as a trademark.